The Moon Book

From the Earth
To the Moon

and

Round the Moon

The Moon Book

From the Earth To the Moon

and

Round the Moon

JULES VERNE

PHOENIX PICK
an imprint of

ARC
MANOR
ROCKVILLE, MARYLAND
2008

ISBN: 978-1-60450-250-3

Published by Phoenix Pick
An Imprint of Arc Manor
P. O. Box 10339
Rockville, MD 20849-0339
www.ArcManor.com

Printed in the United States of America/United Kingdom

From the Earth to the Moon

Contents

ooooooooooooooo

Round the Moon

Contents

ooooooooooooooo

From the Earth To the Moon

I

The Gun Club

D URING the War of the Rebellion, a new and influential club was established in the city of Baltimore in the State of Maryland. It is well known with what energy the taste for military matters became developed among that nation of ship-owners, shopkeepers, and mechanics. Simple tradesmen jumped their counters to become extemporized captains, colonels, and generals, without having ever passed the School of Instruction at West Point; nevertheless; they quickly rivaled their compeers of the old continent, and, like them, carried off victories by dint of lavish expenditure in ammunition, money, and men.

But the point in which the Americans singularly distanced the Europeans was in the science of gunnery. Not, indeed, that their weapons retained a higher degree of perfection than theirs, but that they exhibited unheard-of dimensions, and consequently attained hitherto unheard-of ranges. In point of grazing, plunging, oblique, or enfilading, or point-blank firing, the English, French, and Prussians have nothing to learn; but their cannon, howitzers, and mortars are mere pocket-pistols compared with the formidable engines of the American artillery.

This fact need surprise no one. The Yankees, the first mechanicians in the world, are engineers—just as the Italians are musicians and the Germans metaphysicians—by right of birth. Nothing is more natural, therefore, than to perceive them applying their audacious ingenuity to the science of gunnery. Witness the marvels of Parrott, Dahlgren, and Rodman. The Armstrong, Palliser, and Beaulieu guns were compelled to bow before their transatlantic rivals.

Now when an American has an idea, he directly seeks a second American to share it. If there be three, they elect a president and two secretaries. Given four, they name a keeper of records, and the office is ready for work; five, they convene a general meeting, and the club is fully constituted. So things were managed in Baltimore. The inventor of a new cannon associated himself with the caster and the borer. Thus was formed the nucleus of the "Gun Club." In a single month after its formation it numbered 1,833 effective members and 30,565 corresponding members.

One condition was imposed as a sine qua non upon every candidate for admission into the association, and that was the condition of having designed, or (more or less) perfected a cannon; or, in default of a cannon, at least a firearm of some description. It may, however, be mentioned that mere inventors of revolvers, fire-shooting carbines, and similar small arms, met with little consideration. Artillerists always commanded the chief place of favor.

The estimation in which these gentlemen were held, according to one of the most scientific exponents of the Gun Club, was "proportional to the masses of their guns, and in the direct ratio of the square of the distances attained by their projectiles."

The Gun Club once founded, it is easy to conceive the result of the inventive genius of the Americans. Their military weapons attained colossal proportions, and their projectiles, exceeding the prescribed limits, unfortunately occasionally cut in two some unoffending pedestrians. These inventions, in fact, left far in the rear the timid instruments of European artillery.

It is but fair to add that these Yankees, brave as they have ever proved themselves to be, did not confine themselves to theories and formulae, but that they paid heavily, in propria persona, for their inventions. Among them were to be counted officers of all ranks, from lieutenants to generals; military men of every age, from those who were just making their debut in the profession of arms up to those who had grown old in the gun-carriage. Many had found their rest on the field of battle whose names figured in the "Book of Honor" of the Gun Club; and of those who made good their return the greater proportion bore the marks of their indisputable valor. Crutches, wooden legs, artificial arms, steel hooks, caoutchouc jaws, silver craniums, platinum noses, were all to be found in the collection; and it was calculated by the great statistician Pitcairn that throughout the Gun Club there was not quite one arm between four persons and two legs between six.

Nevertheless, these valiant artillerists took no particular account of these little facts, and felt justly proud when the despatches of a battle returned the number of victims at ten-fold the quantity of projectiles expended.

One day, however—sad and melancholy day!—peace was signed between the survivors of the war; the thunder of the guns gradually ceased, the mortars were silent, the howitzers were muzzled for an indefinite period, the cannon, with muzzles depressed, were returned into the arsenal, the shot were repiled, all bloody reminiscences were effaced; the cotton-plants grew luxuriantly in the well-manured fields, all mourning garments were laid aside, together with grief; and the Gun Club was relegated to profound inactivity.

Some few of the more advanced and inveterate theorists set themselves again to work upon calculations regarding the laws of projectiles. They reverted invariably to gigantic shells and howitzers of unparalleled caliber. Still in default of practical experience what was the value of mere theories? Consequently, the clubrooms became deserted, the servants dozed in the antechambers, the newspapers grew mouldy on the tables, sounds of snoring came from dark corners, and the members of the Gun Club, erstwhile so noisy in their seances, were reduced to silence by this disastrous peace and gave themselves up wholly to dreams of a Platonic kind of artillery.

"This is horrible!" said Tom Hunter one evening, while rapidly carbonizing his wooden legs in the fireplace of the smoking-room; "nothing to do! nothing to look forward to! what a loathsome existence! When again shall the guns arouse us in the morning with their delightful reports?"

"Those days are gone by," said jolly Bilsby, trying to extend his missing arms. "It was delightful once upon a time! One invented a gun, and hardly was it cast, when one hastened to try it in the face of the enemy! Then one returned to camp with a word of encouragement from Sherman or a friendly shake of the hand from McClellan. But now the generals are gone back to their counters; and in place of projectiles, they despatch bales of cotton. By Jove, the future of gunnery in America is lost!"

"Ay! and no war in prospect!" continued the famous James T. Maston, scratching with his steel hook his gutta-percha cranium. "Not a cloud on the horizon! and that too at such a critical period in the progress of the science of artillery! Yes, gentlemen! I who address you have myself this very morning perfected a model (plan, section, elevation, etc.) of a mortar destined to change all the conditions of warfare!"

"No! is it possible?" replied Tom Hunter, his thoughts reverting involuntarily to a former invention of the Hon. J. T. Maston, by which, at its first trial, he had succeeded in killing three hundred and thirty-seven people.

"Fact!" replied he. "Still, what is the use of so many studies worked out, so many difficulties vanquished? It's mere waste of time! The New World seems to have made up its mind to live in peace; and our bellicose Tribune predicts some approaching catastrophes arising out of this scandalous increase of population."

"Nevertheless," replied Colonel Blomsberry, "they are always struggling in Europe to maintain the principle of nationalities."

"Well?"

"Well, there might be some field for enterprise down there; and if they would accept our services—"

"What are you dreaming of?" screamed Bilsby; "work at gunnery for the benefit of foreigners?"

"That would be better than doing nothing here," returned the colonel.

"Quite so," said J. T. Matson; "but still we need not dream of that expedient."

"And why not?" demanded the colonel.

"Because their ideas of progress in the Old World are contrary to our American habits of thought. Those fellows believe that one can't become a general without having served first as an ensign; which is as much as to say that one can't point a gun without having first cast it oneself!"

"Ridiculous!" replied Tom Hunter, whittling with his bowie-knife the arms of his easy chair; "but if that be the case there, all that is left for us is to plant tobacco and distill whale-oil."

"What!" roared J. T. Maston, "shall we not employ these remaining years of our life in perfecting firearms? Shall there never be a fresh opportunity of trying the ranges of projectiles? Shall the air never again be lighted with the glare of our guns? No international difficulty ever arise to enable us to declare war against some transatlantic power? Shall not the French sink one of our steamers, or the English, in defiance of the rights of nations, hang a few of our countrymen?"

"No such luck," replied Colonel Blomsberry; "nothing of the kind is likely to happen; and even if it did, we should not profit by it. American susceptibility is fast declining, and we are all going to the dogs."

"It is too true," replied J. T. Maston, with fresh violence; "there are a thousand grounds for fighting, and yet we don't fight. We save up our arms and legs for the benefit of nations who don't know what to do with them! But stop—without going out of one's way to find a cause for war—did not North America once belong to the English?"

"Undoubtedly," replied Tom Hunter, stamping his crutch with fury.

"Well, then," replied J. T. Maston, "why should not England in her turn belong to the Americans?"

"It would be but just and fair," returned Colonel Blomsberry.

"Go and propose it to the President of the United States," cried J. T. Maston, "and see how he will receive you."

"Bah!" growled Bilsby between the four teeth which the war had left him; "that will never do!"

"By Jove!" cried J. T. Maston, "he mustn't count on my vote at the next election!"

"Nor on ours," replied unanimously all the bellicose invalids.

"Meanwhile," replied J. T. Maston, "allow me to say that, if I cannot get an opportunity to try my new mortars on a real field of battle, I shall say good-by to the members of the Gun Club, and go and bury myself in the prairies of Arkansas!"

"In that case we will accompany you," cried the others.

Matters were in this unfortunate condition, and the club was threatened with approaching dissolution, when an unexpected circumstance occurred to prevent so deplorable a catastrophe.

On the morrow after this conversation every member of the association received a sealed circular couched in the following terms:

BALTIMORE, *October 3.*

The president of the Gun Club has the honor to inform his colleagues that, at the meeting of the 5th instant, he will bring before them a communication of an extremely interesting nature. He requests, therefore, that they will make it convenient to attend in accordance with the present invitation.

Very cordially,
IMPEY BARBICANE, P.G.C.

II

PRESIDENT BARBICANE'S COMMUNICATION

ON the 5th of October, at eight p.m., a dense crowd pressed toward the saloons of the Gun Club at No. 21 Union Square. All the members of the association resident in Baltimore attended the invitation of their president. As regards the corresponding members, notices were delivered by hundreds throughout the streets of the city, and, large as was the great hall, it was quite inadequate to accommodate the crowd of savants. They overflowed into the adjoining rooms, down the narrow passages, into the outer courtyards. There they ran against the vulgar herd who pressed up to the doors, each struggling to reach the front ranks, all eager to learn the nature of the important communication of President Barbicane; all pushing, squeezing, crushing with that perfect freedom of action which is so peculiar to the masses when educated in ideas of "self-government."

On that evening a stranger who might have chanced to be in Baltimore could not have gained admission for love or money into the great hall. That was reserved exclusively for resident or corresponding members; no one else could possibly have obtained a place; and the city magnates, municipal councilors, and "select men" were compelled to mingle with the mere townspeople in order to catch stray bits of news from the interior.

Nevertheless the vast hall presented a curious spectacle. Its immense area was singularly adapted to the purpose. Lofty pillars formed of cannon, superposed upon huge mortars as a base, supported the fine ironwork of the arches, a perfect piece of cast-iron lacework. Trophies of blunderbuses, matchlocks, arquebuses, carbines, all kinds of firearms, ancient and modern, were picturesquely interlaced against the walls. The gas lit up in full glare myriads of revolvers grouped in the form of lustres, while groups of pistols, and candelabra formed of muskets bound together, completed this magnificent display of brilliance. Models of cannon, bronze castings, sights covered with dents, plates battered by the shots of the Gun Club, assortments of rammers and sponges, chaplets of shells, wreaths of projectiles, garlands of howitzers—in short, all the apparatus of the artillerist, enchanted the eye by this wonderful arrangement and induced a kind of belief that their real purpose was ornamental rather than deadly.

At the further end of the saloon the president, assisted by four secretaries, occupied a large platform. His chair, supported by a carved gun-carriage, was modeled upon the ponderous proportions of a 32-inch mortar. It was pointed at an angle of ninety degrees, and suspended upon truncheons, so that the president could balance himself upon it as upon a rocking-chair, a very agreeable fact in the very hot weather. Upon the table (a huge iron plate supported upon six carronades) stood an inkstand of exquisite elegance, made of a beautifully chased Spanish piece, and a sonnette, which, when required, could give forth a report equal to that of a revolver. During violent debates this novel kind of bell scarcely sufficed to drown the clamor of these excitable artillerists.

In front of the table benches arranged in zigzag form, like the circumvallations of a retrenchment, formed a succession of bastions and curtains set apart for the use of the members of the club; and on this especial evening one might say, "All the world was on the ramparts." The president was sufficiently well known, however, for all to be assured that he would not put his colleagues to discomfort without some very strong motive.

Impey Barbicane was a man of forty years of age, calm, cold, austere; of a singularly serious and self-contained demeanor, punctual as a chronometer, of imperturbable temper and immovable character; by no means chivalrous, yet adventurous withal, and always bringing practical ideas to bear upon the very rashest enterprises; an essentially New Englander, a Northern colonist, a descendant of the old anti-Stuart Roundheads, and the implacable enemy of the gentlemen of the South, those ancient cavaliers of the mother country. In a word, he was a Yankee to the backbone.

Barbicane had made a large fortune as a timber merchant. Being nominated director of artillery during the war, he proved himself fertile in invention. Bold in his conceptions, he contributed powerfully to the progress of that arm and gave an immense impetus to experimental researches.

He was personage of the middle height, having, by a rare exception in the Gun Club, all his limbs complete. His strongly marked features seemed drawn by square and rule; and if it be true that, in order to judge a man's character one must look at his profile, Barbicane, so examined, exhibited the most certain indications of energy, audacity, and sang-froid.

At this moment he was sitting in his armchair, silent, absorbed, lost in reflection, sheltered under his high-crowned hat—a kind of black cylinder which always seems firmly screwed upon the head of an American.

Just when the deep-toned clock in the great hall struck eight, Barbicane, as if he had been set in motion by a spring, raised himself up. A profound silence ensued, and the speaker, in a somewhat emphatic tone of voice, commenced as follows:

"My brave, colleagues, too long already a paralyzing peace has plunged the members of the Gun Club in deplorable inactivity. After a period of years full of incidents we have been compelled to abandon our labors, and to stop short on the road of progress. I do not hesitate to state, baldly, that any war which would recall us to arms would be welcome!" (Tremendous applause!) "But war, gentlemen, is impossible under existing circumstances; and, however we may desire it, many years may elapse before our cannon shall again thunder in the field of battle. We must make up our minds, then, to seek in another train of ideas some field for the activity which we all pine for."

The meeting felt that the president was now approaching the critical point, and redoubled their attention accordingly.

"For some months past, my brave colleagues," continued Barbicane, "I have been asking myself whether, while confining ourselves to our own particular objects, we could not enter upon some grand experiment worthy of the nineteenth century; and whether the progress of artillery science would not enable us to carry it out to a successful issue. I have been considering, working, calculating; and the result of my studies is the conviction that we are safe to succeed in an enterprise which to any other country would appear wholly impracticable. This project, the result of long elaboration, is the object of my present communication. It is worthy of yourselves, worthy of the antecedents of the Gun Club; and it cannot fail to make some noise in the world."

A thrill of excitement ran through the meeting.

Barbicane, having by a rapid movement firmly fixed his hat upon his head, calmly continued his harangue:

"There is no one among you, my brave colleagues, who has not seen the Moon, or, at least, heard speak of it. Don't be surprised if I am about to discourse to you regarding the Queen of the Night. It is perhaps reserved for us to become the Columbuses of this unknown world. Only enter into my plans, and second me with all your power, and I will lead you to its conquest, and its name shall be added to those of the thirty-six states which compose this Great Union."

"Three cheers for the Moon!" roared the Gun Club, with one voice.

"The moon, gentlemen, has been carefully studied," continued Barbicane; "her mass, density, and weight; her constitution, motions, distance, as well as her place in the solar system, have all been exactly determined. Selenographic charts have been constructed with a perfection which equals, if it does not even surpass, that of our terrestrial maps. Photography has given us proofs of the incomparable beauty of our satellite; all is known regarding the moon which mathematical science, astronomy, geology, and optics can learn about her. But up to the present moment no direct communication has been established with her."

A violent movement of interest and surprise here greeted this remark of the speaker.

"Permit me," he continued, "to recount to you briefly how certain ardent spirits, starting on imaginary journeys, have penetrated the secrets of our satellite. In the seventeenth century a certain David Fabricius boasted of having seen with his own eyes the inhabitants of the moon. In 1649 a Frenchman, one Jean Baudoin, published a 'Journey performed from the Earth to the Moon by Domingo Gonzalez,' a Spanish adventurer. At the same period Cyrano de Bergerac published that celebrated 'Journeys in the Moon' which met with such success in France. Somewhat later another Frenchman, named Fontenelle, wrote 'The Plurality of Worlds,' a chef-d'oeuvre of its time. About 1835 a small treatise, translated from the New York American, related how Sir John Herschel, having been despatched to the Cape of Good Hope for the purpose of making there some astronomical calculations, had, by means of a telescope brought to perfection by means of internal lighting, reduced the apparent distance of the moon to eighty yards! He then distinctly perceived caverns frequented by hippopotami, green mountains bordered by golden lace-work, sheep with horns of ivory, a white species of deer and inhabitants with membranous wings, like bats. This brochure, the work of an American named Locke, had a great sale. But, to bring this rapid sketch to a close, I will only add that a certain Hans Pfaal, of Rotterdam, launching himself in a balloon filled with a gas extracted from nitrogen, thirty-seven times lighter than hydrogen, reached the moon after a passage of nineteen hours. This journey, like all previous ones, was purely imaginary; still, it was the work of a popular American author—I mean Edgar Poe!"

"Cheers for Edgar Poe!" roared the assemblage, electrified by their president's words.

"I have now enumerated," said Barbicane, "the experiments which I call purely paper ones, and wholly insufficient to establish serious relations with the Queen of the Night. Nevertheless, I am bound to add that some practical geniuses have attempted to establish actual communication with her. Thus, a few days ago, a German geometrician proposed to send a scientific expedition to the steppes of Siberia. There, on those vast plains, they were to describe enormous geometric figures, drawn in characters of reflecting luminosity, among which was the proposition regarding the 'square of the hypothenuse,' commonly called the 'Ass's Bridge' by the French. 'Every intelligent being,' said the geometrician, 'must understand the scientific meaning of that figure. The Selenites, do they exist, will respond by a similar figure; and, a communication being thus once established, it will be easy to form an alphabet which shall enable us to converse with the inhabitants of the moon.' So spoke the German geometrician; but his project was never put into practice, and up to the present day there is no bond in existence between the Earth and her satellite. It is reserved for the practical genius of Americans to establish a communication with the sidereal world. The means of arriving thither are simple, easy, certain, infallible—and that is the purpose of my present proposal."

A storm of acclamations greeted these words. There was not a single person in the whole audience who was not overcome, carried away, lifted out of himself by the speaker's words!

Long-continued applause resounded from all sides.

As soon as the excitement had partially subsided, Barbicane resumed his speech in a somewhat graver voice.

"You know," said he, "what progress artillery science has made during the last few years, and what a degree of perfection firearms of every kind have reached. Moreover, you are well aware that, in general terms, the resisting power of cannon and the expansive force of gunpowder are practically unlimited. Well! starting from this principle, I ask myself whether, supposing sufficient apparatus could be obtained constructed upon the conditions of ascertained resistance, it might not be possible to project a shot up to the moon?"

At these words a murmur of amazement escaped from a thousand panting chests; then succeeded a moment of perfect silence, resembling that profound stillness which precedes the bursting of a thunderstorm. In point of fact, a thunderstorm did peal forth, but it was the thunder of applause, or cries, and of uproar which made the very hall tremble. The president attempted to speak, but could not. It was fully ten minutes before he could make himself heard.

"Suffer me to finish," he calmly continued. "I have looked at the question in all its bearings, I have resolutely attacked it, and by incontrovertible calculations I find that a projectile endowed with an initial velocity of 12,000 yards per second, and aimed at the moon, must necessarily reach it. I have the honor, my brave colleagues, to propose a trial of this little experiment."

III

EFFECT OF THE PRESIDENT'S COMMUNICATION

IT is impossible to describe the effect produced by the last words of the honorable president—the cries, the shouts, the succession of roars, hurrahs, and all the varied vociferations which the American language is capable of supplying. It was a scene of indescribable confusion and uproar. They shouted, they clapped, they stamped on the floor of the hall. All the weapons in the museum discharged at once could not have more violently set in motion the waves of sound. One need not be surprised at this. There are some cannoneers nearly as noisy as their own guns.

Barbicane remained calm in the midst of this enthusiastic clamor; perhaps he was desirous of addressing a few more words to his colleagues, for by his gestures he demanded silence, and his powerful alarum was worn out by its violent reports. No attention, however, was paid to his request. He was presently torn from his seat and passed from the hands of his faithful colleagues into the arms of a no less excited crowd.

Nothing can astound an American. It has often been asserted that the word "impossible" in not a French one. People have evidently been deceived by the dictionary. In America, all is easy, all is simple; and as for mechanical difficulties, they are overcome before they arise. Between Barbicane's proposition and its realization no true Yankee would have allowed even the semblance of a difficulty to be possible. A thing with them is no sooner said than done.

The triumphal progress of the president continued throughout the evening. It was a regular torchlight procession. Irish, Germans, French, Scotch, all the heterogeneous units which make up the population of Maryland shouted in their respective vernaculars; and the "vivas," "hurrahs," and "bravos" were intermingled in inexpressible enthusiasm.

Just at this crisis, as though she comprehended all this agitation regarding herself, the moon shone forth with serene splendor, eclipsing by her intense illumination all the surrounding lights. The Yankees all turned their gaze toward her resplendent orb, kissed their hands, called her by all kinds of endearing names. Between eight o'clock and midnight one optician in Jones'-Fall Street made his fortune by the sale of opera-glasses.

Midnight arrived, and the enthusiasm showed no signs of diminution. It spread equally among all classes of citizens—men of science, shopkeepers, merchants, porters, chair-men, as well as "greenhorns," were stirred in their innermost fibres. A national enterprise was at stake. The whole city, high and low, the quays bordering the Patapsco, the ships lying in the basins, disgorged a crowd drunk with joy, gin, and whisky. Every one chattered, argued, discussed, disputed, applauded, from the gentleman lounging upon the barroom settee with his tumbler of sherry-cobbler before him down to the waterman who got drunk upon his "knock-me-down" in the dingy taverns of Fell Point.

About two A.M., however, the excitement began to subside. President Barbicane reached his house, bruised, crushed, and squeezed almost to a mummy. Hercules could not have resisted a similar outbreak of enthusiasm. The crowd gradually deserted the squares and streets. The four railways from Philadelphia and Washington, Harrisburg and Wheeling, which converge at Baltimore, whirled away the heterogeneous population to the four corners of the United States, and the city subsided into comparative tranquility.

On the following day, thanks to the telegraphic wires, five hundred newspapers and journals, daily, weekly, monthly, or bi-monthly, all took up the question. They examined it under all its different aspects, physical, meteorological, economical, or moral, up to its bearings on politics or civilization. They debated whether the moon was a finished world, or whether it was destined to undergo any further transformation. Did it resemble the earth at the period when the latter was destitute as yet of an atmosphere? What kind of spectacle would its hidden hemisphere present to our terrestrial spheroid? Granting that the question at present was simply that of sending a projectile up to the moon, every one must see that that involved the commencement of a series of experiments. All must hope that some day America would penetrate the deepest secrets of that mysterious orb; and some even seemed to fear lest its conquest should not sensibly derange the equilibrium of Europe.

The project once under discussion, not a single paragraph suggested a doubt of its realization. All the papers, pamphlets, reports—all the journals published by the scientific, literary, and religious societies enlarged upon its advantages; and the Society of Natural History of Boston, the Society of Science and Art of Albany, the Geographical and Statistical Society of New York, the Philosophical Society of Philadelphia, and the Smithsonian of Washington sent innumerable letters of congratulation to the Gun Club, together with offers of immediate assistance and money.

From that day forward Impey Barbicane became one of the greatest citizens of the United States, a kind of Washington of science. A single trait of feeling, taken from many others, will serve to show the point which this homage of a whole people to a single individual attained.

Some few days after this memorable meeting of the Gun Club, the manager of an English company announced, at the Baltimore theatre, the production of "Much ado about Nothing." But the populace, seeing in that title an allusion damaging to Barbicane's project, broke into the auditorium, smashed the benches, and compelled the unlucky director to alter his playbill. Being a sensible man, he bowed to the public will and replaced the offending comedy by "As you like it"; and for many weeks he realized fabulous profits.

IV

REPLY FROM THE OBSERVATORY OF CAMBRIDGE

BARBICANE, however, lost not one moment amid all the enthusiasm of which he had become the object. His first care was to reassemble his colleagues in the board-room of the Gun Club. There, after some discussion, it was agreed to consult the astronomers regarding the astronomical part of the enterprise. Their reply once ascertained, they could then discuss the mechanical means, and nothing should be wanting to ensure the success of this great experiment.

A note couched in precise terms, containing special interrogatories, was then drawn up and addressed to the Observatory of Cambridge in

Massachusetts. This city, where the first university of the United States was founded, is justly celebrated for its astronomical staff. There are to be found assembled all the most eminent men of science. Here is to be seen at work that powerful telescope which enabled Bond to resolve the nebula of Andromeda, and Clarke to discover the satellite of Sirius. This celebrated institution fully justified on all points the confidence reposed in it by the Gun Club. So, after two days, the reply so impatiently awaited was placed in the hands of President Barbicane.

It was couched in the following terms:

THE DIRECTOR OF THE CAMBRIDGE OBSERVATORY TO THE
PRESIDENT OF THE GUN CLUB AT BALTIMORE.

CAMBRIDGE, *October 7.*

On the receipt of your favor of the 6th instant, addressed to the Observatory of Cambridge in the name of the members of the Baltimore Gun Club, our staff was immediately called together, and it was judged expedient to reply as follows:

The questions which have been proposed to it are these—

"1.   Is it possible to transmit a projectile up to the moon?

"2.   What is the exact distance which separates the earth from its satellite?

"3.   What will be the period of transit of the projectile when endowed with sufficient initial velocity? and, consequently, at what moment ought it to be discharged in order that it may touch the moon at a particular point?

"4.   At what precise moment will the moon present herself in the most favorable position to be reached by the projectile?

"5.   What point in the heavens ought the cannon to be aimed at which is intended to discharge the projectile?

"6.   What place will the moon occupy in the heavens at the moment of the projectile's departure?"

Regarding the first question, "Is it possible to transmit a projectile up to the moon?"

ANSWER:—Yes; provided it possess an initial velocity of 1,200 yards per second; calculations prove that to be sufficient. In proportion as we recede from the earth the action of gravitation diminishes in the inverse ratio of the square of the distance; that is to say, at three times a given distance the action is nine times less. Consequently, the weight of a shot will decrease, and will become reduced to zero at the instant that the attraction of the moon exactly counterpoises that of the earth; that is to say at 47/52 of its passage. At that instant the projectile will have no weight whatever; and, if it passes that point, it will fall into the moon by the sole effect of the lunar attraction. The theoretical possibility of the experiment is therefore absolutely demonstrated; its success must depend upon the power of the engine employed.

As to the second question, "What is the exact distance which separates the earth from its satellite?"

ANSWER:—The moon does not describe a circle round the earth, but rather an ellipse, of which our earth occupies one of the foci; the consequence, therefore, is, that at certain times it approaches nearer to, and at others it recedes farther from, the earth; in astronomical language, it is at one time in apogee, at another in perigee. Now the difference between its greatest and its least distance is too considerable to be left out of consideration. In point of fact, in its apogee the moon is 247,552 miles, and in its perigee, 218,657 miles only distant; a fact which makes a difference of 28,895 miles, or more than one-ninth of the entire distance. The perigee distance, therefore, is that which ought to serve as the basis of all calculations.

To the third question.

ANSWER:—If the shot should preserve continuously its initial velocity of 12,000 yards per second, it would require little more than nine hours to reach its destination; but, inasmuch as that initial velocity will be continually decreasing, it will occupy 300,000 seconds, that is 83hrs. 20m. in reaching the point where the attraction of the earth and moon will be in equilibrio. From this point it will fall into the moon in 50,000 seconds, or 13hrs. 53m. 20sec. It will be desirable, therefore, to discharge it 97hrs. 13m. 20sec. before the arrival of the moon at the point aimed at.

Regarding question four, "At what precise moment will the moon present herself in the most favorable position, etc.?"

ANSWER:—After what has been said above, it will be necessary, first of all, to choose the period when the moon will be in perigee, and also the moment when she will be crossing the zenith, which latter event will further diminish the entire distance by a length equal to the radius of the earth, i. e. 3,919 miles; the result of which will be that the final passage remaining to be accomplished will be 214,976 miles. But although the moon passes her perigee every month, she does not reach the zenith always at exactly the same moment. She does not appear under these two conditions simultaneously, except at long intervals of time. It will be necessary, therefore, to wait for the moment when her passage in perigee shall coincide with that in the zenith. Now, by a fortunate circumstance, on the 4th of December in the ensuing year the moon will present these two conditions. At midnight she will be in perigee, that

FROM THE EARTH TO THE MOON

is, at her shortest distance from the earth, and at the same moment she will be crossing the zenith.

On the fifth question, "At what point in the heavens ought the cannon to be aimed?"

ANSWER:—The preceding remarks being admitted, the cannon ought to be pointed to the zenith of the place. Its fire, therefore, will be perpendicular to the plane of the horizon; and the projectile will soonest pass beyond the range of the terrestrial attraction. But, in order that the moon should reach the zenith of a given place, it is necessary that the place should not exceed in latitude the declination of the luminary; in other words, it must be comprised within the degrees 0@ and 28@ of lat. N. or S. In every other spot the fire must necessarily be oblique, which would seriously militate against the success of the experiment.

As to the sixth question, "What place will the moon occupy in the heavens at the moment of the projectile's departure?"

ANSWER:—At the moment when the projectile shall be discharged into space, the moon, which travels daily forward 13@ 10' 35", will be distant from the zenith point by four times that quantity, i. e. by 52@ 41' 20", a space which corresponds to the path which she will describe during the entire journey of the projectile. But, inasmuch as it is equally necessary to take into account the deviation which the rotary motion of the earth will impart to the shot, and as the shot cannot reach the moon until after a deviation equal to 16 radii of the earth, which, calculated upon the moon's orbit, are equal to about eleven degrees, it becomes necessary to add these eleven degrees to those which express the retardation of the moon just mentioned: that is to say, in round numbers, about sixty-four degrees. Consequently, at the moment of firing the visual radius applied to the moon will describe, with the vertical line of the place, an angle of sixty-four degrees.

These are our answers to the questions proposed to the Observatory of Cambridge by the members of the Gun Club:

To sum up—

1st. The cannon ought to be planted in a country situated between 0@ and 28@ of N. or S. lat.

2nd. It ought to be pointed directly toward the zenith of the place.

3rd. The projectile ought to be propelled with an initial velocity of 12,000 yards per second.

4th. It ought to be discharged at 10hrs. 46m. 40sec. of the 1st of December of the ensuing year.

5th. It will meet the moon four days after its discharge, precisely at midnight on the 4th of December, at the moment of its transit across the zenith.

The members of the Gun Club ought, therefore, without delay, to commence the works necessary for such an experiment, and to be prepared to set to work at the moment determined upon; for, if they should suffer this 4th of December to go by, they will not find the moon again under the same conditions of perigee and of zenith until eighteen years and eleven days afterward.

The staff of the Cambridge Observatory place themselves entirely at their disposal in respect of all questions of theoretical astronomy; and herewith add their congratulations to those of all the rest of America.

For the Astronomical Staff,
J. M. BELFAST,
Director of the Observatory of Cambridge.

V

THE ROMANCE OF THE MOON

AN observer endued with an infinite range of vision, and placed in that unknown center around which the entire world revolves, might have beheld myriads of atoms filling all space during the chaotic epoch of the universe. Little by little, as ages went on, a change took place; a general law of attraction manifested itself, to which the hitherto errant atoms became obedient: these atoms combined together chemically according to their affinities, formed themselves into molecules, and composed those nebulous masses with which the depths of the heavens are strewed. These masses became immediately endued with a rotary motion around their own central point. This center, formed of indefinite molecules, began to revolve around its own axis during its gradual condensation; then, following the immutable laws of mechanics, in proportion as its bulk diminished by condensation, its rotary motion became accelerated, and these two effects continuing, the result was the formation of one principal star, the center of the nebulous mass.

By attentively watching, the observer would then have perceived the other molecules of the mass, following the example of this central star, become likewise condensed by gradually accelerated rotation, and gravitating round it in the shape of innumerable stars. Thus was formed the Nebulae, of which astronomers have reckoned up nearly 5,000.

Among these 5,000 nebulae there is one which has received the name of the Milky Way, and which contains eighteen millions of stars, each of which has become the center of a solar world.

If the observer had then specially directed his attention to one of the more humble and less brilliant of these stellar bodies, a star of the fourth class, that which is arrogantly called the Sun, all the phenomena to which the formation of the Universe is to be ascribed would have been successively fulfilled before his eyes. In fact, he would have perceived this sun, as yet in the gaseous state, and composed of moving molecules, revolving round its axis in order to accomplish its work of concentration. This motion, faithful to the laws of mechanics, would have been accelerated with the diminution of its volume; and a moment would have arrived when the centrifugal force would have overpowered the centripetal, which causes the molecules all to tend toward the center.

Another phenomenon would now have passed before the observer's eye, and the molecules situated on the plane of the equator, escaping like a stone from a sling of which the cord had suddenly snapped, would have formed around the sun sundry concentric rings resembling that of Saturn. In their turn, again, these rings of cosmical matter, excited by a rotary motion about the central mass, would have been broken up and decomposed into secondary nebulosities, that is to say, into planets. Similarly he would have observed these planets throw off one or more rings each, which became the origin of the secondary bodies which we call satellites.

Thus, then, advancing from atom to molecule, from molecule to nebulous mass, from that to principal star, from star to sun, from sun to planet, and hence to satellite, we have the whole series of transformations undergone by the heavenly bodies during the first days of the world.

Now, of those attendant bodies which the sun maintains in their elliptical orbits by the great law of gravitation, some few in turn possess satellites. Uranus has eight, Saturn eight, Jupiter four, Neptune possibly three, and the Earth one. This last, one of the least important of the entire solar system, we call the Moon; and it is she whom the daring genius of the Americans professed their intention of conquering.

The moon, by her comparative proximity, and the constantly varying appearances produced by her several phases, has always occupied a considerable share of the attention of the inhabitants of the earth.

From the time of Thales of Miletus, in the fifth century B.C., down to that of Copernicus in the fifteenth and Tycho Brahe in the sixteenth century A.D., observations have been from time to time carried on with more or less correctness, until in the present day the altitudes of the lunar mountains have been determined with exactitude. Galileo explained the phenomena of the lunar light produced during certain of her phases by the existence of mountains, to which he assigned a mean altitude of 27,000 feet. After him Hevelius, an astronomer of Dantzic, reduced the highest elevations to 15,000 feet; but the calculations of Riccioli brought them up again to 21,000 feet.

At the close of the eighteenth century Herschel, armed with a powerful telescope, considerably reduced the preceding measurements. He assigned a height of 11,400 feet to the maximum elevations, and reduced the mean of the different altitudes to little more than 2,400 feet. But Herschel's calculations were in their turn corrected by the observations of Halley, Nasmyth, Bianchini, Gruithuysen, and others; but it was reserved for the labors of Boeer and Maedler finally to solve the question. They succeeded in measuring 1,905 different elevations, of which six exceed 15,000 feet, and twenty-two exceed 14,400 feet. The highest summit of all towers to a height of 22,606 feet above the surface of the lunar disc. At the same period the examination of the moon was completed. She appeared completely riddled with craters, and her essentially volcanic character was apparent at each observation. By the absence of refraction in the rays of the planets occulted by her we conclude that she is absolutely devoid of an atmosphere. The absence of air entails the absence of water. It became, therefore, manifest that the Selenites, to support life under such conditions, must possess a special organization of their own, must differ remarkably from the inhabitants of the earth.

At length, thanks to modern art, instruments of still higher perfection searched the moon without intermission, not leaving a single point of her surface unexplored; and notwithstanding that her diameter measures 2,150 miles, her surface equals the one-fifteenth part of that of our globe, and her bulk the one-forty-ninth part of that of the terrestrial spheroid—not one of her secrets was able to escape the eyes of the astronomers; and these skillful men of science carried to an even greater degree their prodigious observations.

Thus they remarked that, during full moon, the disc appeared scored in certain parts with white lines; and, during the phases, with black. On prosecuting the study of these with still greater precision, they succeeded in obtaining an exact account of the nature of these lines. They were long and narrow furrows sunk between parallel ridges, bordering generally upon the edges of the craters. Their length varied between ten and 100 miles, and their width was about 1,600 yards. Astronomers called them chasms, but they could not get any further. Whether these chasms were the dried-up beds of ancient rivers or not they were unable thoroughly to ascertain.

The Americans, among others, hoped one day or other to determine this geological question. They also undertook to examine the true nature of that system of parallel ramparts discovered on the moon's surface by Gruithuysen, a learned professor of Munich, who considered them to be "a system of fortifications thrown up by the Selenitic engineers." These two points, yet obscure, as well as others, no doubt, could not be definitely settled except by direct communication with the moon.

Regarding the degree of intensity of its light, there was nothing more to learn on this point. It was known that it is 300,000 times weaker than that of the sun, and that its heat has no appreciable effect upon the thermometer. As to the phenomenon known as the "ashy light," it is explained naturally by the effect of the transmission of the solar rays from the earth to the moon, which give the appearance of completeness to the lunar disc, while it presents itself under the crescent form during its first and last phases.

Such was the state of knowledge acquired regarding the earth's satellite, which the Gun Club undertook to perfect in all its aspects, cosmographic, geological, political, and moral.

VI

PERMISSIVE LIMITS OF IGNORANCE AND BELIEF IN THE UNITED STATES

THE immediate result of Barbicane's proposition was to place upon the orders of the day all the astronomical facts relative to the Queen of the Night. Everybody set to work to study assiduously. One would have thought that the moon had just appeared for the first time, and that no one had ever before caught a glimpse of her in the heavens. The papers revived all the old anecdotes in which the "sun of the wolves" played a part; they recalled the influences which the ignorance of past ages ascribed to her; in short, all America was seized with selenomania, or had become moon-mad.

The scientific journals, for their part, dealt more especially with the questions which touched upon the enterprise of the Gun Club. The letter of the Observatory of Cambridge was published by them, and commented upon with unreserved approval.

Until that time most people had been ignorant of the mode in which the distance which separates the moon from the earth is calculated. They took advantage of this fact to explain to them that this distance was obtained by measuring the parallax of the moon. The term parallax proving "caviare to the general," they further explained that it meant the angle formed by the inclination of two straight lines drawn from either extremity of the earth's radius to the moon. On doubts being expressed as to the correctness of this method, they immediately proved that not only was the mean distance 234,347 miles, but that astronomers could not possibly be in error in their estimate by more than seventy miles either way.

To those who were not familiar with the motions of the moon, they demonstrated that she possesses two distinct motions, the first being that of rotation upon her axis, the second being that of revolution round the earth, accomplishing both together in an equal period of time, that is to say, in twenty-seven and one-third days.

The motion of rotation is that which produces day and night on the surface of the moon; save that there is only one day and one night in the lunar month, each lasting three hundred and fifty-four and one-third hours. But, happily for her, the face turned toward the terrestrial globe is illuminated by it with an intensity equal to that of fourteen moons. As to the other face, always invisible to us, it has of necessity three hundred and fifty-four hours of absolute night, tempered only by that "pale glimmer which falls upon it from the stars."

Some well-intentioned, but rather obstinate persons, could not at first comprehend how, if the moon displays invariably the same face to the earth during her revolution, she can describe one turn round herself. To such they answered, "Go into your dining-room, and walk round the table in such a way as to always keep your face turned toward the center; by the time you will have achieved one complete round you will have completed one turn around yourself, since your eye will have traversed successively every point of the room. Well, then, the room is the heavens, the table is the earth, and the moon is yourself." And they would go away delighted.

So, then the moon displays invariably the same face to the earth; nevertheless, to be quite exact, it is necessary to add that, in consequence of certain fluctuations of north and south, and of west and east, termed her libration, she permits rather more than half, that is to say, five-sevenths, to be seen.

As soon as the ignoramuses came to understand as much as the director of the observatory himself knew, they began to worry themselves regarding her revolution round the earth, whereupon twenty scientific reviews immediately came to the rescue. They pointed out to them that the firmament, with its infinitude of stars, may be considered as one vast dial-plate, upon which the moon travels, indicating the true time to all the inhabitants of the earth; that it is during this movement that the Queen of Night exhibits her different phases; that the moon is full when she is in opposition with the sun, that is when the three bodies are on the same straight line, the earth occupying the center; that she is new when she is in conjunction with the sun, that is, when she is between it and the earth; and, lastly that she is in her first or last quarter, when she makes with the sun and the earth an angle of which she herself occupies the apex.

Regarding the altitude which the moon attains above the horizon, the letter of the Cambridge Observatory had said all that was to be said in this respect. Every one knew that this altitude varies according to the latitude of the observer. But the only zones of the globe in which the moon passes the zenith, that is, the point directly over the head of the spectator, are of necessity comprised between the twenty-eighth parallels and the equator. Hence the importance of the advice to try the experiment upon some point of that part of the globe, in order that the projectile might be discharged perpendicularly, and so the soonest escape the action of gravitation. This was an essential condition to the success of the enterprise, and continued actively to engage the public attention.

Regarding the path described by the moon in her revolution round the earth, the Cambridge Observatory had demonstrated that this path is a re-entering curve, not a perfect circle, but an ellipse, of which the earth occupies one of the foci. It was also well understood that it is farthest removed from the earth during its apogee, and approaches most nearly to it at its perigee.

Such was then the extent of knowledge possessed by every American on the subject, and of which no one could decently profess ignorance. Still, while these principles were being rapidly disseminated many errors and illusory fears proved less easy to eradicate.

For instance, some worthy persons maintained that the moon was an ancient comet which, in describing its elongated orbit round the sun, happened to pass near the earth, and became confined within her circle of attraction. These drawing-room astronomers professed to explain the charred aspect of the moon—a disaster which they attributed to the intensity of the solar heat; only, on being reminded that comets have an atmosphere, and that the moon has little or none, they were fairly at a loss for a reply.

Others again, belonging to the doubting class, expressed certain fears as to the position of the moon. They had heard it said that, according to observations made in the time of the Caliphs, her revolution had become accelerated in a certain degree. Hence they concluded, logically enough, that an acceleration of motion ought to be accompanied by a corresponding diminution in the distance separating the two bodies; and that, supposing the double effect to be continued to infinity, the moon would end by one day falling into the earth. However, they became reassured as to the fate of future generations on being apprised that, according to the calculations of Laplace, this acceleration of motion is confined within very restricted limits, and that a proportional diminution of speed will be certain to succeed it. So, then, the stability of the solar system would not be deranged in ages to come.

There remains but the third class, the superstitious. These worthies were not content merely to rest in ignorance; they must know all about things which had no existence whatever, and as to the moon, they had long known all about her. One set regarded her disc as a polished mirror, by means of which people could see each other from different points of the earth and interchange their thoughts. Another set pretended that out of one thousand new moons that had been observed, nine hundred and fifty had been attended with remarkable disturbances, such as cataclysms, revolutions, earthquakes, the deluge, etc. Then they believed in some mysterious influence exercised by her over human destinies—that every Selenite was attached to some inhabitant of the earth by a tie of sympathy; they maintained that the entire vital system is subject to her control, etc. But in time the majority renounced these vulgar errors, and espoused the true side of the question. As for the Yankees, they had no other ambition than to take possession of this new continent of the sky, and to plant upon the summit of its highest elevation the star-spangled banner of the United States of America.

VII

THE HYMN OF THE CANNON-BALL

THE Observatory of Cambridge in its memorable letter had treated the question from a purely astronomical point of view. The mechanical part still remained.

President Barbicane had, without loss of time, nominated a working committee of the Gun Club. The duty of this committee was to resolve the three grand questions of the cannon, the projectile, and the powder. It was composed of four members of great technical knowledge, Barbicane (with a casting vote in case of equality), General Morgan, Major Elphinstone, and J. T. Maston, to whom were confided the functions of secretary. On the 8th of October the committee met at the house of President Barbicane, 3 Republican Street. The meeting was opened by the president himself.

"Gentlemen," said he, "we have to resolve one of the most important problems in the whole of the noble science of gunnery. It might appear, perhaps, the most logical course to devote our first meeting to the discussion of the engine to be employed. Nevertheless, after mature consideration, it has appeared to me that the question of the projectile must take precedence of that of the cannon, and that the dimensions of the latter must necessarily depend on those of the former."

"Suffer me to say a word," here broke in J. T. Maston. Permission having been granted, "Gentlemen," said he with an inspired accent, "our president is right in placing the question of the projectile above all others. The ball we are about to discharge at the moon is our ambassador to her, and I wish to consider it from a moral point of view. The cannon-ball, gentlemen, to my mind, is the most magnificent manifestation of human power. If Providence has created the stars and the planets, man has called the cannon-ball into existence. Let Providence claim the swiftness of electricity and of light, of the stars, the comets, and the planets, of wind and sound—we claim to have invented the swiftness of the cannon-ball, a hundred times superior to that of the swiftest horses or railway train. How glorious will be the moment when, infinitely exceeding all hitherto attained velocities, we shall launch our new projectile with the rapidity of seven miles a second! Shall it not, gentlemen—shall it not be received up there with the honors due to a terrestrial ambassador?"

Overcome with emotion the orator sat down and applied himself to a huge plate of sandwiches before him.

"And now," said Barbicane, "let us quit the domain of poetry and come direct to the question."

"By all means," replied the members, each with his mouth full of sandwich.

"The problem before us," continued the president, "is how to communicate to a projectile a velocity of 12,000 yards per second. Let us at present examine the velocities hitherto attained. General Morgan will be able to enlighten us on this point."

"And the more easily," replied the general, "that during the war I was a member of the committee of experiments. I may say, then, that the 100-

pounder Dahlgrens, which carried a distance of 5,000 yards, impressed upon their projectile an initial velocity of 500 yards a second. The Rodman Columbiad threw a shot weighing half a ton a distance of six miles, with a velocity of 800 yards per second—a result which Armstrong and Palisser have never obtained in England."

"This," replied Barbicane, "is, I believe, the maximum velocity ever attained?"

"It is so," replied the general.

"Ah!" groaned J. T. Maston, "if my mortar had not burst—"

"Yes," quietly replied Barbicane, "but it did burst. We must take, then, for our starting point, this velocity of 800 yards. We must increase it twenty-fold. Now, reserving for another discussion the means of producing this velocity, I will call your attention to the dimensions which it will be proper to assign to the shot. You understand that we have nothing to do here with projectiles weighing at most but half a ton."

"Why not?" demanded the major.

"Because the shot," quickly replied J. T. Maston, "must be big enough to attract the attention of the inhabitants of the moon, if there are any?"

"Yes," replied Barbicane, "and for another reason more important still."

"What mean you?" asked the major.

"I mean that it is not enough to discharge a projectile, and then take no further notice of it; we must follow it throughout its course, up to the moment when it shall reach its goal."

"What?" shouted the general and the major in great surprise.

"Undoubtedly," replied Barbicane composedly, "or our experiment would produce no result."

"But then," replied the major, "you will have to give this projectile enormous dimensions."

"No! Be so good as to listen. You know that optical instruments have acquired great perfection; with certain instruments we have succeeded in obtaining enlargements of 6,000 times and reducing the moon to within forty miles' distance. Now, at this distance, any objects sixty feet square would be perfectly visible.

"If, then, the penetrative power of telescopes has not been further increased, it is because that power detracts from their light; and the moon, which is but a reflecting mirror, does not give back sufficient light to enable us to perceive objects of lesser magnitude."

"Well, then, what do you propose to do?" asked the general. "Would you give your projectile a diameter of sixty feet?"

"Not so."

"Do you intend, then, to increase the luminous power of the moon?"

"Exactly so. If I can succeed in diminishing the density of the atmosphere through which the moon's light has to travel I shall have rendered her light more intense. To effect that object it will be enough to establish a telescope on some elevated mountain. That is what we will do."

"I give it up," answered the major. "You have such a way of simplifying things. And what enlargement do you expect to obtain in this way?"

"One of 48,000 times, which should bring the moon within an apparent distance of five miles; and, in order to be visible, objects need not have a diameter of more than nine feet."

"So, then," cried J. T. Maston, "our projectile need not be more than nine feet in diameter."

"Let me observe, however," interrupted Major Elphinstone, "this will involve a weight such as—"

"My dear major," replied Barbicane, "before discussing its weight permit me to enumerate some of the marvels which our ancestors have achieved in this respect. I don't mean to pretend that the science of gunnery has not advanced, but it is as well to bear in mind that during the middle ages they obtained results more surprising, I will venture to say, than ours. For instance, during the siege of Constantinople by Mahomet II., in 1453, stone shot of 1,900 pounds weight were employed. At Malta, in the time of the knights, there was a gun of the fortress of St. Elmo which threw a projectile weighing 2,500 pounds. And, now, what is the extent of what we have seen ourselves? Armstrong guns discharging shot of 500 pounds, and the Rodman guns projectiles of half a ton! It seems, then, that if projectiles have gained in range, they have lost far more in weight. Now, if we turn our efforts in that direction, we ought to arrive, with the progress on science, at ten times the weight of the shot of Mahomet II. and the Knights of Malta."

"Clearly," replied the major; "but what metal do you calculate upon employing?"

"Simply cast iron," said General Morgan.

"But," interrupted the major, "since the weight of a shot is proportionate to its volume, an iron ball of nine feet in diameter would be of tremendous weight."

"Yes, if it were solid, not if it were hollow."

"Hollow? then it would be a shell?"

"Yes, a shell," replied Barbicane; "decidedly it must be. A solid shot of 108 inches would weigh more than 200,000 pounds, a weight evidently far too great. Still, as we must reserve a certain stability for our projectile, I propose to give it a weight of 20,000 pounds."

"What, then, will be the thickness of the sides?" asked the major.

"If we follow the usual proportion," replied Morgan, "a diameter of 108 inches would require sides of two feet thickness, or less."

"That would be too much," replied Barbicane; "for you will observe that the question is not that of a shot intended to pierce an iron plate; it will suffice to give it sides strong enough to resist the pressure of the gas. The problem, therefore, is this—What thickness ought a cast-iron shell to have in order not to weight more than 20,000 pounds? Our clever secretary will soon enlighten us upon this point."

"Nothing easier." replied the worthy secretary of the committee; and, rapidly tracing a few algebraical formulae upon paper, among which n^2 and x^2 frequently appeared, he presently said:

"The sides will require a thickness of less than two inches."

"Will that be enough?" asked the major doubtfully.

"Clearly not!" replied the president.

"What is to be done, then?" said Elphinstone, with a puzzled air.

"Employ another metal instead of iron."

"Copper?" said Morgan.

"No! that would be too heavy. I have better than that to offer."

"What then?" asked the major.

"Aluminum!" replied Barbicane.

"Aluminum?" cried his three colleagues in chorus.

"Unquestionably, my friends. This valuable metal possesses the whiteness of silver, the indestructibility of gold, the tenacity of iron, the fusibility of copper, the lightness of glass. It is easily wrought, is very widely distributed, forming the base of most of the rocks, is three times lighter than iron, and seems to have been created for the express purpose of furnishing us with the material for our projectile."

"But, my dear president," said the major, "is not the cost price of aluminum extremely high?"

"It was so at its first discovery, but it has fallen now to nine dollars a pound."

"But still, nine dollars a pound!" replied the major, who was not willing readily to give in; "even that is an enormous price."

"Undoubtedly, my dear major; but not beyond our reach."

"What will the projectile weigh then?" asked Morgan.

"Here is the result of my calculations," replied Barbicane. "A shot of 108 inches in diameter, and twelve inches in thickness, would weigh, in cast-iron, 67,440 pounds; cast in aluminum, its weight will be reduced to 19,250 pounds."

"Capital!" cried the major; "but do you know that, at nine dollars a pound, this projectile will cost—"

"One hundred and seventy-three thousand and fifty dollars ($173,050). I know it quite well. But fear not, my friends; the money will not be wanting for our enterprise. I will answer for it. Now what say you to aluminum, gentlemen?"

"Adopted!" replied the three members of the committee. So ended the first meeting. The question of the projectile was definitely settled.

VIII

HISTORY OF THE CANNON

THE resolutions passed at the last meeting produced a great effect out of doors. Timid people took fright at the idea of a shot weighing 20,000 pounds being launched into space; they asked what cannon could ever transmit a sufficient velocity to such a mighty mass. The minutes of the second meeting were destined triumphantly to answer such questions. The following evening the discussion was renewed.

"My dear colleagues," said Barbicane, without further preamble, "the subject now before us is the construction of the engine, its length, its composition, and its weight. It is probable that we shall end by giving it gigantic dimensions; but however great may be the difficulties in the way, our mechanical genius will readily surmount them. Be good enough, then, to give me your attention, and do not hesitate to make objections at the close. I have no fear of them. The problem before us is how to communicate an initial force of 12,000 yards per second to a shell of 108 inches in diameter, weighing 20,000 pounds. Now when a projectile is launched into space, what happens to it? It is acted upon by three independent forces: the resistance of the air, the attraction of the earth, and the force of impulsion with which it is endowed. Let us examine these three forces. The resistance of the air is of little importance. The atmosphere of the earth does not exceed forty miles. Now, with the given rapidity, the projectile will have traversed this in five seconds, and the period is too brief for the resistance of the medium to be regarded otherwise than as insignificant. Proceding, then, to the attraction of the earth, that is, the weight of the shell, we know that this weight will diminish in the inverse ratio of the square of the distance. When a body left to itself falls to the surface of the earth, it falls five feet in the first second; and if the same body were removed 257,542 miles further off, in other words, to the distance of the moon, its fall would be reduced to about half a line in the first second. That is almost equivalent to a state of perfect rest. Our business, then, is to overcome progressively this action of gravitation. The mode of accomplishing that is by the force of impulsion."

"There's the difficulty," broke in the major.

"True," replied the president; "but we will overcome that, for the force of impulsion will depend on the length of the engine and the powder employed, the latter being limited only by the resisting power of the former. Our business, then, to-day is with the dimensions of the cannon."

"Now, up to the present time," said Barbicane, "our longest guns have not exceeded twenty-five feet in length. We shall therefore astonish the world by the dimensions we shall be obliged to adopt. It must evidently be, then, a gun of great range, since the length of the piece will increase the detention of the gas accumulated behind the projectile; but there is no advantage in passing certain limits."

"Quite so," said the major. "What is the rule in such a case?"

"Ordinarily the length of a gun is twenty to twenty-five times the diameter of the shot, and its weight two hundred and thirty-five to two hundred and forty times that of the shot."

"That is not enough," cried J. T. Maston impetuously.

"I agree with you, my good friend; and, in fact, following this proportion for a projectile nine feet in diameter, weighing 30,000 pounds, the gun would only have a length of two hundred and twenty-five feet, and a weight of 7,200,000 pounds."

"Ridiculous!" rejoined Maston. "As well take a pistol."

"I think so too," replied Barbicane; "that is why I propose to quadruple that length, and to construct a gun of nine hundred feet."

The general and the major offered some objections; nevertheless, the proposition, actively supported by the secretary, was definitely adopted.

"But," said Elphinstone, "what thickness must we give it?"

"A thickness of six feet," replied Barbicane.

"You surely don't think of mounting a mass like that upon a carriage?" asked the major.

"It would be a superb idea, though," said Maston.

"But impracticable," replied Barbicane. "No, I think of sinking this engine in the earth alone, binding it with hoops of wrought iron, and finally surrounding it with a thick mass of masonry of stone and cement. The piece once cast, it must be bored with great precision, so as to preclude any possible windage. So there will be no loss whatever of gas, and all the expansive force of the powder will be employed in the propulsion."

"One simple question," said Elphinstone: "is our gun to be rifled?"

"No, certainly not," replied Barbicane; "we require an enormous initial velocity; and you are well aware that a shot quits a rifled gun less rapidly than it does a smooth-bore."

"True," rejoined the major.

The committee here adjourned for a few minutes to tea and sandwiches.

On the discussion being renewed, "Gentlemen," said Barbicane, "we must now take into consideration the metal to be employed. Our cannon must be possessed of great tenacity, great hardness, be infusible by heat, indissoluble, and inoxidable by the corrosive action of acids."

"There is no doubt about that," replied the major; "and as we shall have to employ an immense quantity of metal, we shall not be at a loss for choice."

"Well, then," said Morgan, "I propose the best alloy hitherto known, which consists of one hundred parts of copper, twelve of tin, and six of brass."

"I admit," replied the president, "that this composition has yielded excellent results, but in the present case it would be too expensive, and very difficult to work. I think, then, that we ought to adopt a material excellent in its way and of low price, such as cast iron. What is your advice, major?"

"I quite agree with you," replied Elphinstone.

"In fact," continued Barbicane, "cast iron costs ten times less than bronze; it is easy to cast, it runs readily from the moulds of sand, it is easy of manipulation, it is at once economical of money and of time. In addition, it is excellent as a material, and I well remember that during the war, at the siege of Atlanta, some iron guns fired one thousand rounds at intervals of twenty minutes without injury."

"Cast iron is very brittle, though," replied Morgan.

"Yes, but it possesses great resistance. I will now ask our worthy secretary to calculate the weight of a cast-iron gun with a bore of nine feet and a thickness of six feet of metal."

"In a moment," replied Maston. Then, dashing off some algebraical formulae with marvelous facility, in a minute or two he declared the following result:

"The cannon will weigh 68,040 tons. And, at two cents a pound, it will cost—"

"Two million five hundred and ten thousand seven hundred and one dollars."

Maston, the major, and the general regarded Barbicane with uneasy looks.

"Well, gentlemen," replied the president, "I repeat what I said yesterday. Make yourselves easy; the millions will not be wanting."

With this assurance of their president the committee separated, after having fixed their third meeting for the following evening.

IX

THE QUESTION OF THE POWDERS

THERE remained for consideration merely the question of powders. The public awaited with interest its final decision. The size of the projectile, the length of the cannon being settled, what would be the quantity of powder necessary to produce impulsion?

It is generally asserted that gunpowder was invented in the fourteenth century by the monk Schwartz, who paid for his grand discovery with his life. It is, however, pretty well proved that this story ought to be ranked among the legends of the middle ages. Gunpowder was not invented by any one; it was the lineal successor of the Greek fire, which, like itself, was composed of sulfur and saltpeter. Few persons are acquainted with the mechanical power of gunpowder. Now this is precisely what is necessary to be understood in order to comprehend the importance of the question submitted to the committee.

A litre of gunpowder weighs about two pounds; during combustion it produces 400 litres of gas. This gas, on being liberated and acted upon by temperature raised to 2,400 degrees, occupies a space of 4,000 litres: consequently the volume of powder is to the volume of gas produced by its combustion as 1 to 4,000. One may judge, therefore, of the tremendous pressure on this gas when compressed within a space 4,000 times too confined. All this was, of course, well known to the members of the committee when they met on the following evening.

The first speaker on this occasion was Major Elphinstone, who had been the director of the gunpowder factories during the war.

"Gentlemen," said this distinguished chemist, "I begin with some figures which will serve as the basis of our calculation. The old 24-pounder shot required for its discharge sixteen pounds of powder."

"You are certain of this amount?" broke in Barbicane.

"Quite certain," replied the major. "The Armstrong cannon employs only seventy-five pounds of powder for a projectile of eight hundred pounds, and the Rodman Columbiad uses only one hundred and sixty pounds of powder to send its half ton shot a distance of six miles. These facts cannot be called in question, for I myself raised the point during the depositions taken before the committee of artillery."

"Quite true," said the general.

"Well," replied the major, "these figures go to prove that the quantity of powder is not increased with the weight of the shot; that is to say, if a 24-pounder shot requires sixteen pounds of powder;—in other words, if in ordinary guns we employ a quantity of powder equal to two-thirds of the weight of the projectile, this proportion is not constant. Calculate, and you will see that in place of three hundred and thirty-three pounds of powder, the quantity is reduced to no more than one hundred and sixty pounds."

"What are you aiming at?" asked the president.

"If you push your theory to extremes, my dear major," said J. T. Maston, "you will get to this, that as soon as your shot becomes sufficiently heavy you will not require any powder at all."

"Our friend Maston is always at his jokes, even in serious matters," cried the major; "but let him make his mind easy, I am going presently to propose gunpowder enough to satisfy his artillerist's propensities. I only keep to statistical facts when I say that, during the war, and for the very largest guns, the weight of the powder was reduced, as the result of experience, to a tenth part of the weight of the shot."

"Perfectly correct," said Morgan; "but before deciding the quantity of powder necessary to give the impulse, I think it would be as well—"

"We shall have to employ a large-grained powder," continued the major; "its combustion is more rapid than that of the small."

"No doubt about that," replied Morgan; "but it is very destructive, and ends by enlarging the bore of the pieces."

"Granted; but that which is injurious to a gun destined to perform long service is not so to our Columbiad. We shall run no danger of an explosion; and it is necessary that our powder should take fire instantaneously in order that its mechanical effect may be complete."

"We must have," said Maston, "several touch-holes, so as to fire it at different points at the same time."

"Certainly," replied Elphinstone; "but that will render the working of the piece more difficult. I return then to my large-grained powder, which removes those difficulties. In his Columbiad charges Rodman employed a powder as large as chestnuts, made of willow charcoal, simply dried in cast-iron pans. This powder was hard and glittering, left no trace upon the hand, contained hydrogen and oxygen in large proportion, took fire instantaneously, and, though very destructive, did not sensibly injure the mouth-piece."

Up to this point Barbicane had kept aloof from the discussion; he left the others to speak while he himself listened; he had evidently got an idea. He now simply said, "Well, my friends, what quantity of powder do you propose?"

The three members looked at one another.

"Two hundred thousand pounds." at last said Morgan.

"Five hundred thousand," added the major.

"Eight hundred thousand," screamed Maston.

A moment of silence followed this triple proposal; it was at last broken by the president.

"Gentlemen," he quietly said, "I start from this principle, that the resistance of a gun, constructed under the given conditions, is unlimited. I shall surprise our friend Maston, then, by stigmatizing his calculations as timid; and I propose to double his 800,000 pounds of powder."

"Sixteen hundred thousand pounds?" shouted Maston, leaping from his seat.

"Just so."

"We shall have to come then to my ideal of a cannon half a mile long; for you see 1,600,000 pounds will occupy a space of about 20,000 cubic feet; and since the contents of your cannon do not exceed 54,000 cubic feet, it would be half full; and the bore will not be more than long enough for the gas to communicate to the projectile sufficient impulse."

"Nevertheless," said the president, "I hold to that quantity of powder. Now, 1,600,000 pounds of powder will create 6,000,000,000 litres of gas. Six thousand millions! You quite understand?"

"What is to be done then?" said the general.

"The thing is very simple; we must reduce this enormous quantity of powder, while preserving to it its mechanical power."

"Good; but by what means?"

"I am going to tell you," replied Barbicane quietly.

"Nothing is more easy than to reduce this mass to one quarter of its bulk. You know that curious cellular matter which constitutes the elementary tissues of vegetable? This substance is found quite pure in many bodies, especially in cotton, which is nothing more than the down of the seeds of the cotton plant. Now cotton, combined with cold nitric acid, become transformed into a substance eminently insoluble, combustible, and explosive. It was first discovered in 1832, by Braconnot, a French chemist, who called it xyloidine. In 1838 another Frenchman, Pelouze, investigated its different properties, and finally, in 1846, Schonbein, professor of chemistry at Bale, proposed its employment for purposes of war. This powder, now called pyroxyle, or fulminating cotton, is prepared with great facility by simply plunging cotton for fifteen minutes in nitric acid, then washing it in water, then drying it, and it is ready for use."

"Nothing could be more simple," said Morgan.

"Moreover, pyroxyle is unaltered by moisture—a valuable property to us, inasmuch as it would take several days to charge the cannon. It ignites at 170 degrees in place of 240, and its combustion is so rapid that one may set light to it on the top of the ordinary powder, without the latter having time to ignite."

"Perfect!" exclaimed the major.

"Only it is more expensive."

"What matter?" cried J. T. Maston.

"Finally, it imparts to projectiles a velocity four times superior to that of gunpowder. I will even add, that if we mix it with one-eighth of its own weight of nitrate of potassium, its expansive force is again considerably augmented."

"Will that be necessary?" asked the major.

"I think not," replied Barbicane. "So, then, in place of 1,600,000 pounds of powder, we shall have but 400,000 pounds of fulminating cotton; and since we can, without danger, compress 500 pounds of cotton into twenty-seven cubic feet, the whole quantity will not occupy a height of more than 180 feet within the bore of the Columbiad. In this way the shot will have more than 700 feet of bore to traverse under a force of 6,000,000,000 litres of gas before taking its flight toward the moon."

At this juncture J. T. Maston could not repress his emotion; he flung himself into the arms of his friend with the violence of a projectile, and Barbicane would have been stove in if he had not been boom-proof.

This incident terminated the third meeting of the committee.

Barbicane and his bold colleagues, to whom nothing seemed impossible, had succeeding in solving the complex problems of projectile, cannon, and powder. Their plan was drawn up, and it only remained to put it into execution.

"A mere matter of detail, a bagatelle," said J. T. Maston.

X

ONE ENEMY V. TWENTY-FIVE MILLIONS OF FRIENDS

THE American public took a lively interest in the smallest details of the enterprise of the Gun Club. It followed day by day the discussion of the committee. The most simple preparations for the great experiment, the questions of figures which it involved, the mechanical difficulties to be resolved—in one word, the entire plan of work—roused the popular excitement to the highest pitch.

The purely scientific attraction was suddenly intensified by the following incident:

We have seen what legions of admirers and friends Barbicane's project had rallied round its author. There was, however, one single individual alone in all the States of the Union who protested against the attempt of the Gun Club. He attacked it furiously on every opportunity, and human nature is such that Barbicane felt more keenly the opposition of that one man than he did the applause of all the others. He was well aware of the motive of this antipathy, the origin of this solitary enmity, the cause of its personality and old standing, and in what rivalry of self-love it had its rise.

This persevering enemy the president of the Gun Club had never seen. Fortunate that it was so, for a meeting between the two men would certainly have been attended with serious consequences. This rival was a man of science, like Barbicane himself, of a fiery, daring, and violent disposition; a pure Yankee. His name was Captain Nicholl; he lived at Philadelphia.

Most people are aware of the curious struggle which arose during the Federal war between the guns and armor of iron-plated ships. The result was the entire reconstruction of the navy of both the continents; as the one grew heavier, the other became thicker in proportion. The Merrimac, the Monitor, the Tennessee, the Weehawken discharged enormous projectiles themselves, after having been armor-clad against the projectiles of others. In fact they did to others that which they would not they should do to them—that grand principle of immortality upon which rests the whole art of war.

Now if Barbicane was a great founder of shot, Nicholl was a great forger of plates; the one cast night and day at Baltimore, the other forged day and night at Philadelphia. As soon as ever Barbicane invented a new shot, Nicholl invented a new plate; each followed a current of ideas essentially opposed to the other. Happily for these citizens, so useful to their country, a distance of from fifty to sixty miles separated them from one another, and they had never yet met. Which of these two inventors had the advantage over the other it was difficult to decide from the results obtained. By last accounts, however, it would seem that the armor-plate would in the end have to give way to the shot; nevertheless, there were competent judges who had their doubts on the point.

At the last experiment the cylindro-conical projectiles of Barbicane stuck like so many pins in the Nicholl plates. On that day the Philadelphia iron-forger then believed himself victorious, and could not evince contempt enough for his rival; but when the other afterward substituted for conical shot simple 600-pound shells, at very moderate velocity, the captain was obliged to give in. In fact, these projectiles knocked his best metal plate to shivers.

Matters were at this stage, and victory seemed to rest with the shot, when the war came to an end on the very day when Nicholl had completed a new armor-plate of wrought steel. It was a masterpiece of its kind, and bid defiance to all the projectiles of the world. The captain had it conveyed to the Polygon at Washington, challenging the president of the Gun Club to break it. Barbicane, peace having been declared, declined to try the experiment.

Nicholl, now furious, offered to expose his plate to the shock of any shot, solid, hollow, round, or conical. Refused by the president, who did not choose to compromise his last success.

Nicholl, disgusted by this obstinacy, tried to tempt Barbicane by offering him every chance. He proposed to fix the plate within two hundred yards of the gun. Barbicane still obstinate in refusal. A hundred yards? Not even seventy-five!

"At fifty then!" roared the captain through the newspapers. "At twenty-five yards! and I'll stand behind!"

Barbicane returned for answer that, even if Captain Nicholl would be so good as to stand in front, he would not fire any more.

Nicholl could not contain himself at this reply; threw out hints of cowardice; that a man who refused to fire a cannon-shot was pretty near being afraid of it; that artillerists who fight at six miles distance are substituting mathematical formulae for individual courage.

To these insinuations Barbicane returned no answer; perhaps he never heard of them, so absorbed was he in the calculations for his great enterprise.

When his famous communication was made to the Gun Club, the captain's wrath passed all bounds; with his intense jealousy was mingled a feeling of absolute impotence. How was he to invent anything to beat this 900-feet Columbiad? What armor-plate could ever resist a projectile of 30,000 pounds weight? Overwhelmed at first under this violent shock, he by and by recovered himself, and resolved to crush the proposal by weight of his arguments.

He then violently attacked the labors of the Gun Club, published a number of letters in the newspapers, endeavored to prove Barbicane ignorant of the first principles of gunnery. He maintained that it was absolutely impossible to impress upon any body whatever a velocity of 12,000 yards per second; that even with such a velocity a projectile of such a weight could not transcend the limits of the earth's atmosphere.

Further still, even regarding the velocity to be acquired, and granting it to be sufficient, the shell could not resist the pressure of the gas developed by the ignition of 1,600,000 pounds of powder; and supposing it to resist that pressure, it would be less able to support that temperature; it would melt on quitting the Columbiad, and fall back in a red-hot shower upon the heads of the imprudent spectators.

Barbicane continued his work without regarding these attacks.

Nicholl then took up the question in its other aspects. Without touching upon its uselessness in all points of view, he regarded the experiment as fraught with extreme danger, both to the citizens, who might sanction by their presence so reprehensible a spectacle, and also to the towns in the neighborhood of this deplorable cannon. He also observed that if the projectile did not succeed in reaching its destination (a result absolutely impossible), it must inevitably fall back upon the earth, and that the shock of such a mass, multiplied by the square of its velocity, would seriously endanger every point of the globe. Under the circumstances, therefore, and without interfering with the rights of free citizens, it was a case for the intervention of Government, which ought not to endanger the safety of all for the pleasure of one individual.

In spite of all his arguments, however, Captain Nicholl remained alone in his opinion. Nobody listened to him, and he did not succeed in alienating a single admirer from the president of the Gun Club. The latter did not even take the pains to refute the arguments of his rival.

Nicholl, driven into his last entrenchments, and not able to fight personally in the cause, resolved to fight with money. He published, therefore, in the Richmond Inquirer a series of wagers, conceived in these terms, and on an increasing scale:

No. 1 ($1,000):—That the necessary funds for the experiment of the Gun Club will not be forthcoming.

No. 2 ($2,000):—That the operation of casting a cannon of 900 feet is impracticable, and cannot possibly succeed.

No. 3 ($3,000):—That is it impossible to load the Columbiad, and that the pyroxyle will take fire spontaneously under the pressure of the projectile.

No. 4 ($4,000):—That the Columbiad will burst at the first fire.

No. 5 ($5,000):—That the shot will not travel farther than six miles, and that it will fall back again a few seconds after its discharge.

It was an important sum, therefore, which the captain risked in his invincible obstinacy. He had no less than $15,000 at stake.

Notwithstanding the importance of the challenge, on the 19th of May he received a sealed packet containing the following superbly laconic reply:

"BALTIMORE, *October 19.*
"*Done.*
"BARBICANE."

XI

FLORIDA AND TEXAS

ONE question remained yet to be decided; it was necessary to choose a favorable spot for the experiment. According to the advice of the Observatory of Cambridge, the gun must be fired perpendicularly to the plane of the horizon, that is to say, toward the zenith. Now the moon does not traverse the zenith, except in places situated between 0@ and 28@ of latitude. It became, then, necessary to determine exactly that spot on the globe where the immense Columbiad should be cast.

On the 20th of October, at a general meeting of the Gun Club, Barbicane produced a magnificent map of the United States. "Gentlemen," said he, in opening the discussion, "I presume that we are all agreed that this experiment cannot and ought not to be tried anywhere but within the limits of the soil of the Union. Now, by good fortune, certain frontiers of the United States extend downward as far as the 28th parallel of the north latitude. If you will cast your eye over this map, you will see that we have at our disposal the whole of the southern portion of Texas and Florida."

It was finally agreed, then, that the Columbiad must be cast on the soil of either Texas or Florida. The result, however, of this decision was to create a rivalry entirely without precedent between the different towns of these two States.

The 28th parallel, on reaching the American coast, traverses the peninsula of Florida, dividing it into two nearly equal portions. Then, plunging into the Gulf of Mexico, it subtends the arc formed by the coast of Alabama, Mississippi, and Louisiana; then skirting Texas, off which it cuts an angle, it continues its course over Mexico, crosses the Sonora, Old California, and loses itself in the Pacific Ocean. It was, therefore, only those portions of Texas and Florida which were situated below this parallel which came within the prescribed conditions of latitude.

Florida, in its southern part, reckons no cities of importance; it is simply studded with forts raised against the roving Indians. One solitary town, Tampa Town, was able to put in a claim in favor of its situation.

In Texas, on the contrary, the towns are much more numerous and important. Corpus Christi, in the county of Nueces, and all the cities situated on the Rio Bravo, Laredo, Comalites, San Ignacio on the Web, Rio Grande City on the Starr, Edinburgh in the Hidalgo, Santa Rita, Elpanda, Brownsville in the Cameron, formed an imposing league against the pretensions of Florida. So, scarcely was the decision known, when the Texan and Floridan deputies arrived at Baltimore in an incredibly short space of time. From that very moment President Barbicane and the influential members of the Gun Club were besieged day and night by formidable claims. If seven cities of Greece contended for the honor of having given birth to a Homer, here were two entire States threatening to come to blows about the question of a cannon.

The rival parties promenaded the streets with arms in their hands; and at every occasion of their meeting a collision was to be apprehended which might have been attended with disastrous results. Happily the prudence and address of President Barbicane averted the danger. These personal demonstrations found a division in the newspapers of the different States. The New York Herald and the Tribune supported Texas, while the Times and the American Review espoused the cause of the Floridan deputies. The members of the Gun Club could not decide to which to give the preference.

Texas produced its array of twenty-six counties; Florida replied that twelve counties were better than twenty-six in a country only one-sixth part of the size.

Texas plumed itself upon its 330,000 natives; Florida, with a far smaller territory, boasted of being much more densely populated with 56,000.

The Texans, through the columns of the Herald claimed that some regard should be had to a State which grew the best cotton in all America, produced the best green oak for the service of the navy, and contained the finest oil, besides iron mines, in which the yield was fifty per cent. of pure metal.

To this the American Review replied that the soil of Florida, although not equally rich, afforded the best conditions for the moulding and casting of the Columbiad, consisting as it did of sand and argillaceous earth.

"That may be all very well," replied the Texans; "but you must first get to this country. Now the communications with Florida are difficult, while the coast of Texas offers the bay of Galveston, which possesses a circumference of fourteen leagues, and is capable of containing the navies of the entire world!"

"A pretty notion truly," replied the papers in the interest of Florida, "that of Galveston bay below the 29th parallel! Have we not got the bay of Espiritu Santo, opening precisely upon the 28th degree, and by which ships can reach Tampa Town by direct route?"

"A fine bay; half choked with sand!"

"Choked yourselves!" returned the others.

Thus the war went on for several days, when Florida endeavored to draw her adversary away on to fresh ground; and one morning the Times hinted that, the enterprise being essentially American, it ought not to be attempted upon other than purely American territory.

To these words Texas retorted, "American! are we not as much so as you? Were not Texas and Florida both incorporated into the Union in 1845?"

"Undoubtedly," replied the Times; "but we have belonged to the Americans ever since 1820."

"Yes!" returned the Tribune; "after having been Spaniards or English for two hundred years, you were sold to the United States for five million dollars!"

"Well! and why need we blush for that? Was not Louisiana bought from Napoleon in 1803 at the price of sixteen million dollars?"

"Scandalous!" roared the Texas deputies. "A wretched little strip of country like Florida to dare to compare itself to Texas, who, in place of selling herself, asserted her own independence, drove out the Mexicans in March 2, 1846, and declared herself a federal republic after the victory gained by Samuel Houston, on the banks of the San Jacinto, over the troops of Santa Anna!—a country, in fine, which voluntarily annexed itself to the United States of America!"

"Yes; because it was afraid of the Mexicans!" replied Florida.

"Afraid!" From this moment the state of things became intolerable. A sanguinary encounter seemed daily imminent between the two parties in the streets of Baltimore. It became necessary to keep an eye upon the deputies.

President Barbicane knew not which way to look. Notes, documents, letters full of menaces showered down upon his house. Which side ought he to take? As regarded the appropriation of the soil, the facility of communication, the rapidity of transport, the claims of both States were evenly balanced. As for political prepossessions, they had nothing to do with the question.

This dead block had existed for some little time, when Barbicane resolved to get rid of it all at once. He called a meeting of his colleagues, and laid before them a proposition which, it will be seen, was profoundly sagacious.

"On carefully considering," he said, "what is going on now between Florida and Texas, it is clear that the same difficulties will recur with all the towns of the favored State. The rivalry will descend from State to city, and so on downward. Now Texas possesses eleven towns within the prescribed conditions, which will further dispute the honor and create us new enemies, while Florida has only one. I go in, therefore, for Florida and Tampa Town."

This decision, on being made known, utterly crushed the Texan deputies. Seized with an indescribable fury, they addressed threatening letters to the different members of the Gun Club by name. The magistrates had but one course to take, and they took it. They chartered a special train, forced the Texans into it whether they would or no; and they quitted the city with a speed of thirty miles an hour.

Quickly, however, as they were despatched, they found time to hurl one last and bitter sarcasm at their adversaries.

Alluding to the extent of Florida, a mere peninsula confined between two seas, they pretended that it could never sustain the shock of the discharge, and that it would "bust up" at the very first shot.

"Very well, let it bust up!" replied the Floridans, with a brevity of the days of ancient Sparta.

XII

URBI ET ORBI

THE astronomical, mechanical, and topographical difficulties resolved, finally came the question of finance. The sum required was far too great for any individual, or even any single State, to provide the requisite millions.

President Barbicane undertook, despite of the matter being a purely American affair, to render it one of universal interest, and to request the financial co-operation of all peoples. It was, he maintained, the right and duty of the whole earth to interfere in the affairs of its satellite. The subscription opened at Baltimore extended properly to the whole world—Urbi et orbi.

This subscription was successful beyond all expectation; notwithstanding that it was a question not of lending but of giving the money. It was a purely disinterested operation in the strictest sense of the term, and offered not the slightest chance of profit.

The effect, however, of Barbicane's communication was not confined to the frontiers of the United States; it crossed the Atlantic and Pacific, invading simultaneously Asia and Europe, Africa and Oceanica. The observatories of the Union placed themselves in immediate communication with those of foreign countries. Some, such as those of Paris, Petersburg, Berlin, Stockholm, Hamburg, Malta, Lisbon, Benares, Madras, and others, transmitted their good wishes; the rest maintained a prudent silence, quietly awaiting the result. As for the observatory at Greenwich, seconded as it was by the twenty-two astronomical establishments of Great Britain, it spoke plainly enough. It boldly denied the possibility of success, and pronounced in favor of the theories of Captain Nicholl. But this was nothing more than mere English jealousy.

On the 8th of October President Barbicane published a manifesto full of enthusiasm, in which he made an appeal to "all persons of good will upon the face of the earth." This document, translated into all languages, met with immense success.

Subscription lists were opened in all the principal cities of the Union, with a central office at the Baltimore Bank, 9 Baltimore Street.

In addition, subscriptions were received at the following banks in the different states of the two continents:

- At Vienna, with S. M. de Rothschild.
- At Petersburg, Stieglitz and Co.
- At Paris, The Credit Mobilier.
- At Stockholm, Tottie and Arfuredson.
- At London, N. M. Rothschild and Son.
- At Turin, Ardouin and Co.
- At Berlin, Mendelssohn.
- At Geneva, Lombard, Odier and Co.
- At Constantinople, The Ottoman Bank.
- At Brussels, J. Lambert.
- At Madrid, Daniel Weisweller.
- At Amsterdam, Netherlands Credit Co.
- At Rome, Torlonia and Co.
- At Lisbon, Lecesne.
- At Copenhagen, Private Bank.
- At Rio de Janeiro, Private Bank.
- At Montevideo, Private Bank.
- At Valparaiso and Lima, Thomas la Chambre and Co.
- At Mexico, Martin Daran and Co.

Three days after the manifesto of President Barbicane $4,000,000 were paid into the different towns of the Union. With such a balance the

Gun Club might begin operations at once. But some days later advices were received to the effect that foreign subscriptions were being eagerly taken up. Certain countries distinguished themselves by their liberality; others untied their purse-strings with less facility—a matter of temperament. Figures are, however, more eloquent than words, and here is the official statement of the sums which were paid in to the credit of the Gun Club at the close of the subscription.

Russia paid in as her contingent the enormous sum of 368,733 roubles. No one need be surprised at this, who bears in mind the scientific taste of the Russians, and the impetus which they have given to astronomical studies—thanks to their numerous observatories.

France began by deriding the pretensions of the Americans. The moon served as a pretext for a thousand stale puns and a score of ballads, in which bad taste contested the palm with ignorance. But as formerly the French paid before singing, so now they paid after having had their laugh, and they subscribed for a sum of 1,253,930 francs. At that price they had a right to enjoy themselves a little.

Austria showed herself generous in the midst of her financial crisis. Her public contributions amounted to the sum of 216,000 florins—a perfect godsend.

Fifty-two thousand rix-dollars were the remittance of Sweden and Norway; the amount is large for the country, but it would undoubtedly have been considerably increased had the subscription been opened in Christiana simultaneously with that at Stockholm. For some reason or other the Norwegians do not like to send their money to Sweden.

Prussia, by a remittance of 250,000 thalers, testified her high approval of the enterprise.

Turkey behaved generously; but she had a personal interest in the matter. The moon, in fact, regulates the cycle of her years and her fast of Ramadan. She could not do less than give 1,372,640 piastres; and she gave them with an eagerness which denoted, however, some pressure on the part of the government.

Belgium distinguished herself among the second-rate states by a grant of 513,000 francs—about two centimes per head of her population.

Holland and her colonies interested themselves to the extent of 110,000 florins, only demanding an allowance of five per cent. discount for paying ready money.

Denmark, a little contracted in territory, gave nevertheless 9,000 ducats, proving her love for scientific experiments.

The Germanic Confederation pledged itself to 34,285 florins. It was impossible to ask for more; besides, they would not have given it.

Though very much crippled, Italy found 200,000 lire in the pockets of her people. If she had had Venetia she would have done better; but she had not.

The States of the Church thought that they could not send less than 7,040 Roman crowns; and Portugal carried her devotion to science as far as 30,000 cruzados. It was the widow's mite—eighty-six piastres; but self-constituted empires are always rather short of money.

Two hundred and fifty-seven francs, this was the modest contribution of Switzerland to the American work. One must freely admit that she did not see the practical side of the matter. It did not seem to her that the mere despatch of a shot to the moon could possibly establish any relation of affairs with her; and it did not seem prudent to her to embark her capital in so hazardous an enterprise. After all, perhaps she was right.

As to Spain, she could not scrape together more than 110 reals. She gave as an excuse that she had her railways to finish. The truth is, that science is not favorably regarded in that country, it is still in a backward state; and moreover, certain Spaniards, not by any means the least educated, did not form a correct estimate of the bulk of the projectile compared with that of the moon. They feared that it would disturb the established order of things. In that case it were better to keep aloof; which they did to the tune of some reals.

There remained but England; and we know the contemptuous antipathy with which she received Barbicane's proposition. The English have but one soul for the whole twenty-six millions of inhabitants which Great Britain contains. They hinted that the enterprise of the Gun Club was contrary to the "principle of non-intervention." And they did not subscribe a single farthing.

At this intimation the Gun Club merely shrugged its shoulders and returned to its great work. When South America, that is to say, Peru, Chili, Brazil, the provinces of La Plata and Columbia, had poured forth their quota into their hands, the sum of $300,000, it found itself in possession of a considerable capital, of which the following is a statement:

United States subscriptions, ------------------ $4,000,000
Foreign subscriptions ---------------------- $1,446,675
Total, ------------------------------------- $5,446,675

Such was the sum which the public poured into the treasury of the Gun Club.

Let no one be surprised at the vastness of the amount. The work of casting, boring, masonry, the transport of workmen, their establishment in an almost uninhabited country, the construction of furnaces and workshops, the plant, the powder, the projectile, and incipient expenses, would, according to the estimates, absorb nearly the whole. Certain cannon-shots in the Federal war cost one thousand dollars apiece. This one of President Barbicane, unique in the annals of gunnery, might well cost five thousand times more.

On the 20th of October a contract was entered into with the manufactory at Coldspring, near New York, which during the war had furnished the largest Parrott, cast-iron guns. It was stipulated between the contracting parties that the manufactory of Coldspring should engage to transport to Tampa Town, in southern Florida, the necessary materials for casting the Columbiad. The work was bound to be completed at latest by the 15th of October following, and the cannon delivered in good condition under penalty of a forfeit of one hundred dollars a day to the moment when the moon should again present herself under the same conditions—that is to say, in eighteen years and eleven days.

The engagement of the workmen, their pay, and all the necessary details of the work, devolved upon the Coldspring Company.

This contract, executed in duplicate, was signed by Barbicane, president of the Gun Club, of the one part, and T. Murchison director of the Coldspring manufactory, of the other, who thus executed the deed on behalf of their respective principals.

XIII

Stones Hill

WHEN the decision was arrived at by the Gun Club, to the disparagement of Texas, every one in America, where reading is a universal acquirement, set to work to study the geography of Florida. Never before had there been such a sale for works like "Bertram's Travels in Florida," "Roman's Natural History of East and West Florida," "William's Territory of Florida," and "Cleland on the Cultivation of the Sugar-Cane in Florida." It became necessary to issue fresh editions of these works.

Barbicane had something better to do than to read. He desired to see things with his own eyes, and to mark the exact position of the proposed gun. So, without a moment's loss of time, he placed at the disposal of the Cambridge Observatory the funds necessary for the construction of a telescope, and entered into negotiations with the house of Breadwill and Co., of Albany, for the construction of an aluminum projectile of the required size. He then quitted Baltimore, accompanied by J. T. Maston, Major Elphinstone, and the manager of the Coldspring factory.

On the following day, the four fellow-travelers arrived at New Orleans. There they immediately embarked on board the Tampico, a despatch-boat belonging to the Federal navy, which the government had placed at their disposal; and, getting up steam, the banks of Louisiana speedily disappeared from sight.

The passage was not long. Two days after starting, the Tampico, having made four hundred and eighty miles, came in sight of the coast of Florida. On a nearer approach Barbicane found himself in view of a low, flat country of somewhat barren aspect. After coasting along a series of creeks abounding in lobsters and oysters, the Tampico entered the bay of Espiritu Santo, where she finally anchored in a small natural harbor, formed by the embouchure of the River Hillisborough, at seven P.M., on the 22d of October.

Our four passengers disembarked at once. "Gentlemen," said Barbicane, "we have no time to lose; tomorrow we must obtain horses, and proceed to reconnoiter the country."

Barbicane had scarcely set his foot on shore when three thousand of the inhabitants of Tampa Town came forth to meet him, an honor due to the president who had signalized their country by his choice.

Declining, however, every kind of ovation, Barbicane ensconced himself in a room of the Franklin Hotel.

On the morrow some of the small horses of the Spanish breed, full of vigor and of fire, stood snorting under his windows; but instead of four steeds, here were fifty, together with their riders. Barbicane descended with his three fellow-travelers; and much astonished were they all to find themselves in the midst of such a cavalcade. He remarked that every horseman carried a carbine slung across his shoulders and pistols in his holsters.

On expressing his surprise at these preparations, he was speedily enlightened by a young Floridan, who quietly said:

"Sir, there are Seminoles there."

"What do you mean by Seminoles?"

"Savages who scour the prairies. We thought it best, therefore, to escort you on your road."

"Pooh!" cried J. T. Maston, mounting his steed.

"All right," said the Floridan; "but it is true enough, nevertheless."

"Gentlemen," answered Barbicane, "I thank you for your kind attention; but it is time to be off."

It was five A.M. when Barbicane and his party, quitting Tampa Town, made their way along the coast in the direction of Alifia Creek. This little river falls into Hillisborough Bay twelve miles above Tampa Town. Barbicane and his escort coasted along its right bank to the eastward. Soon the waves of the bay disappeared behind a bend of rising ground, and the Floridan "champagne" alone offered itself to view.

Florida, discovered on Palm Sunday, in 1512, by Juan Ponce de Leon, was originally named Pascha Florida. It little deserved that designation, with its dry and parched coasts. But after some few miles of tract the nature of the soil gradually changes and the country shows itself worthy of the name. Cultivated plains soon appear, where are united all the productions of the northern and tropical floras, terminating in prairies abounding with pineapples and yams, tobacco, rice, cotton-plants, and sugar-canes, which extend beyond reach of sight, flinging their riches broadcast with careless prodigality.

Barbicane appeared highly pleased on observing the progressive elevation of the land; and in answer to a question of J. T. Maston, replied:

"My worthy friend, we cannot do better than sink our Columbiad in these high grounds."

"To get nearer the moon, perhaps?" said the secretary of the Gun Club.

"Not exactly," replied Barbicane, smiling; "do you not see that among these elevated plateaus we shall have a much easier work of it? No struggles with the water-springs, which will save us long expensive tubings; and we shall be working in daylight instead of down a deep and narrow well. Our business, then, is to open our trenches upon ground some hundreds of yards above the level of the sea."

"You are right, sir," struck in Murchison, the engineer; "and, if I mistake not, we shall ere long find a suitable spot for our purpose."

"I wish we were at the first stroke of the pickaxe," said the president.

"And I wish we were at the last," cried J. T. Maston.

About ten A.M. the little band had crossed a dozen miles. To fertile plains succeeded a region of forests. There perfumes of the most varied kinds mingled together in tropical profusion. These almost impenetrable forests were composed of pomegranates, orange-trees, citrons, figs, olives, apricots, bananas, huge vines, whose blossoms and fruits rivaled each other in color and perfume. Beneath the odorous shade of these magnificent trees fluttered and warbled a little world of brilliantly plumaged birds.

J. T. Maston and the major could not repress their admiration on finding themselves in the presence of the glorious beauties of this wealth of nature. President Barbicane, however, less sensitive to these wonders, was in haste to press forward; the very luxuriance of the country was displeasing to him. They hastened onward, therefore, and were compelled to ford several rivers, not without danger, for they were infested with huge alligators from fifteen to eighteen feet long. Maston courageously menaced them with his steel hook, but he only succeeded in frightening some pelicans and teal, while tall flamingos stared stupidly at the party.

At length these denizens of the swamps disappeared in their turn; smaller trees became thinly scattered among less dense thickets—a few isolated groups detached in the midst of endless plains over which ranged herds of startled deer.

"At last," cried Barbicane, rising in his stirrups, "here we are at the region of pines!"

"Yes! and of savages too," replied the major.

In fact, some Seminoles had just came in sight upon the horizon; they rode violently backward and forward on their fleet horses, brandishing their spears or discharging their guns with a dull report. These hostile demonstrations, however, had no effect upon Barbicane and his companions.

They were then occupying the center of a rocky plain, which the sun scorched with its parching rays. This was formed by a considerable elevation of the soil, which seemed to offer to the members of the Gun Club all the conditions requisite for the construction of their Columbiad.

"Halt!" said Barbicane, reining up. "Has this place any local appellation?"

"It is called Stones Hill," replied one of the Floridans.

Barbicane, without saying a word, dismounted, seized his instruments, and began to note his position with extreme exactness. The little band, drawn up in the rear, watched his proceedings in profound silence.

At this moment the sun passed the meridian. Barbicane, after a few moments, rapidly wrote down the result of his observations, and said:

"This spot is situated eighteen hundred feet above the level of the sea, in 27@ 7' N. lat. and 5@ 7' W. long. of the meridian of Washington. It appears to me by its rocky and barren character to offer all the conditions requisite for our experiment. On that plain will be raised our magazines, workshops, furnaces, and workmen's huts; and here, from this very spot," said he, stamping his foot on the summit of Stones Hill, "hence shall our projectile take its flight into the regions of the Solar World."

XIV

PICKAXE AND TROWEL

THE same evening Barbicane and his companions returned to Tampa Town; and Murchison, the engineer, re-embarked on board the Tampico for New Orleans. His object was to enlist an army of workmen, and to collect together the greater part of the materials. The members of the Gun Club remained at Tampa Town, for the purpose of setting on foot the preliminary works by the aid of the people of the country.

Eight days after its departure, the Tampico returned into the bay of Espiritu Santo, with a whole flotilla of steamboats. Murchison had succeeded in assembling together fifteen hundred artisans. Attracted by the high pay and considerable bounties offered by the Gun Club, he had enlisted a choice legion of stokers, iron-founders, lime-burners, miners, brickmakers, and artisans of every trade, without distinction of color. As many of these people brought their families with them, their departure resembled a perfect emigration.

On the 31st of October, at ten o'clock in the morning, the troop disembarked on the quays of Tampa Town; and one may imagine the activity which pervaded that little town, whose population was thus doubled in a single day.

During the first few days they were busy discharging the cargo brought by the flotilla, the machines, and the rations, as well as a large number of huts constructed of iron plates, separately pieced and numbered. At the same period Barbicane laid the first sleepers of a railway fifteen miles in length, intended to unite Stones Hill with Tampa Town. On the first of November Barbicane quitted Tampa Town with a detachment of workmen; and on the following day the whole town of huts was erected round Stones Hill. This they enclosed with palisades; and in respect of energy and activity, it might have been mistaken for one of the great cities of the Union. Everything was placed under a complete system of discipline, and the works were commenced in most perfect order.

The nature of the soil having been carefully examined, by means of repeated borings, the work of excavation was fixed for the 4th of November.

On that day Barbicane called together his foremen and addressed them as follows: "You are well aware, my friends, of the object with which I have assembled you together in this wild part of Florida. Our business is to construct a cannon measuring nine feet in its interior diameter, six feet thick, and with a stone revetment of nineteen and a half feet in thickness. We have, therefore, a well of sixty feet in diameter to dig down to a depth of nine hundred feet. This great work must be completed within eight months, so that you have 2,543,400 cubic feet of earth to excavate in 255 days; that is to say, in round numbers, 2,000 cubic feet per day. That which would present no difficulty to a thousand navvies working in open country will be of course more troublesome in a comparatively confined space. However, the thing must be done, and I reckon for its accomplishment upon your courage as much as upon your skill."

At eight o'clock the next morning the first stroke of the pickaxe was struck upon the soil of Florida; and from that moment that prince of tools was never inactive for one moment in the hands of the excavators. The gangs relieved each other every three hours.

On the 4th of November fifty workmen commenced digging, in the very center of the enclosed space on the summit of Stones Hill, a circular hole sixty feet in diameter. The pickaxe first struck upon a kind of black earth, six inches in thickness, which was speedily disposed of. To this earth succeeded two feet of fine sand, which was carefully laid aside as being valuable for serving the casting of the inner mould. After the sand appeared some compact white clay, resembling the chalk of Great Britain, which extended down to a depth of four feet. Then the iron of the picks struck upon the hard bed of the soil; a kind of rock formed of petrified shells, very dry, very solid, and which the picks could with difficulty penetrate. At this point the excavation exhibited a depth of six and a half feet and the work of the masonry was begun.

At the bottom of the excavation they constructed a wheel of oak, a kind of circle strongly bolted together, and of immense strength. The center of this wooden disc was hollowed out to a diameter equal to the exterior diameter of the Columbiad. Upon this wheel rested the first layers of the masonry, the stones of which were bound together by hydraulic cement, with irresistible tenacity. The workmen, after laying the stones from the circumference to the center, were thus enclosed within a kind of well twenty-one feet in diameter. When this work was accomplished, the miners resumed their picks and cut away the rock from underneath the wheel itself, taking care to support it as they advanced upon blocks of great thickness. At every two feet which the hole gained in depth they successively withdrew the blocks. The wheel then sank little by little, and with it the massive ring of masonry, on the upper bed of which the masons labored incessantly, always reserving some vent holes to permit the escape of gas during the operation of the casting.

This kind of work required on the part of the workmen extreme nicety and minute attention. More than one, in digging underneath the wheel, was dangerously injured by the splinters of stone. But their ardor never relaxed, night or day. By day they worked under the rays of the scorching sun; by night, under the gleam of the electric light. The sounds of the picks against the rock, the bursting of mines, the grinding of the machines, the wreaths of smoke scattered through the air, traced around Stones Hill a circle of terror which the herds of buffaloes and the war parties of the Seminoles never ventured to pass. Nevertheless, the works advanced regularly, as the steam-cranes actively removed the rubbish. Of unexpected obstacles there was little account; and with regard to foreseen difficulties, they were speedily disposed of.

At the expiration of the first month the well had attained the depth assigned for that lapse of time, namely, 112 feet. This depth was doubled in December, and trebled in January.

During the month of February the workmen had to contend with a sheet of water which made its way right across the outer soil. It became necessary to employ very powerful pumps and compressed-air engines to drain it off, so as to close up the orifice from whence it issued; just as one stops a leak on board ship. They at last succeeded in getting the upper hand of these untoward streams; only, in consequence of the loosening of the soil, the wheel partly gave way, and a slight partial settlement ensued. This accident cost the life of several workmen.

No fresh occurrence thenceforward arrested the progress of the operation; and on the tenth of June, twenty days before the expiration of the period fixed by Barbicane, the well, lined throughout with its facing of stone, had attained the depth of 900 feet. At the bottom the masonry rested upon a massive block measuring thirty feet in thickness, while on the upper portion it was level with the surrounding soil.

President Barbicane and the members of the Gun Club warmly congratulated their engineer Murchison; the cyclopean work had been accomplished with extraordinary rapidity.

During these eight months Barbicane never quitted Stones Hill for a single instant. Keeping ever close by the work of excavation, he busied himself incessantly with the welfare and health of his workpeople, and was singularly fortunate in warding off the epidemics common to large communities of men, and so disastrous in those regions of the globe which are exposed to the influences of tropical climates.

Many workmen, it is true, paid with their lives for the rashness inherent in these dangerous labors; but these mishaps are impossible to be avoided, and they are classed among the details with which the Americans trouble themselves but little. They have in fact more regard for human nature in general than for the individual in particular.

Nevertheless, Barbicane professed opposite principles to these, and put them in force at every opportunity. So, thanks to his care, his intelligence, his useful intervention in all difficulties, his prodigious and humane sagacity, the average of accidents did not exceed that of transatlantic countries, noted for their excessive precautions—France, for instance, among others, where they reckon about one accident for every two hundred thousand francs of work.

XV

THE FETE OF THE CASTING

DURING the eight months which were employed in the work of excavation the preparatory works of the casting had been carried on simultaneously with extreme rapidity. A stranger arriving at Stones Hill would have been surprised at the spectacle offered to his view.

At 600 yards from the well, and circularly arranged around it as a central point, rose 1,200 reverberating ovens, each six feet in diameter, and separated from each other by an interval of three feet. The circumference occupied by these 1,200 ovens presented a length of two miles. Being all constructed on the same plan, each with its high quadrangular chimney, they produced a most singular effect.

It will be remembered that on their third meeting the committee had decided to use cast iron for the Columbiad, and in particular the white description. This metal, in fact, is the most tenacious, the most ductile, and the most malleable, and consequently suitable for all moulding operations; and when smelted with pit coal, is of superior quality for all engineering works requiring great resisting power, such as cannon, steam boilers, hydraulic presses, and the like.

Cast iron, however, if subjected to only one single fusion, is rarely sufficiently homogeneous; and it requires a second fusion completely to refine it by dispossessing it of its last earthly deposits. So long before being forwarded to Tampa Town, the iron ore, molten in the great furnaces of Coldspring, and brought into contact with coal and silicium heated to a high temperature, was carburized and transformed into cast iron. After this first operation, the metal was sent on to Stones Hill. They had, however, to deal with 136,000,000 pounds of iron, a quantity far too costly to send by railway. The cost of transport would have been double that of material. It appeared preferable to freight vessels at New York, and to load them with the iron in bars. This, however, required not less than sixty-eight vessels of 1,000 tons, a veritable fleet, which, quitting New York on the 3rd of May, on the 10th of the same month ascended the Bay of Espiritu Santo, and discharged their cargoes, without dues, in the port at Tampa Town. Thence the iron was transported by rail to Stones Hill, and about the middle of January this enormous mass of metal was delivered at its destination.

It will easily be understood that 1,200 furnaces were not too many to melt simultaneously these 60,000 tons of iron. Each of these furnaces contained nearly 140,000 pounds weight of metal. They were all built after the model of those which served for the casting of the Rodman gun; they were trapezoidal in shape, with a high elliptical arch. These furnaces, constructed of fireproof brick, were especially adapted for burning pit coal, with a flat bottom upon which the iron bars were laid. This bottom, inclined at an angle of 25 degrees, allowed the metal to flow into the receiving troughs; and the 1,200 converging trenches carried the molten metal down to the central well.

The day following that on which the works of the masonry and boring had been completed, Barbicane set to work upon the central mould. His object now was to raise within the center of the well, and with a coincident axis, a cylinder 900 feet high, and nine feet in diameter, which should exactly fill up the space reserved for the bore of the Columbiad. This cylinder was composed of a mixture of clay and sand, with the addition of a little hay and straw. The space left between the mould and the masonry was intended to be filled up by the molten metal, which would thus form the walls six feet in thickness. This cylinder, in order to maintain its equilibrium, had to be bound by iron bands, and firmly fixed at certain intervals by cross-clamps fastened into the stone lining; after the castings these would be buried in the block of metal, leaving no external projection.

This operation was completed on the 8th of July, and the run of the metal was fixed for the following day.

"This fete of the casting will be a grand ceremony," said J. T. Maston to his friend Barbicane.

"Undoubtedly," said Barbicane; "but it will not be a public fete"

"What! will you not open the gates of the enclosure to all comers?"

"I must be very careful, Maston. The casting of the Columbiad is an extremely delicate, not to say a dangerous operation, and I should prefer its being done privately. At the discharge of the projectile, a fete if you like—till then, no!"

The president was right. The operation involved unforeseen dangers, which a great influx of spectators would have hindered him from averting. It was necessary to preserve complete freedom of movement. No one was admitted within the enclosure except a delegation of members of the Gun Club, who had made the voyage to Tampa Town. Among these was the brisk Bilsby, Tom Hunter, Colonel Blomsberry, Major Elphinstone, General Morgan, and the rest of the lot to whom the casting of the Columbiad was a matter of personal interest. J. T. Maston became their cicerone. He omitted no point of detail; he conducted them throughout the magazines, workshops, through the midst of the engines, and compelled them to visit the whole 1,200 furnaces one after the other. At the end of the twelve-hundredth visit they were pretty well knocked up.

The casting was to take place at twelve o'clock precisely. The previous evening each furnace had been charged with 114,000 pounds weight of metal in bars disposed cross-ways to each other, so as to allow the hot air to circulate freely between them. At daybreak the 1,200 chimneys vomited their torrents of flame into the air, and the ground was agitated with dull tremblings. As many pounds of metal as there were to cast, so many pounds of coal were there to burn. Thus there were 68,000 tons of coal which projected in the face of the sun a thick curtain of smoke. The heat soon became insupportable within the circle of furnaces, the rumbling of which resembled the rolling of thunder. The powerful ventilators added their continuous blasts and saturated with oxygen the glowing plates. The operation, to be successful, required to be conducted with great rapidity. On a signal given by a cannon-shot each furnace was to give vent to the molten iron and completely to empty itself. These arrangements made, foremen and workmen waited the preconcerted moment with an impatience mingled with a certain amount of emotion. Not a soul remained within the enclosure. Each superintendent took his post by the aperture of the run.

Barbicane and his colleagues, perched on a neighboring eminence, assisted at the operation. In front of them was a piece of artillery ready to give fire on the signal from the engineer. Some minutes before midday the first driblets of metal began to flow; the reservoirs filled little by little; and, by the time that the whole melting was completely accomplished, it was kept in abeyance for a few minutes in order to facilitate the separation of foreign substances.

Twelve o'clock struck! A gunshot suddenly pealed forth and shot its flame into the air. Twelve hundred melting-troughs were simultaneously opened and twelve hundred fiery serpents crept toward the central well, unrolling their incandescent curves. There, down they plunged with a terrific noise into a depth of 900 feet. It was an exciting and a magnificent spectacle. The ground trembled, while these molten waves, launching into the sky their wreaths of smoke, evaporated the moisture of the mould and hurled it upward through the vent-holes of the stone lining in the form of dense vapor-clouds. These artificial clouds unrolled their thick spirals to a height of 1,000 yards into the air. A savage, wandering somewhere beyond the limits of the horizon, might have believed that some new crater was forming in the bosom of Florida, although there was neither any eruption, nor typhoon, nor storm, nor struggle of the elements, nor any of those terrible phenomena which nature is capable of producing. No, it was man alone who had produced these reddish vapors, these gigantic flames worthy of a volcano itself, these tremendous vibrations resembling the shock of an earthquake, these reverberations rivaling those of hurricanes and storms; and it was his hand which precipitated into an abyss, dug by himself, a whole Niagara of molten metal!

XVI

The Columbiad

HAD the casting succeeded? They were reduced to mere conjecture. There was indeed every reason to expect success, since the mould has absorbed the entire mass of the molten metal; still some considerable time must elapse before they could arrive at any certainty upon the matter.

The patience of the members of the Gun Club was sorely tried during this period of time. But they could do nothing. J. T. Maston escaped roasting by a miracle. Fifteen days after the casting an immense column of smoke was still rising in the open sky and the ground burned the soles of the feet within a radius of two hundred feet round the summit of Stones Hill. It was impossible to approach nearer. All they could do was to wait with what patience they might.

"Here we are at the 10th of August," exclaimed J. T. Maston one morning, "only four months to the 1st of December! We shall never be ready in time!" Barbicane said nothing, but his silence covered serious irritation.

However, daily observations revealed a certain change going on in the state of the ground. About the 15th of August the vapors ejected had sensibly diminished in intensity and thickness. Some days afterward the earth exhaled only a slight puff of smoke, the last breath of the monster enclosed within its circle of stone. Little by little the belt of heat contracted, until on the 22nd of August, Barbicane, his colleagues, and the engineer were enabled to set foot on the iron sheet which lay level upon the summit of Stones Hill.

"At last!" exclaimed the president of the Gun Club, with an immense sigh of relief.

The work was resumed the same day. They proceeded at once to extract the interior mould, for the purpose of clearing out the boring of the piece. Pickaxes and boring irons were set to work without intermission. The clayey and sandy soils had acquired extreme hardness under the action of the heat; but, by the aid of the machines, the rubbish on being dug out was rapidly carted away on railway wagons; and such was the ardor of the work, so persuasive the arguments of Barbicane's dollars, that by the 3rd of September all traces of the mould had entirely disappeared.

Immediately the operation of boring was commenced; and by the aid of powerful machines, a few weeks later, the inner surface of the immense tube had been rendered perfectly cylindrical, and the bore of the piece had acquired a thorough polish.

At length, on the 22d of September, less than a twelvemonth after Barbicane's original proposition, the enormous weapon, accurately bored, and exactly vertically pointed, was ready for work. There was only the moon now to wait for; and they were pretty sure that she would not fail in the rendezvous.

The ecstasy of J. T. Maston knew no bounds, and he narrowly escaped a frightful fall while staring down the tube. But for the strong hand of Colonel Blomsberry, the worthy secretary, like a modern Erostratus, would have found his death in the depths of the Columbiad.

The cannon was then finished; there was no possible doubt as to its perfect completion. So, on the 6th of October, Captain Nicholl opened an account between himself and President Barbicane, in which he debited himself to the latter in the sum of two thousand dollars. One may believe that the captain's wrath was increased to its highest point, and must have made him seriously ill. However, he had still three bets of three, four, and five thousand dollars, respectively; and if he gained two out of these, his position would not be very bad. But the money question did not enter into his calculations; it was the success of his rival in casting a cannon against which iron plates sixty feet thick would have been ineffectual, that dealt him a terrible blow.

After the 23rd of September the enclosure of Stones hill was thrown open to the public; and it will be easily imagined what was the concourse of visitors to this spot! There was an incessant flow of people to and from Tampa Town and the place, which resembled a procession, or rather, in fact, a pilgrimage.

It was already clear to be seen that, on the day of the experiment itself, the aggregate of spectators would be counted by millions; for they were already arriving from all parts of the earth upon this narrow strip of promontory. Europe was emigrating to America.

Up to that time, however, it must be confessed, the curiosity of the numerous comers was but scantily gratified. Most had counted upon witnessing the spectacle of the casting, and they were treated to nothing but smoke. This was sorry food for hungry eyes; but Barbicane would admit no one to that operation. Then ensued grumbling, discontent, murmurs; they blamed the president, taxed him with dictatorial conduct. His proceedings were declared "un-American." There was very nearly a riot round Stones Hill; but Barbicane remained inflexible. When, however, the Columbiad was entirely finished, this state of closed doors could no longer be maintained; besides it would have been bad taste, and even imprudence, to affront the public feeling. Barbicane, therefore, opened the enclosure to all comers; but, true to his practical disposition, he determined to coin money out of the public curiosity.

It was something, indeed, to be enabled to contemplate this immense Columbiad; but to descend into its depths, this seemed to the Americans the ne plus ultra of earthly felicity. Consequently, there was not one curious spectator who was not willing to give himself the treat of visiting the interior of this great metallic abyss. Baskets suspended from steam-cranes permitted them to satisfy their curiosity. There was a perfect mania. Women, children, old men, all made it a point of duty to penetrate the mysteries of the colossal gun. The fare for the descent was fixed at five dollars per head; and despite this high charge, during the two months which preceded the experiment, the influx of visitors enabled the Gun Club to pocket nearly five hundred thousand dollars!

It is needless to say that the first visitors of the Columbiad were the members of the Gun Club. This privilege was justly reserved for that illustrious body. The ceremony took place on the 25th of September. A basket of honor took down the president, J. T. Maston, Major Elphinstone, General Morgan, Colonel Blomsberry, and other members of the club, to the number of ten in all. How hot it was at the bottom of that long tube of metal! They were half suffocated. But what delight! What ecstasy! A table had been laid with six covers on the massive stone which formed the bottom of the Columbiad, and lighted by a jet of electric light resembling that of day itself. Numerous exquisite dishes, which seemed to descend from heaven, were placed successively before the guests, and the richest wines of France flowed in profusion during this splendid repast, served nine hundred feet beneath the surface of the earth!

The festival was animated, not to say somewhat noisy. Toasts flew backward and forward. They drank to the earth and to her satellite, to the Gun Club, the Union, the Moon, Diana, Phoebe, Selene, the "peaceful courier of the night!" All the hurrahs, carried upward upon the sonorous waves of the immense acoustic tube, arrived with the sound of thunder at its mouth; and the multitude ranged round Stones Hill heartily united their shouts with those of the ten revelers hidden from view at the bottom of the gigantic Columbiad.

J. T. Maston was no longer master of himself. Whether he shouted or gesticulated, ate or drank most, would be a difficult matter to determine. At all events, he would not have given his place up for an empire, "not even if the cannon—loaded, primed, and fired at that very moment—were to blow him in pieces into the planetary world."

XVII

A Telegraphic Dispatch

THE great works undertaken by the Gun Club had now virtually come to an end; and two months still remained before the day for the discharge of the shot to the moon. To the general impatience these two months appeared as long as years! Hitherto the smallest details of the operation had been daily chronicled by the journals, which the public devoured with eager eyes.

Just at this moment a circumstance, the most unexpected, the most extraordinary and incredible, occurred to rouse afresh their panting spirits, and to throw every mind into a state of the most violent excitement.

One day, the 30th of September, at 3:47 P.M., a telegram, transmitted by cable from Valentia (Ireland) to Newfoundland and the American Mainland, arrived at the address of President Barbicane.

The president tore open the envelope, read the dispatch, and, despite his remarkable powers of self-control, his lips turned pale and his eyes grew dim, on reading the twenty words of this telegram.

Here is the text of the dispatch, which figures now in the archives of the Gun Club:

FRANCE, PARIS,
30 September, 4 A.M.

Barbicane, Tampa Town, Florida, United States.

Substitute for your spherical shell a cylindro-conical projectile. I shall go inside. Shall arrive by steamer Atlanta.

MICHEL ARDAN.

XVIII

The Passenger of the Atlanta

IF this astounding news, instead of flying through the electric wires, had simply arrived by post in the ordinary sealed envelope, Barbicane would not have hesitated a moment. He would have held his tongue about it, both as a measure of prudence, and in order not to have to reconsider his plans. This telegram might be a cover for some jest, especially as it came from a Frenchman. What human being would ever have conceived the idea of such a journey? and, if such a person really existed, he must be an idiot, whom one would shut up in a lunatic ward, rather than within the walls of the projectile.

The contents of the dispatch, however, speedily became known; for the telegraphic officials possessed but little discretion, and Michel Ardan's proposition ran at once throughout the several States of the Union. Barbicane, had, therefore, no further motives for keeping silence. Consequently, he called together such of his colleagues as were at the moment in Tampa Town, and without any expression of his own opinions simply read to them the laconic text itself. It was received with every possible variety of expressions of doubt, incredulity, and derision from every one, with the exception of J. T. Maston, who exclaimed, "It is a grand idea, however!"

When Barbicane originally proposed to send a shot to the moon every one looked upon the enterprise as simple and practicable enough—a mere question of gunnery; but when a person, professing to be a reasonable being, offered to take passage within the projectile, the whole thing became a farce, or, in plainer language a humbug.

One question, however, remained. Did such a being exist? This telegram flashed across the depths of the Atlantic, the designation of the vessel on board which he was to take his passage, the date assigned for his speedy arrival, all combined to impart a certain character of reality to the proposal. They must get some clearer notion of the matter. Scattered groups of inquirers at length condensed themselves into a compact crowd, which made straight for the residence of President Barbicane. That worthy individual was keeping quiet with the intention of watching events as they arose. But he had forgotten to take into account the public impatience; and it was with no pleasant countenance that he watched the population of Tampa Town gathering under his windows. The murmurs and vociferations below presently obliged him to appear. He came forward, therefore, and on silence being procured, a citizen put point-blank to him the following question: "Is the person mentioned in the telegram, under the name of Michel Ardan, on his way here? Yes or no."

"Gentlemen," replied Barbicane, "I know no more than you do."

"We must know," roared the impatient voices.

"Time will show," calmly replied the president.

"Time has no business to keep a whole country in suspense," replied the orator. "Have you altered the plans of the projectile according to the request of the telegram?"

"Not yet, gentlemen; but you are right! we must have better information to go by. The telegraph must complete its information."

"To the telegraph!" roared the crowd.

Barbicane descended; and heading the immense assemblage, led the way to the telegraph office. A few minutes later a telegram was dispatched to the secretary of the underwriters at Liverpool, requesting answers to the following queries:

"About the ship Atlanta—when did she leave Europe? Had she on board a Frenchman named Michel Ardan?"

Two hours afterward Barbicane received information too exact to leave room for the smallest remaining doubt.

"The steamer Atlanta from Liverpool put to sea on the 2nd of October, bound for Tampa Town, having on board a Frenchman borne on the list of passengers by the name of Michel Ardan."

That very evening he wrote to the house of Breadwill and Co., requesting them to suspend the casting of the projectile until the receipt of further orders. On the 10th of October, at nine A.M., the semaphores of the Bahama Canal signaled a thick smoke on the horizon. Two hours later a large steamer exchanged signals with them./ the name of the Atlanta flew at once over Tampa Town. At four o'clock the English vessel entered the Bay of Espiritu Santo. At five it crossed the passage of Hillisborough Bay at full steam. At six she cast anchor at Port Tampa. The anchor had scarcely caught the sandy bottom when five hundred boats surrounded the Atlanta, and the steamer was taken by assault. Barbicane was the first to set foot on deck, and in a voice of which he vainly tried to conceal the emotion, called "Michel Ardan."

"Here!" replied an individual perched on the poop.

Barbicane, with arms crossed, looked fixedly at the passenger of the Atlanta.

He was a man of about forty-two years of age, of large build, but slightly round-shouldered. His massive head momentarily shook a shock of reddish hair, which resembled a lion's mane. His face was short with a broad forehead, and furnished with a moustache as bristly as a cat's, and little patches of yellowish whiskers upon full cheeks. Round, wildish eyes, slightly near-sighted, completed a physiognomy essentially feline. His nose was firmly shaped, his mouth particularly sweet in expression, high forehead, intelligent and furrowed with wrinkles like a newly-plowed field. The body was powerfully developed and firmly fixed upon long legs. Muscular arms, and a general air of decision gave him the appearance of a hardy, jolly, companion. He was dressed in a suit of ample dimensions, loose neckerchief, open shirtcollar, disclosing a robust neck; his cuffs were invariably unbuttoned, through which appeared a pair of red hands.

On the bridge of the steamer, in the midst of the crowd, he bustled to and fro, never still for a moment, "dragging his anchors," as the sailors say, gesticulating, making free with everybody, biting his nails with nervous avidity. He was one of those originals which nature sometimes invents in the freak of a moment, and of which she then breaks the mould.

Among other peculiarities, this curiosity gave himself out for a sublime ignoramus, "like Shakespeare," and professed supreme contempt for all scientific men. Those "fellows," as he called them, "are only fit to mark the points, while we play the game." He was, in fact, a thorough Bohemian, adventurous, but not an adventurer; a hare-brained fellow, a kind of Icarus, only possessing relays of wings. For the rest, he was ever in scrapes, ending invariably by falling on his feet, like those little figures which they sell for children's toys. In a few words, his motto was "I have my opinions," and the love of the impossible constituted his ruling passion.

Such was the passenger of the Atlanta, always excitable, as if boiling under the action of some internal fire by the character of his physical organization. If ever two individuals offered a striking contrast to each other, these were certainly Michel Ardan and the Yankee Barbicane; both, moreover, being equally enterprising and daring, each in his own way.

The scrutiny which the president of the Gun Club had instituted regarding this new rival was quickly interrupted by the shouts and hurrahs of the crowd. The cries became at last so uproarious, and the popular enthusiasm assumed so personal a form, that Michel Ardan, after having shaken hands some thousands of times, at the imminent risk of leaving his fingers behind him, was fain at last to make a bolt for his cabin.

Barbicane followed him without uttering a word.

"You are Barbicane, I suppose?" said Michel Ardan, in a tone of voice in which he would have addressed a friend of twenty years' standing.

"Yes," replied the president of the Gun Club.

"All right! how d'ye do, Barbicane? how are you getting on—pretty well? that's right."

"So," said Barbicane without further preliminary, "you are quite determined to go."

"Quite decided."

"Nothing will stop you?"

"Nothing. Have you modified your projectile according to my telegram."

"I waited for your arrival. But," asked Barbicane again, "have you carefully reflected?"

"Reflected? have I any time to spare? I find an opportunity of making a tour in the moon, and I mean to profit by it. There is the whole gist of the matter."

Barbicane looked hard at this man who spoke so lightly of his project with such complete absence of anxiety. "But, at least," said he, "you have some plans, some means of carrying your project into execution?"

"Excellent, my dear Barbicane; only permit me to offer one remark: My wish is to tell my story once for all, to everybody, and then have done with it; then there will be no need for recapitulation. So, if you have no objection, assemble your friends, colleagues, the whole town, all Florida, all America if you like, and to-morrow I shall be ready to explain my plans and answer any objections whatever that may be advanced. You may rest assured I shall wait without stirring. Will that suit you?"

"All right," replied Barbicane.

So saying, the president left the cabin and informed the crowd of the proposal of Michel Ardan. His words were received with clappings of hands and shouts of joy. They had removed all difficulties. To-morrow every one would contemplate at his ease this European hero. However, some of the spectators, more infatuated than the rest, would not leave the deck of the Atlanta. They passed the night on board. Among others J. T. Maston got his hook fixed in the combing of the poop, and it pretty nearly required the capstan to get it out again.

"He is a hero! a hero!" he cried, a theme of which he was never tired of ringing the changes; "and we are only like weak, silly women, compared with this European!"

As to the president, after having suggested to the visitors it was time to retire, he re-entered the passenger's cabin, and remained there till the bell of the steamer made it midnight.

But then the two rivals in popularity shook hands heartily and parted on terms of intimate friendship.

XIX

A MONSTER MEETING

O N the following day Barbicane, fearing that indiscreet questions might be put to Michel Ardan, was desirous of reducing the number of the audience to a few of the initiated, his own colleagues for instance. He might as well have tried to check the Falls of Niagara! he was compelled, therefore, to give up the idea, and let his new friend run the chances of a public conference. The place chosen for this monster meeting was a vast plain situated in the rear of the town. In a few hours, thanks to the help of the shipping in port, an immense roofing of canvas was stretched over the parched prairie, and protected it from the burning rays of the sun. There three hundred thousand people braved for many hours the stifling heat while awaiting the arrival of the Frenchman. Of this crowd of spectators a first set could both see and hear; a second set saw badly and heard nothing at all; and as for the third, it could neither see nor hear anything at all. At three o'clock Michel Ardan made his appearance, accompanied by the principal members of the Gun Club. He was supported on his right by President Barbicane, and on his left by J. T. Maston, more radiant than the midday sun, and nearly as ruddy. Ardan mounted a platform, from the top of which his view extended over a sea of black hats.

He exhibited not the slightest embarrassment; he was just as gay, familiar, and pleasant as if he were at home. To the hurrahs which greeted him he replied by a graceful bow; then, waving his hands to request silence, he spoke in perfectly correct English as follows:

"Gentlemen, despite the very hot weather I request your patience for a short time while I offer some explanations regarding the projects which seem to have so interested you. I am neither an orator nor a man of science, and I had no idea of addressing you in public; but my friend Barbicane has told me that you would like to hear me, and I am quite at your service. Listen to me, therefore, with your six hundred thousand ears, and please excuse the faults of the speaker. Now pray do not forget that you see before you a perfect ignoramus whose ignorance goes so far that he cannot even understand the difficulties! It seemed to him that it was a matter quite simple, natural, and easy to take one's place in a projectile and start for the moon! That journey must be undertaken sooner or later; and, as for the mode of locomotion adopted, it follows simply the law of progress. Man began by walking on all-fours; then, one fine day, on two feet; then in a carriage; then in a stage-coach; and lastly by railway. Well, the projectile is the vehicle of the future, and the planets themselves are nothing else! Now some of you, gentlemen, may imagine that the velocity we propose to impart to it is extravagant. It is nothing of the kind. All the stars exceed it in rapidity, and the earth herself is at this moment carrying us round the sun at three times as rapid a rate, and yet she is a mere lounger on the way compared with many others of the planets! And her velocity is constantly decreasing. Is it not evident, then, I ask you, that there will some day appear velocities far greater than these, of which light or electricity will probably be the mechanical agent?

"Yes, gentlemen," continued the orator, "in spite of the opinions of certain narrow-minded people, who would shut up the human race upon this globe, as within some magic circle which it must never outstep, we shall one day travel to the moon, the planets, and the stars, with the same facility, rapidity, and certainty as we now make the voyage from Liverpool to New York! Distance is but a relative expression, and must end by being reduced to zero."

The assembly, strongly predisposed as they were in favor of the French hero, were slightly staggered at this bold theory. Michel Ardan perceived the fact.

"Gentlemen," he continued with a pleasant smile, "you do not seem quite convinced. Very good! Let us reason the matter out. Do you know how long it would take for an express train to reach the moon? Three hundred days; no more! And what is that? The distance is no more than nine times the circumference of the earth; and there are no sailors or travelers, of even moderate activity, who have not made longer journeys than that in their lifetime. And now consider that I shall be only ninety-seven hours on my journey. Ah! I see you are reckoning that the moon is a long way off from the earth, and that one must think twice before making the experiment. What would you say, then, if we were talking of going to Neptune, which revolves at a distance of more than two thousand seven hundred and twenty millions of miles from the sun! And yet what is that compared with the distance of the fixed stars, some of which, such as Arcturus, are billions of miles distant from us? And then you talk of the distance which separates the planets from the sun! And there are people who affirm that such a thing as distance exists. Absurdity, folly, idiotic nonsense! Would you know what I think of our own solar universe? Shall I tell you my theory? It is very simple! In my opinion the solar system is a solid homogeneous body; the planets which compose it are in actual contact with each other; and whatever space exists between them is nothing more than the space which separates the molecules of the densest metal, such as silver, iron, or platinum! I have the right, therefore, to affirm, and I repeat, with the conviction which must penetrate all your minds, 'Distance is but an empty name; distance does not really exist!'"

"Hurrah!" cried one voice (need it be said it was that of J. T. Maston). "Distance does not exist!" And overcome by the energy of his movements, he nearly fell from the platform to the ground. He just escaped a severe fall, which would have proved to him that distance was by no means an empty name.

"Gentlemen," resumed the orator, "I repeat that the distance between the earth and her satellite is a mere trifle, and undeserving of serious consideration. I am convinced that before twenty years are over one-half of our earth will have paid a visit to the moon. Now, my worthy friends, if you have any question to put to me, you will, I fear, sadly embarrass a poor man like myself; still I will do my best to answer you."

Up to this point the president of the Gun Club had been satisfied with the turn which the discussion had assumed. It became now, however, desirable to divert Ardan from questions of a practical nature, with which he was doubtless far less conversant. Barbicane, therefore, hastened to get in a word, and began by asking his new friend whether he thought that the moon and the planets were inhabited.

"You put before me a great problem, my worthy president," replied the orator, smiling. "Still, men of great intelligence, such as Plutarch, Swedenborg, Bernardin de St. Pierre, and others have, if I mistake not, pronounced in the affirmative. Looking at the question from the natural philosopher's point of view, I should say that nothing useless existed in the world; and, replying to your question by another, I should venture to assert, that if these worlds are habitable, they either are, have been, or will be inhabited."

"No one could answer more logically or fairly," replied the president. "The question then reverts to this: Are these worlds habitable? For my own part I believe they are."

"For myself, I feel certain of it," said Michel Ardan.

"Nevertheless," retorted one of the audience, "there are many arguments against the habitability of the worlds. The conditions of life must evidently be greatly modified upon the majority of them. To mention only the planets, we should be either broiled alive in some, or frozen to death in others, according as they are more or less removed from the sun."

"I regret," replied Michel Ardan, "that I have not the honor of personally knowing my contradictor, for I would have attempted to answer him. His objection has its merits, I admit; but I think we may successfully combat it, as well as all others which affect the habitability of other worlds. If I were a natural philosopher, I would tell him that if less of caloric were set in motion upon the planets which are nearest to the sun, and more, on the contrary, upon those which are farthest removed from it, this simple fact would alone suffice to equalize the heat, and to render the temperature of those worlds supportable by beings organized like ourselves. If I were a naturalist, I would tell him that, according to some illustrious men of science, nature has furnished us with instances upon the earth of animals existing under very varying conditions of life; that fish respire in a medium fatal to other animals; that amphibious creatures possess a double existence very difficult of explanation; that certain denizens of the seas maintain life at enormous depths, and there support a pressure equal to that of fifty or sixty atmospheres without being crushed; that several aquatic insects, insensible to temperature, are met with equally among boiling springs and in the frozen plains of the Polar Sea; in fine, that we cannot help recognizing in nature a diversity of means of operation oftentimes incomprehensible, but not the less real. If I were a chemist, I would tell him that the aerolites, bodies evidently formed exteriorly of our terrestrial globe, have, upon analysis, revealed indisputable traces of carbon, a substance which owes its origin solely to organized beings, and which, according to the experiments of Reichenbach, must necessarily itself have been endued with animation. And lastly, were I a theologian, I would tell him that the scheme of the Divine Redemption, according to St. Paul, seems to be applicable, not merely to the earth, but to all the celestial worlds. But, unfortunately, I am neither theologian, nor chemist, nor naturalist, nor philosopher; therefore, in my absolute ignorance of the great laws which govern the universe, I confine myself to saying in reply, 'I do not know whether the worlds are inhabited or not: and since I do not know, I am going to see!'"

Whether Michel Ardan's antagonist hazarded any further arguments or not it is impossible to say, for the uproarious shouts of the crowd would not allow any expression of opinion to gain a hearing. On silence being restored, the triumphant orator contented himself with adding the following remarks:

"Gentlemen, you will observe that I have but slightly touched upon this great question. There is another altogether different line of argument in favor of the habitability of the stars, which I omit for the present. I only desire to call attention to one point. To those who maintain that the planets are not inhabited one may reply: You might be perfectly in the right, if you could only show that the earth is the best possible world, in spite of what Voltaire has said. She has but one satellite, while Jupiter, Uranus, Saturn, Neptune have each several, an advantage by no means to be despised. But that which renders our own globe so uncomfortable is the inclination of its axis to the plane of its orbit. Hence the inequality of days and nights; hence the disagreeable diversity of the seasons. On the surface of our unhappy spheroid we are always either too hot or too cold; we are frozen in winter, broiled in summer; it is the planet of rheumatism, coughs, bronchitis; while on the surface of Jupiter, for example, where the axis is but slightly inclined, the inhabitants may enjoy uniform temperatures. It possesses zones of perpetual springs, summers, autumns, and winters; every Jovian may choose for himself what climate he likes, and there spend the whole of his life in security from all variations of temperature. You will, I am sure, readily admit this superiority of Jupiter over our own planet, to say nothing of his years, which each equal twelve of ours! Under such auspices and such marvelous conditions of existence, it appears to me that the inhabitants of so fortunate a world must be in every respect superior to ourselves. All we require, in order to attain such perfection, is the mere trifle of having an axis of rotation less inclined to the plane of its orbit!"

"Hurrah!" roared an energetic voice, "let us unite our efforts, invent the necessary machines, and rectify the earth's axis!"

A thunder of applause followed this proposal, the author of which was, of course, no other than J. T. Maston. And, in all probability, if the truth must be told, if the Yankees could only have found a point of application for it, they would have constructed a lever capable of raising the earth and rectifying its axis. It was just this deficiency which baffled these daring mechanicians.

XX

ATTACK AND RIPOSTE

As soon as the excitement had subsided, the following words were heard uttered in a strong and determined voice:

"Now that the speaker has favored us with so much imagination, would he be so good as to return to his subject, and give us a little practical view of the question?"

All eyes were directed toward the person who spoke. He was a little dried-up man, of an active figure, with an American "goatee" beard. Profiting by the different movements in the crowd, he had managed by degrees to gain the front row of spectators. There, with arms crossed and stern gaze, he watched the hero of the meeting. After having put his question he remained silent, and appeared to take no notice of the thousands of looks directed toward himself, nor of the murmur of disapprobation excited by his words. Meeting at first with no reply, he repeated his question with marked emphasis, adding, "We are here to talk about the moon and not about the earth."

"You are right, sir," replied Michel Ardan; "the discussion has become irregular. We will return to the moon."

"Sir," said the unknown, "you pretend that our satellite is inhabited. Very good, but if Selenites do exist, that race of beings assuredly must live without breathing, for—I warn you for your own sake—there is not the smallest particle of air on the surface of the moon."

At this remark Ardan pushed up his shock of red hair; he saw that he was on the point of being involved in a struggle with this person upon the very gist of the whole question. He looked sternly at him in his turn and said:

"Oh! so there is no air in the moon? And pray, if you are so good, who ventures to affirm that?

"The men of science."

"Really?"

"Really."

"Sir," replied Michel, "pleasantry apart, I have a profound respect for men of science who do possess science, but a profound contempt for men of science who do not."

"Do you know any who belong to the latter category?"

"Decidedly. In France there are some who maintain that, mathematically, a bird cannot possibly fly; and others who demonstrate theoretically that fishes were never made to live in water."

"I have nothing to do with persons of that description, and I can quote, in support of my statement, names which you cannot refuse deference to."

"Then, sir, you will sadly embarrass a poor ignorant, who, besides, asks nothing better than to learn."

"Why, then, do you introduce scientific questions if you have never studied them?" asked the unknown somewhat coarsely.

"For the reason that 'he is always brave who never suspects danger.' I know nothing, it is true; but it is precisely my very weakness which constitutes my strength."

"Your weakness amounts to folly," retorted the unknown in a passion.

"All the better," replied our Frenchman, "if it carries me up to the moon."

Barbicane and his colleagues devoured with their eyes the intruder who had so boldly placed himself in antagonism to their enterprise. Nobody knew him, and the president, uneasy as to the result of so free a discussion, watched his new friend with some anxiety. The meeting began to be somewhat fidgety also, for the contest directed their attention to the dangers, if not the actual impossibilities, of the proposed expedition.

"Sir," replied Ardan's antagonist, "there are many and incontrovertible reasons which prove the absence of an atmosphere in the moon. I might say that, a priori, if one ever did exist, it must have been absorbed by the earth; but I prefer to bring forward indisputable facts."

"Bring them forward then, sir, as many as you please."

"You know," said the stranger, "that when any luminous rays cross a medium such as the air, they are deflected out of the straight line; in other words, they undergo refraction. Well! When stars are occulted by the moon, their rays, on grazing the edge of her disc, exhibit not the least deviation, nor offer the slightest indication of refraction. It follows, therefore, that the moon cannot be surrounded by an atmosphere.

"In point of fact," replied Ardan, "this is your chief, if not your only argument; and a really scientific man might be puzzled to answer it. For myself, I will simply say that it is defective, because it assumes that the angular diameter of the moon has been completely determined, which is not the case. But let us proceed. Tell me, my dear sir, do you admit the existence of volcanoes on the moon's surface?"

"Extinct, yes! In activity, no!"

"These volcanoes, however, were at one time in a state of activity?"

"True, but, as they furnish themselves the oxygen necessary for combustion, the mere fact of their eruption does not prove the presence of an atmosphere."

"Proceed again, then; and let us set aside this class of arguments in order to come to direct observations. In 1715 the astronomers Louville and Halley, watching the eclipse of the 3rd of May, remarked some very extraordinary scintillations. These jets of light, rapid in nature, and of frequent recurrence, they attributed to thunderstorms generated in the lunar atmosphere."

"In 1715," replied the unknown, "the astronomers Louville and Halley mistook for lunar phenomena some which were purely terrestrial, such as meteoric or other bodies which are generated in our own atmosphere. This was the scientific explanation at the time of the facts; and that is my answer now."

"On again, then," replied Ardan; "Herschel, in 1787, observed a great number of luminous points on the moon's surface, did he not?"

"Yes! but without offering any solution of them. Herschel himself never inferred from them the necessity of a lunar atmosphere. And I may add that Baeer and Maedler, the two great authorities upon the moon, are quite agreed as to the entire absence of air on its surface."

A movement was here manifest among the assemblage, who appeared to be growing excited by the arguments of this singular personage.

"Let us proceed," replied Ardan, with perfect coolness, "and come to one important fact. A skillful French astronomer, M. Laussedat, in watching the eclipse of July 18, 1860, probed that the horns of the lunar crescent were rounded and truncated. Now, this appearance could only have been produced by a deviation of the solar rays in traversing the atmosphere of the moon. There is no other possible explanation of the facts."

"But is this established as a fact?"

"Absolutely certain!"

A counter-movement here took place in favor of the hero of the meeting, whose opponent was now reduced to silence. Ardan resumed the conversation; and without exhibiting any exultation at the advantage he had gained, simply said:

"You see, then, my dear sir, we must not pronounce with absolute positiveness against the existence of an atmosphere in the moon. That atmosphere is, probably, of extreme rarity; nevertheless at the present day science generally admits that it exists."

"Not in the mountains, at all events," returned the unknown, unwilling to give in.

"No! but at the bottom of the valleys, and not exceeding a few hundred feet in height."

"In any case you will do well to take every precaution, for the air will be terribly rarified."

"My good sir, there will always be enough for a solitary individual; besides, once arrived up there, I shall do my best to economize, and not to breathe except on grand occasions!"

A tremendous roar of laughter rang in the ears of the mysterious interlocutor, who glared fiercely round upon the assembly.

"Then," continued Ardan, with a careless air, "since we are in accord regarding the presence of a certain atmosphere, we are forced to admit the presence of a certain quantity of water. This is a happy consequence for me. Moreover, my amiable contradictor, permit me to submit to you one further observation. We only know one side of the moon's disc; and if there is but little air on the face presented to us, it is possible that there is plenty on the one turned away from us."

"And for what reason?"

"Because the moon, under the action of the earth's attraction, has assumed the form of an egg, which we look at from the smaller end. Hence it follows, by Hausen's calculations, that its center of gravity is situated in the other hemisphere. Hence it results that the great mass of air and water must have been drawn away to the other face of our satellite during the first days of its creation."

"Pure fancies!" cried the unknown.

"No! Pure theories! which are based upon the laws of mechanics, and it seems difficult to me to refute them. I appeal then to this meeting, and I put it to them whether life, such as exists upon the earth, is possible on the surface of the moon?"

Three hundred thousand auditors at once applauded the proposition. Ardan's opponent tried to get in another word, but he could not obtain a hearing. Cries and menaces fell upon him like hail.

"Enough! enough!" cried some.

"Drive the intruder off!" shouted others.

"Turn him out!" roared the exasperated crowd.

But he, holding firmly on to the platform, did not budge an inch, and let the storm pass on, which would soon have assumed formidable proportions, if Michel Ardan had not quieted it by a gesture. He was too chivalrous to abandon his opponent in an apparent extremity.

"You wished to say a few more words?" he asked, in a pleasant voice.

"Yes, a thousand; or rather, no, only one! If you persevere in your enterprise, you must be a—"

"Very rash person! How can you treat me as such? me, who have demanded a cylindro-conical projectile, in order to prevent turning round and round on my way like a squirrel?"

"But, unhappy man, the dreadful recoil will smash you to pieces at your starting."

"My dear contradictor, you have just put your finger upon the true and only difficulty; nevertheless, I have too good an opinion of the industrial genius of the Americans not to believe that they will succeed in overcoming it."

"But the heat developed by the rapidity of the projectile in crossing the strata of air?"

"Oh! the walls are thick, and I shall soon have crossed the atmosphere."

"But victuals and water?"

"I have calculated for a twelvemonth's supply, and I shall be only four days on the journey."

"But for air to breathe on the road?"

"I shall make it by a chemical process."

"But your fall on the moon, supposing you ever reach it?"

"It will be six times less dangerous than a sudden fall upon the earth, because the weight will be only one-sixth as great on the surface of the moon."

"Still it will be enough to smash you like glass!"

"What is to prevent my retarding the shock by means of rockets conveniently placed, and lighted at the right moment?"

"But after all, supposing all difficulties surmounted, all obstacles removed, supposing everything combined to favor you, and granting that you may arrive safe and sound in the moon, how will you come back?"

"I am not coming back!"

At this reply, almost sublime in its very simplicity, the assembly became silent. But its silence was more eloquent than could have been its cries of enthusiasm. The unknown profited by the opportunity and once more protested:

"You will inevitably kill yourself!" he cried; "and your death will be that of a madman, useless even to science!"

"Go on, my dear unknown, for truly your prophecies are most agreeable!"

"It really is too much!" cried Michel Ardan's adversary. "I do not know why I should continue so frivolous a discussion! Please yourself about this insane expedition! We need not trouble ourselves about you!"

"Pray don't stand upon ceremony!"

"No! another person is responsible for your act."

"Who, may I ask?" demanded Michel Ardan in an imperious tone.

"The ignoramus who organized this equally absurd and impossible experiment!"

The attack was direct. Barbicane, ever since the interference of the unknown, had been making fearful efforts of self-control; now, however, seeing himself directly attacked, he could restrain himself no longer. He rose suddenly, and was rushing upon the enemy who thus braved him to the face, when all at once he found himself separated from him.

The platform was lifted by a hundred strong arms, and the president of the Gun Club shared with Michel Ardan triumphal honors. The shield was heavy, but the bearers came in continuous relays, disputing, struggling, even fighting among themselves in their eagerness to lend their shoulders to this demonstration.

However, the unknown had not profited by the tumult to quit his post. Besides he could not have done it in the midst of that compact crowd. There he held on in the front row with crossed arms, glaring at President Barbicane.

The shouts of the immense crowd continued at their highest pitch throughout this triumphant march. Michel Ardan took it all with evident pleasure. His face gleamed with delight. Several times the platform seemed seized with pitching and rolling like a weatherbeaten ship. But the two heros of the meeting had good sea-legs. They never stumbled; and their vessel arrived without dues at the port of Tampa Town.

Michel Ardan managed fortunately to escape from the last embraces of his vigorous admirers. He made for the Hotel Franklin, quickly gained his chamber, and slid under the bedclothes, while an army of a hundred thousand men kept watch under his windows.

During this time a scene, short, grave, and decisive, took place between the mysterious personage and the president of the Gun Club.

Barbicane, free at last, had gone straight at his adversary.

"Come!" he said shortly.

The other followed him on the quay; and the two presently found themselves alone at the entrance of an open wharf on Jones' Fall.

The two enemies, still mutually unknown, gazed at each other.

"Who are you?" asked Barbicane.

"Captain Nicholl!"

"So I suspected. Hitherto chance has never thrown you in my way."

"I am come for that purpose."

"You have insulted me."

"Publicly!"

"And you will answer to me for this insult?"

"At this very moment."

"No! I desire that all that passes between us shall be secret. Their is a wood situated three miles from Tampa, the wood of Skersnaw. Do you know it?"

"I know it."

"Will you be so good as to enter it to-morrow morning at five o'clock, on one side?"

"Yes! if you will enter at the other side at the same hour."

"And you will not forget your rifle?" said Barbicane.

"No more than you will forget yours?" replied Nicholl.

These words having been coldly spoken, the president of the Gun Club and the captain parted. Barbicane returned to his lodging; but instead of snatching a few hours of repose, he passed the night in endeavoring to discover a means of evading the recoil of the projectile, and resolving the difficult problem proposed by Michel Ardan during the discussion at the meeting.

XXI

How a Frenchman Manages an Affair

WHILE the contract of this duel was being discussed by the president and the captain—this dreadful, savage duel, in which each adversary became a man-hunter—Michel Ardan was resting from the fatigues of his triumph. Resting is hardly an appropriate expression, for American beds rival marble or granite tables for hardness.

Ardan was sleeping, then, badly enough, tossing about between the cloths which served him for sheets, and he was dreaming of making a more comfortable couch in his projectile when a frightful noise disturbed his dreams. Thundering blows shook his door. They seemed to be caused by some iron instrument. A great deal of loud talking was distinguishable in this racket, which was rather too early in the morning. "Open the door," some one shrieked, "for heaven's sake!" Ardan saw no reason for complying with a demand so roughly expressed. However, he got up and opened the door just as it was giving way before the blows of this determined visitor. The secretary of the Gun Club burst into the room. A bomb could not have made more noise or have entered the room with less ceremony.

"Last night," cried J. T. Maston, ex abrupto, "our president was publicly insulted during the meeting. He provoked his adversary, who is none other than Captain Nicholl! They are fighting this morning in the wood of Skersnaw. I heard all the particulars from the mouth of Barbicane himself. If he is killed, then our scheme is at an end. We must prevent his duel; and one man alone has enough influence over Barbicane to stop him, and that man is Michel Ardan."

While J. T. Maston was speaking, Michel Ardan, without interrupting him, had hastily put on his clothes; and, in less than two minutes, the two friends were making for the suburbs of Tampa Town with rapid strides.

It was during this walk that Maston told Ardan the state of the case. He told him the real causes of the hostility between Barbicane and Nicholl; how it was of old date, and why, thanks to unknown friends, the president and the captain had, as yet, never met face to face. He added that it arose simply from a rivalry between iron plates and shot, and, finally, that the scene at the meeting was only the long-wished-for opportunity for Nicholl to pay off an old grudge.

Nothing is more dreadful than private duels in America. The two adversaries attack each other like wild beasts. Then it is that they might well covet those wonderful properties of the Indians of the prairies—their quick intelligence, their ingenious cunning, their scent of the enemy. A single mistake, a moment's hesitation, a single false step may cause death. On these occasions Yankees are often accompanied by their dogs, and keep up the struggle for hours.

"What demons you are!" cried Michel Ardan, when his companion had depicted this scene to him with much energy.

"Yes, we are," replied J. T. modestly; "but we had better make haste."

Though Michel Ardan and he had crossed the plains still wet with dew, and had taken the shortest route over creeks and ricefields, they could not reach Skersnaw in under five hours and a half.

Barbicane must have passed the border half an hour ago.

There was an old bushman working there, occupied in selling fagots from trees that had been leveled by his axe.

Maston ran toward him, saying, "Have you seen a man go into the wood, armed with a rifle? Barbicane, the president, my best friend?"

The worthy secretary of the Gun Club thought that his president must be known by all the world. But the bushman did not seem to understand him.

"A hunter?" said Ardan.

"A hunter? Yes," replied the bushman.

"Long ago?"

"About an hour."

"Too late!" cried Maston.

"Have you heard any gunshots?" asked Ardan.

"No!"

"Not one?"

"Not one! that hunter did not look as if he knew how to hunt!"

"What is to be done?" said Maston.

"We must go into the wood, at the risk of getting a ball which is not intended for us."

"Ah!" cried Maston, in a tone which could not be mistaken, "I would rather have twenty balls in my own head than one in Barbicane's."

"Forward, then," said Ardan, pressing his companion's hand.

A few moments later the two friends had disappeared in the copse. It was a dense thicket, in which rose huge cypresses, sycamores, tulip-trees, olives, tamarinds, oaks, and magnolias. These different trees had interwoven their branches into an inextricable maze, through which the eye could not penetrate. Michel Ardan and Maston walked side by side in silence through the tall grass, cutting themselves a path through the strong creepers, casting curious glances on the bushes, and momentarily expecting to hear the sound of rifles. As for the traces which Barbicane ought to have left of his passage through the wood, there was not a vestige of them visible: so they followed the barely perceptible paths along which Indians had tracked some enemy, and which the dense foliage darkly overshadowed.

After an hour spent in vain pursuit the two stopped in intensified anxiety.

"It must be all over," said Maston, discouraged. "A man like Barbicane would not dodge with his enemy, or ensnare him, would not even maneuver! He is too open, too brave. He has gone straight ahead, right into the danger, and doubtless far enough from the bushman for the wind to prevent his hearing the report of the rifles."

"But surely," replied Michel Ardan, "since we entered the wood we should have heard!"

"And what if we came too late?" cried Maston in tones of despair.

For once Ardan had no reply to make, he and Maston resuming their walk in silence. From time to time, indeed, they raised great shouts, calling alternately Barbicane and Nicholl, neither of whom, however, answered their cries. Only the birds, awakened by the sound, flew past them and disappeared among the branches, while some frightened deer fled precipitately before them.

For another hour their search was continued. The greater part of the wood had been explored. There was nothing to reveal the presence of the combatants. The information of the bushman was after all doubtful, and Ardan was about to propose their abandoning this useless pursuit, when all at once Maston stopped.

"Hush!" said he, "there is some one down there!"

"Some one?" repeated Michel Ardan.

"Yes; a man! He seems motionless. His rifle is not in his hands. What can he be doing?"

"But can you recognize him?" asked Ardan, whose short sight was of little use to him in such circumstances.

"Yes! yes! He is turning toward us," answered Maston.

"And it is?"

"Captain Nicholl!"

"Nicholl?" cried Michel Ardan, feeling a terrible pang of grief.

"Nicholl unarmed! He has, then, no longer any fear of his adversary!"

"Let us go to him," said Michel Ardan, "and find out the truth."

But he and his companion had barely taken fifty steps, when they paused to examine the captain more attentively. They expected to find a bloodthirsty man, happy in his revenge.

On seeing him, they remained stupefied.

A net, composed of very fine meshes, hung between two enormous tulip-trees, and in the midst of this snare, with its wings entangled, was a poor little bird, uttering pitiful cries, while it vainly struggled to escape. The bird-catcher who had laid this snare was no human being, but a venomous spider, peculiar to that country, as large as a pigeon's egg, and armed with enormous claws. The hideous creature, instead of rushing on its prey, had beaten a sudden retreat and taken refuge in the upper branches of the tulip-tree, for a formidable enemy menaced its stronghold.

Here, then, was Nicholl, his gun on the ground, forgetful of danger, trying if possible to save the victim from its cobweb prison. At last it was accomplished, and the little bird flew joyfully away and disappeared.

Nicholl lovingly watched its flight, when he heard these words pronounced by a voice full of emotion:

"You are indeed a brave man."

He turned. Michel Ardan was before him, repeating in a different tone:

"And a kindhearted one!"

"Michel Ardan!" cried the captain. "Why are you here?"

"To press your hand, Nicholl, and to prevent you from either killing Barbicane or being killed by him."

"Barbicane!" returned the captain. "I have been looking for him for the last two hours in vain. Where is he hiding?"

"Nicholl!" said Michel Ardan, "this is not courteous! we ought always to treat an adversary with respect; rest assureed if Barbicane is still alive we shall find him all the more easily; because if he has not, like you, been amusing himself with freeing oppressed birds, he must be looking for you. When we have found him, Michel Ardan tells you this, there will be no duel between you."

"Between President Barbicane and myself," gravely replied Nicholl, "there is a rivalry which the death of one of us—"

"Pooh, pooh!" said Ardan. "Brave fellows like you indeed! you shall not fight!"

"I will fight, sir!"

"No!"

"Captain," said J. T. Maston, with much feeling, "I am a friend of the president's, his alter ego, his second self; if you really must kill some one, shoot me! it will do just as well!"

"Sir," Nicholl replied, seizing his rifle convulsively, "these jokes—"

"Our friend Maston is not joking," replied Ardan. "I fully understand his idea of being killed himself in order to save his friend. But neither he nor Barbicane will fall before the balls of Captain Nicholl. Indeed I have so attractive a proposal to make to the two rivals, that both will be eager to accept it."

"What is it?" asked Nicholl with manifest incredulity.

"Patience!" exclaimed Ardan. "I can only reveal it in the presence of Barbicane."

"Let us go in search of him then!" cried the captain.

The three men started off at once; the captain having discharged his rifle threw it over his shoulder, and advanced in silence. Another half hour passed, and the pursuit was still fruitless. Maston was oppressed by sinister forebodings. He looked fiercely at Nicholl, asking himself whether the captain's vengeance had already been satisfied, and the unfortunate Barbicane, shot, was perhaps lying dead on some bloody track. The same thought seemed to occur to Ardan; and both were casting inquiring glances on Nicholl, when suddenly Maston paused.

The motionless figure of a man leaning against a gigantic catalpa twenty feet off appeared, half-veiled by the foliage.

"It is he!" said Maston.

Barbicane never moved. Ardan looked at the captain, but he did not wince. Ardan went forward crying:

"Barbicane! Barbicane!"

No answer! Ardan rushed toward his friend; but in the act of seizing his arms, he stopped short and uttered a cry of surprise.

Barbicane, pencil in hand, was tracing geometrical figures in a memorandum book, while his unloaded rifle lay beside him on the ground.

Absorbed in his studies, Barbicane, in his turn forgetful of the duel, had seen and heard nothing.

When Ardan took his hand, he looked up and stared at his visitor in astonishment.

"Ah, it is you!" he cried at last. "I have found it, my friend, I have found it!"

"What?"

"My plan!"

"What plan?"

"The plan for countering the effect of the shock at the departure of the projectile!"

"Indeed?" said Michel Ardan, looking at the captain out of the corner of his eye.

"Yes! water! simply water, which will act as a spring—ah! Maston," cried Barbicane, "you here also?"

"Himself," replied Ardan; "and permit me to introduce to you at the same time the worthy Captain Nicholl!"

"Nicholl!" cried Barbicane, who jumped up at once. "Pardon me, captain, I had quite forgotten—I am ready!"

Michel Ardan interfered, without giving the two enemies time to say anything more.

"Thank heaven!" said he. "It is a happy thing that brave men like you two did not meet sooner! we should now have been mourning for one or other of you. But, thanks to Providence, which has interfered, there is now no further cause for alarm. When one forgets one's anger in mechanics or in cobwebs, it is a sign that the anger is not dangerous."

Michel Ardan then told the president how the captain had been found occupied.

"I put it to you now," said he in conclusion, "are two such good fellows as you are made on purpose to smash each other's skulls with shot?"

There was in "the situation" somewhat of the ridiculous, something quite unexpected; Michel Ardan saw this, and determined to effect a reconciliation.

"My good friends," said he, with his most bewitching smile, "this is nothing but a misunderstanding. Nothing more! well! to prove that it is all over between you, accept frankly the proposal I am going to make to you."

"Make it," said Nicholl.

"Our friend Barbicane believes that his projectile will go straight to the moon?"

"Yes, certainly," replied the president.

"And our friend Nicholl is persuaded it will fall back upon the earth?"

"I am certain of it," cried the captain.

"Good!" said Ardan. "I cannot pretend to make you agree; but I suggest this: Go with me, and so see whether we are stopped on our journey."

"What?" exclaimed J. T. Maston, stupefied.

The two rivals, on this sudden proposal, looked steadily at each other. Barbicane waited for the captain's answer. Nicholl watched for the decision of the president.

"Well?" said Michel. "There is now no fear of the shock!"

"Done!" cried Barbicane.

But quickly as he pronounced the word, he was not before Nicholl.

"Hurrah! bravo! hip! hip! hurrah!" cried Michel, giving a hand to each of the late adversaries. "Now that it is all settled, my friends, allow me to treat you after French fashion. Let us be off to breakfast!"

XXII

THE NEW CITIZEN OF THE UNITED STATES

THAT same day all America heard of the affair of Captain Nicholl and President Barbicane, as well as its singular denouement. From that day forth, Michel Ardan had not one moment's rest. Deputations from all corners of the Union harassed him without cessation or intermission. He was compelled to receive them all, whether he would or no. How many hands he shook, how many people he was "hail-fellow-well-met" with, it is impossible to guess! Such a triumphal result would have intoxicated any other man; but he managed to keep himself in a state of delightful semi-tipsiness.

Among the deputations of all kinds which assailed him, that of "The Lunatics" were careful not to forget what they owed to the future conqueror of the moon. One day, certain of these poor people, so numerous in America, came to call upon him, and requested permission to return with him to their native country.

"Singular hallucination!" said he to Barbicane, after having dismissed the deputation with promises to convey numbers of messages to friends in the moon. "Do you believe in the influence of the moon upon distempers?"

"Scarcely!"

"No more do I, despite some remarkable recorded facts of history. For instance, during an epidemic in 1693, a large number of persons died at the very moment of an eclipse. The celebrated Bacon always fainted during an eclipse. Charles VI relapsed six times into madness during the year 1399, sometimes during the new, sometimes during the full moon. Gall observed that insane persons underwent an accession of their disorder twice in every month, at the epochs of new and full moon. In fact, numerous observations made upon fevers, somnambulisms, and other human maladies, seem to prove that the moon does exercise some mysterious influence upon man."

"But the how and the wherefore?" asked Barbicane.

"Well, I can only give you the answer which Arago borrowed from Plutarch, which is nineteen centuries old. 'Perhaps the stories are not true!'"

In the height of his triumph, Michel Ardan had to encounter all the annoyances incidental to a man of celebrity. Managers of entertainments wanted to exhibit him. Barnum offered him a million dollars to make a tour of the United States in his show. As for his photographs, they were sold of all size, and his portrait taken in every imaginable posture. More than half a million copies were disposed of in an incredibly short space of time.

But it was not only the men who paid him homage, but the women as well. He might have married well a hundred times over, if he had been willing to settle in life. The old maids, in particular, of forty years and upward, and dry in proportion, devoured his photographs day and night. They would have married him by hundreds, even if he had imposed upon them the condition of accompanying him into space. He had, however, no intention of transplanting a race of Franco-Americans upon the surface of the moon.

He therefore declined all offers.

As soon as he could withdraw from these somewhat embarrassing demonstrations, he went, accompanied by his friends, to pay a visit to the Columbiad. He was highly gratified by his inspection, and made the descent to the bottom of the tube of this gigantic machine which was presently to launch him to the regions of the moon. It is necessary here to mention a proposal of J. T. Maston's. When the secretary of the Gun Club found that Barbicane and Nicholl accepted the proposal of Michel Ardan, he determined to join them, and make one of a smug party of four. So one day he determined to be admitted as one of the travelers. Barbicane, pained at having to refuse him, gave him clearly to understand that the projectile could not possibly contain so many passengers. Maston, in despair, went in search of Michel Ardan, who counseled him to resign himself to the situation, adding one or two arguments ad hominem.

"You see, old fellow," he said, "you must not take what I say in bad part; but really, between ourselves, you are in too incomplete a condition to appear in the moon!"

"Incomplete?" shrieked the valiant invalid.

"Yes, my dear fellow! imagine our meeting some of the inhabitants up there! Would you like to give them such a melancholy notion of what goes on down here? to teach them what war is, to inform them that we employ our time chiefly in devouring each other, in smashing arms and legs, and that too on a globe which is capable of supporting a hundred billions of inhabitants, and which actually does contain nearly two hundred millions? Why, my worthy friend, we should have to turn you out of doors!"

"But still, if you arrive there in pieces, you will be as incomplete as I am."

"Unquestionably," replied Michel Ardan; "but we shall not."

In fact, a preparatory experiment, tried on the 18th of October, had yielded the best results and caused the most well-grounded hopes of success. Barbicane, desirous of obtaining some notion of the effect of the shock at the moment of the projectile's departure, had procured a 38-inch mortar from the arsenal of Pensacola. He had this placed on the bank of Hillisborough Roads, in order that the shell might fall back into the sea, and the shock be thereby destroyed. His object was to ascertain the extent of the shock of departure, and not that of the return.

A hollow projectile had been prepared for this curious experiment. A thick padding fastened upon a kind of elastic network, made of the best steel, lined the inside of the walls. It was a veritable nest most carefully wadded.

"What a pity I can't find room in there," said J. T. Maston, regretting that his height did not allow of his trying the adventure.

Within this shell were shut up a large cat, and a squirrel belonging to J. T. Maston, and of which he was particularly fond. They were desirous, however, of ascertaining how this little animal, least of all others subject to giddiness, would endure this experimental voyage.

The mortar was charged with 160 pounds of powder, and the shell placed in the chamber. On being fired, the projectile rose with great velocity, described a majestic parabola, attained a height of about a thousand feet, and with a graceful curve descended in the midst of the vessels that lay there at anchor.

Without a moment's loss of time a small boat put off in the direction of its fall; some divers plunged into the water and attached ropes to the handles of the shell, which was quickly dragged on board. Five minutes did not elapse between the moment of enclosing the animals and that of unscrewing the coverlid of their prison.

Ardan, Barbicane, Maston, and Nicholl were present on board the boat, and assisted at the operation with an interest which may readily be comprehended. Hardly had the shell been opened when the cat leaped out, slightly bruised, but full of life, and exhibiting no signs whatever of having made an aerial expedition. No trace, however, of the squirrel could be discovered. The truth at last became apparent—the cat had eaten its fellow-traveler!

J. T. Maston grieved much for the loss of his poor squirrel, and proposed to add its case to that of other martyrs to science.

After this experiment all hesitation, all fear disappeared. Besides, Barbicane's plans would ensure greater perfection for his projectile, and go far to annihilate altogether the effects of the shock. Nothing now remained but to go!

Two days later Michel Ardan received a message from the President of the United States, an honor of which he showed himself especially sensible.

After the example of his illustrious fellow-countryman, the Marquis de la Fayette, the government had decreed to him the title of "Citizen of the United States of America."

XXIII

THE PROJECTILE-VEHICLE

ON the completion of the Columbiad the public interest centered in the projectile itself, the vehicle which was destined to carry the three hardy adventurers into space.

The new plans had been sent to Breadwill and Co., of Albany, with the request for their speedy execution. The projectile was consequently cast on the 2nd of November, and immediately forwarded by the Eastern Railway to Stones Hill, which it reached without accident on the 10th of that month, where Michel Ardan, Barbicane, and Nicholl were waiting impatiently for it.

The projectile had now to be filled to the depth of three feet with a bed of water, intended to support a water-tight wooden disc, which worked easily within the walls of the projectile. It was upon this kind of raft that the travelers were to take their place. This body of water was divided by horizontal partitions, which the shock of the departure would have to break in succession. Then each sheet of the water, from the lowest to the highest, running off into escape tubes toward the top of the projectile, constituted a kind of spring; and the wooden disc, supplied with extremely powerful plugs, could not strike the lowest plate except after breaking successively the different partitions. Undoubtedly the travelers would still have to encounter a violent recoil after the complete escapement of the water; but the first shock would be almost entirely destroyed by this powerful spring. The upper parts of the walls were lined with a thick padding of leather, fastened upon springs of the best steel, behind which the escape tubes were completely concealed; thus all imaginable precautions had been taken for averting the first shock; and if they did get crushed, they must, as Michel Ardan said, be made of very bad materials.

The entrance into this metallic tower was by a narrow aperture contrived in the wall of the cone. This was hermetically closed by a plate of aluminum, fastened internally by powerful screw-pressure. The travelers could therefore quit their prison at pleasure, as soon as they should reach the moon.

Light and view were given by means of four thick lenticular glass scuttles, two pierced in the circular wall itself, the third in the bottom, the fourth in the top. These scuttles then were protected against the shock of departure by plates let into solid grooves, which could easily be opened outward by unscrewing them from the inside. Reservoirs firmly fixed contained water and the necessary provisions; and fire and light were procurable by means of gas, contained in a special reservoir under a pressure of several atmospheres. They had only to turn a tap, and for six hours the gas would light and warm this comfortable vehicle.

There now remained only the question of air; for allowing for the consumption of air by Barbicane, his two companions, and two dogs which he proposed taking with him, it was necessary to renew the air of the projectile. Now air consists principally of twenty-one parts of oxygen and seventy-nine of nitrogen. The lungs absorb the oxygen, which is indispensable for the support of life, and reject the nitrogen. The air expired loses nearly five per cent. of the former and contains nearly an equal volume of carbonic acid, produced by the combustion of the elements of the blood. In an airtight enclosure, then, after a certain time, all the oxygen of the air will be replaced by the carbonic acid—a gas fatal to life. There were two things to be done then—first, to replace the absorbed oxygen; secondly, to destroy the expired carbonic acid; both easy enough to do, by means of chlorate of potassium and caustic potash. The former is a salt which appears under the form of white crystals; when raised to a temperature of 400 degrees it is transformed into chlorure of potassium, and the oxygen which it contains is entirely liberated. Now twenty-eight pounds of chlorate of potassium produces seven pounds of oxygen, or 2,400 litres—the quantity necessary for the travelers during twenty-four hours.

Caustic potash has a great affinity for carbonic acid; and it is sufficient to shake it in order for it to seize upon the acid and form bicarbonate of potassium. By these two means they would be enabled to restore to the vitiated air its life- supporting properties.

It is necessary, however, to add that the experiments had hitherto been made in anima vili. Whatever its scientific accuracy was, they were at present ignorant how it would answer with human beings. The honor of putting it to the proof was energetically claimed by J. T. Maston.

"Since I am not to go," said the brave artillerist, "I may at least live for a week in the projectile."

It would have been hard to refuse him; so they consented to his wish. A sufficient quantity of chlorate of potassium and of caustic potash was placed at his disposal, together with provisions for eight days. And having shaken hands with his friends, on the 12th of November, at six o'clock A.M., after strictly informing them not to open his prison before the 20th, at six o'clock P.M., he slid down the projectile, the plate of which was at once hermetically sealed. What did he do with himself during that week? They could get no information. The thickness of the walls of the projectile prevented any sound reaching from the inside to the outside. On the 20th of November, at six P.M. exactly, the plate was opened. The friends of J. T. Maston had been all along in a state of much anxiety; but they were promptly reassured on hearing a jolly voice shouting a boisterous hurrah.

Presently afterward the secretary of the Gun Club appeared at the top of the cone in a triumphant attitude. He had grown fat!

XXIV

The Telescope of the Rocky Mountains

ON the 20th of October in the preceding year, after the close of the subscription, the president of the Gun Club had credited the Observatory of Cambridge with the necessary sums for the construction of a gigantic optical instrument. This instrument was designed for the purpose of rendering visible on the surface of the moon any object exceeding nine feet in diameter.

At the period when the Gun Club essayed their great experiment, such instruments had reached a high degree of perfection, and produced some magnificent results. Two telescopes in particular, at this time, were possessed of remarkable power and of gigantic dimensions. The first, constructed by Herschel, was thirty-six feet in length, and had an object-glass of four feet six inches; it possessed a magnifying power of 6,000. The second was raised in Ireland, in Parsonstown Park, and belongs to Lord Rosse. The length of this tube is forty-eight feet, and the diameter of its object-glass six feet; it magnifies 6,400 times, and required an immense erection of brick work and masonry for the purpose of working it, its weight being twelve and a half tons.

Still, despite these colossal dimensions, the actual enlargements scarcely exceeded 6,000 times in round numbers; consequently, the moon was brought within no nearer an apparent distance than thirty-nine miles; and objects of less than sixty feet in diameter, unless they were of very considerable length, were still imperceptible.

In the present case, dealing with a projectile nine feet in diameter and fifteen feet long, it became necessary to bring the moon within an apparent distance of five miles at most; and for that purpose to establish a magnifying power of 48,000 times.

Such was the question proposed to the Observatory of Cambridge, There was no lack of funds; the difficulty was purely one of construction.

After considerable discussion as to the best form and principle of the proposed instrument the work was finally commenced. According to the calculations of the Observatory of Cambridge, the tube of the new reflector would require to be 280 feet in length, and the object-glass sixteen feet in diameter. Colossal as these dimensions may appear, they were diminutive in comparison with the 10,000 foot telescope proposed by the astronomer Hooke only a few years ago!

Regarding the choice of locality, that matter was promptly determined. The object was to select some lofty mountain, and there are not many of these in the United States. In fact there are but two chains of moderate elevation, between which runs the magnificent Mississippi, the "king of rivers" as these Republican Yankees delight to call it.

Eastwards rise the Appalachians, the very highest point of which, in New Hampshire, does not exceed the very moderate altitude of 5,600 feet.

On the west, however, rise the Rocky Mountains, that immense range which, commencing at the Straights of Magellan, follows the western coast of Southern America under the name of the Andes or the Cordilleras, until it crosses the Isthmus of Panama, and runs up the whole of North America to the very borders of the Polar Sea. The highest elevation of this range still does not exceed 10,700 feet. With this elevation, nevertheless, the Gun Club were compelled to be content, inasmuch as they had determined that both telescope and Columbiad should be erected within the limits of the Union. All the necessary apparatus was consequently sent on to the summit of Long's Peak, in the territory of Missouri.

Neither pen nor language can describe the difficulties of all kinds which the American engineers had to surmount, of the prodigies of daring and skill which they accomplished. They had to raise enormous stones, massive pieces of wrought iron, heavy corner-clamps and huge portions of cylinder, with an object-glass weighing nearly 30,000 pounds, above the line of perpetual snow for more than 10,000 feet in height, after crossing desert prairies, impenetrable forests, fearful rapids, far from all centers of population, and in the midst of savage regions, in which every detail of life becomes an almost insoluble problem. And yet, notwithstanding these innumerable obstacles, American genius triumphed. In less than a year after the commencement of the works, toward the close of September, the gigantic reflector rose into the air to a height of 280 feet. It was raised by means of an enormous iron crane; an ingenious mechanism allowed it to be easily worked toward all the points of the heavens, and to follow the stars from the one horizon to the other during their journey through the heavens.

It had cost $400,000. The first time it was directed toward the moon the observers evinced both curiosity and anxiety. What were they about to discover in the field of this telescope which magnified objects 48,000 times? Would they perceive peoples, herds of lunar animals, towns, lakes, seas? No! there was nothing which science had not already discovered! and on all the points of its disc the volcanic nature of the moon became determinable with the utmost precision.

But the telescope of the Rocky Mountains, before doing its duty to the Gun Club, rendered immense services to astronomy. Thanks to its penetrative power, the depths of the heavens were sounded to the utmost extent; the apparent diameter of a great number of stars was accurately measured; and Mr. Clark, of the Cambridge staff, resolved the Crab nebula in Taurus, which the reflector of Lord Rosse had never been able to decompose.

XXV

FINAL DETAILS

IT was the 22nd of November; the departure was to take place in ten days. One operation alone remained to be accomplished to bring all to a happy termination; an operation delicate and perilous, requiring infinite precautions, and against the success of which Captain Nicholl had laid his third bet. It was, in fact, nothing less than the loading of the Columbiad, and the introduction into it of 400,000 pounds of gun-cotton. Nicholl had

96

thought, not perhaps without reason, that the handling of such formidable quantities of pyroxyle would, in all probability, involve a grave catastrophe; and at any rate, that this immense mass of eminently inflammable matter would inevitably ignite when submitted to the pressure of the projectile.

There were indeed dangers accruing as before from the carelessness of the Americans, but Barbicane had set his heart on success, and took all possible precautions. In the first place, he was very careful as to the transportation of the gun-cotton to Stones Hill. He had it conveyed in small quantities, carefully packed in sealed cases. These were brought by rail from Tampa Town to the camp, and from thence were taken to the Columbiad by barefooted workmen, who deposited them in their places by means of cranes placed at the orifice of the cannon. No steam-engine was permitted to work, and every fire was extinguished within two miles of the works.

Even in November they feared to work by day, lest the sun's rays acting on the gun-cotton might lead to unhappy results. This led to their working at night, by light produced in a vacuum by means of Ruhmkorff's apparatus, which threw an artificial brightness into the depths of the Columbiad. There the cartridges were arranged with the utmost regularity, connected by a metallic thread, destined to communicate to them all simultaneously the electric spark, by which means this mass of gun-cotton was eventually to be ignited.

By the 28th of November eight hundred cartridges had been placed in the bottom of the Columbiad. So far the operation had been successful! But what confusion, what anxieties, what struggles were undergone by President Barbicane! In vain had he refused admission to Stones Hill; every day the inquisitive neighbors scaled the palisades, some even carrying their imprudence to the point of smoking while surrounded by bales of gun-cotton. Barbicane was in a perpetual state of alarm. J. T. Maston seconded him to the best of his ability, by giving vigorous chase to the intruders, and carefully picking up the still lighted cigar ends which the Yankees threw about. A somewhat difficult task! seeing that more than 300,000 persons were gathered round the enclosure. Michel Ardan had volunteered to superintend the transport of the cartridges to the mouth of the Columbiad; but the president, having surprised him with an enormous cigar in his mouth, while he was hunting out the rash spectators to whom he himself offered so dangerous an example, saw that he could not trust this fearless smoker, and was therefore obliged to mount a special guard over him.

At last, Providence being propitious, this wonderful loading came to a happy termination, Captain Nicholl's third bet being thus lost. It remained now to introduce the projectile into the Columbiad, and to place it on its soft bed of gun-cotton.

But before doing this, all those things necessary for the journey had to be carefully arranged in the projectile vehicle. These necessaries were numerous; and had Ardan been allowed to follow his own wishes, there would have been no space remaining for the travelers. It is impossible to conceive of half the things this charming Frenchman wished to convey to the moon. A veritable stock of useless trifles! But Barbicane interfered and refused admission to anything not absolutely needed. Several thermometers, barometers, and telescopes were packed in the instrument case.

The travelers being desirous of examing the moon carefully during their voyage, in order to facilitate their studies, they took with them Boeer and Moeller's excellent Mappa Selenographica, a masterpiece of patience and observation, which they hoped would enable them to identify those physical features in the moon, with which they were acquainted. This map reproduced with scrupulous fidelity the smallest details of the lunar surface which faces the earth; the mountains, valleys, craters, peaks, and ridges were all represented, with their exact dimensions, relative positions, and names; from the mountains Doerfel and Leibnitz on the eastern side of the disc, to the Mare frigoris of the North Pole.

They took also three rifles and three fowling-pieces, and a large quantity of balls, shot, and powder.

"We cannot tell whom we shall have to deal with," said Michel Ardan. "Men or beasts may possibly object to our visit. It is only wise to take all precautions."

These defensive weapons were accompanied by pickaxes, crowbars, saws, and other useful implements, not to mention clothing adapted to every temperature, from that of polar regions to that of the torrid zone.

Ardan wished to convey a number of animals of different sorts, not indeed a pair of every known species, as he could not see the necessity of acclimatizing serpents, tigers, alligators, or any other noxious beasts in the moon. "Nevertheless," he said to Barbicane, "some valuable and useful beasts, bullocks, cows, horses, and donkeys, would bear the journey very well, and would also be very useful to us."

"I dare say, my dear Ardan," replied the president, "but our projectile-vehicle is no Noah's ark, from which it differs both in dimensions and object. Let us confine ourselves to possibilities."

After a prolonged discussion, it was agreed that the travelers should restrict themselves to a sporting-dog belonging to Nicholl, and to a large Newfoundland. Several packets of seeds were also included among the necessaries. Michel Ardan, indeed, was anxious to add some sacks full of earth to sow them in; as it was, he took a dozen shrubs carefully wrapped up in straw to plant in the moon.

The important question of provisions still remained; it being necessary to provide against the possibility of their finding the moon absolutely barren. Barbicane managed so successfully, that he supplied them with sufficient rations for a year. These consisted of preserved meats and vegetables, reduced by strong hydraulic pressure to the smallest possible dimensions. They were also supplied with brandy, and took water enough for two months, being confident, from astronomical observations, that there was no lack of water on the moon's surface. As to provisions, doubtless the inhabitants of the earth would find nourishment somewhere in the moon. Ardan never questioned this; indeed, had he done so, he would never have undertaken the journey.

"Besides," he said one day to his friends, "we shall not be completely abandoned by our terrestrial friends; they will take care not to forget us."

"No, indeed!" replied J. T. Maston.

"Nothing would be simpler," replied Ardan; "the Columbiad will be always there. Well! whenever the moon is in a favorable condition as to the zenith, if not to the perigee, that is to say about once a year, could you not send us a shell packed with provisions, which we might expect on some appointed day?"

"Hurrah! hurrah!" cried J. T. Matson; "what an ingenious fellow! what a splendid idea! Indeed, my good friends, we shall not forget you!"

"I shall reckon upon you! Then, you see, we shall receive news regularly from the earth, and we shall indeed be stupid if we hit upon no plan for communicating with our good friends here!"

These words inspired such confidence, that Michel Ardan carried all the Gun Club with him in his enthusiasm. What he said seemed so simple and so easy, so sure of success, that none could be so sordidly attached to this earth as to hesitate to follow the three travelers on their lunar expedition.

All being ready at last, it remained to place the projectile in the Columbiad, an operation abundantly accompanied by dangers and difficulties.

The enormous shell was conveyed to the summit of Stones Hill. There, powerful cranes raised it, and held it suspended over the mouth of the cylinder.

It was a fearful moment! What if the chains should break under its enormous weight? The sudden fall of such a body would inevitably cause the gun-cotton to explode!

Fortunately this did not happen; and some hours later the projectile-vehicle descended gently into the heart of the cannon and rested on its couch of pyroxyle, a veritable bed of explosive eider-down. Its pressure had no result, other than the more effectual ramming down of the charge in the Columbiad.

"I have lost," said the captain, who forthwith paid President Barbicane the sum of three thousand dollars.

Barbicane did not wish to accept the money from one of his fellow-travelers, but gave way at last before the determination of Nicholl, who wished before leaving the earth to fulfill all his engagements.

"Now," said Michel Ardan, "I have only one thing more to wish for you, my brave captain."

"What is that?" asked Nicholl.

"It is that you may lose your two other bets! Then we shall be sure not to be stopped on our journey!"

XXVI

FIRE!

THE first of December had arrived! the fatal day! for, if the projectile were not discharged that very night at 10h. 48m. 40s. P.M., more than eighteen years must roll by before the moon would again present herself under the same conditions of zenith and perigee.

The weather was magnificent. Despite the approach of winter, the sun shone brightly, and bathed in its radiant light that earth which three of its denizens were about to abandon for a new world.

How many persons lost their rest on the night which preceded this long-expected day! All hearts beat with disquietude, save only the heart of Michel Ardan. That imperturbable personage came and went with his habitual business-like air, while nothing whatever denoted that any unusual matter preoccupied his mind.

After dawn, an innumerable multitude covered the prairie which extends, as far as the eye can reach, round Stones Hill. Every quarter of an hour the railway brought fresh accessions of sightseers; and, according to the statement of the Tampa Town Observer, not less than five millions of spectators thronged the soil of Florida.

For a whole month previously, the mass of these persons had bivouacked round the enclosure, and laid the foundations for a town which was afterward called "Ardan's Town." The whole plain was covered with huts, cottages, and tents. Every nation under the sun was represented there; and every language might be heard spoken at the same time. It was a perfect Babel re-enacted. All the various classes of American society were mingled together in terms of absolute equality. Bankers, farmers, sailors, cotton-planters, brokers, merchants, watermen, magistrates, elbowed each other in the most free-and-easy way. Louisiana Creoles fraternized with farmers from Indiana; Kentucky and Tennessee gentlemen and haughty Virginians conversed with trappers and the half-savages of the lakes and butchers from Cincinnati. Broad-brimmed white hats and Panamas, blue-cotton trousers, light-colored stockings, cambric frills, were all here displayed; while upon shirt-fronts, wristbands, and neckties, upon every finger, even upon the very ears, they wore an assortment of rings, shirt-pins, brooches, and trinkets, of which the value only equaled the execrable taste. Women, children, and servants, in equally expensive dress, surrounded their husbands, fathers, or masters, who resembled the patriarchs of tribes in the midst of their immense households.

At meal-times all fell to work upon the dishes peculiar to the Southern States, and consumed with an appetite that threatened speedy exhaustion of the victualing powers of Florida, fricasseed frogs, stuffed monkey, fish chowder, underdone 'possum, and raccoon steaks. And as for the liquors which accompanied this indigestible repast! The shouts, the vociferations that resounded through the bars and taverns decorated with glasses, tankards, and bottles of marvelous shape, mortars for pounding sugar, and bundles of straws! "Mint-julep" roars one of the barmen; "Claret sangaree!" shouts another; "Cocktail!" "Brandy-smash!" "Real mint-julep in the new style!" All these cries intermingled produced a bewildering and deafening hubbub.

But on this day, 1st of December, such sounds were rare. No one thought of eating or drinking, and at four P.M. there were vast numbers of spectators who had not even taken their customary lunch! And, a still more significant fact, even the national passion for play seemed quelled for the time under the general excitement of the hour.

Up till nightfall, a dull, noiseless agitation, such as precedes great catastrophes, ran through the anxious multitude. An indescribable uneasiness pervaded all minds, an indefinable sensation which oppressed the heart. Every one wished it was over.

However, about seven o'clock, the heavy silence was dissipated. The moon rose above the horizon. Millions of hurrahs hailed her appearance. She was punctual to the rendezvous, and shouts of welcome greeted her on all sides, as her pale beams shone gracefully in the clear heavens. At this moment the three intrepid travelers appeared. This was the signal for renewed cries of still greater intensity. Instantly the vast assemblage, as with one accord, struck up the national hymn of the United States, and

"Yankee Doodle," sung by five million of hearty throats, rose like a roaring tempest to the farthest limits of the atmosphere. Then a profound silence reigned throughout the crowd.

The Frenchman and the two Americans had by this time entered the enclosure reserved in the center of the multitude. They were accompanied by the members of the Gun Club, and by deputations sent from all the European Observatories. Barbicane, cool and collected, was giving his final directions. Nicholl, with compressed lips, his arms crossed behind his back, walked with a firm and measured step. Michel Ardan, always easy, dressed in thorough traveler's costume, leathern gaiters on his legs, pouch by his side, in loose velvet suit, cigar in mouth, was full of inexhaustible gayety, laughing, joking, playing pranks with J. T. Maston. In one word, he was the thorough "Frenchman" (and worse, a "Parisian") to the last moment.

Ten o'clock struck! The moment had arrived for taking their places in the projectile! The necessary operations for the descent, and the subsequent removal of the cranes and scaffolding that inclined over the mouth of the Columbiad, required a certain period of time.

Barbicane had regulated his chronometer to the tenth part of a second by that of Murchison the engineer, who was charged with the duty of firing the gun by means of an electric spark. Thus the travelers enclosed within the projectile were enabled to follow with their eyes the impassive needle which marked the precise moment of their departure.

The moment had arrived for saying "good-by!" The scene was a touching one. Despite his feverish gayety, even Michel Ardan was touched. J. T. Maston had found in his own dry eyes one ancient tear, which he had doubtless reserved for the occasion. He dropped it on the forehead of his dear president.

"Can I not go?" he said, "there is still time!"

"Impossible, old fellow!" replied Barbicane. A few moments later, the three fellow-travelers had ensconced themselves in the projectile, and screwed down the plate which covered the entrance-aperture. The mouth of the Columbiad, now completely disencumbered, was open entirely to the sky.

The moon advanced upward in a heaven of the purest clearness, outshining in her passage the twinkling light of the stars. She passed over the constellation of the Twins, and was now nearing the halfway point between the horizon and the zenith. A terrible silence weighed upon the entire scene! Not a breath of wind upon the earth! not a sound of breathing from the countless chests of the spectators! Their hearts seemed afraid to beat! All eyes were fixed upon the yawning mouth of the Columbiad.

Murchison followed with his eye the hand of his chronometer. It wanted scarce forty seconds to the moment of departure, but each second seemed to last an age! At the twentieth there was a general shudder, as it occurred to the minds of that vast assemblage that the bold travelers shut up within the projectile were also counting those terrible seconds. Some few cries here and there escaped the crowd.

"Thirty-five!—thirty-six!—thirty-seven!—thirty-eight!—thirty-nine!—forty! FIRE!!!"

Instantly Murchison pressed with his finger the key of the electric battery, restored the current of the fluid, and discharged the spark into the breech of the Columbiad.

An appalling unearthly report followed instantly, such as can be compared to nothing whatever known, not even to the roar of thunder, or the blast of volcanic explosions! No words can convey the slightest idea of the terrific sound! An immense spout of fire shot up from the bowels of the earth as from a crater. The earth heaved up, and with great difficulty some few spectators obtained a momentary glimpse of the projectile victoriously cleaving the air in the midst of the fiery vapors!

XXVII

FOUL WEATHER

AT the moment when that pyramid of fire rose to a prodigious height into the air, the glare of flame lit up the whole of Florida; and for a moment day superseded night over a considerable extent of the country. This immense canopy of fire was perceived at a distance of one hundred miles out at sea, and more than one ship's captain entered in his log the appearance of this gigantic meteor.

The discharge of the Columbiad was accompanied by a perfect earthquake. Florida was shaken to its very depths. The gases of the powder, expanded by heat, forced back the atmospheric strata with tremendous violence, and this artificial hurricane rushed like a water-spout through the air.

Not a single spectator remained on his feet! Men, women children, all lay prostrate like ears of corn under a tempest. There ensued a terrible tumult; a large number of persons were seriously injured. J. T. Maston, who, despite all dictates of prudence, had kept in advance of the mass, was pitched back 120 feet, shooting like a projectile over the heads of his fellow-citizens. Three hundred thousand persons remained deaf for a time, and as though struck stupefied.

As soon as the first effects were over, the injured, the deaf, and lastly, the crowd in general, woke up with frenzied cries. "Hurrah for Ardan! Hurrah for Barbicane! Hurrah for Nicholl!" rose to the skies. Thousands of persons, noses in air, armed with telescopes and race-glasses, were questioning space, forgetting all contusions and emotions in the one idea of watching for the projectile. They looked in vain! It was no longer to be seen, and they were obliged to wait for telegrams from Long's Peak. The director of the Cambridge Observatory was at his post on the Rocky Mountains; and to him, as a skillful and persevering astronomer, all observations had been confided.

But an unforeseen phenomenon came in to subject the public impatience to a severe trial.

The weather, hitherto so fine, suddenly changed; the sky became heavy with clouds. It could not have been otherwise after the terrible derangement of the atmospheric strata, and the dispersion of the enormous quantity of vapor arising from the combustion of 200,000 pounds of pyroxyle!

On the morrow the horizon was covered with clouds—a thick and impenetrable curtain between earth and sky, which unhappily extended as far as the Rocky Mountains. It was a fatality! But since man had chosen so to disturb the atmosphere, he was bound to accept the consequences of his experiment.

Supposing, now, that the experiment had succeeded, the travelers having started on the 1st of December, at 10h. 46m. 40s. P.M., were due on the 4th at 0h. P.M. at their destination. So that up to that time it would have been very difficult after all to have observed, under such conditions, a body so small as the shell. Therefore they waited with what patience they might.

From the 4th to the 6th of December inclusive, the weather remaining much the same in America, the great European instruments of Herschel, Rosse, and Foucault, were constantly directed toward the moon, for the weather was then magnificent; but the comparative weakness of their glasses prevented any trustworthy observations being made.

On the 7th the sky seemed to lighten. They were in hopes now, but their hope was of but short duration, and at night again thick clouds hid the starry vault from all eyes.

Matters were now becoming serious, when on the 9th the sun reappeared for an instant, as if for the purpose of teasing the Americans. It was received with hisses; and wounded, no doubt, by such a reception, showed itself very sparing of its rays.

On the 10th, no change! J. T. Maston went nearly mad, and great fears were entertained regarding the brain of this worthy individual, which had hitherto been so well preserved within his gutta-percha cranium.

But on the 11th one of those inexplicable tempests peculiar to those intertropical regions was let loose in the atmosphere. A terrific east wind swept away the groups of clouds which had been so long gathering, and at night the semi-disc of the orb of night rode majestically amid the soft constellations of the sky.

XXVIII

A New Star

THAT very night, the startling news so impatiently awaited, burst like a thunderbolt over the United States of the Union, and thence, darting across the ocean, ran through all the telegraphic wires of the globe. The projectile had been detected, thanks to the gigantic reflector of Long's Peak! Here is the note received by the director of the Observatory of Cambridge. It contains the scientific conclusion regarding this great experiment of the Gun Club.

LONG'S PEAK, *December 12.*

TO THE OFFICERS OF THE OBSERVATORY OF CAMBRIDGE.

The projectile discharged by the Columbiad at Stones Hill has been detected by Messrs. Belfast and J. T. Maston, 12th of December, at 8:47 P.M., the moon having entered her last quarter. This projectile has not arrived at its destination. It has passed by the side; but sufficiently near to be retained by the lunar attraction.

The rectilinear movement has thus become changed into a circular motion of extreme velocity, and it is now pursuing an elliptical orbit round the moon, of which it has become a true satellite.

The elements of this new star we have as yet been unable to determine; we do not yet know the velocity of its passage. The distance which separates it from the surface of the moon may be estimated at about 2,833 miles.

However, two hypotheses come here into our consideration.

1. Either the attraction of the moon will end by drawing them into itself, and the travelers will attain their destination; or,

2. The projectile, following an immutable law, will continue to gravitate round the moon till the end of time.

At some future time, our observations will be able to determine this point, but till then the experiment of the Gun Club can have no other result than to have provided our solar system with a new star.

J. BELFAST.

To how many questions did this unexpected denouement give rise? What mysterious results was the future reserving for the investigation of science? At all events, the names of Nicholl, Barbicane, and Michel Ardan were certain to be immortalized in the annals of astronomy!

When the dispatch from Long's Peak had once become known, there was but one universal feeling of surprise and alarm. Was it possible to go to the aid of these bold travelers? No! for they had placed themselves beyond the pale of humanity, by crossing the limits imposed by the Creator on his earthly creatures. They had air enough for two months; they had victuals enough for twelve;—but after that? There was only one man who would not admit that the situation was desperate—he alone had confidence; and that was their devoted friend J. T. Maston.

Besides, he never let them get out of sight. His home was henceforth the post at Long's Peak; his horizon, the mirror of that immense reflector. As soon as the moon rose above the horizon, he immediately caught her in the field of the telescope; he never let her go for an instant out of his sight, and followed her assiduously in her course through the stellar spaces. He watched with untiring patience the passage of the projectile across her silvery disc, and really the worthy man remained in perpetual communication with his three friends, whom he did not despair of seeing again some day.

"Those three men," said he, "have carried into space all the resources of art, science, and industry. With that, one can do anything; and you will see that, some day, they will come out all right."

■■■■■■■■■■

Round the Moon

A Sequel to
From the Earth to the Moon

PRELIMINARY CHAPTER

The First Part of this Work,
And Serving as a Preface to the Second

During the year 186-, the whole world was greatly excited by a scientific experiment unprecedented in the annals of science. The members of the Gun Club, a circle of artillerymen formed at Baltimore after the American war, conceived the idea of putting themselves in communication with the moon!—yes, with the moon—by sending to her a projectile. Their president, Barbicane, the promoter of the enterprise, having consulted the astronomers of the Cambridge Observatory upon the subject, took all necessary means to ensure the success of this extraordinary enterprise, which had been declared practicable by the majority of competent judges. After setting on foot a public subscription, which realized nearly 1,200,000, they began the gigantic work.

According to the advice forwarded from the members of the Observatory, the gun destined to launch the projectile had to be fixed in a country situated between the 0 and 28th degrees of north or south latitude, in order to aim at the moon when at the zenith; and its initiatory velocity was fixed at twelve thousand yards to the second. Launched on the 1st of December, at 10hrs. 46m. 40s. P.M., it ought to reach the moon four days after its departure, that is on the 5th of December, at midnight precisely, at the moment of her attaining her perigee, that is her nearest distance from the earth, which is exactly 86,410 leagues (French), or 238,833 miles mean distance (English).

The principal members of the Gun Club, President Barbicane, Major Elphinstone, the secretary Joseph T. Maston, and other learned men, held several meetings, at which the shape and composition of the projectile were discussed, also the position and nature of the gun, and the quality and quantity of powder to be used. It was decided: First, that the projectile should be a shell made of aluminum with a diameter of 108 inches and a thickness of twelve inches to its walls; and should weigh 19,250 pounds. Second, that the gun should be a Columbiad cast in iron,

900 feet long, and run perpendicularly into the earth. Third, that the charge should contain 400,000 pounds of gun-cotton, which, giving out six billions of litres of gas in rear of the projectile, would easily carry it toward the orb of night.

These questions determined President Barbicane, assisted by Murchison the engineer, to choose a spot situated in Florida, in 27@ 7' North latitude, and 77@ 3' West (Greenwich) longitude. It was on this spot, after stupendous labor, that the Columbiad was cast with full success. Things stood thus, when an incident took place which increased the interest attached to this great enterprise a hundredfold.

A Frenchman, an enthusiastic Parisian, as witty as he was bold, asked to be enclosed in the projectile, in order that he might reach the moon, and reconnoiter this terrestrial satellite. The name of this intrepid adventurer was Michel Ardan. He landed in America, was received with enthusiasm, held meetings, saw himself carried in triumph, reconciled President Barbicane to his mortal enemy, Captain Nicholl, and, as a token of reconciliation, persuaded them both to start with him in the projectile. The proposition being accepted, the shape of the projectile was slightly altered. It was made of a cylindro-conical form. This species of aerial car was lined with strong springs and partitions to deaden the shock of departure. It was provided with food for a year, water for some months, and gas for some days. A self-acting apparatus supplied the three travelers with air to breathe. At the same time, on one of the highest points of the Rocky Mountains, the Gun Club had a gigantic telescope erected, in order that they might be able to follow the course of the projectile through space. All was then ready.

On the 30th of November, at the hour fixed upon, from the midst of an extraordinary crowd of spectators, the departure took place, and for the first time, three human beings quitted the terrestrial globe, and launched into inter-planetary space with almost a certainty of reaching their destination. These bold travelers, Michel Ardan, President Barbicane, and Captain Nicholl, ought to make the passage in ninety-seven hours, thirteen minutes, and twenty seconds. Consequently, their arrival on the lunar disc could not take place until the 5th of December at twelve at night, at the exact moment when the moon should be full, and not on the 4th, as some badly informed journalists had announced.

But an unforeseen circumstance, viz., the detonation produced by the Columbiad, had the immediate effect of troubling the terrestrial atmosphere, by accumulating a large quantity of vapor, a phenomenon which excited universal indignation, for the moon was hidden from the eyes of the watchers for several nights.

The worthy Joseph T. Maston, the staunchest friend of the three travelers, started for the Rocky Mountains, accompanied by the Hon. J. Belfast, director of the Cambridge Observatory, and reached the station of Long's Peak, where the telescope was erected which brought the moon within an apparent distance of two leagues. The honorable secretary of the Gun Club wished himself to observe the vehicle of his daring friends.

The accumulation of the clouds in the atmosphere prevented all observation on the 5th, 6th, 7th, 8th, 9th, and 10th of December. Indeed it was thought that all observations would have to be put off to the 3d of January in the following year; for the moon entering its last quarter on the 11th, would then only present an ever-decreasing portion of her disc, insufficient to allow of their following the course of the projectile.

At length, to the general satisfaction, a heavy storm cleared the atmosphere on the night of the 11th and 12th of December, and the moon, with half-illuminated disc, was plainly to be seen upon the black sky.

That very night a telegram was sent from the station of Long's Peak by Joseph T. Maston and Belfast to the gentlemen of the Cambridge Observatory, announcing that on the 11th of December at 8h. 47m. P.M., the projectile launched by the Columbiad of Stones Hill had been detected by Messrs. Belfast and Maston—that it had deviated from its course from some unknown cause, and had not reached its destination; but that it had passed near enough to be retained by the lunar attraction; that its rectilinear movement had been changed to a circular one, and that following an elliptical orbit round the star of night it had become its satellite. The telegram added that the elements of this new star had not yet been calculated; and indeed three observations made upon a star in three different positions are necessary to determine these elements. Then it showed that the distance separating the projectile from the lunar surface "might" be reckoned at about 2,833 miles.

It ended with the double hypothesis: either the attraction of the moon would draw it to herself, and the travelers thus attain their end; or that the projectile, held in one immutable orbit, would gravitate around the lunar disc to all eternity.

With such alternatives, what would be the fate of the travelers? Certainly they had food for some time. But supposing they did succeed in their rash enterprise, how would they return? Could they ever return? Should they hear from them? These questions, debated by the most learned pens of the day, strongly engrossed the public attention.

It is advisable here to make a remark which ought to be well considered by hasty observers. When a purely speculative discovery is announced to the public, it cannot be done with too much prudence. No one is obliged to discover either a planet, a comet, or a satellite; and whoever makes a mistake in such a case exposes himself justly to the derision of the mass. Far better is it to wait; and that is what the impatient Joseph T. Maston should have done before sending this telegram forth to the world, which, according to his idea, told the whole result of the enterprise. Indeed this telegram contained two sorts of errors, as was proved eventually. First, errors of observation, concerning the distance of the projectile from the surface of the moon, for on the 11th of December it was impossible to see it; and what Joseph T. Maston had seen, or thought he saw, could not have been the projectile of the Columbiad. Second, errors of theory on the fate in store for the said projectile; for in making it a satellite of the moon, it was putting it in direct contradiction of all mechanical laws.

One single hypothesis of the observers of Long's Peak could ever be realized, that which foresaw the case of the travelers (if still alive) uniting their efforts with the lunar attraction to attain the surface of the disc.

Now these men, as clever as they were daring, had survived the terrible shock consequent on their departure, and it is their journey in the projectile car which is here related in its most dramatic as well as in its most singular details. This recital will destroy many illusions and surmises; but it will give a true idea of the singular changes in store for such an enterprise; it will bring out the scientific instincts of Barbicane, the industrious resources of Nicholl, and the audacious humor of Michel Ardan. Besides this, it will prove that their worthy friend, Joseph T. Maston, was wasting his time, while leaning over the gigantic telescope he watched the course of the moon through the starry space.

I

Twenty Minutes Past Ten
To Forty-Seven Minutes Past Ten P. M.

As ten o'clock struck, Michel Ardan, Barbicane, and Nicholl, took leave of the numerous friends they were leaving on the earth. The two dogs, destined to propagate the canine race on the lunar continents, were already shut up in the projectile.

The three travelers approached the orifice of the enormous cast-iron tube, and a crane let them down to the conical top of the projectile. There, an opening made for the purpose gave them access to the aluminum car. The tackle belonging to the crane being hauled from outside, the mouth of the Columbiad was instantly disencumbered of its last supports.

Nicholl, once introduced with his companions inside the projectile, began to close the opening by means of a strong plate, held in position by powerful screws. Other plates, closely fitted, covered the lenticular glasses, and the travelers, hermetically enclosed in their metal prison, were plunged in profound darkness.

"And now, my dear companions," said Michel Ardan, "let us make ourselves at home; I am a domesticated man and strong in housekeeping. We are bound to make the best of our new lodgings, and make ourselves comfortable. And first let us try and see a little. Gas was not invented for moles."

So saying, the thoughtless fellow lit a match by striking it on the sole of his boot; and approached the burner fixed to the receptacle, in which the carbonized hydrogen, stored at high pressure, sufficed for the lighting and warming of the projectile for a hundred and forty-four hours, or six days and six nights. The gas caught fire, and thus lighted the projectile looked like a comfortable room with thickly padded walls, furnished with a circular divan, and a roof rounded in the shape of a dome.

Michel Ardan examined everything, and declared himself satisfied with his installation.

"It is a prison," said he, "but a traveling prison; and, with the right of putting my nose to the window, I could well stand a lease of a hundred years.

You smile, Barbicane. Have you any arriere-pensee? Do you say to yourself, 'This prison may be our tomb?' Tomb, perhaps; still I would not change it for Mahomet's, which floats in space but never advances an inch!"

While Michel Ardan was speaking, Barbicane and Nicholl were making their last preparations.

Nicholl's chronometer marked twenty minutes past ten P.M. when the three travelers were finally enclosed in their projectile. This chronometer was set within the tenth of a second by that of Murchison the engineer. Barbicane consulted it.

"My friends," said he, "it is twenty minutes past ten. At forty-seven minutes past ten Murchison will launch the electric spark on the wire which communicates with the charge of the Columbiad. At that precise moment we shall leave our spheroid. Thus we still have twenty-seven minutes to remain on the earth."

"Twenty-six minutes thirteen seconds," replied the methodical Nicholl.

"Well!" exclaimed Michel Ardan, in a good-humored tone, "much may be done in twenty-six minutes. The gravest questions of morals and politics may be discussed, and even solved. Twenty-six minutes well employed are worth more than twenty-six years in which nothing is done. Some seconds of a Pascal or a Newton are more precious than the whole existence of a crowd of raw simpletons—"

"And you conclude, then, you everlasting talker?" asked Barbicane.

"I conclude that we have twenty-six minutes left," replied Ardan.

"Twenty-four only," said Nicholl.

"Well, twenty-four, if you like, my noble captain," said Ardan; "twenty-four minutes in which to investigate—"

"Michel," said Barbicane, "during the passage we shall have plenty of time to investigate the most difficult questions. For the present we must occupy ourselves with our departure."

"Are we not ready?"

"Doubtless; but there are still some precautions to be taken, to deaden as much as possible the first shock."

"Have we not the water-cushions placed between the partition-breaks, whose elasticity will sufficiently protect us?"

"I hope so, Michel," replied Barbicane gently, "but I am not sure."

"Ah, the joker!" exclaimed Michel Ardan. "He hopes!—He is not sure!—and he waits for the moment when we are encased to make this deplorable admission! I beg to be allowed to get out!"

"And how?" asked Barbicane.

"Humph!" said Michel Ardan, "it is not easy; we are in the train, and the guard's whistle will sound before twenty-four minutes are over."

"Twenty," said Nicholl.

For some moments the three travelers looked at each other. Then they began to examine the objects imprisoned with them.

"Everything is in its place," said Barbicane. "We have now to decide how we can best place ourselves to resist the shock. Position cannot be an indifferent matter; and we must, as much as possible, prevent the rush of blood to the head."

"Just so," said Nicholl.

"Then," replied Michel Ardan, ready to suit the action to the word, "let us put our heads down and our feet in the air, like the clowns in the grand circus."

"No," said Barbicane, "let us stretch ourselves on our sides; we shall resist the shock better that way. Remember that, when the projectile starts, it matters little whether we are in it or before it; it amounts to much the same thing."

"If it is only 'much the same thing,' I may cheer up," said Michel Ardan.

"Do you approve of my idea, Nicholl?" asked Barbicane.

"Entirely," replied the captain. "We've still thirteen minutes and a half."

"That Nicholl is not a man," exclaimed Michel; "he is a chronometer with seconds, an escape, and eight holes."

But his companions were not listening; they were taking up their last positions with the most perfect coolness. They were like two methodical travelers in a car, seeking to place themselves as comfortably as possible.

We might well ask ourselves of what materials are the hearts of these Americans made, to whom the approach of the most frightful danger added no pulsation.

Three thick and solidly-made couches had been placed in the projectile. Nicholl and Barbicane placed them in the center of the disc forming the floor. There the three travelers were to stretch themselves some moments before their departure.

During this time, Ardan, not being able to keep still, turned in his narrow prison like a wild beast in a cage, chatting with his friends, speaking to the dogs Diana and Satellite, to whom, as may be seen, he had given significant names.

"Ah, Diana! Ah, Satellite!" he exclaimed, teasing them; "so you are going to show the moon-dogs the good habits of the dogs of the earth! That will do honor to the canine race! If ever we do come down again, I will bring a cross type of 'moon-dogs,' which will make a stir!"

"If there are dogs in the moon," said Barbicane.

"There are," said Michel Ardan, "just as there are horses, cows, donkeys, and chickens. I bet that we shall find chickens."

"A hundred dollars we shall find none!" said Nicholl.

"Done, my captain!" replied Ardan, clasping Nicholl's hand. "But, by the bye, you have already lost three bets with our president, as the necessary funds for the enterprise have been found, as the operation of casting has been successful, and lastly, as the Columbiad has been loaded without accident, six thousand dollars."

"Yes," replied Nicholl. "Thirty-seven minutes six seconds past ten."

"It is understood, captain. Well, before another quarter of an hour you will have to count nine thousand dollars to the president; four thousand because the Columbiad will not burst, and five thousand because the projectile will rise more than six miles in the air."

"I have the dollars," replied Nicholl, slapping the pocket of this coat. "I only ask to be allowed to pay."

"Come, Nicholl. I see that you are a man of method, which I could never be; but indeed you have made a series of bets of very little advantage to yourself, allow me to tell you."

"And why?" asked Nicholl.

"Because, if you gain the first, the Columbiad will have burst, and the projectile with it; and Barbicane will no longer be there to reimburse your dollars."

"My stake is deposited at the bank in Baltimore," replied Barbicane simply; "and if Nicholl is not there, it will go to his heirs."

"Ah, you practical men!" exclaimed Michel Ardan; "I admire you the more for not being able to understand you."

"Forty-two minutes past ten!" said Nicholl.

"Only five minutes more!" answered Barbicane.

"Yes, five little minutes!" replied Michel Ardan; "and we are enclosed in a projectile, at the bottom of a gun 900 feet long! And under this projectile are rammed 400,000 pounds of gun-cotton, which is equal to 1,600,000 pounds of ordinary powder! And friend Murchison, with his chronometer in hand, his eye fixed on the needle, his finger on the electric apparatus, is counting the seconds preparatory to launching us into interplanetary space."

"Enough, Michel, enough!" said Barbicane, in a serious voice; "let us prepare. A few instants alone separate us from an eventful moment. One clasp of the hand, my friends."

"Yes," exclaimed Michel Ardan, more moved than he wished to appear; and the three bold companions were united in a last embrace.

"God preserve us!" said the religious Barbicane.

Michel Ardan and Nicholl stretched themselves on the couches placed in the center of the disc.

"Forty-seven minutes past ten!" murmured the captain.

"Twenty seconds more!" Barbicane quickly put out the gas and lay down by his companions, and the profound silence was only broken by the ticking of the chronometer marking the seconds.

Suddenly a dreadful shock was felt, and the projectile, under the force of six billions of litres of gas, developed by the combustion of pyroxyle, mounted into space.

II

The First Half-Hour

WHAT had happened? What effect had this frightful shock produced? Had the ingenuity of the constructors of the projectile obtained any happy result? Had the shock been deadened, thanks to the springs, the four plugs, the water-cushions, and the partition-breaks? Had they been able to subdue the frightful pressure of the initiatory speed of more than 11,000 yards, which was enough to traverse Paris or New York in a second? This was evidently the question suggested to the thousand spectators of this moving scene. They forgot the aim of the journey, and thought only of the travelers. And if one of them—Joseph T. Maston for example—could have cast one glimpse into the projectile, what would he have seen?

Nothing then. The darkness was profound. But its cylindro-conical partitions had resisted wonderfully. Not a rent or a dent anywhere! The wonderful projectile was not even heated under the intense deflagration of the powder, nor liquefied, as they seemed to fear, in a shower of aluminum.

The interior showed but little disorder; indeed, only a few objects had been violently thrown toward the roof; but the most important seemed not to have suffered from the shock at all; their fixtures were intact.

On the movable disc, sunk down to the bottom by the smashing of the partition-breaks and the escape of the water, three bodies lay apparently lifeless. Barbicane, Nicholl, and Michel Ardan—did they still breathe? or was the projectile nothing now but a metal coffin, bearing three corpses into space?

Some minutes after the departure of the projectile, one of the bodies moved, shook its arms, lifted its head, and finally succeeded in getting on its knees. It was Michel Ardan. He felt himself all over, gave a sonorous "Hem!" and then said:

"Michel Ardan is whole. How about the others?"

The courageous Frenchman tried to rise, but could not stand. His head swam, from the rush of blood; he was blind; he was a drunken man.

"Bur-r!" said he. "It produces the same effect as two bottles of Corton, though perhaps less agreeable to swallow." Then, passing his hand several times across his forehead and rubbing his temples, he called in a firm voice:

"Nicholl! Barbicane!"

He waited anxiously. No answer; not even a sigh to show that the hearts of his companions were still beating. He called again. The same silence.

"The devil!" he exclaimed. "They look as if they had fallen from a fifth story on their heads. Bah!" he added, with that imperturbable confidence which nothing could check, "if a Frenchman can get on his knees, two Americans ought to be able to get on their feet. But first let us light up."

Ardan felt the tide of life return by degrees. His blood became calm, and returned to its accustomed circulation. Another effort restored his equilibrium. He succeeded in rising, drew a match from his pocket, and approaching the burner lighted it. The receiver had not suffered at all. The gas had not escaped. Besides, the smell would have betrayed it; and in that case Michel Ardan could not have carried a lighted match with impunity through the space filled with hydrogen. The gas mixing with the air would have produced a detonating mixture, and the explosion would have finished what the shock had perhaps begun. When the burner was lit, Ardan leaned over the bodies of his companions: they were lying one on the other, an inert mass, Nicholl above, Barbicane underneath.

Ardan lifted the captain, propped him up against the divan, and began to rub vigorously. This means, used with judgment, restored Nicholl, who opened his eyes, and instantly recovering his presence of mind, seized Ardan's hand and looked around him.

"And Barbicane?" said he.

"Each in turn," replied Michel Ardan. "I began with you, Nicholl, because you were on the top. Now let us look to Barbicane." Saying which, Ardan and Nicholl raised the president of the Gun Club and laid him on the divan. He seemed to have suffered more than either of his companions; he was bleeding, but Nicholl was reassured by finding that the hemorrhage came from a slight wound on the shoulder, a mere graze, which he bound up carefully.

Still, Barbicane was a long time coming to himself, which frightened his friends, who did not spare friction.

"He breathes though," said Nicholl, putting his ear to the chest of the wounded man.

"Yes," replied Ardan, "he breathes like a man who has some notion of that daily operation. Rub, Nicholl; let us rub harder." And the two improvised practitioners worked so hard and so well that Barbicane recovered his senses. He opened his eyes, sat up, took his two friends by the hands, and his first words were—

"Nicholl, are we moving?"

Nicholl and Ardan looked at each other; they had not yet troubled themselves about the projectile; their first thought had been for the traveler, not for the car.

"Well, are we really moving?" repeated Michel Ardan.

"Or quietly resting on the soil of Florida?" asked Nicholl.

"Or at the bottom of the Gulf of Mexico?" added Michel Ardan.

"What an idea!" exclaimed the president.

And this double hypothesis suggested by his companions had the effect of recalling him to his senses. In any case they could not decide on the position of the projectile. Its apparent immovability, and the want of communication with the outside, prevented them from solving the question. Perhaps the projectile was unwinding its course through space. Perhaps after a short rise it had fallen upon the earth, or even in the Gulf of Mexico—a fall which the narrowness of the peninsula of Florida would render not impossible.

The case was serious, the problem interesting, and one that must be solved as soon as possible. Thus, highly excited, Barbicane's moral energy triumphed over physical weakness, and he rose to his feet. He listened. Outside was perfect silence; but the thick padding was enough to intercept all sounds coming from the earth. But one circumstance struck Barbicane, viz., that the temperature inside the projectile was singularly high. The president drew a thermometer from its case and consulted it. The instrument showed 81@ Fahr.

"Yes," he exclaimed, "yes, we are moving! This stifling heat, penetrating through the partitions of the projectile, is produced by its friction on the atmospheric strata. It will soon diminish, because we are already floating in space, and after having nearly stifled, we shall have to suffer intense cold."

"What!" said Michel Ardan. "According to your showing, Barbicane, we are already beyond the limits of the terrestrial atmosphere?"

"Without a doubt, Michel. Listen to me. It is fifty-five minutes past ten; we have been gone about eight minutes; and if our initiatory speed has not been checked by the friction, six seconds would be enough for us to pass through the forty miles of atmosphere which surrounds the globe."

"Just so," replied Nicholl; "but in what proportion do you estimate the diminution of speed by friction?"

"In the proportion of one-third, Nicholl. This diminution is considerable, but according to my calculations it is nothing less. If, then, we had an initiatory speed of 12,000 yards, on leaving the atmosphere this speed would be reduced to 9,165 yards. In any case we have already passed through this interval, and—"

"And then," said Michel Ardan, "friend Nicholl has lost his two bets: four thousand dollars because the Columbiad did not burst; five thousand dollars because the projectile has risen more than six miles. Now, Nicholl, pay up."

"Let us prove it first," said the captain, "and we will pay afterward. It is quite possible that Barbicane's reasoning is correct, and that I have lost my nine thousand dollars. But a new hypothesis presents itself to my mind, and it annuls the wager."

"What is that?" asked Barbicane quickly.

"The hypothesis that, for some reason or other, fire was never set to the powder, and we have not started at all."

"My goodness, captain," exclaimed Michel Ardan, "that hypothesis is not worthy of my brain! It cannot be a serious one. For have we not been half annihilated by the shock? Did I not recall you to life? Is not the president's shoulder still bleeding from the blow it has received?"

"Granted," replied Nicholl; "but one question."

"Well, captain?"

"Did you hear the detonation, which certainly ought to be loud?"

"No," replied Ardan, much surprised; "certainly I did not hear the detonation."

"And you, Barbicane?"

"Nor I, either."

"Very well," said Nicholl.

"Well now," murmured the president "why did we not hear the detonation?"

The three friends looked at each other with a disconcerted air. It was quite an inexplicable phenomenon. The projectile had started, and consequently there must have been a detonation.

"Let us first find out where we are," said Barbicane, "and let down this panel."

This very simple operation was soon accomplished.

The nuts which held the bolts to the outer plates of the right-hand scuttle gave way under the pressure of the English wrench. These bolts were pushed outside, and the buffers covered with India-rubber stopped up the holes which let them through. Immediately the outer plate fell back upon its hinges like a porthole, and the lenticular glass which closed the scuttle appeared. A similar one was let into the thick partition on the opposite side of the projectile, another in the top of the dome, and finally a fourth in the middle of the base. They could, therefore, make observations in four different directions; the firmament by the side and most direct windows, the earth or the moon by the upper and under openings in the projectile.

Barbicane and his two companions immediately rushed to the uncovered window. But it was lit by no ray of light. Profound darkness surrounded them, which, however, did not prevent the president from exclaiming:

"No, my friends, we have not fallen back upon the earth; no, nor are we submerged in the Gulf of Mexico. Yes! we are mounting into space. See those stars shining in the night, and that impenetrable darkness heaped up between the earth and us!"

"Hurrah! hurrah!" exclaimed Michel Ardan and Nicholl in one voice.

Indeed, this thick darkness proved that the projectile had left the earth, for the soil, brilliantly lit by the moon-beams would have been visible to the travelers, if they had been lying on its surface. This darkness also showed that the projectile had passed the atmospheric strata, for the diffused light spread in the air would have been reflected on the metal walls, which reflection was wanting. This light would have lit the window, and the window was dark. Doubt was no longer possible; the travelers had left the earth.

"I have lost," said Nicholl.

"I congratulate you," replied Ardan.

"Here are the nine thousand dollars," said the captain, drawing a roll of paper dollars from his pocket.

"Will you have a receipt for it?" asked Barbicane, taking the sum.

"If you do not mind," answered Nicholl; "it is more business-like."

And coolly and seriously, as if he had been at his strong-box, the president drew forth his notebook, tore out a blank leaf, wrote a proper receipt in pencil, dated and signed it with the usual flourish,[1] and gave it to the captain, who carefully placed it in his pocketbook. Michel Ardan, taking off his hat, bowed to his two companions without speaking. So much formality under such circumstances left him speechless. He had never before seen anything so "American."

This affair settled, Barbicane and Nicholl had returned to the window, and were watching the constellations. The stars looked like bright points on the black sky. But from that side they could not see the orb of

---

1   This is a purely French habit.

night, which, traveling from east to west, would rise by degrees toward the zenith. Its absence drew the following remark from Ardan:

"And the moon; will she perchance fail at our rendezvous?"

"Do not alarm yourself," said Barbicane; "our future globe is at its post, but we cannot see her from this side; let us open the other."

"As Barbicane was about leaving the window to open the opposite scuttle, his attention was attracted by the approach of a brilliant object. It was an enormous disc, whose colossal dimension could not be estimated. Its face, which was turned to the earth, was very bright. One might have thought it a small moon reflecting the light of the large one. She advanced with great speed, and seemed to describe an orbit round the earth, which would intersect the passage of the projectile. This body revolved upon its axis, and exhibited the phenomena of all celestial bodies abandoned in space.

"Ah!" exclaimed Michel Ardan, "What is that? another projectile?"

Barbicane did not answer. The appearance of this enormous body surprised and troubled him. A collision was possible, and might be attended with deplorable results; either the projectile would deviate from its path, or a shock, breaking its impetus, might precipitate it to earth; or, lastly, it might be irresistibly drawn away by the powerful asteroid. The president caught at a glance the consequences of these three hypotheses, either of which would, one way or the other, bring their experiment to an unsuccessful and fatal termination. His companions stood silently looking into space. The object grew rapidly as it approached them, and by an optical illusion the projectile seemed to be throwing itself before it.

"By Jove!" exclaimed Michel Ardan, "we shall run into one another!"

Instinctively the travelers drew back. Their dread was great, but it did not last many seconds. The asteroid passed several hundred yards from the projectile and disappeared, not so much from the rapidity of its course, as that its face being opposite the moon, it was suddenly merged into the perfect darkness of space.

"A happy journey to you," exclaimed Michel Ardan, with a sigh of relief. "Surely infinity of space is large enough for a poor little projectile to walk through without fear. Now, what is this portentous globe which nearly struck us?"

"I know," replied Barbicane.

"Oh, indeed! you know everything."

"It is," said Barbicane, "a simple meteorite, but an enormous one, which the attraction of the earth has retained as a satellite."

"Is it possible!" exclaimed Michel Ardan; "the earth then has two moons like Neptune?"

"Yes, my friends, two moons, though it passes generally for having only one; but this second moon is so small, and its speed so great, that the inhabitants of the earth cannot see it. It was by noticing disturbances that a French astronomer, M. Petit, was able to determine the existence of this second satellite and calculate its elements. According to his observations, this meteorite will accomplish its revolution around the earth in three hours and twenty minutes, which implies a wonderful rate of speed."

"Do all astronomers admit the existence of this satellite?" asked Nicholl.

"No," replied Barbicane; "but if, like us, they had met it, they could no longer doubt it. Indeed, I think that this meteorite, which, had it struck the projectile, would have much embarrassed us, will give us the means of deciding what our position in space is."

"How?" said Ardan.

"Because its distance is known, and when we met it, we were exactly four thousand six hundred and fifty miles from the surface of the terrestrial globe."

"More than two thousand French leagues," exclaimed Michel Ardan. "That beats the express trains of the pitiful globe called the earth."

"I should think so," replied Nicholl, consulting his chronometer; "it is eleven o'clock, and it is only thirteen minutes since we left the American continent."

"Only thirteen minutes?" said Barbicane.

"Yes," said Nicholl; "and if our initiatory speed of twelve thousand yards has been kept up, we shall have made about twenty thousand miles in the hour."

"That is all very well, my friends," said the president, "but the insoluble question still remains. Why did we not hear the detonation of the Columbiad?"

For want of an answer the conversation dropped, and Barbicane began thoughtfully to let down the shutter of the second side. He succeeded; and through the uncovered glass the moon filled the projectile with a brilliant light. Nicholl, as an economical man, put out the gas, now useless, and whose brilliancy prevented any observation of the inter-planetary space.

The lunar disc shone with wonderful purity. Her rays, no longer filtered through the vapory atmosphere of the terrestrial globe, shone through the glass, filling the air in the interior of the projectile with silvery reflections. The black curtain of the firmament in reality heightened the moon's brilliancy, which in this void of ether unfavorable to diffusion did not eclipse the neighboring stars. The heavens, thus seen, presented quite a new aspect, and one which the human eye could never dream of. One may conceive the interest with which these bold men watched the orb of night, the great aim of their journey.

In its motion the earth's satellite was insensibly nearing the zenith, the mathematical point which it ought to attain ninety-six hours later. Her mountains, her plains, every projection was as clearly discernible to their eyes as if they were observing it from some spot upon the earth; but its light was developed through space with wonderful intensity. The disc shone like a platinum mirror. Of the earth flying from under their feet, the travelers had lost all recollection.

It was captain Nicholl who first recalled their attention to the vanishing globe.

"Yes," said Michel Ardan, "do not let us be ungrateful to it. Since we are leaving our country, let our last looks be directed to it. I wish to see the earth once more before it is quite hidden from my eyes."

To satisfy his companions, Barbicane began to uncover the window at the bottom of the projectile, which would allow them to observe the earth direct. The disc, which the force of the projection had beaten down to the base, was removed, not without difficulty. Its fragments, placed carefully against a wall, might serve again upon occasion. Then a circular gap appeared, nineteen inches in diameter, hollowed out of the lower part of the projectile. A glass cover, six inches thick and strengthened with upper fastenings, closed it tightly. Beneath was fixed an aluminum plate, held in place by bolts. The screws being undone, and the bolts let go, the plate fell down, and visible communication was established between the interior and the exterior.

Michel Ardan knelt by the glass. It was cloudy, seemingly opaque.

"Well!" he exclaimed, "and the earth?"

"The earth?" said Barbicane. "There it is."

"What! that little thread; that silver crescent?"

"Doubtless, Michel. In four days, when the moon will be full, at the very time we shall reach it, the earth will be new, and will only appear to us as a slender crescent which will soon disappear, and for some days will be enveloped in utter darkness."

"That the earth?" repeated Michel Ardan, looking with all his eyes at the thin slip of his native planet.

The explanation given by President Barbicane was correct. The earth, with respect to the projectile, was entering its last phase. It was in its octant, and showed a crescent finely traced on the dark background of the sky. Its light, rendered bluish by the thick strata of the atmosphere was less intense than that of the crescent moon, but it was of considerable dimensions, and looked like an enormous arch stretched across the firmament. Some parts brilliantly lighted, especially on its concave part, showed the presence of high mountains, often disappearing behind thick spots, which are never seen on the lunar disc. They were rings of clouds placed concentrically round the terrestrial globe.

While the travelers were trying to pierce the profound darkness, a brilliant cluster of shooting stars burst upon their eyes. Hundreds of meteorites, ignited by the friction of the atmosphere, irradiated the shadow of the luminous train, and lined the cloudy parts of the disc with their fire. At this period the earth was in its perihelion, and the month of December is so propitious to these shooting stars, that astronomers have counted as many as twenty-four thousand in an hour. But Michel Ardan, disdaining scientific reasonings, preferred thinking that the earth was thus saluting the departure of her three children with her most brilliant fireworks.

Indeed this was all they saw of the globe lost in the solar world, rising and setting to the great planets like a simple morning or evening star! This globe, where they had left all their affections, was nothing more than a fugitive crescent!

Long did the three friends look without speaking, though united in heart, while the projectile sped onward with an ever-decreasing speed. Then an irresistible drowsiness crept over their brain. Was it weariness of body and mind? No doubt; for after the over-excitement of those last hours passed upon earth, reaction was inevitable.

"Well," said Nicholl, "since we must sleep, let us sleep."

And stretching themselves on their couches, they were all three soon in a profound slumber.

But they had not forgotten themselves more than a quarter of an hour, when Barbicane sat up suddenly, and rousing his companions with a loud voice, exclaimed—

"I have found it!"

"What have you found?" asked Michel Ardan, jumping from his bed.

"The reason why we did not hear the detonation of the Columbiad."

"And it is—?" said Nicholl.

"Because our projectile traveled faster than the sound!"

III

THEIR PLACE OF SHELTER

THIS curious but certainly correct explanation once given, the three friends returned to their slumbers. Could they have found a calmer or more peaceful spot to sleep in? On the earth, houses, towns, cottages, and country feel every shock given to the exterior of the globe. On sea, the vessels rocked by the waves are still in motion; in the air, the balloon oscillates incessantly on the fluid strata of divers densities. This projectile alone, floating in perfect space, in the midst of perfect silence, offered perfect repose.

Thus the sleep of our adventurous travelers might have been indefinitely prolonged, if an unexpected noise had not awakened them at about seven o'clock in the morning of the 2nd of December, eight hours after their departure.

This noise was a very natural barking.

"The dogs! it is the dogs!" exclaimed Michel Ardan, rising at once.

"They are hungry," said Nicholl.

"By Jove!" replied Michel, "we have forgotten them."

"Where are they?" asked Barbicane.

They looked and found one of the animals crouched under the divan. Terrified and shaken by the initiatory shock, it had remained in the corner till its voice returned with the pangs of hunger. It was the amiable Diana, still very confused, who crept out of her retreat, though not without much persuasion, Michel Ardan encouraging her with most gracious words.

"Come, Diana," said he: "come, my girl! thou whose destiny will be marked in the cynegetic annals; thou whom the pagans would have given as companion to the god Anubis, and Christians as friend to St. Roch; thou who art rushing into interplanetary space, and wilt perhaps be the Eve of all Selenite dogs! come, Diana, come here."

Diana, flattered or not, advanced by degrees, uttering plaintive cries.

"Good," said Barbicane: "I see Eve, but where is Adam?"

"Adam?" replied Michel; "Adam cannot be far off; he is there somewhere; we must call him. Satellite! here, Satellite!"

But Satellite did not appear. Diana would not leave off howling. They found, however, that she was not bruised, and they gave her a pie, which silenced her complaints. As to Satellite, he seemed quite lost. They had to hunt a long time before finding him in one of the upper compartments of the projectile, whither some unaccountable shock must have violently hurled him. The poor beast, much hurt, was in a piteous state.

"The devil!" said Michel.

They brought the unfortunate dog down with great care. Its skull had been broken against the roof, and it seemed unlikely that he could recover from such a shock. Meanwhile, he was stretched comfortably on a cushion. Once there, he heaved a sigh.

"We will take care of you," said Michel; "we are responsible for your existence. I would rather lose an arm than a paw of my poor Satellite."

Saying which, he offered some water to the wounded dog, who swallowed it with avidity.

This attention paid, the travelers watched the earth and the moon attentively. The earth was now only discernible by a cloudy disc ending in a crescent, rather more contracted than that of the previous evening; but its expanse was still enormous, compared with that of the moon, which was approaching nearer and nearer to a perfect circle.

"By Jove!" said Michel Ardan, "I am really sorry that we did not start when the earth was full, that is to say, when our globe was in opposition to the sun."

"Why?" said Nicholl.

"Because we should have seen our continents and seas in a new light—the first resplendent under the solar rays, the latter cloudy as represented on some maps of the world. I should like to have seen those poles of the earth on which the eye of man has never yet rested."

"I dare say," replied Barbicane; "but if the earth had been full, the moon would have been new; that is to say, invisible, because of the rays of the sun. It is better for us to see the destination we wish to reach, than the point of departure."

"You are right, Barbicane," replied Captain Nicholl; "and, besides, when we have reached the moon, we shall have time during the long lunar nights to consider at our leisure the globe on which our likenesses swarm."

"Our likenesses!" exclaimed Michel Ardan; "They are no more our likenesses than the Selenites are! We inhabit a new world, peopled by ourselves—the projectile! I am Barbicane's likeness, and Barbicane is Nicholl's. Beyond us, around us, human nature is at an end, and we are the only population of this microcosm until we become pure Selenites."

"In about eighty-eight hours," replied the captain.

"Which means to say?" asked Michel Ardan.

"That it is half-past eight," replied Nicholl.

"Very well," retorted Michel; "then it is impossible for me to find even the shadow of a reason why we should not go to breakfast."

Indeed the inhabitants of the new star could not live without eating, and their stomachs were suffering from the imperious laws of hunger. Michel Ardan, as a Frenchman, was declared chief cook, an important function, which raised no rival. The gas gave sufficient heat for the culinary apparatus, and the provision box furnished the elements of this first feast.

The breakfast began with three bowls of excellent soup, thanks to the liquefaction in hot water of those precious cakes of Liebig, prepared from the best parts of the ruminants of the Pampas. To the soup succeeded some beefsteaks, compressed by an hydraulic press, as tender and succulent as if brought straight from the kitchen of an English eating-house. Michel, who was imaginative, maintained that they were even "red."

Preserved vegetables ("fresher than nature," said the amiable Michel) succeeded the dish of meat; and was followed by some cups of tea with bread and butter, after the American fashion.

The beverage was declared exquisite, and was due to the infusion of the choicest leaves, of which the emperor of Russia had given some chests for the benefit of the travelers.

And lastly, to crown the repast, Ardan had brought out a fine bottle of Nuits, which was found "by chance" in the provision-box. The three friends drank to the union of the earth and her satellite.

And, as if he had not already done enough for the generous wine which he had distilled on the slopes of Burgundy, the sun chose to be part of the party. At this moment the projectile emerged from the conical shadow cast by the terrestrial globe, and the rays of the radiant orb struck the lower disc of the projectile direct occasioned by the angle which the moon's orbit makes with that of the earth.

"The sun!" exclaimed Michel Ardan.

"No doubt," replied Barbicane; "I expected it."

"But," said Michel, "the conical shadow which the earth leaves in space extends beyond the moon?"

"Far beyond it, if the atmospheric refraction is not taken into consideration," said Barbicane. "But when the moon is enveloped in this shadow, it is because the centers of the three stars, the sun, the earth, and the moon, are all in one and the same straight line. Then the nodes coincide with the phases of the moon, and there is an eclipse. If we had started when there was an eclipse of the moon, all our passage would have been in the shadow, which would have been a pity."

"Why?"

"Because, though we are floating in space, our projectile, bathed in the solar rays, will receive light and heat. It economizes the gas, which is in every respect a good economy."

Indeed, under these rays which no atmosphere can temper, either in temperature or brilliancy, the projectile grew warm and bright, as if it had passed suddenly from winter to summer. The moon above, the sun beneath, were inundating it with their fire.

"It is pleasant here," said Nicholl.

"I should think so," said Michel Ardan. "With a little earth spread on our aluminum planet we should have green peas in twenty-four hours. I have but one fear, which is that the walls of the projectile might melt."

"Calm yourself, my worthy friend," replied Barbicane; "the projectile withstood a very much higher temperature than this as it slid through the strata of the atmosphere. I should not be surprised if it did not look like a meteor on fire to the eyes of the spectators in Florida."

"But then J. T. Maston will think we are roasted!"

"What astonishes me," said Barbicane, "is that we have not been. That was a danger we had not provided for."

"I feared it," said Nicholl simply.

"And you never mentioned it, my sublime captain," exclaimed Michel Ardan, clasping his friend's hand.

Barbicane now began to settle himself in the projectile as if he was never to leave it. One must remember that this aerial car had a base with a superficies of fifty-four square feet. Its height to the roof was twelve feet. Carefully laid out in the inside, and little encumbered by instruments and traveling utensils, which each had their particular place, it left the three travelers a certain freedom of movement. The thick window inserted in the bottom could bear any amount of weight, and Barbicane and his companions walked upon it as if it were solid plank; but the sun striking it directly with its rays lit the interior of the projectile from beneath, thus producing singular effects of light.

They began by investigating the state of their store of water and provisions, neither of which had suffered, thanks to the care taken to deaden the shock. Their provisions were abundant, and plentiful enough to last the three travelers for more than a year. Barbicane wished to be cautious, in case the projectile should land on a part of the moon which was utterly barren. As to water and the reserve of brandy, which consisted of fifty gallons, there was only enough for two months; but according to the last observations of astronomers, the moon had a low, dense, and thick atmosphere, at least in the deep valleys, and there springs and streams could not fail. Thus, during their passage, and for the first year of their settlement on the lunar continent, these adventurous explorers would suffer neither hunger nor thirst.

Now about the air in the projectile. There, too, they were secure. Reiset and Regnaut's apparatus, intended for the production of oxygen, was supplied with chlorate of potassium for two months. They necessarily consumed a certain quantity of gas, for they were obliged to keep the producing substance at a temperature of above 400@. But there again they were all safe. The apparatus only wanted a little care. But it was not enough to renew the oxygen; they must absorb the carbonic acid produced by expiration. During the last twelve hours the atmosphere of the projectile had become charged with this deleterious gas. Nicholl discovered the state of the air by observing Diana panting painfully. The carbonic acid, by a phenomenon similar to that produced in the famous Grotto del Cane, had collected at the bottom of the projectile owing to its weight. Poor Diana, with her head low, would suffer before her masters from the presence of this gas. But Captain Nicholl hastened to remedy this state of things, by placing on the floor several receivers containing caustic potash, which he shook about for a time, and this substance, greedy of carbonic acid, soon completely absorbed it, thus purifying the air.

An inventory of instruments was then begun. The thermometers and barometers had resisted, all but one minimum thermometer, the glass of which was broken. An excellent aneroid was drawn from the wadded box which contained it and hung on the wall. Of course it was only affected by and marked the pressure of the air inside the projectile, but it also showed the quantity of moisture which it contained. At that moment its needle oscillated between 25.24 and 25.08.

It was fine weather.

Barbicane had also brought several compasses, which he found intact. One must understand that under present conditions their needles were acting wildly, that is without any constant direction. Indeed, at the distance they were from the earth, the magnetic pole could have no perceptible action upon the apparatus; but the box placed on the lunar disc might perhaps exhibit some strange phenomena. In any case it would be interesting to see whether the earth's satellite submitted like herself to its magnetic influence.

A hypsometer to measure the height of the lunar mountains, a sextant to take the height of the sun, glasses which would be useful as they neared the moon, all these instruments were carefully looked over, and pronounced good in spite of the violent shock.

As to the pickaxes and different tools which were Nicholl's especial choice; as to the sacks of different kinds of grain and shrubs which Michel

Ardan hoped to transplant into Selenite ground, they were stowed away in the upper part of the projectile. There was a sort of granary there, loaded with things which the extravagant Frenchman had heaped up. What they were no one knew, and the good-tempered fellow did not explain. Now and then he climbed up by cramp-irons riveted to the walls, but kept the inspection to himself. He arranged and rearranged, he plunged his hand rapidly into certain mysterious boxes, singing in one of the falsest of voices an old French refrain to enliven the situation.

Barbicane observed with some interest that his guns and other arms had not been damaged. These were important, because, heavily loaded, they were to help lessen the fall of the projectile, when drawn by the lunar attraction (after having passed the point of neutral attraction) on to the moon's surface; a fall which ought to be six times less rapid than it would have been on the earth's surface, thanks to the difference of bulk. The inspection ended with general satisfaction, when each returned to watch space through the side windows and the lower glass coverlid.

There was the same view. The whole extent of the celestial sphere swarmed with stars and constellations of wonderful purity, enough to drive an astronomer out of his mind! On one side the sun, like the mouth of a lighted oven, a dazzling disc without a halo, standing out on the dark background of the sky! On the other, the moon returning its fire by reflection, and apparently motionless in the midst of the starry world. Then, a large spot seemingly nailed to the firmament, bordered by a silvery cord; it was the earth! Here and there nebulous masses like large flakes of starry snow; and from the zenith to the nadir, an immense ring formed by an impalpable dust of stars, the "Milky Way," in the midst of which the sun ranks only as a star of the fourth magnitude. The observers could not take their eyes from this novel spectacle, of which no description could give an adequate idea. What reflections it suggested! What emotions hitherto unknown awoke in their souls! Barbicane wished to begin the relation of his journey while under its first impressions, and hour after hour took notes of all facts happening in the beginning of the enterprise. He wrote quietly, with his large square writing, in a business-like style.

During this time Nicholl, the calculator, looked over the minutes of their passage, and worked out figures with unparalleled dexterity. Michel Ardan chatted first with Barbicane, who did not answer him, and then with Nicholl, who did not hear him, with Diana, who understood none of his theories, and lastly with himself, questioning and answering, going and coming, busy with a thousand details; at one time bent over the lower glass, at another roosting in the heights of the projectile, and always singing. In this microcosm he represented French loquacity and excitability, and we beg you to believe that they were well represented. The day, or rather (for the expression is not correct) the lapse of twelve hours, which forms a day upon the earth, closed with a plentiful supper carefully prepared. No accident of any nature had yet happened to shake the travelers' confidence; so, full of hope, already sure of success, they slept peacefully, while the projectile under an uniformly decreasing speed was crossing the sky.

IV

A Little Algebra

THE night passed without incident. The word "night," however, is scarcely applicable.

The position of the projectile with regard to the sun did not change. Astronomically, it was daylight on the lower part, and night on the upper; so when during this narrative these words are used, they represent the lapse of time between rising and setting of the sun upon the earth.

The travelers' sleep was rendered more peaceful by the projectile's excessive speed, for it seemed absolutely motionless. Not a motion betrayed its onward course through space. The rate of progress, however rapid it might be, cannot produce any sensible effect on the human frame when it takes place in a vacuum, or when the mass of air circulates with the body which is carried with it. What inhabitant of the earth perceives its speed, which, however, is at the rate of 68,000 miles per hour? Motion under such conditions is "felt" no more than repose; and when a body is in repose it will remain so as long as no strange force displaces it; if moving, it will not stop unless an obstacle comes in its way. This indifference to motion or repose is called inertia.

Barbicane and his companions might have believed themselves perfectly stationary, being shut up in the projectile; indeed, the effect would have been the same if they had been on the outside of it. Had it not been for the moon, which was increasing above them, they might have sworn that they were floating in complete stagnation.

That morning, the 3rd of December, the travelers were awakened by a joyous but unexpected noise; it was the crowing of a cock which sounded through the car. Michel Ardan, who was the first on his feet, climbed to the top of the projectile, and shutting a box, the lid of which was partly open, said in a low voice, "Will you hold your tongue? That creature will spoil my design!"

But Nicholl and Barbicane were awake.

"A cock!" said Nicholl.

"Why no, my friends," Michel answered quickly; "it was I who wished to awake you by this rural sound." So saying, he gave vent to a splendid cock-a-doodledoo, which would have done honor to the proudest of poultry-yards.

The two Americans could not help laughing.

"Fine talent that," said Nicholl, looking suspiciously at his companion.

"Yes," said Michel; "a joke in my country. It is very Gallic; they play the cock so in the best society."

Then turning the conversation:

"Barbicane, do you know what I have been thinking of all night?"

"No," answered the president.

"Of our Cambridge friends. You have already remarked that I am an ignoramus in mathematical subjects; and it is impossible for me to find out how the savants of the observatory were able to calculate what initiatory speed the projectile ought to have on leaving the Columbiad in order to attain the moon."

"You mean to say," replied Barbicane, "to attain that neutral point where the terrestrial and lunar attractions are equal; for, starting from that point, situated about nine-tenths of the distance traveled over, the projectile would simply fall upon the moon, on account of its weight."

"So be it," said Michel; "but, once more; how could they calculate the initiatory speed?"

"Nothing can be easier," replied Barbicane.

"And you knew how to make that calculation?" asked Michel Ardan.

"Perfectly. Nicholl and I would have made it, if the observatory had not saved us the trouble."

"Very well, old Barbicane," replied Michel; "they might have cut off my head, beginning at my feet, before they could have made me solve that problem."

"Because you do not know algebra," answered Barbicane quietly.

"Ah, there you are, you eaters of x^1; you think you have said all when you have said 'Algebra.'"

"Michel," said Barbicane, "can you use a forge without a hammer, or a plow without a plowshare?"

"Hardly."

"Well, algebra is a tool, like the plow or the hammer, and a good tool to those who know how to use it."

"Seriously?"

"Quite seriously."

"And can you use that tool in my presence?"

"If it will interest you."

"And show me how they calculated the initiatory speed of our car?"

"Yes, my worthy friend; taking into consideration all the elements of the problem, the distance from the center of the earth to the center of the moon, of the radius of the earth, of its bulk, and of the bulk of the moon, I can tell exactly what ought to be the initiatory speed of the projectile, and that by a simple formula."

"Let us see."

"You shall see it; only I shall not give you the real course drawn by the projectile between the moon and the earth in considering their motion round the sun. No, I shall consider these two orbs as perfectly motionless, which will answer all our purpose."

"And why?"

"Because it will be trying to solve the problem called 'the problem of the three bodies,' for which the integral calculus is not yet far enough advanced."

"Then," said Michel Ardan, in his sly tone, "mathematics have not said their last word?"

"Certainly not," replied Barbicane.

"Well, perhaps the Selenites have carried the integral calculus farther than you have; and, by the bye, what is this 'integral calculus?'"

"It is a calculation the converse of the differential," replied Barbicane seriously.

"Much obliged; it is all very clear, no doubt."

"And now," continued Barbicane, "a slip of paper and a bit of pencil, and before a half-hour is over I will have found the required formula."

Half an hour had not elapsed before Barbicane, raising his head, showed Michel Ardan a page covered with algebraical signs, in which the general formula for the solution was contained.

"Well, and does Nicholl understand what that means?"

"Of course, Michel," replied the captain. "All these signs, which seem cabalistic to you, form the plainest, the clearest, and the most logical language to those who know how to read it."

"And you pretend, Nicholl," asked Michel, "that by means of these hieroglyphics, more incomprehensible than the Egyptian Ibis, you can find what initiatory speed it was necessary to give the projectile?"

"Incontestably," replied Nicholl; "and even by this same formula I can always tell you its speed at any point of its transit."

"On your word?"

"On my word."

"Then you are as cunning as our president."

"No, Michel; the difficult part is what Barbicane has done; that is, to get an equation which shall satisfy all the conditions of the problem. The remainder is only a question of arithmetic, requiring merely the knowledge of the four rules."

"That is something!" replied Michel Ardan, who for his life could not do addition right, and who defined the rule as a Chinese puzzle, which allowed one to obtain all sorts of totals.

"The expression v zero, which you see in that equation, is the speed which the projectile will have on leaving the atmosphere."

"Just so," said Nicholl; "it is from that point that we must calculate the velocity, since we know already that the velocity at departure was exactly one and a half times more than on leaving the atmosphere."

"I understand no more," said Michel.

"It is a very simple calculation," said Barbicane.

"Not as simple as I am," retorted Michel.

"That means, that when our projectile reached the limits of the terrestrial atmosphere it had already lost one-third of its initiatory speed."

"As much as that?"

"Yes, my friend; merely by friction against the atmospheric strata. You understand that the faster it goes the more resistance it meets with from the air."

"That I admit," answered Michel; "and I understand it, although your x's and zero's, and algebraic formula, are rattling in my head like nails in a bag."

"First effects of algebra," replied Barbicane; "and now, to finish, we are going to prove the given number of these different expressions, that is, work out their value."

"Finish me!" replied Michel.

Barbicane took the paper, and began to make his calculations with great rapidity. Nicholl looked over and greedily read the work as it proceeded.

"That's it! that's it!" at last he cried.

"Is it clear?" asked Barbicane.

"It is written in letters of fire," said Nicholl.

"Wonderful fellows!" muttered Ardan.

"Do you understand it at last?" asked Barbicane.

"Do I understand it?" cried Ardan; "my head is splitting with it."

"And now," said Nicholl, "to find out the speed of the projectile when it leaves the atmosphere, we have only to calculate that."

The captain, as a practical man equal to all difficulties, began to write with frightful rapidity. Divisions and multiplications grew under his fingers; the figures were like hail on the white page. Barbicane watched him, while Michel Ardan nursed a growing headache with both hands.

"Very well?" asked Barbicane, after some minutes' silence.

"Well!" replied Nicholl; every calculation made, v zero, that is to say, the speed necessary for the projectile on leaving the atmosphere, to enable it to reach the equal point of attraction, ought to be—"

"Yes?" said Barbicane.

"Twelve thousand yards."

"What!" exclaimed Barbicane, starting; "you say—"

"Twelve thousand yards."

"The devil!" cried the president, making a gesture of despair.

"What is the matter?" asked Michel Ardan, much surprised.

"What is the matter! why, if at this moment our speed had already diminished one-third by friction, the initiatory speed ought to have been—"

"Seventeen thousand yards."

"And the Cambridge Observatory declared that twelve thousand yards was enough at starting; and our projectile, which only started with that speed—"

"Well?" asked Nicholl.

"Well, it will not be enough."

"Good."

"We shall not be able to reach the neutral point."

"The deuce!"

"We shall not even get halfway."

"In the name of the projectile!" exclaimed Michel Ardan, jumping as if it was already on the point of striking the terrestrial globe.

"And we shall fall back upon the earth!"

V

THE COLD OF SPACE

THIS revelation came like a thunderbolt. Who could have expected such an error in calculation? Barbicane would not believe it. Nicholl revised his figures: they were exact. As to the formula which had determined them, they could not suspect its truth; it was evident that an initiatory velocity of seventeen thousand yards in the first second was necessary to enable them to reach the neutral point.

The three friends looked at each other silently. There was no thought of breakfast. Barbicane, with clenched teeth, knitted brows, and hands clasped convulsively, was watching through the window. Nicholl had crossed his arms, and was examining his calculations. Michel Ardan was muttering:

"That is just like these scientific men: they never do anything else. I would give twenty pistoles if we could fall upon the Cambridge Observatory and crush it, together with the whole lot of dabblers in figures which it contains."

Suddenly a thought struck the captain, which he at once communicated to Barbicane.

"Ah!" said he; "it is seven o'clock in the morning; we have already been gone thirty-two hours; more than half our passage is over, and we are not falling that I am aware of."

Barbicane did not answer, but after a rapid glance at the captain, took a pair of compasses wherewith to measure the angular distance of the terrestrial globe; then from the lower window he took an exact observation, and noticed that the projectile was apparently stationary. Then rising and wiping his forehead, on which large drops of perspiration were standing, he put some figures on paper. Nicholl understood that the president was deducting from the terrestrial diameter the projectile's distance from the earth. He watched him anxiously.

"No," exclaimed Barbicane, after some moments, "no, we are not falling! no, we are already more than 50,000 leagues from the earth. We have passed the point at which the projectile would have stopped if its speed had only been 12,000 yards at starting. We are still going up."

"That is evident," replied Nicholl; "and we must conclude that our initial speed, under the power of the 400,000 pounds of gun-cotton, must have exceeded the required 12,000 yards. Now I can understand how, after thirteen minutes only, we met the second satellite, which gravitates round the earth at more than 2,000 leagues' distance."

"And this explanation is the more probable," added Barbicane, "because, in throwing off the water enclosed between its partition-breaks, the projectile found itself lightened of a considerable weight."

"Just so," said Nicholl.

"Ah, my brave Nicholl, we are saved!"

"Very well then," said Michel Ardan quietly; "as we are safe, let us have breakfast."

Nicholl was not mistaken. The initial speed had been, very fortunately, much above that estimated by the Cambridge Observatory; but the Cambridge Observatory had nevertheless made a mistake.

The travelers, recovered from this false alarm, breakfasted merrily. If they ate a good deal, they talked more. Their confidence was greater after than before "the incident of the algebra."

"Why should we not succeed?" said Michel Ardan; "why should we not arrive safely? We are launched; we have no obstacle before us, no stones in the way; the road is open, more so than that of a ship battling with the sea; more open than that of a balloon battling with the wind; and if a ship can reach its destination, a balloon go where it pleases, why cannot our projectile attain its end and aim?"

"It will attain it," said Barbicane.

"If only to do honor to the Americans," added Michel Ardan, "the only people who could bring such an enterprise to a happy termination, and the only one which could produce a President Barbicane. Ah, now we are no longer uneasy, I begin to think, What will become of us? We shall get right royally weary."

Barbicane and Nicholl made a gesture of denial.

"But I have provided for the contingency, my friends," replied Michel; "you have only to speak, and I have chess, draughts, cards, and dominoes at your disposal; nothing is wanting but a billiard-table."

"What!" exclaimed Barbicane; "you brought away such trifles?"

"Certainly," replied Michel, "and not only to distract ourselves, but also with the laudable intention of endowing the Selenite smoking divans with them."

"My friend," said Barbicane, "if the moon is inhabited, its inhabitants must have appeared some thousands of years before those of the earth, for we cannot doubt that their star is much older than ours. If then these Selenites have existed their hundreds of thousands of years, and if their brain is of the same organization of the human brain, they have already invented all that we have invented, and even what we may invent in future ages. They have nothing to learn from us, and we have everything to learn from them."

"What!" said Michel; "you believe that they have artists like Phidias, Michael Angelo, or Raphael?"

"Yes."

"Poets like Homer, Virgil, Milton, Lamartine, and Hugo?"

"I am sure of it."

"Philosophers like Plato, Aristotle, Descartes, Kant?"

"I have no doubt of it."

"Scientific men like Archimedes, Euclid, Pascal, Newton?"

"I could swear it."

"Comic writers like Arnal, and photographers like—like Nadar?"

"Certain."

"Then, friend Barbicane, if they are as strong as we are, and even stronger—these Selenites—why have they not tried to communicate with the earth? why have they not launched a lunar projectile to our terrestrial regions?"

"Who told you that they have never done so?" said Barbicane seriously.

"Indeed," added Nicholl, "it would be easier for them than for us, for two reasons; first, because the attraction on the moon's surface is six times less than on that of the earth, which would allow a projectile to rise more easily; secondly, because it would be enough to send such a projectile only at 8,000 leagues instead of 80,000, which would require the force of projection to be ten times less strong."

"Then," continued Michel, "I repeat it, why have they not done it?"

"And I repeat," said Barbicane; "who told you that they have not done it?"

"When?"

"Thousands of years before man appeared on earth."

"And the projectile—where is the projectile? I demand to see the projectile."

"My friend," replied Barbicane, "the sea covers five-sixths of our globe. From that we may draw five good reasons for supposing that the lunar projectile, if ever launched, is now at the bottom of the Atlantic or the Pacific, unless it sped into some crevasse at that period when the crust of the earth was not yet hardened."

"Old Barbicane," said Michel, "you have an answer for everything, and I bow before your wisdom. But there is one hypothesis that would suit me better than all the others, which is, the Selenites, being older than we, are wiser, and have not invented gunpowder."

At this moment Diana joined in the conversation by a sonorous barking. She was asking for her breakfast.

"Ah!" said Michel Ardan, "in our discussion we have forgotten Diana and Satellite."

Immediately a good-sized pie was given to the dog, which devoured it hungrily.

"Do you see, Barbicane," said Michel, "we should have made a second Noah's ark of this projectile, and borne with us to the moon a couple of every kind of domestic animal."

"I dare say; but room would have failed us."

"Oh!" said Michel, "we might have squeezed a little."

"The fact is," replied Nicholl, "that cows, bulls, and horses, and all ruminants, would have been very useful on the lunar continent, but unfortunately the car could neither have been made a stable nor a shed."

"Well, we might have at least brought a donkey, only a little donkey; that courageous beast which old Silenus loved to mount. I love those old donkeys; they are the least favored animals in creation; they are not only beaten while alive, but even after they are dead."

"How do you make that out?" asked Barbicane. "Why," said Michel, "they make their skins into drums."

Barbicane and Nicholl could not help laughing at this ridiculous remark. But a cry from their merry companion stopped them. The latter was leaning over the spot where Satellite lay. He rose, saying:

"My good Satellite is no longer ill."

"Ah!" said Nicholl.

"No," answered Michel, "he is dead! There," added he, in a piteous tone, "that is embarrassing. I much fear, my poor Diana, that you will leave no progeny in the lunar regions!"

Indeed the unfortunate Satellite had not survived its wound. It was quite dead. Michel Ardan looked at his friends with a rueful countenance.

"One question presents itself," said Barbicane. "We cannot keep the dead body of this dog with us for the next forty-eight hours."

"No! certainly not," replied Nicholl; "but our scuttles are fixed on hinges; they can be let down. We will open one, and throw the body out into space."

The president thought for some moments, and then said:

"Yes, we must do so, but at the same time taking very great precautions."

"Why?" asked Michel.

"For two reasons which you will understand," answered Barbicane. "The first relates to the air shut up in the projectile, and of which we must lose as little as possible."

"But we manufacture the air?"

"Only in part. We make only the oxygen, my worthy Michel; and with regard to that, we must watch that the apparatus does not furnish the oxygen in too great a quantity; for an excess would bring us very serious physiological troubles. But if we make the oxygen, we do not make the azote, that medium which the lungs do not absorb, and which ought to remain intact; and that azote will escape rapidly through the open scuttles."

"Oh! the time for throwing out poor Satellite?" said Michel.

"Agreed; but we must act quickly."

"And the second reason?" asked Michel.

"The second reason is that we must not let the outer cold, which is excessive, penetrate the projectile or we shall be frozen to death."

"But the sun?"

"The sun warms our projectile, which absorbs its rays; but it does not warm the vacuum in which we are floating at this moment. Where there is no air, there is no more heat than diffused light; and the same with darkness; it is cold where the sun's rays do not strike direct. This temperature is only the temperature produced by the radiation of the stars; that is to say, what the terrestrial globe would undergo if the sun disappeared one day."

"Which is not to be feared," replied Nicholl.

"Who knows?" said Michel Ardan. "But, in admitting that the sun does not go out, might it not happen that the earth might move away from it?"

"There!" said Barbicane, "there is Michel with his ideas."

"And," continued Michel, "do we not know that in 1861 the earth passed through the tail of a comet? Or let us suppose a comet whose power of attraction is greater than that of the sun. The terrestrial orbit will bend toward the wandering star, and the earth, becoming its satellite, will be drawn such a distance that the rays of the sun will have no action on its surface."

"That might happen, indeed," replied Barbicane, "but the consequences of such a displacement need not be so formidable as you suppose."

"And why not?"

"Because the heat and cold would be equalized on our globe. It has been calculated that, had our earth been carried along in its course by the comet of 1861, at its perihelion, that is, its nearest approach to the sun, it would have undergone a heat 28,000 times greater than that of summer. But this heat, which is sufficient to evaporate the waters, would have formed a thick ring of cloud, which would have modified that excessive temperature; hence the compensation between the cold of the aphelion and the heat of the perihelion."

"At how many degrees," asked Nicholl, "is the temperature of the planetary spaces estimated?"

"Formerly," replied Barbicane, "it was greatly exaggerated; but now, after the calculations of Fourier, of the French Academy of Science, it is not supposed to exceed 60@ Centigrade below zero."

"Pooh!" said Michel, "that's nothing!"

"It is very much," replied Barbicane; "the temperature which was observed in the polar regions, at Melville Island and Fort Reliance, that is 76@ Fahrenheit below zero."

"If I mistake not," said Nicholl, "M. Pouillet, another savant, estimates the temperature of space at 250@ Fahrenheit below zero. We shall, however, be able to verify these calculations for ourselves."

"Not at present; because the solar rays, beating directly upon our thermometer, would give, on the contrary, a very high temperature. But, when we arrive in the moon, during its fifteen days of night at either face, we shall have leisure to make the experiment, for our satellite lies in a vacuum."

"What do you mean by a vacuum?" asked Michel. "Is it perfectly such?"

"It is absolutely void of air."

"And is the air replaced by nothing whatever?"

"By the ether only," replied Barbicane.

"And pray what is the ether?"

"The ether, my friend, is an agglomeration of imponderable atoms, which, relatively to their dimensions, are as far removed from each other as the celestial bodies are in space. It is these atoms which, by their vibratory motion, produce both light and heat in the universe."

They now proceeded to the burial of Satellite. They had merely to drop him into space, in the same way that sailors drop a body into the sea; but, as President Barbicane suggested, they must act quickly, so as to lose as little as possible of that air whose elasticity would rapidly have spread it into space. The bolts of the right scuttle, the opening of which measured about twelve inches across, were carefully drawn, while Michel, quite grieved, prepared to launch his dog into space. The glass, raised by a powerful lever, which enabled it to overcome the pressure of the inside air on the walls of the projectile, turned rapidly on its hinges, and Satellite was thrown out. Scarcely a particle of air could have escaped, and the operation was so successful that later on Barbicane did not fear to dispose of the rubbish which encumbered the car.

VI

QUESTION AND ANSWER

ON the 4th of December, when the travelers awoke after fifty-four hours' journey, the chronometer marked five o'clock of the terrestrial morning. In time it was just over five hours and forty minutes, half of that assigned to their sojourn in the projectile; but they had already accomplished nearly seven-tenths of the way. This peculiarity was due to their regularly decreasing speed.

Now when they observed the earth through the lower window, it looked like nothing more than a dark spot, drowned in the solar rays. No more crescent, no more cloudy light! The next day, at midnight, the earth would be new, at the very moment when the moon would be full. Above, the orb of night was nearing the line followed by the projectile, so as to meet it at the given hour. All around the black vault was studded with brilliant points, which seemed to move slowly; but, at the great distance they were from them, their relative size did not seem to change. The sun and stars appeared exactly as they do to us upon earth. As to the moon, she was considerably larger; but the travelers' glasses, not very powerful, did not allow them as yet to make any useful observations upon her surface, or reconnoiter her topographically or geologically.

Thus the time passed in never-ending conversations all about the moon. Each one brought forward his own contingent of particular facts; Barbicane and Nicholl always serious, Michel Ardan always enthusiastic. The projectile, its situation, its direction, incidents which might happen, the precautions necessitated by their fall on to the moon, were inexhaustible matters of conjecture.

As they were breakfasting, a question of Michel's, relating to the projectile, provoked rather a curious answer from Barbicane, which is worth repeating. Michel, supposing it to be roughly stopped, while still under its formidable initial speed, wished to know what the consequences of the stoppage would have been.

"But," said Barbicane, "I do not see how it could have been stopped."

"But let us suppose so," said Michel.

"It is an impossible supposition," said the practical Barbicane; "unless that impulsive force had failed; but even then its speed would diminish by degrees, and it would not have stopped suddenly."

"Admit that it had struck a body in space."

"What body?"

"Why that enormous meteor which we met."

"Then," said Nicholl, "the projectile would have been broken into a thousand pieces, and we with it."

"More than that," replied Barbicane; "we should have been burned to death."

"Burned?" exclaimed Michel, "by Jove! I am sorry it did not happen, 'just to see.'"

"And you would have seen," replied Barbicane. "It is known now that heat is only a modification of motion. When water is warmed—that is to say, when heat is added to it—its particles are set in motion."

"Well," said michel, "that is an ingenious theory!"

"And a true one, my worthy friend; for it explains every phenomenon of caloric. Heat is but the motion of atoms, a simple oscillation of the particles of a body. When they apply the brake to a train, the train comes to a stop; but what becomes of the motion which it had previously possessed? It is transformed into heat, and the brake becomes hot. Why do they grease the axles of the wheels? To prevent their heating, because this heat would be generated by the motion which is thus lost by transformation."

"Yes, I understand," replied Michel, "perfectly. For example, when I have run a long time, when I am swimming, when I am perspiring in large drops, why am I obliged to stop? Simply because my motion is changed into heat."

Barbicane could not help smiling at Michel's reply; then, returning to his theory, said:

"Thus, in case of a shock, it would have been with our projectile as with a ball which falls in a burning state after having struck the metal plate; it is its motion which is turned into heat. Consequently I affirm that, if our projectile had struck the meteor, its speed thus suddenly checked would have raised a heat great enough to turn it into vapor instantaneously."

"Then," asked Nicholl, "what would happen if the earth's motion were to stop suddenly?"

"Her temperature would be raised to such a pitch," said Barbicane, "that she would be at once reduced to vapor."

"Well," said Michel, "that is a way of ending the earth which will greatly simplify things."

"And if the earth fell upon the sun?" asked Nicholl.

"According to calculation," replied Barbicane, "the fall would develop a heat equal to that produced by 16,000 globes of coal, each equal in bulk to our terrestrial globe."

"Good additional heat for the sun," replied Michel Ardan, "of which the inhabitants of Uranus or Neptune would doubtless not complain; they must be perished with cold on their planets."

"Thus, my friends," said Barbicane, "all motion suddenly stopped produces heat. And this theory allows us to infer that the heat of the solar disc is fed by a hail of meteors falling incessantly on its surface. They have even calculated—"

"Oh, dear!" murmured Michel, "the figures are coming."

"They have even calculated," continued the imperturbable Barbicane, "that the shock of each meteor on the sun ought to produce a heat equal to that of 4,000 masses of coal of an equal bulk."

"And what is the solar heat?" asked Michel.

"It is equal to that produced by the combustion of a stratum of coal surrounding the sun to a depth of forty-seven miles."

"And that heat—"

"Would be able to boil two billions nine hundred millions of cubic myriameters[2] of water."

"And it does not roast us!" exclaimed Michel.

"No," replied Barbicane, "because the terrestrial atmosphere absorbs four-tenths of the solar heat; besides, the quantity of heat intercepted by the earth is but a billionth part of the entire radiation."

"I see that all is for the best," said Michel, "and that this atmosphere is a useful invention; for it not only allows us to breathe, but it prevents us from roasting."

"Yes!" said Nicholl, "unfortunately, it will not be the same in the moon."

"Bah!" said Michel, always hopeful. "If there are inhabitants, they must breathe. If there are no longer any, they must have left enough oxygen for three people, if only at the bottom of ravines, where its own weight will cause it to accumulate, and we will not climb the mountains; that is all." And Michel, rising, went to look at the lunar disc, which shone with intolerable brilliancy.

"By Jove!" said he, "it must be hot up there!"

"Without considering," replied Nicholl, "that the day lasts 360 hours!"

"And to compensate that," said Barbicane, "the nights have the same length; and as heat is restored by radiation, their temperature can only be that of the planetary space."

"A pretty country, that!" exclaimed Michel. "Never mind! I wish I was there! Ah! my dear comrades, it will be rather curious to have the earth for our moon, to see it rise on the horizon, to recognize the shape of its continents, and to say to oneself, 'There is America, there is Europe;' then to follow it when it is about to lose itself in the sun's rays! By the bye, Barbicane, have the Selenites eclipses?"

"Yes, eclipses of the sun," replied Barbicane, "when the centers of the three orbs are on a line, the earth being in the middle. But they are only partial, during which the earth, cast like a screen upon the solar disc, allows the greater portion to be seen."

"And why," asked Nicholl, "is there no total eclipse? Does not the cone of the shadow cast by the earth extend beyond the moon?"

"Yes, if we do not take into consideration the refraction produced by the terrestrial atmosphere. No, if we take that refraction into consideration. Thus let (lower case delta) be the horizontal parallel, and p the apparent semidiameter—"

"Oh!" said Michel. "Do speak plainly, you man of algebra!"

"Very well, replied Barbicane; "in popular language the mean distance from the moon to the earth being sixty terrestrial radii, the length of the

---

2   The myriameter is equal to rather more than 10,936 cubic yards English.

cone of the shadow, on account of refraction, is reduced to less than forty-two radii. The result is that when there are eclipses, the moon finds itself beyond the cone of pure shadow, and that the sun sends her its rays, not only from its edges, but also from its center."

"Then," said Michel, in a merry tone, "why are there eclipses, when there ought not to be any?"

"Simply because the solar rays are weakened by this refraction, and the atmosphere through which they pass extinguished the greater part of them!"

"That reason satisfies me," replied Michel. "Besides we shall see when we get there. Now, tell me, Barbicane, do you believe that the moon is an old comet?"

"There's an idea!"

"Yes," replied Michel, with an amiable swagger, "I have a few ideas of that sort."

"But that idea does not spring from Michel," answered Nicholl.

"Well, then, I am a plagiarist."

"No doubt about it. According to the ancients, the Arcadians pretend that their ancestors inhabited the earth before the moon became her satellite. Starting from this fact, some scientific men have seen in the moon a comet whose orbit will one day bring it so near to the earth that it will be held there by its attraction."

"Is there any truth in this hypothesis?" asked Michel.

"None whatever," said Barbicane, "and the proof is, that the moon has preserved no trace of the gaseous envelope which always accompanies comets."

"But," continued Nicholl, "Before becoming the earth's satellite, could not the moon, when in her perihelion, pass so near the sun as by evaporation to get rid of all those gaseous substances?"

"It is possible, friend Nicholl, but not probable."

"Why not?"

"Because—Faith I do not know."

"Ah!" exclaimed Michel, "what hundred of volumes we might make of all that we do not know!"

"Ah! indeed. What time is it?" asked Barbicane.

"Three o'clock," answered Nicholl.

"How time goes," said Michel, "in the conversation of scientific men such as we are! Certainly, I feel I know too much! I feel that I am becoming a well!"

Saying which, Michel hoisted himself to the roof of the projectile, "to observe the moon better," he pretended. During this time his companions were watching through the lower glass. Nothing new to note!

When Michel Ardan came down, he went to the side scuttle; and suddenly they heard an exclamation of surprise!

"What is it?" asked Barbicane.

The president approached the window, and saw a sort of flattened sack floating some yards from the projectile. This object seemed as motionless as the projectile, and was consequently animated with the same ascending movement.

"What is that machine?" continued Michel Ardan. "Is it one of the bodies which our projectile keeps within its attraction, and which will accompany it to the moon?"

"What astonishes me," said Nicholl, "is that the specific weight of the body, which is certainly less than that of the projectile, allows it to keep so perfectly on a level with it."

"Nicholl," replied Barbicane, after a moment's reflection, "I do not know what the object it, but I do know why it maintains our level."

"And why?"

"Because we are floating in space, my dear captain, and in space bodies fall or move (which is the same thing) with equal speed whatever be their weight or form; it is the air, which by its resistance creates these differences in weight. When you create a vacuum in a tube, the objects you send through it, grains of dust or grains of lead, fall with the same rapidity. Here in space is the same cause and the same effect."

"Just so," said Nicholl, "and everything we throw out of the projectile will accompany it until it reaches the moon."

"Ah! fools that we are!" exclaimed Michel.

"Why that expletive?" asked Barbicane.

"Because we might have filled the projectile with useful objects, books, instruments, tools, etc. We could have thrown them all out, and all would have followed in our train. But happy thought! Why cannot we walk outside like the meteor? Why cannot we launch into space through the scuttle? What enjoyment it would be to feel oneself thus suspended in ether, more favored than the birds who must use their wings to keep themselves up!"

"Granted," said Barbicane, "but how to breathe?"

"Hang the air, to fail so inopportunely!"

"But if it did not fail, Michel, your density being less than that of the projectile, you would soon be left behind."

"Then we must remain in our car?"

"We must!"

"Ah!" exclaimed Michel, in a load voice.

"What is the matter," asked Nicholl.

"I know, I guess, what this pretended meteor is! It is no asteroid which is accompanying us! It is not a piece of a planet."

"What is it then?" asked Barbicane.

"It is our unfortunate dog! It is Diana's husband!"

Indeed, this deformed, unrecognizable object, reduced to nothing, was the body of Satellite, flattened like a bagpipe without wind, and ever mounting, mounting!

VII

A MOMENT OF INTOXICATION

THUS a phenomenon, curious but explicable, was happening under these strange conditions.

Every object thrown from the projectile would follow the same course and never stop until it did. There was a subject for conversation which the whole evening could not exhaust.

Besides, the excitement of the three travelers increased as they drew near the end of their journey. They expected unforseen incidents, and new phenomena; and nothing would have astonished them in the frame of mind they then were in. Their overexcited imagination went faster than the projectile, whose speed was evidently diminishing, though insensibly to themselves. But the moon grew larger to their eyes, and they fancied if they stretched out their hands they could seize it.

The next day, the 5th of November, at five in the morning, all three were on foot. That day was to be the last of their journey, if all calculations were true. That very night, at twelve o'clock, in eighteen hours, exactly at the full moon, they would reach its brilliant disc. The next midnight would see that journey ended, the most extraordinary of ancient or modern times. Thus from the first of the morning, through the scuttles silvered by its rays, they saluted the orb of night with a confident and joyous hurrah.

The moon was advancing majestically along the starry firmament. A few more degrees, and she would reach the exact point where her meeting with the projectile was to take place.

According to his own observations, Barbicane reckoned that they would land on her northern hemisphere, where stretch immense plains, and where mountains are rare. A favorable circumstance if, as they thought, the lunar atmosphere was stored only in its depths.

"Besides," observed Michel Ardan, "a plain is easier to disembark upon than a mountain. A Selenite, deposited in Europe on the summit of Mont Blanc, or in Asia on the top of the Himalayas, would not be quite in the right place."

"And," added Captain Nicholl, "on a flat ground, the projectile will remain motionless when it has once touched; whereas on a declivity it would roll like an avalanche, and not being squirrels we should not come out safe and sound. So it is all for the best."

Indeed, the success of the audacious attempt no longer appeared doubtful. But Barbicane was preoccupied with one thought; but not wishing to make his companions uneasy, he kept silence on this subject.

The direction the projectile was taking toward the moon's northern hemisphere, showed that her course had been slightly altered. The discharge, mathematically calculated, would carry the projectile to the very center of the lunar disc. If it did not land there, there must have been some deviation. What had caused it? Barbicane could neither imagine nor determine the importance of the deviation, for there were no points to go by.

He hoped, however, that it would have no other result than that of bringing them nearer the upper border of the moon, a region more suitable for landing.

Without imparting his uneasiness to his companions, Barbicane contented himself with constantly observing the moon, in order to see whether the course of the projectile would not be altered; for the situation would have been terrible if it failed in its aim, and being carried beyond the disc should be launched into interplanetary space. At that moment, the moon, instead of appearing flat like a disc, showed its convexity. If the sun's rays had struck it obliquely, the shadow thrown would have brought out the high mountains, which would have been clearly detached. The eye might have gazed into the crater's gaping abysses, and followed the capricious fissures which wound through the immense plains. But all relief was as yet leveled in intense brilliancy. They could scarcely distinguish those large spots which give the moon the appearance of a human face.

"Face, indeed!" said Michel Ardan; "but I am sorry for the amiable sister of Apollo. A very pitted face!"

But the travelers, now so near the end, were incessantly observing this new world. They imagined themselves walking through its unknown countries, climbing its highest peaks, descending into its lowest depths.

Here and there they fancied they saw vast seas, scarcely kept together under so rarefied an atmosphere, and water-courses emptying the mountain tributaries. Leaning over the abyss, they hoped to catch some sounds from that orb forever mute in the solitude of space. That last day left them.

They took down the most trifling details. A vague uneasiness took possession of them as they neared the end. This uneasiness would have been doubled had they felt how their speed had decreased. It would have seemed to them quite insufficient to carry them to the end. It was because the projectile then "weighed" almost nothing. Its weight was ever decreasing, and would be entirely annihilated on that line where the lunar and terrestrial attractions would neutralize each other.

But in spite of his preoccupation, Michel Ardan did not forget to prepare the morning repast with his accustomed punctuality. They ate with a good appetite. Nothing was so excellent as the soup liquefied by the heat of the gas; nothing better than the preserved meat. Some glasses of good French wine crowned the repast, causing Michel Ardan to remark that the lunar vines, warmed by that ardent sun, ought to distill even more generous wines; that is, if they existed. In any case, the far-seeing Frenchman had taken care not to forget in his collection some precious cuttings of the Medoc and Cote d'Or, upon which he founded his hopes.

Reiset and Regnaut's apparatus worked with great regularity. Not an atom of carbonic acid resisted the potash; and as to the oxygen, Captain Nicholl said "it was of the first quality." The little watery vapor enclosed in the projectile mixing with the air tempered the dryness; and many apartments in London, Paris, or New York, and many theaters, were certainly not in such a healthy condition.

But that it might act with regularity, the apparatus must be kept in perfect order; so each morning Michel visited the escape regulators, tried the taps, and regulated the heat of the gas by the pyrometer. Everything had gone well up to that time, and the travelers, imitating the worthy Joseph T. Maston, began to acquire a degree of embonpoint which would have rendered them unrecognizable if their imprisonment had been prolonged to some months. In a word, they behaved like chickens in a coop; they were getting fat.

In looking through the scuttle Barbicane saw the specter of the dog, and other divers objects which had been thrown from the projectile, obstinately following them. Diana howled lugubriously on seeing the remains of Satellite, which seemed as motionless as if they reposed on solid earth.

"Do you know, my friends," said Michel Ardan, "that if one of us had succumbed to the shock consequent on departure, we should have had a great deal of trouble to bury him? What am I saying? to etherize him, as here ether takes the place of earth. You see the accusing body would have followed us into space like a remorse."

"That would have been sad," said Nicholl.

"Ah!" continued Michel, "what I regret is not being able to take a walk outside. What voluptuousness to float amid this radiant ether, to bathe oneself in it, to wrap oneself in the sun's pure rays. If Barbicane had only thought of furnishing us with a diving apparatus and an air-pump, I could have ventured out and assumed fanciful attitudes of feigned monsters on the top of the projectile."

"Well, old Michel," replied Barbicane, "you would not have made a feigned monster long, for in spite of your diver's dress, swollen by the expansion of air within you, you would have burst like a shell, or rather like a balloon which has risen too high. So do not regret it, and do not forget this—as long as we float in space, all sentimental walks beyond the projectile are forbidden."

Michel Ardan allowed himself to be convinced to a certain extent. He admitted that the thing was difficult but not impossible, a word which he never uttered.

The conversation passed from this subject to another, not failing him for an instant. It seemed to the three friends as though, under present conditions, ideas shot up in their brains as leaves shoot at the first warmth of spring. They felt bewildered. In the middle of the questions and answers which crossed each other, Nicholl put one question which did not find an immediate solution.

"Ah, indeed!" said he; "it is all very well to go to the moon, but how to get back again?"

His two interlocutors looked surprised. One would have thought that this possibility now occurred to them for the first time.

"What do you mean by that, Nicholl?" asked Barbicane gravely.

"To ask for means to leave a country," added Michel, "When we have not yet arrived there, seems to me rather inopportune."

"I do not say that, wishing to draw back," replied Nicholl; "but I repeat my question, and I ask, 'How shall we return?'"

"I know nothing about it," answered Barbicane.

"And I," said Michel, "if I had known how to return, I would never have started."

"There's an answer!" cried Nicholl.

"I quite approve of Michel's words," said Barbicane; "and add, that the question has no real interest. Later, when we think it is advisable to return, we will take counsel together. If the Columbiad is not there, the projectile will be."

"That is a step certainly. A ball without a gun!"

"The gun," replied Barbicane, "can be manufactured. The powder can be made. Neither metals, saltpeter, nor coal can fail in the depths of the moon, and we need only go 8,000 leagues in order to fall upon the terrestrial globe by virtue of the mere laws of weight."

"Enough," said Michel with animation. "Let it be no longer a question of returning: we have already entertained it too long. As to communicating with our former earthly colleagues, that will not be difficult."

"And how?"

"By means of meteors launched by lunar volcanoes."

"Well thought of, Michel," said Barbicane in a convinced tone of voice. "Laplace has calculated that a force five times greater than that of our gun would suffice to send a meteor from the moon to the earth, and there is not one volcano which has not a greater power of propulsion than that."

"Hurrah!" exclaimed Michel; "these meteors are handy postmen, and cost nothing. And how we shall be able to laugh at the post-office administration! But now I think of it—"

"What do you think of?"

"A capital idea. Why did we not fasten a thread to our projectile, and we could have exchanged telegrams with the earth?"

"The deuce!" answered Nicholl. "Do you consider the weight of a thread 250,000 miles long nothing?"

"As nothing. They could have trebled the Columbiad's charge; they could have quadrupled or quintupled it!" exclaimed Michel, with whom the verb took a higher intonation each time.

"There is but one little objection to make to your proposition," replied Barbicane, "which is that, during the rotary motion of the globe, our thread would have wound itself round it like a chain on a capstan, and that it would inevitably have brought us to the ground."

"By the thirty-nine stars of the Union!" said Michel, "I have nothing but impracticable ideas to-day; ideas worthy of J. T. Maston. But I have a notion that, if we do not return to earth, J. T. Maston will be able to come to us."

"Yes, he'll come," replied Barbicane; "he is a worthy and a courageous comrade. Besides, what is easier? Is not the Columbiad still buried in the soil of Florida? Is cotton and nitric acid wanted wherewith to manufacture the pyroxyle? Will not the moon pass the zenith of Florida? In eighteen years' time will she not occupy exactly the same place as to-day?"

"Yes," continued Michel, "yes, Maston will come, and with him our friends Elphinstone, Blomsberry, all the members of the Gun Club, and they will be well received. And by and by they will run trains of projectiles between the earth and the moon! Hurrah for J. T. Maston!"

It is probable that, if the Hon. J. T. Maston did not hear the hurrahs uttered in his honor, his ears at least tingled. What was he doing then? Doubtless, posted in the Rocky Mountains, at the station of Long's Peak, he was trying to find the invisible projectile gravitating in space. If he was thinking of his dear companions, we must allow that they were not far behind him; and that, under the influence of a strange excitement, they were devoting to him their best thoughts.

But whence this excitement, which was evidently growing upon the tenants of the projectile? Their sobriety could not be doubted. This strange irritation of the brain, must it be attributed to the peculiar circumstances under which they found themselves, to their proximity to the orb of night, from which only a few hours separated them, to some secret influence of the moon acting upon their nervous system? Their faces were as rosy as if they had been exposed to the roaring flames of an oven; their voices resounded in loud accents; their words escaped like a champagne cork driven out by carbonic acid; their gestures became annoying, they wanted so much room to perform them; and, strange to say, they none of them noticed this great tension of the mind.

"Now," said Nicholl, in a short tone, "now that I do not know whether we shall ever return from the moon, I want to know what we are going to do there?"

"What we are going to do there?" replied Barbicane, stamping with his foot as if he was in a fencing saloon; "I do not know."

"You do not know!" exclaimed Michel, with a bellow which provoked a sonorous echo in the projectile.

"No, I have not even thought about it," retorted Barbicane, in the same loud tone.

"Well, I know," replied Michel.

"Speak, then," cried Nicholl, who could no longer contain the growling of his voice.

"I shall speak if it suits me," exclaimed Michel, seizing his companions' arms with violence.

"It must suit you," said Barbicane, with an eye on fire and a threatening hand. "It was you who drew us into this frightful journey, and we want to know what for."

"Yes," said the captain, "now that I do not know where I am going, I want to know why I am going."

"Why?" exclaimed Michel, jumping a yard high, "why? To take possession of the moon in the name of the United States; to add a fortieth

State to the Union; to colonize the lunar regions; to cultivate them, to people them, to transport thither all the prodigies of art, of science, and industry; to civilize the Selenites, unless they are more civilized than we are; and to constitute them a republic, if they are not already one!"

"And if there are no Selenites?" retorted Nicholl, who, under the influence of this unaccountable intoxication, was very contradictory.

"Who said that there were no Selenites?" exclaimed Michel in a threatening tone.

"I do," howled Nicholl.

"Captain," said Michel, "do not repreat that insolence, or I will knock your teeth down your throat!"

The two adversaries were going to fall upon each other, and the incoherent discussion threatened to merge into a fight, when Barbicane intervened with one bound.

"Stop, miserable men," said he, separating his two companions; "if there are no Selenites, we will do without them."

"Yes," exclaimed Michel, who was not particular; "yes, we will do without them. We have only to make Selenites. Down with the Selenites!"

"The empire of the moon belongs to us," said Nicholl.

"Let us three constitute the republic."

"I will be the congress," cried Michel.

"And I the senate," retorted Nicholl.

"And Barbicane, the president," howled Michel.

"Not a president elected by the nation," replied Barbicane.

"Very well, a president elected by the congress," cried Michel; "and as I am the congress, you are unanimously elected!"

"Hurrah! hurrah! hurrah! for President Barbicane," exclaimed Nicholl.

"Hip! hip! hip!" vociferated Michel Ardan.

Then the president and the senate struck up in a tremendous voice the popular song "Yankee Doodle," while from the congress resounded the masculine tones of the "Marseillaise."

Then they struck up a frantic dance, with maniacal gestures, idiotic stampings, and somersaults like those of the boneless clowns in the circus. Diana, joining in the dance, and howling in her turn, jumped to the top of the projectile. An unaccountable flapping of wings was then heard amid most fantastic cock-crows, while five or six hens fluttered like bats against the walls.

Then the three traveling companions, acted upon by some unaccountable influence above that of intoxication, inflamed by the air which had set their respiratory apparatus on fire, fell motionless to the bottom of the projectile.

VIII

AT SEVENTY-EIGHT THOUSAND
FIVE HUNDRED AND FOURTEEN LEAGUES

WHAT had happened? Whence the cause of this singular intoxication, the consequences of which might have been very disastrous? A simple blunder of Michel's, which, fortunately, Nicholl was able to correct in time.

After a perfect swoon, which lasted some minutes, the captain, recovering first, soon collected his scattered senses. Although he had breakfasted only two hours before, he felt a gnawing hunger, as if he had not eaten anything for several days. Everything about him, stomach and brain, were overexcited to the highest degree. He got up and demanded from Michel a supplementary repast. Michel, utterly done up, did not answer.

Nicholl then tried to prepare some tea destined to help the absorption of a dozen sandwiches. He first tried to get some fire, and struck a match sharply. What was his surprise to see the sulphur shine with so extraordinary a brilliancy as to be almost unbearable to the eye. From the gas-burner which he lit rose a flame equal to a jet of electric light.

A revelation dawned on Nicholl's mind. That intensity of light, the physiological troubles which had arisen in him, the overexcitement of all his moral and quarrelsome faculties—he understood all.

"The oxygen!" he exclaimed.

And leaning over the air apparatus, he saw that the tap was allowing the colorless gas to escape freely, life-giving, but in its pure state producing the gravest disorders in the system. Michel had blunderingly opened the tap of the apparatus to the full.

Nicholl hastened to stop the escape of oxygen with which the atmosphere was saturated, which would have been the death of the travelers, not by suffocation, but by combustion. An hour later, the air less charged with it restored the lungs to their normal condition. By degrees the three friends recovered from their intoxication; but they were obliged to sleep themselves sober over their oxygen as a drunkard does over his wine.

When Michel learned his share of the responsibility of this incident, he was not much disconcerted. This unexpected drunkenness broke the monotony of the journey. Many foolish things had been said while under its influence, but also quickly forgotten.

"And then," added the merry Frenchman, "I am not sorry to have tasted a little of this heady gas. Do you know, my friends, that a curious establishment might be founded with rooms of oxygen, where people whose system is weakened could for a few hours live a more active life. Fancy parties where the room was saturated with this heroic fluid, theaters where it should be kept at high pressure; what passion in the souls of the actors and spectators! what fire, what enthusiasm! And if, instead of an assembly only a whole people could be saturated, what activity in its functions, what a supplement to life it would derive. From an exhausted nation they might make a great and strong one, and I know more than one state in old Europe which ought to put itself under the regime of oxygen for the sake of its health!"

Michel spoke with so much animation that one might have fancied that the tap was still too open. But a few words from Barbicane soon shattered his enthusiasm.

"That is all very well, friend Michel," said he, "but will you inform us where these chickens came from which have mixed themselves up in our concert?"

"Those chickens?"

"Yes."

Indeed, half a dozen chickens and a fine cock were walking about, flapping their wings and chattering.

"Ah, the awkward things!" exclaimed Michel. "The oxygen has made them revolt."

"But what do you want to do with these chickens?" asked Barbicane.

"To acclimatize them in the moon, by Jove!"

"Then why did you hide them?"

"A joke, my worthy president, a simple joke, which has proved a miserable failure. I wanted to set them free on the lunar continent, without saying anything. Oh, what would have been your amazement on seeing these earthly-winged animals pecking in your lunar fields!"

"You rascal, you unmitigated rascal," replied Barbicane, "you do not want oxygen to mount to the head. You are always what we were under the influence of the gas; you are always foolish!"

"Ah, who says that we were not wise then?" replied Michel Ardan.

After this philosophical reflection, the three friends set about restoring the order of the projectile. Chickens and cock were reinstated in their coop. But while proceeding with this operation, Barbicane and his two companions had a most desired perception of a new phenomenon. From the moment of leaving the earth, their own weight, that of the projectile, and the objects it enclosed, had been subject to an increasing diminution.

If they could not prove this loss of the projectile, a moment would arrive when it would be sensibly felt upon themselves and the utensils and instruments they used.

It is needless to say that a scale would not show this loss; for the weight destined to weight the object would have lost exactly as much as the object itself; but a spring steelyard for example, the tension of which was independent of the attraction, would have given a just estimate of this loss.

We know that the attraction, otherwise called the weight, is in proportion to the densities of the bodies, and inversely as the squares of the distances. Hence this effect: If the earth had been alone in space, if the other celestial bodies had been suddenly annihilated, the projectile, according to Newton's laws, would weigh less as it got farther from the earth, but without ever losing its weight entirely, for the terrestrial attraction would always have made itself felt, at whatever distance.

But, in reality, a time must come when the projectile would no longer be subject to the law of weight, after allowing for the other celestial bodies whose effect could not be set down as zero. Indeed, the projectile's course was being traced between the earth and the moon. As it distanced the earth, the terrestrial attraction diminished: but the lunar attraction rose in proportion. There must come a point where these two attractions would neutralize each other: the projectile would possess weight no longer. If the moon's and the earth's densities had been equal, this point would have been at an equal distance between the two orbs. But taking the different densities into consideration, it was easy to reckon that this point would be situated at 47/60ths of the whole journey, i.e., at 78,514 leagues from the earth. At this point, a body having no principle of speed or displacement in itself, would remain immovable forever, being attracted equally by both orbs, and not being drawn more toward one than toward the other.

Now if the projectile's impulsive force had been correctly calculated, it would attain this point without speed, having lost all trace of weight, as well as all the objects within it. What would happen then? Three hypotheses presented themselves.

1. Either it would retain a certain amount of motion, and pass the point of equal attraction, and fall upon the moon by virtue of the excess of the lunar attraction over the terrestrial.

2. Or, its speed failing, and unable to reach the point of equal attraction, it would fall upon the moon by virtue of the excess of the lunar attraction over the terrestrial.

3. Or, lastly, animated with sufficient speed to enable it to reach the neutral point, but not sufficient to pass it, it would remain forever suspended in that spot like the pretended tomb of Mahomet, between the zenith and the nadir.

Such was their situation; and Barbicane clearly explained the consequences to his traveling companions, which greatly interested them. But how should they know when the projectile had reached this neutral point situated at that distance, especially when neither themselves, nor the objects enclosed in the projectile, would be any longer subject to the laws of weight?

Up to this time, the travelers, while admitting that this action was constantly decreasing, had not yet become sensible to its total absence.

But that day, about eleven o'clock in the morning, Nicholl having accidentally let a glass slip from his hand, the glass, instead of falling, remained suspended in the air.

"Ah!" exclaimed Michel Ardan, "that is rather an amusing piece of natural philosophy."

And immediately divers other objects, firearms and bottles, abandoned to themselves, held themselves up as by enchantment. Diana too, placed in space by Michel, reproduced, but without any trick, the wonderful suspension practiced by Caston and Robert Houdin. Indeed the dog did not seem to know that she was floating in air.

The three adventurous companions were surprised and stupefied, despite their scientific reasonings. They felt themselves being carried into the domain of wonders! they felt that weight was really wanting to their bodies. If they stretched out their arms, they did not attempt to fall. Their heads shook on their shoulders. Their feet no longer clung to the floor of the projectile. They were like drunken men having no stability in themselves.

Fancy has depicted men without reflection, others without shadow. But here reality, by the neutralizations of attractive forces, produced men in whom nothing had any weight, and who weighed nothing themselves.

Suddenly Michel, taking a spring, left the floor and remained suspended in the air, like Murillo's monk of the Cusine des Anges.

The two friends joined him instantly, and all three formed a miraculous "Ascension" in the center of the projectile.

"Is it to be believed? is it probable? is it possible?" exclaimed Michel; "and yet it is so. Ah! if Raphael had seen us thus, what an 'Assumption' he would have thrown upon canvas!"

"The 'Assumption' cannot last," replied Barbicane. "If the projectile passes the neutral point, the lunar attraction will draw us to the moon."

"Then our feet will be upon the roof," replied Michel.

"No," said Barbicane, "because the projectile's center of gravity is very low; it will only turn by degrees."

"Then all our portables will be upset from top to bottom, that is a fact."

"Calm yourself, Michel," replied Nicholl; "no upset is to be feared; not a thing will move, for the projectile's evolution will be imperceptible."

"Just so," continued Barbicane; "and when it has passed the point of equal attraction, its base, being the heavier, will draw it perpendicularly to the moon; but, in order that this phenomenon should take place, we must have passed the neutral line."

"Pass the neutral line," cried Michel; "then let us do as the sailors do when they cross the equator."

A slight side movement brought Michel back toward the padded side; thence he took a bottle and glasses, placed them "in space" before his companions, and, drinking merrily, they saluted the line with a triple hurrah. The influence of these attractions scarcely lasted an hour; the travelers felt themselves insensibly drawn toward the floor, and Barbicane fancied that the conical end of the projectile was varying a little from its normal direction toward the moon. By an inverse motion the base was approaching first; the lunar attraction was prevailing over the terrestrial; the fall toward the moon was beginning, almost imperceptibly as yet, but by degrees the attractive force would become stronger, the fall would be more decided, the projectile, drawn by its base, would turn its cone to the earth, and fall with ever-increasing speed on to the surface of the Selenite continent; their destination would then be attained. Now nothing could prevent the success of their enterprise, and Nicholl and Michel Ardan shared Barbicane's joy.

Then they chatted of all the phenomena which had astonished them one after the other, particularly the neutralization of the laws of weight. Michel Ardan, always enthusiastic, drew conclusions which were purely fanciful.

"Ah, my worthy friends," he exclaimed, "what progress we should make if on earth we could throw off some of that weight, some of that chain which binds us to her; it would be the prisoner set at liberty; no more fatigue of either arms or legs. Or, if it is true that in order to fly on the earth's surface, to keep oneself suspended in the air merely by the play of the muscles, there requires a strength a hundred and fifty times greater than that which we possess, a simple act of volition, a caprice, would bear us into space, if attraction did not exist."

"Just so," said Nicholl, smiling; "if we could succeed in suppressing weight as they suppress pain by anaesthesia, that would change the face of modern society!"

"Yes," cried Michel, full of his subject, "destroy weight, and no more burdens!"

"Well said," replied Barbicane; "but if nothing had any weight, nothing would keep in its place, not even your hat on your head, worthy Michel; nor your house, whose stones only adhere by weight; nor a boat, whose stability on the waves is only caused by weight; not even the ocean, whose waves would no longer be equalized by terrestrial attraction; and lastly, not even the atmosphere, whose atoms, being no longer held in their places, would disperse in space!"

"That is tiresome," retorted Michel; "nothing like these matter-of-fact people for bringing one back to the bare reality."

"But console yourself, Michel," continued Barbicane, "for if no orb exists from whence all laws of weight are banished, you are at least going to visit one where it is much less than on the earth."

"The moon?"

"Yes, the moon, on whose surface objects weigh six times less than on the earth, a phenomenon easy to prove."

"And we shall feel it?" asked Michel.

"Evidently, as two hundred pounds will only weigh thirty pounds on the surface of the moon."

"And our muscular strength will not diminish?"

"Not at all; instead of jumping one yard high, you will rise eighteen feet high."

"But we shall be regular Herculeses in the moon!" exclaimed Michel.

"Yes," replied Nicholl; "for if the height of the Selenites is in proportion to the density of their globe, they will be scarcely a foot high."

"Lilliputians!" ejaculated Michel; "I shall play the part of Gulliver. We are going to realize the fable of the giants. This is the advantage of leaving one's own planet and over-running the solar world."

"One moment, Michel," answered Barbicane; "if you wish to play the part of Gulliver, only visit the inferior planets, such as Mercury, Venus, or Mars, whose density is a little less than that of the earth; but do not venture into the great planets, Jupiter, Saturn, Uranus, Neptune; for there the order will be changed, and you will become Lilliputian."

"And in the sun?"

"In the sun, if its density is thirteen hundred and twenty-four thousand times greater, and the attraction is twenty-seven times greater than on the surface of our globe, keeping everything in proportion, the inhabitants ought to be at least two hundred feet high."

"By Jove!" exclaimed Michel; "I should be nothing more than a pigmy, a shrimp!"

"Gulliver with the giants," said Nicholl.

"Just so," replied Barbicane.

"And it would not be quite useless to carry some pieces of artillery to defend oneself."

"Good," replied Nicholl; "your projectiles would have no effect on the sun; they would fall back upon the earth after some minutes."

"That is a strong remark."

"It is certain," replied Barbicane; "the attraction is so great on this enormous orb, that an object weighing 70,000 pounds on the earth would weigh but 1,920 pounds on the surface of the sun. If you were to fall upon it you would weigh—let me see—about 5,000 pounds, a weight which you would never be able to raise again."

"The devil!" said Michel; "one would want a portable crane. However, we will be satisfied with the moon for the present; there at least we shall cut a great figure. We will see about the sun by and by."

IX

THE CONSEQUENCES OF A DEVIATION

BARBICANE had now no fear of the issue of the journey, at least as far as the projectile's impulsive force was concerned; its own speed would carry it beyond the neutral line; it would certainly not return to earth; it would certainly not remain motionless on the line of attraction. One single hypothesis remained to be realized, the arrival of the projectile at its destination by the action of the lunar attraction.

It was in reality a fall of 8,296 leagues on an orb, it is true, where weight could only be reckoned at one sixth of terrestrial weight; a formidable fall, nevertheless, and one against which every precaution must be taken without delay.

These precautions were of two sorts, some to deaden the shock when the projectile should touch the lunar soil, others to delay the fall, and consequently make it less violent.

To deaden the shock, it was a pity that Barbicane was no longer able to employ the means which had so ably weakened the shock at departure, that is to say, by water used as springs and the partition breaks.

The partitions still existed, but water failed, for they could not use their reserve, which was precious, in case during the first days the liquid element should be found wanting on lunar soil.

And indeed this reserve would have been quite insufficient for a spring. The layer of water stored in the projectile at the time of starting upon their journey occupied no less than three feet in depth, and spread over a surface of not less than fifty-four square feet. Besides, the cistern did not contain one-fifth part of it; they must therefore give up this efficient means of deadening the shock of arrival. Happily, Barbicane, not content with employing water, had furnished the movable disc with strong spring plugs, destined to lessen the shock against the base after the breaking of the horizontal partitions. These plugs still existed; they had only to readjust them and replace the movable disc; every piece, easy to handle, as their weight was now scarcely felt, was quickly mounted.

The different pieces were fitted without trouble, it being only a matter of bolts and screws; tools were not wanting, and soon the reinstated disc lay on steel plugs, like a table on its legs. One inconvenience resulted from the replacing of the disc, the lower window was blocked up; thus it was impossible for the travelers to observe the moon from that opening while they were being precipitated perpendicularly upon her; but they were obliged to give it up; even by the side openings they could still see vast lunar regions, as an aeronaut sees the earth from his car.

This replacing of the disc was at least an hour's work. It was past twelve when all preparations were finished. Barbicane took fresh observations on the inclination of the projectile, but to his annoyance it had not turned over sufficiently for its fall; it seemed to take a curve parallel to the lunar disc. The orb of night shone splendidly into space, while opposite, the orb of day blazed with fire.

Their situation began to make them uneasy.

"Are we reaching our destination?" said Nicholl.

"Let us act as if we were about reaching it," replied Barbicane.

"You are sceptical," retorted Michel Ardan. "We shall arrive, and that, too, quicker than we like."

This answer brought Barbicane back to his preparations, and he occupied himself with placing the contrivances intended to break their descent. We may remember the scene of the meeting held at Tampa Town, in Florida, when Captain Nicholl came forward as Barbicane's enemy and Michel Ardan's adversary. To Captain Nicholl's maintaining that the projectile would smash like glass, Michel replied that he would break their fall by means of rockets properly placed.

Thus, powerful fireworks, taking their starting-point from the base and bursting outside, could, by producing a recoil, check to a certain degree the projectile's speed. These rockets were to burn in space, it is true; but oxygen would not fail them, for they could supply themselves with it, like the lunar volcanoes, the burning of which has never yet been stopped by the want of atmosphere round the moon.

Barbicane had accordingly supplied himself with these fireworks, enclosed in little steel guns, which could be screwed on to the base of the projectile. Inside, these guns were flush with the bottom; outside, they protruded about eighteen inches. There were twenty of them. An opening left in the disc allowed them to light the match with which each was provided. All the effect was felt outside. The burning mixture had already been rammed into each gun. They had, then, nothing to do but raise the metallic buffers fixed in the base, and replace them by the guns, which fitted closely in their places.

This new work was finished about three o'clock, and after taking all these precautions there remained but to wait. But the projectile was perceptibly nearing the moon, and evidently succumbed to her influence to a certain degree; though its own velocity also drew it in an oblique direction. From these conflicting influences resulted a line which might become a tangent. But it was certain that the projectile would not fall directly on the moon; for its lower part, by reason of its weight, ought to be turned toward her.

Barbicane's uneasiness increased as he saw his projectile resist the influence of gravitation. The Unknown was opening before him, the Unknown in interplanetary space. The man of science thought he had foreseen the only three hypotheses possible—the return to the earth, the return to the moon, or stagnation on the neutral line; and here a fourth hypothesis, big with all the terrors of the Infinite, surged up inopportunely. To face it without flinching, one must be a resolute savant like Barbicane, a phlegmatic being like Nicholl, or an audacious adventurer like Michel Ardan.

Conversation was started upon this subject. Other men would have considered the question from a practical point of view; they would have asked themselves whither their projectile carriage was carrying them. Not so with these; they sought for the cause which produced this effect.

"So we have become diverted from our route," said Michel; "but why?"

"I very much fear," answered Nicholl, "that, in spite of all precautions taken, the Columbiad was not fairly pointed. An error, however small, would be enough to throw us out of the moon's attraction."

"Then they must have aimed badly?" asked Michel.

"I do not think so," replied Barbicane. "The perpendicularity of the gun was exact, its direction to the zenith of the spot incontestible; and the moon passing to the zenith of the spot, we ought to reach it at the full. There is another reason, but it escapes me."

"Are we not arriving too late?" asked Nicholl.

"Too late?" said Barbicane.

"Yes," continued Nicholl. "The Cambridge Observatory's note says that the transit ought to be accomplished in ninety-seven hours thirteen minutes and twenty seconds; which means to say, that sooner the moon will not be at the point indicated, and later it will have passed it."

"True," replied Barbicane. "But we started the 1st of December, at thirteen minutes and twenty-five seconds to eleven at night; and we ought to arrive on the 5th at midnight, at the exact moment when the moon would be full; and we are now at the 5th of December. It is now half-past three in the evening; half-past eight ought to see us at the end of our journey. Why do we not arrive?"

"Might it not be an excess of speed?" answered Nicholl; "for we know now that its initial velocity was greater than they supposed."

"No! a hundred times, no!" replied Barbicane. "An excess of speed, if the direction of the projectile had been right, would not have prevented us reaching the moon. No, there has been a deviation. We have been turned out of our course."

"By whom? by what?" asked Nicholl.

"I cannot say," replied Barbicane.

"Very well, then, Barbicane," said Michel, "do you wish to know my opinion on the subject of finding out this deviation?"

"Speak."

"I would not give half a dollar to know it. That we have deviated is a fact. Where we are going matters little; we shall soon see. Since we are being borne along in space we shall end by falling into some center of attraction or other."

Michel Ardan's indifference did not content Barbicane. Not that he was uneasy about the future, but he wanted to know at any cost why his projectile had deviated.

But the projectile continued its course sideways to the moon, and with it the mass of things thrown out. Barbicane could even prove, by the elevations which served as landmarks upon the moon, which was only two thousand leagues distant, that its speed was becoming uniform—fresh proof that there was no fall. Its impulsive force still prevailed over the lunar attraction, but the projectile's course was certainly bringing it nearer to the moon, and they might hope that at a nearer point the weight, predominating, would cause a decided fall.

The three friends, having nothing better to do, continued their observations; but they could not yet determine the topographical position of the satellite; every relief was leveled under the reflection of the solar rays.

They watched thus through the side windows until eight o'clock at night. The moon had grown so large in their eyes that it filled half of the firmament. The sun on one side, and the orb of night on the other, flooded the projectile with light.

At that moment Barbicane thought he could estimate the distance which separated them from their aim at no more than 700 leagues. The speed of the projectile seemed to him to be more than 200 yards, or about 170 leagues a second. Under the centripetal force, the base of the projectile tended toward the moon; but the centrifugal still prevailed; and it was probable that its rectilineal course would be changed to a curve of some sort, the nature of which they could not at present determine.

Barbicane was still seeking the solution of his insoluble problem. Hours passed without any result. The projectile was evidently nearing the moon, but it was also evident that it would never reach her. As to the nearest distance at which it would pass her, that must be the result of two forces, attraction and repulsion, affecting its motion.

"I ask but one thing," said Michel; "that we may pass near enough to penetrate her secrets."

"Cursed be the thing that has caused our projectile to deviate from its course," cried Nicholl.

And, as if a light had suddenly broken in upon his mind, Barbicane answered, "Then cursed be the meteor which crossed our path."

"What?" said Michel Ardan.

"What do you mean?" exclaimed Nicholl.

"I mean," said Barbicane in a decided tone, "I mean that our deviation is owing solely to our meeting with this erring body."

"But it did not even brush us as it passed," said Michel.

"What does that matter? Its mass, compared to that of our projectile, was enormous, and its attraction was enough to influence our course."

"So little?" cried Nicholl.

"Yes, Nicholl; but however little it might be," replied Barbicane, "in a distance of 84,000 leagues, it wanted no more to make us miss the moon."

X

THE OBSERVERS OF THE MOON

BARBICANE had evidently hit upon the only plausible reason of this deviation. However slight it might have been, it had sufficed to modify the course of the projectile. It was a fatality. The bold attempt had miscarried by a fortuitous circumstance; and unless by some exceptional event, they could now never reach the moon's disc.

Would they pass near enough to be able to solve certain physical and geological questions until then insoluble? This was the question, and the only one, which occupied the minds of these bold travelers. As to the fate in store for themselves, they did not even dream of it.

But what would become of them amid these infinite solitudes, these who would soon want air? A few more days, and they would fall stifled in this wandering projectile. But some days to these intrepid fellows was a century; and they devoted all their time to observe that moon which they no longer hoped to reach.

The distance which had then separated the projectile from the satellite was estimated at about two hundred leagues. Under these conditions, as regards the visibility of the details of the disc, the travelers were farther from the moon than are the inhabitants of earth with their powerful telescopes.

Indeed, we know that the instrument mounted by Lord Rosse at Parsonstown, which magnifies 6,500 times, brings the moon to within an apparent distance of sixteen leagues. And more than that, with the powerful one set up at Long's Peak, the orb of night, magnified 48,000 times, is brought to within less than two leagues, and objects having a diameter of thirty feet are seen very distinctly. So that, at this distance, the topographical details of the moon, observed without glasses, could not be determined with precision. The eye caught the vast outline of those immense depressions inappropriately called "seas," but they could not recognize their nature. The prominence of the mountains disappeared under the splendid irradiation produced by the reflection of the solar rays. The eye, dazzled as if it was leaning over a bath of molten silver, turned from it involuntarily; but the oblong form of the orb was quite clear. It appeared like a gigantic egg, with the small end turned toward the earth. Indeed the moon, liquid and pliable in the first days of its formation, was originally a perfect sphere; but being soon drawn within the attraction of the earth, it became elongated under the influence of gravitation. In becoming a satellite, she lost her native purity of form; her center of gravity was in advance of the center of her figure; and from this fact some savants draw the conclusion that the air and water had taken refuge on the opposite surface of the moon, which is never seen from the earth. This alteration in the primitive form of the satellite was only perceptible for a few moments. The distance of the projectile from the moon diminished very rapidly under its speed, though that was much less than its initial velocity—but eight or nine times greater than that which propels our express trains. The oblique course of the projectile, from its very obliquity, gave Michel Ardan some hopes of striking the lunar disc at some point or other. He could not think that they would never reach it. No! he could not believe it; and this opinion he often repeated. But Barbicane, who was a better judge, always answered him with merciless logic.

"No, Michel, no! We can only reach the moon by a fall, and we are not falling. The centripetal force keeps us under the moon's influence, but the centrifugal force draws us irresistibly away from it."

This was said in a tone which quenched Michel Ardan's last hope.

The portion of the moon which the projectile was nearing was the northern hemisphere, that which the selenographic maps place below; for these maps are generally drawn after the outline given by the glasses, and we know that they reverse the objects. Such was the Mappa Selenographica of Boeer and Moedler which Barbicane consulted. This northern hemisphere presented vast plains, dotted with isolated mountains.

At midnight the moon was full. At that precise moment the travelers should have alighted upon it, if the mischievous meteor had not diverted their course. The orb was exactly in the condition determined by the Cambridge Observatory. It was mathematically at its perigee, and at the zenith of the twenty-eighth parallel. An observer placed at the bottom of the enormous Columbiad, pointed perpendicularly to the horizon, would have framed the moon in the mouth of the gun. A straight line drawn through the axis of the piece would have passed through the center of the orb of night. It is needless to say, that during the night of the 5th-6th of December, the travelers took not an instant's rest. Could they close their eyes when so near this new world? No! All their feelings were concentrated in one single thought:—See! Representatives of the earth, of humanity, past and present, all centered in them! It is through their eyes that the human race look at these lunar regions, and penetrate the secrets of their satellite! A strange emotion filled their hearts as they went from one window to the other. Their observations, reproduced by

Barbicane, were rigidly determined. To take them, they had glasses; to correct them, maps.

As regards the optical instruments at their disposal, they had excellent marine glasses specially constructed for this journey. They possessed magnifying powers of 100. They would thus have brought the moon to within a distance (apparent) of less than 2,000 leagues from the earth. But then, at a distance which for three hours in the morning did not exceed sixty-five miles, and in a medium free from all atmospheric disturbances, these instruments could reduce the lunar surface to within less than 1,500 yards!

XI

FANCY AND REALITY

"Have you ever seen the moon?" asked a professor, ironically, of one of his pupils.

"No, sir!" replied the pupil, still more ironically, "but I must say I have heard it spoken of."

In one sense, the pupil's witty answer might be given by a large majority of sublunary beings. How many people have heard speak of the moon who have never seen it—at least through a glass or a telescope! How many have never examined the map of their satellite!

In looking at a selenographic map, one peculiarity strikes us. Contrary to the arrangement followed for that of the Earth and Mars, the continents occupy more particularly the southern hemisphere of the lunar globe. These continents do not show such decided, clear, and regular boundary lines as South America, Africa, and the Indian peninsula. Their angular, capricious, and deeply indented coasts are rich in gulfs and peninsulas. They remind one of the confusion in the islands of the Sound, where the land is excessively indented. If navigation ever existed on the surface of the moon, it must have been wonderfully difficult and dangerous; and we may well pity the Selenite sailors and hydrographers; the former, when they came upon these perilous coasts, the latter when they took the soundings of its stormy banks.

We may also notice that, on the lunar sphere, the south pole is much more continental than the north pole. On the latter, there is but one slight strip of land separated from other continents by vast seas. Toward the south, continents clothe almost the whole of the hemisphere. It is even possible that the Selenites have already planted the flag on one of their poles, while Franklin, Ross, Kane, Dumont, d'Urville, and Lambert have never yet been able to attain that unknown point of the terrestrial globe.

As to islands, they are numerous on the surface of the moon. Nearly all oblong or circular, and as if traced with the compass, they seem to form one vast archipelago, equal to that charming group lying between Greece and Asia Minor, and which mythology in ancient times adorned with most graceful legends. Involuntarily the names of Naxos, Tenedos, and Carpathos, rise before the mind, and we seek vainly for Ulysses' vessel or the "clipper" of the Argonauts. So at least it was in Michel Ardan's eyes. To him it was a Grecian archipelago that he saw on the map. To the eyes of his matter-of-fact companions, the aspect of these coasts recalled rather the parceled-out land of New Brunswick and Nova Scotia, and where the Frenchman discovered traces of the heroes of fable, these Americans were marking the most favorable points for the establishment of stores in the interests of lunar commerce and industry.

After wandering over these vast continents, the eye is attracted by the still greater seas. Not only their formation, but their situation and aspect remind one of the terrestrial oceans; but again, as on earth, these seas occupy the greater portion of the globe. But in point of fact, these are not liquid spaces, but plains, the nature of which the travelers hoped soon to determine. Astronomers, we must allow, have graced these pretended seas with at least odd names, which science has respected up to the present time. Michel Ardan was right when he compared this map to a "Tendre card," got up by a Scudary or a Cyrano de Bergerac. "Only," said he, "it is no longer the sentimental card of the seventeenth century, it is the card of life, very neatly divided into two parts, one feminine, the other masculine; the right hemisphere for woman, the left for man."

In speaking thus, Michel made his prosaic companions shrug their shoulders. Barbicane and Nicholl looked upon the lunar map from a very different point of view to that of their fantastic friend. Nevertheless, their fantastic friend was a little in the right. Judge for yourselves.

In the left hemisphere stretches the "Sea of Clouds," where human reason is so often shipwrecked. Not far off lies the "Sea of Rains," fed by all the fever of existence. Near this is the "Sea of Storms," where man is ever fighting against his passions, which too often gain the victory. Then, worn out by deceit, treasons, infidelity, and the whole body of terrestrial misery, what does he find at the end of his career? that vast "Sea of Humors," barely softened by some drops of the waters from the "Gulf of Dew!"

Clouds, rain, storms, and humors—does the life of man contain aught but these? and is it not summed up in these four words?

The right hemisphere, "dedicated to the ladies," encloses smaller seas, whose significant names contain every incident of a feminine existence. There is the "Sea of Serenity," over which the young girl bends; "The Lake of Dreams," reflecting a joyous future; "The Sea of Nectar," with its waves of tenderness and breezes of love; "The Sea of Fruitfulness;" "The Sea of Crises;" then the "Sea of Vapors," whose dimensions are perhaps a little too confined; and lastly, that vast "Sea of Tranquillity," in which every false passion, every useless dream, every unsatisfied desire is at length absorbed, and whose waves emerge peacefully into the "Lake of Death!"

What a strange succession of names! What a singular division of the moon's two hemispheres, joined to one another like man and woman, and forming that sphere of life carried into space! And was not the fantastic Michel right in thus interpreting the fancies of the ancient astronomers? But while his imagination thus roved over "the seas," his grave companions were considering things more geographically. They were learning this new world by heart. They were measuring angles and diameters.

XII

OROGRAPHIC DETAILS

THE course taken by the projectile, as we have before remarked, was bearing it toward the moon's northern hemisphere. The travelers were far from the central point which they would have struck, had their course not been subject to an irremediable deviation. It was past midnight; and Barbicane then estimated the distance at seven hundred and fifty miles, which was a little greater than the length of the lunar radius, and which would diminish as it advanced nearer to the North Pole. The projectile was then not at the altitude of the equator; but across the tenth parallel, and from that latitude, carefully taken on the map to the pole, Barbicane and his two companions were able to observe the moon under the most favorable conditions. Indeed, by means of glasses, the above-named distance was reduced to little more than fourteen miles. The telescope of the Rocky Mountains brought the moon much nearer; but the terrestrial atmosphere singularly lessened its power. Thus Barbicane, posted in his projectile, with the glasses to his eyes, could seize upon details which were almost imperceptible to earthly observers.

"My friends," said the president, in a serious voice, "I do not know whither we are going; I do not know if we shall ever see the terrestrial globe again. Nevertheless, let us proceed as if our work would one day by useful to our fellow-men. Let us keep our minds free from every other consideration. We are astronomers; and this projectile is a room in the Cambridge University, carried into space. Let us make our observations!"

This said, work was begun with great exactness; and they faithfully reproduced the different aspects of the moon, at the different distances which the projectile reached.

At the time that the projectile was as high as the tenth parallel, north latitude, it seemed rigidly to follow the twentieth degree, east longitude. We must here make one important remark with regard to the map by which they were taking observations. In the selenographical maps where, on account of the reversing of the objects by the glasses, the south is above and the north below, it would seem natural that, on account of that inversion, the east should be to the left hand, and the west to the right. But it is not so. If the map were turned upside down, showing the moon as we see her, the east would be to the left, and the west to the right, contrary to that which exists on terrestrial maps. The following is the reason of this anomaly. Observers in the northern hemisphere (say in Europe) see the moon in the south—according to them. When they take observations, they turn their backs to the north, the reverse position to that which they occupy when they study a terrestrial map. As they turn their backs to the north, the east is on their left, and the west to their right. To observers in the southern hemisphere (Patagonia for example), the moon's west would be quite to their left, and the east to their right, as the south is behind them. Such is the reason of the apparent reversing of these two cardinal points, and we must bear it in mind in order to be able to follow President Barbicane's observations.

With the help of Boeer and Moedler's Mappa Selenographica, the travelers were able at once to recognize that portion of the disc enclosed within the field of their glasses.

"What are we looking at, at this moment?" asked Michel.

"At the northern part of the 'Sea of Clouds,'" answered Barbicane. "We are too far off to recognize its nature. Are these plains composed of arid sand, as the first astronomer maintained? Or are they nothing but immense forests, according to M. Warren de la Rue's opinion, who gives the moon an atmosphere, though a very low and a very dense one?

That we shall know by and by. We must affirm nothing until we are in a position to do so."

This "Sea of Clouds" is rather doubtfully marked out upon the maps. It is supposed that these vast plains are strewn with blocks of lava from the neighboring volcanoes on its right, Ptolemy, Purbach, Arzachel. But the projectile was advancing, and sensibly nearing it. Soon there appeared the heights which bound this sea at this northern limit. Before them rose a mountain radiant with beauty, the top of which seemed lost in an eruption of solar rays.

"That is—?" asked Michel.

"Copernicus," replied Barbicane.

"Let us see Copernicus."

This mount, situated in 9@ north latitude and 20@ east longitude, rose to a height of 10,600 feet above the surface of the moon. It is quite visible from the earth; and astronomers can study it with ease, particularly during the phase between the last quarter and the new moon, because then the shadows are thrown lengthways from east to west, allowing them to measure the heights.

This Copernicus forms the most important of the radiating system, situated in the southern hemisphere, according to Tycho Brahe. It rises isolated like a gigantic lighthouse on that portion of the "Sea of Clouds," which is bounded by the "Sea of Tempests," thus lighting by its splendid rays two oceans at a time. It was a sight without an equal, those long luminous trains, so dazzling in the full moon, and which, passing the boundary chain on the north, extends to the "Sea of Rains." At one o'clock of the terrestrial morning, the projectile, like a balloon borne into space, overlooked the top of this superb mount. Barbicane could recognize perfectly its chief features. Copernicus is comprised in the series of ringed mountains of the first order, in the division of great circles. Like Kepler and Aristarchus, which overlook the "Ocean of Tempests," sometimes it appeared like a brilliant point through the cloudy light, and was taken for a volcano in activity. But it is only an extinct one—like all on that side of the moon. Its circumference showed a diameter of about twenty-two leagues. The glasses discovered traces of stratification produced by successive eruptions, and the neighborhood was strewn with volcanic remains which still choked some of the craters.

"There exist," said Barbicane, "several kinds of circles on the surface of the moon, and it is easy to see that Copernicus belongs to the radiating class. If we were nearer, we should see the cones bristling on the inside, which in former times were so many fiery mouths. A curious arrangement, and one without an exception on the lunar disc, is that the interior surface of these circles is the reverse of the exterior, and contrary to the form taken by terrestrial craters. It follows, then, that the general curve of the bottom of these circles gives a sphere of a smaller diameter than that of the moon."

"And why this peculiar disposition?" asked Nicholl.

"We do not know," replied Barbicane.

"What splendid radiation!" said Michel. "One could hardly see a finer spectacle, I think."

"What would you say, then," replied Barbicane, "if chance should bear us toward the southern hemisphere?"

"Well, I should say that it was still more beautiful," retorted Michel Ardan.

At this moment the projectile hung perpendicularly over the circle. The circumference of Copernicus formed almost a perfect circle, and its steep escarpments were clearly defined. They could even distinguish a second ringed enclosure. Around spread a grayish plain, of a wild aspect, on which every relief was marked in yellow. At the bottom of the circle, as if enclosed in a jewel case, sparkled for one instant two or three eruptive cones, like enormous dazzling gems. Toward the north the escarpments were lowered by a depression which would probably have given access to the interior of the crater.

In passing over the surrounding plains, Barbicane noticed a great number of less important mountains; and among others a little ringed one called Guy Lussac, the breadth of which measured twelve miles.

Toward the south, the plain was very flat, without one elevation, without one projection. Toward the north, on the contrary, till where it was bounded by the "Sea of Storms," it resembled a liquid surface agitated by a storm, of which the hills and hollows formed a succession of waves suddenly congealed. Over the whole of this, and in all directions, lay the luminous lines, all converging to the summit of Copernicus.

The travelers discussed the origin of these strange rays; but they could not determine their nature any more than terrestrial observers.

"But why," said Nicholl, "should not these rays be simply spurs of mountains which reflect more vividly the light of the sun?"

"No," replied Barbicane; "if it was so, under certain conditions of the moon, these ridges would cast shadows, and they do not cast any."

And indeed, these rays only appeared when the orb of day was in opposition to the moon, and disappeared as soon as its rays became oblique.

"But how have they endeavored to explain these lines of light?" asked Michel; "for I cannot believe that savants would ever be stranded for want of an explanation."

"Yes," replied Barbicane; "Herschel has put forward an opinion, but he did not venture to affirm it."

"Never mind. What was the opinion?"

"He thought that these rays might be streams of cooled lava which shone when the sun beat straight upon them. It may be so; but nothing can be less certain. Besides, if we pass nearer to Tycho, we shall be in a better position to find out the cause of this radiation."

"Do you know, my friends, what that plain, seen from the height we are at, resembles?" said Michel.

"No," replied Nicholl.

"Very well; with all those pieces of lava lengthened like rockets, it resembles an immense game of spelikans thrown pellmell. There wants but the hook to pull them out one by one."

"Do be serious," said Barbicane.

"Well, let us be serious," replied Michel quietly; "and instead of spelikans, let us put bones. This plain, would then be nothing but an immense cemetery, on which would repose the mortal remains of thousands of extinct generations. Do you prefer that high-flown comparison?"

"One is as good as the other," retorted Barbicane.

"My word, you are difficult to please," answered Michel.

"My worthy friend," continued the matter-of-fact Barbicane, "it matters but little what it resembles, when we do not know what it is."

"Well answered," exclaimed Michel. "That will teach me to reason with savants."

But the projectile continued to advance with almost uniform speed around the lunar disc. The travelers, we may easily imagine, did not dream of taking a moment's rest. Every minute changed the landscape which fled from beneath their gaze. About half past one o'clock in the morning, they caught a glimpse of the tops of another mountain. Barbicane, consulting his map, recognized Eratosthenes.

It was a ringed mountain nine thousand feet high, and one of those circles so numerous on this satellite. With regard to this, Barbicane related Kepler's singular opinion on the formation of circles. According to that celebrated mathematician, these crater-like cavities had been dug by the hand of man.

"For what purpose?" asked Nicholl.

"For a very natural one," replied Barbicane. "The Selenites might have undertaken these immense works and dug these enormous holes for a refuge and shield from the solar rays which beat upon them during fifteen consecutive days."

"The Selenites are not fools," said Michel.

"A singular idea," replied Nicholl; "but it is probable that Kepler did not know the true dimensions of these circles, for the digging of them would have been the work of giants quite impossible for the Selenites."

"Why? if weight on the moon's surface is six times less than on the earth?" said Michel.

"But if the Selenites are six times smaller?" retorted Nicholl.

"And if there are no Selenites?" added Barbicane.

This put an end to the discussion.

Soon Eratosthenes disappeared under the horizon without the projectile being sufficiently near to allow close observation. This mountain separated the Apennines from the Carpathians. In the lunar orography they have discerned some chains of mountains, which are chiefly distributed over the northern hemisphere. Some, however, occupy certain portions of the southern hemisphere also.

About two o'clock in the morning Barbicane found that they were above the twentieth lunar parallel. The distance of the projectile from the moon was not more than six hundred miles. Barbicane, now perceiving that the projectile was steadily approaching the lunar disc, did not despair; if not of reaching her, at least of discovering the secrets of her configuration.

XIII

Lunar Landscapes

At half-past two in the morning, the projectile was over the thirteenth lunar parallel and at the effective distance of five hundred miles, reduced by the glasses to five. It still seemed impossible, however, that it could ever touch any part of the disc. Its motive speed, comparatively so moderate, was inexplicable to President Barbicane. At that distance from the moon it must have been considerable, to enable it to bear up against her attraction. Here was a phenomenon the cause of which escaped them again. Besides, time failed them to investigate the cause. All lunar relief was defiling under the eyes of the travelers, and they would not lose a single detail.

Under the glasses the disc appeared at the distance of five miles. What would an aeronaut, borne to this distance from the earth, distinguish on its surface? We cannot say, since the greatest ascension has not been more than 25,000 feet.

This, however, is an exact description of what Barbicane and his companions saw at this height. Large patches of different colors appeared on the disc. Selenographers are not agreed upon the nature of these colors. There are several, and rather vividly marked. Julius Schmidt pretends that, if the terrestrial oceans were dried up, a Selenite observer could not distinguish on the globe a greater diversity of shades between the oceans and the continental plains than those on the moon present to a terrestrial observer. According to him, the color common to the vast plains known by the name of "seas" is a dark gray mixed with green and brown. Some of the large craters present the same appearance. Barbicane knew this opinion of the German selenographer, an opinion shared by Boeer and Moedler. Observation has proved that right was on their side, and not on that of some astronomers who admit the existence of only gray on the moon's surface. In some parts green was very distinct, such as springs, according to Julius Schmidt, from the seas of "Serenity and Humors." Barbicane also noticed large craters, without any interior cones, which shed a bluish tint similar to the reflection of a sheet of steel freshly polished. These colors belonged really to the lunar disc, and did not result, as some astronomers say, either from the imperfection in the objective of the glasses or from the interposition of the terrestrial atmosphere.

Not a doubt existed in Barbicane's mind with regard to it, as he observed it through space, and so could not commit any optical error. He considered the establishment of this fact as an acquisition to science. Now, were these shades of green, belonging to tropical vegetation, kept up by a low dense atmosphere? He could not yet say.

Farther on, he noticed a reddish tint, quite defined. The same shade had before been observed at the bottom of an isolated enclosure, known by the name of Lichtenburg's circle, which is situated near the Hercynian mountains, on the borders of the moon; but they could not tell the nature of it.

They were not more fortunate with regard to another peculiarity of the disc, for they could not decide upon the cause of it.

Michel Ardan was watching near the president, when he noticed long white lines, vividly lighted up by the direct rays of the sun. It was a succession of luminous furrows, very different from the radiation of Copernicus not long before; they ran parallel with each other.

Michel, with his usual readiness, hastened to exclaim:

"Look there! cultivated fields!"

"Cultivated fields!" replied Nicholl, shrugging his shoulders.

"Plowed, at all events," retorted Michel Ardan; "but what laborers those Selenites must be, and what giant oxen they must harness to their plow to cut such furrows!"

"They are not furrows," said Barbicane; "they are rifts."

"Rifts? stuff!" replied Michel mildly; "but what do you mean by 'rifts' in the scientific world?"

Barbicane immediately enlightened his companion as to what he knew about lunar rifts. He knew that they were a kind of furrow found on every part of the disc which was not mountainous; that these furrows, generally isolated, measured from 400 to 500 leagues in length; that their breadth varied from 1,000 to 1,500 yards, and that their borders were strictly parallel; but he knew nothing more either of their formation or their nature.

Barbicane, through his glasses, observed these rifts with great attention. He noticed that their borders were formed of steep declivities; they were long parallel ramparts, and with some small amount of imagination he might have admitted the existence of long lines of fortifications, raised by Selenite engineers. Of these different rifts some were perfectly straight, as if cut by a line; others were slightly curved, though still keeping their borders parallel; some crossed each other, some cut through craters; here they wound through ordinary cavities, such as Posidonius or Petavius; there they wound through the seas, such as the "Sea of Serenity."

These natural accidents naturally excited the imaginations of these terrestrial astronomers. The first observations had not discovered these rifts. Neither Hevelius, Cassin, La Hire, nor Herschel seemed to have known them. It was Schroeter who in 1789 first drew attention to them. Others followed who studied them, as Pastorff, Gruithuysen, Boeer, and Moedler. At this time their number amounts to seventy; but, if they have been counted, their nature has not yet been determined; they are certainly not fortifications, any more than they are the ancient beds of dried-up rivers; for, on one side, the waters, so slight on the moon's surface, could never have worn such drains for themselves; and, on the other, they often cross craters of great elevation.

We must, however, allow that Michel Ardan had "an idea," and that, without knowing it, he coincided in that respect with Julius Schmidt.

"Why," said he, "should not these unaccountable appearances be simply phenomena of vegetation?"

"What do you mean?" asked Barbicane quickly.

"Do not excite yourself, my worthy president," replied Michel; "might it not be possible that the dark lines forming that bastion were rows of trees regularly placed?"

"You stick to your vegetation, then?" said Barbicane.

"I like," retorted Michel Ardan, "to explain what you savants cannot explain; at least my hypotheses has the advantage of indicating why these rifts disappear, or seem to disappear, at certain seasons."

"And for what reason?"

"For the reason that the trees become invisible when they lose their leaves, and visible again when they regain them."

"Your explanation is ingenious, my dear companion," replied Barbicane, "but inadmissible."

"Why?"

"Because, so to speak, there are no seasons on the moon's surface, and that, consequently, the phenomena of vegetation of which you speak cannot occur."

Indeed, the slight obliquity of the lunar axis keeps the sun at an almost equal height in every latitude. Above the equatorial regions the radiant orb almost invariably occupies the zenith, and does not pass the limits of the horizon in the polar regions; thus, according to each region, there reigns a perpetual winter, spring, summer, or autumn, as in the planet Jupiter, whose axis is but little inclined upon its orbit.

What origin do they attribute to these rifts? That is a question difficult to solve. They are certainly anterior to the formation of craters and circles, for several have introduced themselves by breaking through their circular ramparts. Thus it may be that, contemporary with the later geological epochs, they are due to the expansion of natural forces.

But the projectile had now attained the fortieth degree of lunar latitude, at a distance not exceeding 40 miles. Through the glasses objects appeared to be only four miles distant.

At this point, under their feet, rose Mount Helicon, 1,520 feet high, and round about the left rose moderate elevations, enclosing a small portion of the "Sea of Rains," under the name of the Gulf of Iris. The terrestrial atmosphere would have to be one hundred and seventy times more transparent than it is, to allow astronomers to make perfect observations on the moon's surface; but in the void in which the projectile floated no fluid interposed itself between the eye of the observer and the object observed. And more, Barbicane found himself carried to a greater distance than the most powerful telescopes had ever done before, either that of Lord Rosse or that of the Rocky Mountains. He was, therefore, under extremely favorable conditions for solving that great question of the habitability of the moon; but the solution still escaped him; he could distinguish nothing but desert beds, immense plains, and toward the north, arid mountains. Not a work betrayed the hand of man; not a ruin marked his course; not a group of animals was to be seen indicating life, even in an inferior degree. In no part was there life, in no part was there an appearance of vegetation. Of the three kingdoms which share the terrestrial globe between them, one alone was represented on the lunar and that the mineral.

"Ah, indeed!" said Michel Ardan, a little out of countenance; "then you see no one?"

"No," answered Nicholl; "up to this time, not a man, not an animal, not a tree! After all, whether the atmosphere has taken refuge at the bottom of cavities, in the midst of the circles, or even on the opposite face of the moon, we cannot decide."

"Besides," added Barbicane, "even to the most piercing eye a man cannot be distinguished farther than three and a half miles off; so that, if there are any Selenites, they can see our projectile, but we cannot see them."

Toward four in the morning, at the height of the fiftieth parallel, the distance was reduced to 300 miles. To the left ran a line of mountains capriciously shaped, lying in the full light. To the right, on the contrary, lay a black hollow resembling a vast well, unfathomable and gloomy, drilled into the lunar soil.

This hole was the "Black Lake"; it was Pluto, a deep circle which can be conveniently studied from the earth, between the last quarter and the new moon, when the shadows fall from west to east.

This black color is rarely met with on the surface of the satellite. As yet it has only been recognized in the depths of the circle of Endymion, to the east of the "Cold Sea," in the northern hemisphere, and at the bottom of Grimaldi's circle, on the equator, toward the eastern border of the orb.

Pluto is an annular mountain, situated in 51@ north latitude, and 9@ east longitude. Its circuit is forty-seven miles long and thirty-two broad.

Barbicane regretted that they were not passing directly above this vast opening. There was an abyss to fathom, perhaps some mysterious phenomenon to surprise; but the projectile's course could not be altered. They must rigidly submit. They could not guide a balloon, still less a projectile, when once enclosed within its walls. Toward five in the morning the northern limits of the "Sea of Rains" was at length passed. The mounts of Condamine and Fontenelle remained—one on the right, the other on the left. That part of the disc beginning with 60@ was becoming quite mountainous. The glasses brought them to within two miles, less than that separating the summit of Mont Blanc from the level of the sea. The whole region was bristling with spikes and circles. Toward the 60@ Philolaus stood predominant at a height of 5,550 feet with its elliptical crater, and seen from this distance, the disc showed a very fantastical appearance. Landscapes were presented to the eye under very different conditions from those on the earth, and also very inferior to them.

The moon having no atmosphere, the consequences arising from the absence of this gaseous envelope have already been shown. No twilight on her surface; night following day and day following night with the suddenness of a lamp which is extinguished or lighted amid profound darkness—no transition from cold to heat, the temperature falling in an instant from boiling point to the cold of space.

Another consequence of this want of air is that absolute darkness reigns where the sun's rays do not penetrate. That which on earth is called diffusion of light, that luminous matter which the air holds in suspension, which creates the twilight and the daybreak, which produces the umbrae and penumbrae, and all the magic of chiaro-oscuro, does not exist on the moon. Hence the harshness of contrasts, which only admit of two colors, black and white. If a Selenite were to shade his eyes from the sun's rays, the sky would seem absolutely black, and the stars would shine to him as on the darkest night. Judge of the impression produced on Barbicane and his three friends by this strange scene! Their eyes were confused. They could no longer grasp the respective distances of the different plains. A lunar landscape without the softening of the phenomena of chiaro-oscuro could not be rendered by an earthly landscape painter; it would be spots of ink on a white page—nothing more.

This aspect was not altered even when the projectile, at the height of 80@, was only separated from the moon by a distance of fifty miles; nor even when, at five in the morning, it passed at less than twenty-five miles from the mountain of Gioja, a distance reduced by the glasses to a quarter of a mile. It seemed as if the moon might be touched by the hand! It seemed impossible that, before long, the projectile would not strike her, if only at the north pole, the brilliant arch of which was so distinctly visible on the black sky.

Michel Ardan wanted to open one of the scuttles and throw himself on to the moon's surface! A very useless attempt; for if the projectile could not attain any point whatever of the satellite, Michel, carried along by its motion, could not attain it either.

At that moment, at six o'clock, the lunar pole appeared. The disc only presented to the travelers' gaze one half brilliantly lit up, while the other disappeared in the darkness. Suddenly the projectile passed the line of demarcation between intense light and absolute darkness, and was plunged in profound night!

XIV

THE NIGHT OF THREE HUNDRED AND FIFTY-FOUR HOURS AND A HALF

AT the moment when this phenomenon took place so rapidly, the projectile was skirting the moon's north pole at less than twenty-five miles distance. Some seconds had sufficed to plunge it into the absolute darkness of space. The transition was so sudden, without shade, without gradation of light, without attenuation of the luminous waves, that the orb seemed to have been extinguished by a powerful blow.

"Melted, disappeared!" Michel Ardan exclaimed, aghast.

Indeed, there was neither reflection nor shadow. Nothing more was to be seen of that disc, formerly so dazzling. The darkness was complete. and rendered even more so by the rays from the stars. It was "that blackness" in which the lunar nights are insteeped, which last three hundred and fifty-four hours and a half at each point of the disc, a long night resulting from the equality of the translatory and rotary movements of the moon. The projectile, immerged in the conical shadow of the satellite, experienced the action of the solar rays no more than any of its invisible points.

In the interior, the obscurity was complete. They could not see each other. Hence the necessity of dispelling the darkness. However desirous Barbicane might be to husband the gas, the reserve of which was small, he was obliged to ask from it a fictitious light, an expensive brilliancy which the sun then refused.

"Devil take the radiant orb!" exclaimed Michel Ardan, "which forces us to expend gas, instead of giving us his rays gratuitously."

"Do not let us accuse the sun," said Nicholl, "it is not his fault, but that of the moon, which has come and placed herself like a screen between us and it."

"It is the sun!" continued Michel.

"It is the moon!" retorted Nicholl.

An idle dispute, which Barbicane put an end to by saying:

"My friends, it is neither the fault of the sun nor of the moon; it is the fault of the projectile, which, instead of rigidly following its course, has awkwardly missed it. To be more just, it is the fault of that unfortunate meteor which has so deplorably altered our first direction."

"Well," replied Michel Ardan, "as the matter is settled, let us have break-fast. After a whole night of watching it is fair to build ourselves up a little."

This proposal meeting with no contradiction, Michel prepared the re-past in a few minutes. But they ate for eating's sake, they drank without toasts, without hurrahs. The bold travelers being borne away into gloomy space, without their accustomed cortege of rays, felt a vague uneasiness in their hearts. The "strange" shadow so dear to Victor Hugo's pen bound them on all sides. But they talked over the interminable night of three hundred and fifty-four hours and a half, nearly fifteen days, which the law of physics has imposed on the inhabitants of the moon.

Barbicane gave his friends some explanation of the causes and the consequences of this curious phenomenon.

"Curious indeed," said they; "for, if each hemisphere of the moon is deprived of solar light for fifteen days, that above which we now float does not even enjoy during its long night any view of the earth so beauti-fully lit up. In a word she has no moon (applying this designation to our globe) but on one side of her disc. Now if this were the case with the earth—if, for example, Europe never saw the moon, and she was only visible at the antipodes, imagine to yourself the astonishment of a Euro-pean on arriving in Australia."

"They would make the voyage for nothing but to see the moon!" replied Michel.

"Very well!" continued Barbicane, "that astonishment is reserved for the Selenites who inhabit the face of the moon opposite to the earth, a face which is ever invisible to our countrymen of the terrestrial globe."

"And which we should have seen," added Nicholl, "if we had arrived here when the moon was new, that is to say fifteen days later."

"I will add, to make amends," continued Barbicane, "that the inhabit-ants of the visible face are singularly favored by nature, to the detriment of their brethren on the invisible face. The latter, as you see, have dark nights of 354 hours, without one single ray to break the darkness. The other, on the contrary, when the sun which has given its light for fifteen days sinks below the horizon, see a splendid orb rise on the opposite horizon. It is the earth, which is thirteen times greater than the diminutive moon that we know—the earth which developes itself at a diameter of two degrees, and which sheds a light thirteen times greater than that qualified by at-mospheric strata—the earth which only disappears at the moment when the sun reappears in its turn!"

"Nicely worded!" said Michel, "slightly academical perhaps."

"It follows, then," continued Barbicane, without knitting his brows, "that the visible face of the disc must be very agreeable to inhabit, since it always looks on either the sun when the moon is full, or on the earth when the moon is new."

"But," said Nicholl, "that advantage must be well compensated by the insupportable heat which the light brings with it."

"The inconvenience, in that respect, is the same for the two faces, for the earth's light is evidently deprived of heat. But the invisible face is still more searched by the heat than the visible face. I say that for you, Nicholl, because Michel will probably not understand."

"Thank you," said Michel.

"Indeed," continued Barbicane, "when the invisible face receives at the same time light and heat from the sun, it is because the moon is new; that is to say, she is situated between the sun and the earth. It follows, then, considering the position which she occupies in opposition when full, that she is nearer to the sun by twice her distance from the earth; and that distance may be estimated at the two-hundredth part of that which separates the sun from the earth, or in round numbers 400,000 miles. So that invisible face is so much nearer to the sun when she receives its rays."

"Quite right," replied Nicholl.

"On the contrary," continued Barbicane.

"One moment," said Michel, interrupting his grave companion.

"What do you want?"

"I ask to be allowed to continue the explanation."

"And why?"

"To prove that I understand."

"Get along with you," said Barbicane, smiling.

"On the contrary," said Michel, imitating the tone and gestures of the president, "on the contrary, when the visible face of the moon is lit by the sun, it is because the moon is full, that is to say, opposite the sun with regard to the earth. The distance separating it from the radiant orb is then increased in round numbers to 400,000 miles, and the heat which she receives must be a little less."

"Very well said!" exclaimed Barbicane. "Do you know, Michel, that, for an amateur, you are intelligent."

"Yes," replied Michel coolly, "we are all so on the Boulevard des Italiens."

Barbicane gravely grasped the hand of his amiable companion, and continued to enumerate the advantages reserved for the inhabitants of the visible face.

Among others, he mentioned eclipses of the sun, which only take place on this side of the lunar disc; since, in order that they may take place, it is necessary for the moon to be in opposition. These eclipses, caused by the interposition of the earth between the moon and the sun, can last two hours; during which time, by reason of the rays refracted by its atmosphere, the terrestrial globe can appear as nothing but a black point upon the sun.

"So," said Nicholl, "there is a hemisphere, that invisible hemisphere which is very ill supplied, very ill treated, by nature."

"Never mind," replied Michel; "if we ever become Selenites, we will inhabit the visible face. I like the light."

"Unless, by any chance," answered Nicholl, "the atmosphere should be condensed on the other side, as certain astronomers pretend."

"That would be a consideration," said Michel.

Breakfast over, the observers returned to their post. They tried to see through the darkened scuttles by extinguishing all light in the projectile; but not a luminous spark made its way through the darkness.

One inexplicable fact preoccupied Barbicane. Why, having passed within such a short distance of the moon—about twenty-five miles only— why the projectile had not fallen? If its speed had been enormous, he could have understood that the fall would not have taken place; but, with a relatively moderate speed, that resistance to the moon's attraction could not be explained. Was the projectile under some foreign influence? Did some kind of body retain it in the ether? It was quite evident that it could never reach any point of the moon. Whither was it going? Was it going farther from, or nearing, the disc? Was it being borne in that profound darkness through the infinity of space? How could they learn, how calculate, in the midst of this night? All these questions made Barbicane uneasy, but he could not solve them.

Certainly, the invisible orb was there, perhaps only some few miles off; but neither he nor his companions could see it. If there was any noise on its surface, they could not hear it. Air, that medium of sound, was wanting to transmit the groanings of that moon which the Arabic legends call "a man already half granite, and still breathing."

One must allow that that was enough to aggravate the most patient observers. It was just that unknown hemisphere which was stealing from their sight. That face which fifteen days sooner, or fifteen days later, had been, or would be, splendidly illuminated by the solar rays, was then being lost in utter darkness. In fifteen days where would the projectile be? Who could say? Where would the chances of conflicting attractions have drawn it to? The disappointment of the travelers in the midst of this utter darkness may be imagined. All observation of the lunar disc was impossible. The constellations alone claimed all their attention; and we must allow that the astronomers Faye, Charconac, and Secchi, never found themselves in circumstances so favorable for their observation.

Indeed, nothing could equal the splendor of this starry world, bathed in limpid ether. Its diamonds set in the heavenly vault sparkled magnificently. The eye took in the firmament from the Southern Cross to the North Star, those two constellations which in 12,000 years, by reason of the succession of equinoxes, will resign their part of the polar stars, the one to Canopus in the southern hemisphere, the other to Wega in the northern. Imagination loses itself in this sublime Infinity, amid which the projectile was gravitating, like a new star created by the hand of man. From a natural cause, these constellations shone with a soft luster; they did not twinkle, for there was no atmosphere which, by the intervention of its layers unequally dense and of different degrees of humidity, produces this scintillation. These stars were soft eyes, looking out into the dark night, amid the silence of absolute space.

Long did the travelers stand mute, watching the constellated firmament, upon which the moon, like a vast screen, made an enormous black hole. But at length a painful sensation drew them from their watchings. This was an intense cold, which soon covered the inside of the glass of the scuttles with a thick coating of ice. The sun was no longer warming the projectile with its direct rays, and thus it was losing the heat stored up in its walls by degrees. This heat was rapidly evaporating into space by radiation, and a considerably lower temperature was the result. The humidity of the interior was changed into ice upon contact with the glass, preventing all observation.

Nicholl consulted the thermometer, and saw that it had fallen to seventeen degrees (Centigrade) below zero.[3] So that, in spite of the many reasons for economizing, Barbicane, after having begged light from the gas, was also obliged to beg for heat. The projectile's low temperature was no longer endurable. Its tenants would have been frozen to death.

"Well!" observed Michel, "we cannot reasonably complain of the monotony of our journey! What variety we have had, at least in temperature. Now we are blinded with light and saturated with heat, like the Indians of the Pampas! now plunged into profound darkness, amid the cold, like the Esquimaux of the north pole. No, indeed! we have no right to complain; nature does wonders in our honor."

"But," asked Nicholl, "what is the temperature outside?"

"Exactly that of the planetary space," replied Barbicane.

"Then," continued Michel Ardan, "would not this be the time to make the experiment which we dared not attempt when we were drowned in the sun's rays?

3   1@ Fahrenheit.

"It is now or never," replied Barbicane, "for we are in a good position to verify the temperature of space, and see if Fourier or Pouillet's calculations are exact."

"In any case it is cold," said Michel. "See! the steam of the interior is condensing on the glasses of the scuttles. If the fall continues, the vapor of our breath will fall in snow around us."

"Let us prepare a thermometer," said Barbicane.

We may imagine that an ordinary thermometer would afford no result under the circumstances in which this instrument was to be exposed. The mercury would have been frozen in its ball, as below 42@ Fahrenheit below zero it is no longer liquid. But Barbicane had furnished himself with a spirit thermometer on Wafferdin's system, which gives the minima of excessively low temperatures.

Before beginning the experiment, this instrument was compared with an ordinary one, and then Barbicane prepared to use it.

"How shall we set about it?" asked Nicholl.

"Nothing is easier," replied Michel Ardan, who was never at a loss. "We open the scuttle rapidly; throw out the instrument; it follows the projectile with exemplary docility; and a quarter of an hour after, draw it in."

"With the hand?" asked Barbicane.

"With the hand," replied Michel.

"Well, then, my friend, do not expose yourself," answered Barbicane, "for the hand that you draw in again will be nothing but a stump frozen and deformed by the frightful cold."

"Really!"

"You will feel as if you had had a terrible burn, like that of iron at a white heat; for whether the heat leaves our bodies briskly or enters briskly, it is exactly the same thing. Besides, I am not at all certain that the objects we have thrown out are still following us."

"Why not?" asked Nicholl.

"Because, if we are passing through an atmosphere of the slightest density, these objects will be retarded. Again, the darkness prevents our seeing if they still float around us. But in order not to expose ourselves to the loss of our thermometer, we will fasten it, and we can then more easily pull it back again."

Barbicane's advice was followed. Through the scuttle rapidly opened, Nicholl threw out the instrument, which was held by a short cord, so that it might be more easily drawn up. The scuttle had not been opened more than a second, but that second had sufficed to let in a most intense cold.

"The devil!" exclaimed Michel Ardan, "it is cold enough to freeze a white bear."

Barbicane waited until half an hour had elapsed, which was more than time enough to allow the instrument to fall to the level of the surrounding temperature. Then it was rapidly pulled in.

Barbicane calculated the quantity of spirits of wine overflowed into the little vial soldered to the lower part of the instrument, and said:

"A hundred and forty degrees Centigrade[4] below zero!"

M. Pouillet was right and Fourier wrong. That was the undoubted temperature of the starry space. Such is, perhaps, that of the lunar continents, when the orb of night has lost by radiation all the heat which fifteen days of sun have poured into her.

XV

HYPERBOLA OR PARABOLA

WE may, perhaps, be astonished to find Barbicane and his companions so little occupied with the future reserved for them in their metal prison which was bearing them through the infinity of space. Instead of asking where they were going, they passed their time making experiments, as if they had been quietly installed in their own study.

We might answer that men so strong-minded were above such anxieties—that they did not trouble themselves about such trifles—and that they had something else to do than to occupy their minds with the future.

The truth was that they were not masters of their projectile; they could neither check its course, nor alter its direction.

A sailor can change the head of his ship as he pleases; an aeronaut can give a vertical motion to his balloon. They, on the contrary, had no power over their vehicle. Every maneuver was forbidden. Hence the inclination to let things alone, or as the sailors say, "let her run."

Where did they find themselves at this moment, at eight o'clock in the morning of the day called upon the earth the 6th of December? Very certainly in the neighborhood of the moon, and even near enough for her to look to them like an enormous black screen upon the firmament. As to the distance which separated them, it was impossible to estimate it. The projectile, held by some unaccountable force, had been within four miles of grazing the satellite's north pole.

4   218 degrees Fahrenheit below zero.

But since entering the cone of shadow these last two hours, had the distance increased or diminished? Every point of mark was wanting by which to estimate both the direction and the speed of the projectile.

Perhaps it was rapidly leaving the disc, so that it would soon quit the pure shadow. Perhaps, again, on the other hand, it might be nearing it so much that in a short time it might strike some high point on the invisible hemisphere, which would doubtlessly have ended the journey much to the detriment of the travelers.

A discussion arose on this subject, and Michel Ardan, always ready with an explanation, gave it as his opinion that the projectile, held by the lunar attraction, would end by falling on the surface of the terrestrial globe like an aerolite.

"First of all, my friend," answered Barbicane, "every aerolite does not fall to the earth; it is only a small proportion which do so; and if we had passed into an aerolite, it does not necessarily follow that we should ever reach the surface of the moon."

"But how if we get near enough?" replied Michel.

"Pure mistake," replied Barbicane. "Have you not seen shooting stars rush through the sky by thousands at certain seasons?"

"Yes."

"Well, these stars, or rather corpuscles, only shine when they are heated by gliding over the atmospheric layers. Now, if they enter the atmosphere, they pass at least within forty miles of the earth, but they seldom fall upon it. The same with our projectile. It may approach very near to the moon, and not yet fall upon it."

"But then," asked Michel, "I shall be curious to know how our erring vehicle will act in space?"

"I see but two hypotheses," replied Barbicane, after some moments' reflection.

"What are they?"

"The projectile has the choice between two mathematical curves, and it will follow one or the other according to the speed with which it is animated, and which at this moment I cannot estimate."

"Yes," said Nicholl, "it will follow either a parabola or a hyperbola."

"Just so," replied Barbicane. "With a certain speed it will assume the parabola, and with a greater the hyperbola."

"I like those grand words," exclaimed Michel Ardan; "one knows directly what they mean. And pray what is your parabola, if you please?"

"My friend," answered the captain, "the parabola is a curve of the second order, the result of the section of a cone intersected by a plane parallel to one of the sides."

"Ah! ah!" said Michel, in a satisfied tone.

"It is very nearly," continued Nicholl, "the course described by a bomb launched from a mortar."

"Perfect! And the hyperbola?"

"The hyperbola, Michel, is a curve of the second order, produced by the intersection of a conic surface and a plane parallel to its axis, and constitutes two branches separated one from the other, both tending indefinitely in the two directions."

"Is it possible!" exclaimed Michel Ardan in a serious tone, as if they had told him of some serious event. "What I particularly like in your definition of the hyperbola (I was going to say hyperblague) is that it is still more obscure than the word you pretend to define."

Nicholl and Barbicane cared little for Michel Ardan's fun. They were deep in a scientific discussion. What curve would the projectile follow? was their hobby. One maintained the hyperbola, the other the parabola. They gave each other reasons bristling with x. Their arguments were couched in language which made Michel jump. The discussion was hot, and neither would give up his chosen curve to his adversary.

This scientific dispute lasted so long that it made Michel very impatient.

"Now, gentlemen cosines, will you cease to throw parabolas and hyperbolas at each other's heads? I want to understand the only interesting question in the whole affair. We shall follow one or the other of these curves? Good. But where will they lead us to?"

"Nowhere," replied Nicholl.

"How, nowhere?"

"Evidently," said Barbicane, "they are open curves, which may be prolonged indefinitely."

"Ah, savants!" cried Michel; "and what are either the one or the other to us from the moment we know that they equally lead us into infinite space?"

Barbicane and Nicholl could not forbear smiling. They had just been creating "art for art's sake." Never had so idle a question been raised at such an inopportune moment. The sinister truth remained that, whether hyperbolically or parabolically borne away, the projectile would never again meet either the earth or the moon.

What would become of these bold travelers in the immediate future? If they did not die of hunger, if they did not die of thirst, in some days, when the gas failed, they would die from want of air, unless the cold had killed them first. Still, important as it was to economize the gas, the excessive lowness of the surrounding temperature obliged them to consume a certain quantity. Strictly speaking, they could do without its light, but not without its heat. Fortunately the caloric generated by

Reiset's and Regnaut's apparatus raised the temperature of the interior of the projectile a little, and without much expenditure they were able to keep it bearable.

But observations had now become very difficult. the dampness of the projectile was condensed on the windows and congealed immediately. This cloudiness had to be dispersed continually. In any case they might hope to be able to discover some phenomena of the highest interest.

But up to this time the disc remained dumb and dark. It did not answer the multiplicity of questions put by these ardent minds; a matter which drew this reflection from Michel, apparently a just one:

"If ever we begin this journey over again, we shall do well to choose the time when the moon is at the full."

"Certainly," said Nicholl, "that circumstance will be more favorable. I allow that the moon, immersed in the sun's rays, will not be visible during the transit, but instead we should see the earth, which would be full. And what is more, if we were drawn round the moon, as at this moment, we should at least have the advantage of seeing the invisible part of her disc magnificently lit."

"Well said, Nicholl," replied Michel Ardan. "What do you think, Barbicane?"

"I think this," answered the grave president: "If ever we begin this journey again, we shall start at the same time and under the same conditions. Suppose we had attained our end, would it not have been better to have found continents in broad daylight than a country plunged in utter darkness? Would not our first installation have been made under better circumstances? Yes, evidently. As to the invisible side, we could have visited it in our exploring expeditions on the lunar globe. So that the time of the full moon was well chosen. But we ought to have arrived at the end; and in order to have so arrived, we ought to have suffered no deviation on the road."

"I have nothing to say to that," answered Michel Ardan. "Here is, however, a good opportunity lost of observing the other side of the moon."

But the projectile was now describing in the shadow that incalculable course which no sight-mark would allow them to ascertain. Had its direction been altered, either by the influence of the lunar attraction, or by the action of some unknown star? Barbicane could not say. But a change had taken place in the relative position of the vehicle; and Barbicane verified it about four in the morning.

The change consisted in this, that the base of the projectile had turned toward the moon's surface, and was so held by a perpendicular passing through its axis. The attraction, that is to say the weight, had brought about this alteration. The heaviest part of the projectile inclined toward the invisible disc as if it would fall upon it.

Was it falling? Were the travelers attaining that much desired end? No. And the observation of a sign-point, quite inexplicable in itself, showed Barbicane that his projectile was not nearing the moon, and that it had shifted by following an almost concentric curve.

This point of mark was a luminous brightness, which Nicholl sighted suddenly, on the limit of the horizon formed by the black disc. This point could not be confounded with a star. It was a reddish incandescence which increased by degrees, a decided proof that the projectile was shifting toward it and not falling normally on the surface of the moon.

"A volcano! it is a volcano in action!" cried Nicholl; "a disemboweling of the interior fires of the moon! That world is not quite extinguished."

"Yes, an eruption," replied Barbicane, who was carefully studying the phenomenon through his night glass. "What should it be, if not a volcano?"

"But, then," said Michel Ardan, "in order to maintain that combustion, there must be air. So the atmosphere does surround that part of the moon."

"Perhaps so," replied Barbicane, "but not necessarily.

The volcano, by the decomposition of certain substances, can provide its own oxygen, and thus throw flames into space. It seems to me that the deflagration, by the intense brilliancy of the substances in combustion, is produced in pure oxygen. We must not be in a hurry to proclaim the existence of a lunar atmosphere."

The fiery mountain must have been situated about the 45@ south latitude on the invisible part of the disc; but, to Barbicane's great displeasure, the curve which the projectile was describing was taking it far from the point indicated by the eruption. Thus he could not determine its nature exactly. Half an hour after being sighted, this luminous point had disappeared behind the dark horizon; but the verification of this phenomenon was of considerable consequence in their selenographic studies. It proved that all heat had not yet disappeared from the bowels of this globe; and where heat exists, who can affirm that the vegetable kingdom, nay, even the animal kingdom itself, has not up to this time resisted all destructive influences? The existence of this volcano in eruption, unmistakably seen by these earthly savants, would doubtless give rise to many theories favorable to the grave question of the habitability of the moon.

Barbicane allowed himself to be carried away by these reflections. He forgot himself in a deep reverie in which the mysterious destiny of the lunar world was uppermost. He was seeking to combine together the facts observed up to that time, when a new incident recalled him briskly to reality. This incident was more than a cosmical phenomenon; it was a threatened danger, the consequence of which might be disastrous in the extreme.

Suddenly, in the midst of the ether, in the profound darkness, an enormous mass appeared. It was like a moon, but an incandescent moon whose brilliancy was all the more intolerable as it cut sharply on the frightful darkness of space. This mass, of a circular form, threw a light which filled the projectile. The forms of Barbicane, Nicholl, and Michel Ardan, bathed in its white sheets, assumed that livid spectral appearance which physicians produce with the fictitious light of alcohol impregnated with salt.

"By Jove!" cried Michel Ardan, "we are hideous. What is that ill-conditioned moon?"

"A meteor," replied Barbicane.

"A meteor burning in space?"

"Yes."

This shooting globe suddenly appearing in shadow at a distance of at most 200 miles, ought, according to Barbicane, to have a diameter of 2,000 yards. It advanced at a speed of about one mile and a half per second. It cut the projectile's path and must reach it in some minutes. As it approached it grew to enormous proportions.

Imagine, if possible, the situation of the travelers! It is impossible to describe it. In spite of their courage, their sang-froid, their carelessness of danger, they were mute, motionless with stiffened limbs, a prey to frightful terror. Their projectile, the course of which they could not alter, was rushing straight on this ignited mass, more intense than the open mouth of an oven. It seemed as though they were being precipitated toward an abyss of fire.

Barbicane had seized the hands of his two companions, and all three looked through their half-open eyelids upon that asteroid heated to a white heat. If thought was not destroyed within them, if their brains still worked amid all this awe, they must have given themselves up for lost.

Two minutes after the sudden appearance of the meteor (to them two centuries of anguish) the projectile seemed almost about to strike it, when the globe of fire burst like a bomb, but without making any noise in that void where sound, which is but the agitation of the layers of air, could not be generated.

Nicholl uttered a cry, and he and his companions rushed to the scuttle. What a sight! What pen can describe it? What palette is rich enough in colors to reproduce so magnificent a spectacle?

It was like the opening of a crater, like the scattering of an immense conflagration. Thousands of luminous fragments lit up and irradiated space with their fires. Every size, every color, was there intermingled. There were rays of yellow and pale yellow, red, green, gray—a crown of fireworks of all colors. Of the enormous and much-dreaded globe there remained nothing but these fragments carried in all directions, now become asteroids in their turn, some flaming like a sword, some surrounded by a whitish cloud, and others leaving behind them trains of brilliant cosmical dust.

These incandescent blocks crossed and struck each other, scattering still smaller fragments, some of which struck the projectile. Its left scuttle was even cracked by a violent shock. It seemed to be floating amid a hail of howitzer shells, the smallest of which might destroy it instantly.

The light which saturated the ether was so wonderfully intense, that Michel, drawing Barbicane and Nicholl to his window, exclaimed, "The invisible moon, visible at last!"

And through a luminous emanation, which lasted some seconds, the whole three caught a glimpse of that mysterious disc which the eye of man now saw for the first time. What could they distinguish at a distance which they could not estimate? Some lengthened bands along the disc, real clouds formed in the midst of a very confined atmosphere, from which emerged not only all the mountains, but also projections of less importance; its circles, its yawning craters, as capriciously placed as on the visible surface. Then immense spaces, no longer arid plains, but real seas, oceans, widely distributed, reflecting on their liquid surface all the dazzling magic of the fires of space; and, lastly, on the surface of the continents, large dark masses, looking like immense forests under the rapid illumination of a brilliance.

Was it an illusion, a mistake, an optical illusion? Could they give a scientific assent to an observation so superficially obtained? Dared they pronounce upon the question of its habitability after so slight a glimpse of the invisible disc?

But the lightnings in space subsided by degrees; its accidental brilliancy died away; the asteroids dispersed in different directions and were extinguished in the distance.

The ether returned to its accustomed darkness; the stars, eclipsed for a moment, again twinkled in the firmament, and the disc, so hastily discerned, was again buried in impenetrable night.

XVI

THE SOUTHERN HEMISPHERE

THE projectile had just escaped a terrible danger, and a very unforseen one. Who would have thought of such an encounter with meteors? These erring bodies might create serious perils for the travelers. They were to them so many sandbanks upon that sea of ether which, less fortunate than sailors, they could not escape. But did these adventurers complain of space? No, not since nature had given them the splendid sight of a cosmical meteor bursting from expansion, since this inimitable firework, which no Ruggieri could imitate, had lit up for some seconds the invisible glory of the moon. In that flash, continents, seas, and forests had become visible to them. Did an atmosphere, then, bring to this unknown face its life-giving atoms? Questions still insoluble, and forever closed against human curiosity!

It was then half-past three in the afternoon. The projectile was following its curvilinear direction round the moon. Had its course again been altered by the meteor? It was to be feared so. But the projectile must describe a curve unalterably determined by the laws of mechanical reasoning. Barbicane was inclined to believe that this curve would be rather a parabola than a hyperbola. But admitting the parabola, the projectile must quickly have passed through the cone of shadow projected into space opposite the sun. This cone, indeed, is very narrow, the angular diameter of the moon being so little when compared with the diameter of the orb of day; and up to this time the projectile had been floating in this deep shadow. Whatever had been its speed (and it could not have been insignificant), its period of occultation continued. That was evident, but perhaps that would not have been the case in a supposedly rigidly parabolical trajectory—a new problem which tormented Barbicane's brain, imprisoned as he was in a circle of unknowns which he could not unravel.

Neither of the travelers thought of taking an instant's repose. Each one watched for an unexpected fact, which might throw some new light on their uranographic studies. About five o'clock, Michel Ardan distributed, under the name of dinner, some pieces of bread and cold meat, which were quickly swallowed without either of them abandoning their scuttle, the glass of which was incessantly encrusted by the condensation of vapor.

About forty-five minutes past five in the evening, Nicholl, armed with his glass, sighted toward the southern border of the moon, and in the direction followed by the projectile, some bright points cut upon the dark shield of the sky. They looked like a succession of sharp points lengthened into a tremulous line. They were very bright. Such appeared the terminal line of the moon when in one of her octants.

They could not be mistaken. It was no longer a simple meteor. This luminous ridge had neither color nor motion. Nor was it a volcano in eruption. And Barbicane did not hesitate to pronounce upon it.

"The sun!" he exclaimed.

"What! the sun?" answered Nicholl and Michel Ardan.

"Yes, my friends, it is the radiant orb itself lighting up the summit of the mountains situated on the southern borders of the moon. We are evidently nearing the south pole."

"After having passed the north pole," replied Michel. "We have made the circuit of our satellite, then?"

"Yes, my good Michel."

"Then, no more hyperbolas, no more parabolas, no more open curves to fear?"

"No, but a closed curve."

"Which is called—"

"An ellipse. Instead of losing itself in interplanetary space, it is probable that the projectile will describe an elliptical orbit around the moon."

"Indeed!"

"And that it will become her satellite."

"Moon of the moon!" cried Michel Ardan.

"Only, I would have you observe, my worthy friend," replied Barbicane, "that we are none the less lost for that."

"Yes, in another manner, and much more pleasantly," answered the careless Frenchman with his most amiable smile.

XVII

TYCHO

AT six in the evening the projectile passed the south pole at less than forty miles off, a distance equal to that already reached at the north pole. The elliptical curve was being rigidly carried out.

At this moment the travelers once more entered the blessed rays of the sun. They saw once more those stars which move slowly from east to west. The radiant orb was saluted by a triple hurrah. With its light it also sent heat, which soon pierced the metal walls. The glass resumed its accustomed appearance. The layers of ice melted as if by enchantment; and immediately, for economy's sake, the gas was put out, the air apparatus alone consuming its usual quantity.

"Ah!" said Nicholl, "these rays of heat are good. With what impatience must the Selenites wait the reappearance of the orb of day."

"Yes," replied Michel Ardan, "imbibing as it were the brilliant ether, light and heat, all life is contained in them."

At this moment the bottom of the projectile deviated somewhat from the lunar surface, in order to follow the slightly lengthened elliptical orbit. From this point, had the earth been at the full, Barbicane and his companions could have seen it, but immersed in the sun's irradiation she was quite invisible. Another spectacle attracted their attention, that of the southern part of the moon, brought by the glasses to within 450 yards. They did not again leave the scuttles, and noted every detail of this fantastical continent.

Mounts Doerful and Leibnitz formed two separate groups very near the south pole. The first group extended from the pole to the eighty-fourth parallel, on the eastern part of the orb; the second occupied the eastern border, extending from the 65@ of latitude to the pole.

On their capriciously formed ridge appeared dazzling sheets, as mentioned by Pere Secchi. With more certainty than the illustrious Roman astronomer, Barbicane was enabled to recognize their nature.

"They are snow," he exclaimed.

"Snow?" repeated Nicholl.

"Yes, Nicholl, snow; the surface of which is deeply frozen. See how they reflect the luminous rays. Cooled lava would never give out such intense reflection. There must then be water, there must be air on the moon. As little as you please, but the fact can no longer be contested." No, it could not be. And if ever Barbicane should see the earth again, his notes will bear witness to this great fact in his selenographic observations.

These mountains of Doerful and Leibnitz rose in the midst of plains of a medium extent, which were bounded by an indefinite succession of circles and annular ramparts. These two chains are the only ones met with in this region of circles. Comparatively but slightly marked, they throw up here and there some sharp points, the highest summit of which attains an altitude of 24,600 feet.

But the projectile was high above all this landscape, and the projections disappeared in the intense brilliancy of the disc. And to the eyes of the travelers there reappeared that original aspect of the lunar landscapes, raw in tone, without gradation of colors, and without degrees of shadow, roughly black and white, from the want of diffusion of light.

But the sight of this desolate world did not fail to captivate them by its very strangeness. They were moving over this region as if they had been borne on the breath of some storm, watching heights defile under their feet, piercing the cavities with their eyes, going down into the rifts, climbing the ramparts, sounding these mysterious holes, and leveling all cracks. But no trace of vegetation, no appearance of cities; nothing but stratification, beds of lava, overflowings polished like immense mirrors, reflecting the sun's rays with overpowering brilliancy. Nothing belonging to a living world—everything to a dead world, where avalanches, rolling from the summits of the mountains, would disperse noiselessly at the bottom of the abyss, retaining the motion, but wanting the sound. In any case it was the image of death, without its being possible even to say that life had ever existed there.

Michel Ardan, however, thought he recognized a heap of ruins, to which he drew Barbicane's attention. It was about the 80th parallel, in 30@ longitude. This heap of stones, rather regularly placed, represented a vast fortress, overlooking a long rift, which in former days had served as a bed to the rivers of prehistorical times. Not far from that, rose to a height of 17,400 feet the annular mountain of Short, equal to the Asiatic Caucasus. Michel Ardan, with his accustomed ardor, maintained "the evidences" of his fortress. Beneath it he discerned the dismantled ramparts of a town; here the still intact arch of a portico, there two or three columns lying under their base; farther on, a succession of arches which must have supported the conduit of an aqueduct; in another part the sunken pillars of a gigantic bridge, run into the thickest parts of the rift. He distinguished all this, but with so much imagination in his glance, and through glasses so fantastical, that we must mistrust his observation. But who could affirm, who would dare to say, that the amiable fellow did not really see that which his two companions would not see?

Moments were too precious to be sacrificed in idle discussion. The selenite city, whether imaginary or not, had already disappeared afar off. The distance of the projectile from the lunar disc was on the increase, and the details of the soil were being lost in a confused jumble. The reliefs, the circles, the craters, and the plains alone remained, and still showed their boundary lines distinctly. At this moment, to the left, lay extended one of the finest circles of lunar orography, one of the curiosities of this continent. It was Newton, which Barbicane recognized without trouble, by referring to the Mappa Selenographica.

Newton is situated in exactly 77@ south latitude, and 16@ east longitude. It forms an annular crater, the ramparts of which, rising to a height of 21,300 feet, seemed to be impassable.

Barbicane made his companions observe that the height of this mountain above the surrounding plain was far from equaling the depth of its crater. This enormous hole was beyond all measurement, and formed a gloomy abyss, the bottom of which the sun's rays could never reach. There, according to Humboldt, reigns utter darkness, which the light of the sun and the earth cannot break. Mythologists could well have made it the mouth of hell.

"Newton," said Barbicane, "is the most perfect type of these annular mountains, of which the earth possesses no sample. They prove that the moon's formation, by means of cooling, is due to violent causes; for while, under the pressure of internal fires the reliefs rise to considerable height, the depths withdraw far below the lunar level."

"I do not dispute the fact," replied Michel Ardan.

Some minutes after passing Newton, the projectile directly overlooked the annular mountains of Moret. It skirted at some distance the summits of Blancanus, and at about half-past seven in the evening reached the circle of Clavius.

This circle, one of the most remarkable of the disc, is situated in 58@ south latitude, and 15@ east longitude. Its height is estimated at 22,950 feet. The travelers, at a distance of twenty-four miles (reduced to four by their glasses) could admire this vast crater in its entirety.

"Terrestrial volcanoes," said Barbicane, "are but mole-hills compared with those of the moon. Measuring the old craters formed by the first eruptions of Vesuvius and Etna, we find them little more than three miles in breadth. In France the circle of Cantal measures six miles across; at Ceyland the circle of the island is forty miles, which is considered the largest on the globe. What are these diameters against that of Clavius, which we overlook at this moment?"

"What is its breadth?" asked Nicholl.

"It is 150 miles," replied Barbicane. "This circle is certainly the most important on the moon, but many others measure 150, 100, or 75 miles."

"Ah! my friends," exclaimed Michel, "can you picture to yourselves what this now peaceful orb of night must have been when its craters, filled with thunderings, vomited at the same time smoke and tongues of flame. What a wonderful spectacle then, and now what decay! This moon is nothing more than a thin carcase of fireworks, whose squibs, rockets, serpents, and suns, after a superb brilliancy, have left but sadly broken cases. Who can say the cause, the reason, the motive force of these cataclysms?"

Barbicane was not listening to Michel Ardan; he was contemplating these ramparts of Clavius, formed by large mountains spread over several miles. At the bottom of the immense cavity burrowed hundreds of small extinguished craters, riddling the soil like a colander, and overlooked by a peak 15,000 feet high.

Around the plain appeared desolate. Nothing so arid as these reliefs, nothing so sad as these ruins of mountains, and (if we may so express ourselves) these fragments of peaks and mountains which strewed the soil. The satellite seemed to have burst at this spot.

The projectile was still advancing, and this movement did not subside. Circles, craters, and uprooted mountains succeeded each other incessantly. No more plains; no more seas. A never ending Switzerland and Norway. And lastly, in the canter of this region of crevasses, the most splendid mountain on the lunar disc, the dazzling Tycho, in which posterity will ever preserve the name of the illustrious Danish astronomer.

In observing the full moon in a cloudless sky no one has failed to remark this brilliant point of the southern hemisphere. Michel Ardan used every metaphor that his imagination could supply to designate it by. To him this Tycho was a focus of light, a center of irradiation, a crater vomiting rays. It was the tire of a brilliant wheel, an asteria enclosing the disc with its silver tentacles, an enormous eye filled with flames, a glory carved for Pluto's head, a star launched by the Creator's hand, and crushed against the face of the moon!

Tycho forms such a concentration of light that the inhabitants of the earth can see it without glasses, though at a distance of 240,000 miles! Imagine, then, its intensity to the eye of observers placed at a distance of only fifty miles! Seen through this pure ether, its brilliancy was so intolerable that Barbicane and his friends were obliged to blacken their glasses with the gas smoke before they could bear the splendor. Then silent, scarcely uttering an interjection of admiration, they gazed, they contemplated. All their feelings, all their impressions, were concentrated in that look, as under any violent emotion all life is concentrated at the heart.

Tycho belongs to the system of radiating mountains, like Aristarchus and Copernicus; but it is of all the most complete and decided, showing unquestionably the frightful volcanic action to which the formation of the moon is due. Tycho is situated in 43@ south latitude, and 12@ east longitude. Its center is occupied by a crater fifty miles broad. It assumes a slightly elliptical form, and is surrounded by an enclosure of annular ramparts, which on the east and west overlook the outer plain from a height of

15,000 feet. It is a group of Mont Blancs, placed round one common center and crowned by radiating beams.

What this incomparable mountain really is, with all the projections converging toward it, and the interior excrescences of its crater, photography itself could never represent. Indeed, it is during the full moon that Tycho is seen in all its splendor. Then all shadows disappear, the foreshortening of perspective disappears, and all proofs become white—a disagreeable fact: for this strange region would have been marvelous if reproduced with photographic exactness. It is but a group of hollows, craters, circles, a network of crests; then, as far as the eye could see, a whole volcanic network cast upon this encrusted soil. One can then understand that the bubbles of this central eruption have kept their first form. Crystallized by cooling, they have stereotyped that aspect which the moon formerly presented when under the Plutonian forces.

The distance which separated the travelers from the annular summits of Tycho was not so great but that they could catch the principal details. Even on the causeway forming the fortifications of Tycho, the mountains hanging on to the interior and exterior sloping flanks rose in stories like gigantic terraces. They appeared to be higher by 300 or 400 feet to the west than to the east. No system of terrestrial encampment could equal these natural fortifications. A town built at the bottom of this circular cavity would have been utterly inaccessible.

Inaccessible and wonderfully extended over this soil covered with picturesque projections! Indeed, nature had not left the bottom of this crater flat and empty. It possessed its own peculiar orography, a mountainous system, making it a world in itself. The travelers could distinguish clearly cones, central hills, remarkable positions of the soil, naturally placed to receive the chefs-d'oeuvre of Selenite architecture. There was marked out the place for a temple, here the ground of a forum, on this spot the plan of a palace, in another the plateau for a citadel; the whole overlooked by a central mountain of 1,500 feet. A vast circle, in which ancient Rome could have been held in its entirety ten times over.

"Ah!" exclaimed Michel Ardan, enthusiastic at the sight; "what a grand town might be constructed within that ring of mountains! A quiet city, a peaceful refuge, beyond all human misery. How calm and isolated those misanthropes, those haters of humanity might live there, and all who have a distaste for social life!"

"All! It would be too small for them," replied Barbicane simply.

XVIII

GRAVE QUESTIONS

BUT the projectile had passed the enceinte of Tycho, and Barbicane and his two companions watched with scrupulous attention the brilliant rays which the celebrated mountain shed so curiously over the horizon.

What was this radiant glory? What geological phenomenon had designed these ardent beams? This question occupied Barbicane's mind.

Under his eyes ran in all directions luminous furrows, raised at the edges and concave in the center, some twelve miles, others thirty miles broad. These brilliant trains extended in some places to within 600 miles of Tycho, and seemed to cover, particularly toward the east, the northeast and the north, the half of the southern hemisphere. One of these jets extended as far as the circle of Neander, situated on the 40th meridian. Another, by a slight curve, furrowed the "Sea of Nectar," breaking against the chain of Pyrenees, after a circuit of 800 miles. Others, toward the west, covered the "Sea of Clouds" and the "Sea of Humors" with a luminous network. What was the origin of these sparkling rays, which shone on the plains as well as on the reliefs, at whatever height they might be? All started from a common center, the crater of Tycho. They sprang from him. Herschel attributed their brilliancy to currents of lava congealed by the cold; an opinion, however, which has not been generally adopted. Other astronomers have seen in these inexplicable rays a kind of moraines, rows of erratic blocks, which had been thrown up at the period of Tycho's formation.

"And why not?" asked Nicholl of Barbicane, who was relating and rejecting these different opinions.

"Because the regularity of these luminous lines, and the violence necessary to carry volcanic matter to such distances, is inexplicable."

"Eh! by Jove!" replied Michel Ardan, "it seems easy enough to me to explain the origin of these rays."

"Indeed?" said Barbicane.

"Indeed," continued Michel. "It is enough to say that it is a vast star, similar to that produced by a ball or a stone thrown at a square of glass!"

"Well!" replied Barbicane, smiling. "And what hand would be powerful enough to throw a ball to give such a shock as that?"

"The hand is not necessary," answered Nicholl, not at all confounded; "and as to the stone, let us suppose it to be a comet."

"Ah! those much-abused comets!" exclaimed Barbicane. "My brave Michel, your explanation is not bad; but your comet is useless. The shock which produced that rent must have some from the inside of the star. A violent contraction of the lunar crust, while cooling, might suffice to imprint this gigantic star."

"A contraction! something like a lunar stomach-ache." said Michel Ardan.

"Besides," added Barbicane, "this opinion is that of an English savant, Nasmyth, and it seems to me to sufficiently explain the radiation of these mountains."

"That Nasmyth was no fool!" replied Michel.

Long did the travelers, whom such a sight could never weary, admire the splendors of Tycho. Their projectile, saturated with luminous gleams in the double irradiation of sun and moon, must have appeared like an incandescent globe. They had passed suddenly from excessive cold to intense heat. Nature was thus preparing them to become Selenites. Become Selenites! That idea brought up once more the question of the habitability of the moon. After what they had seen, could the travelers solve it? Would they decide for or against it? Michel Ardan persuaded his two friends to form an opinion, and asked them directly if they thought that men and animals were represented in the lunar world.

"I think that we can answer," said Barbicane; "but according to my idea the question ought not to be put in that form. I ask it to be put differently."

"Put it your own way," replied Michel.

"Here it is," continued Barbicane. "The problem is a double one, and requires a double solution. Is the moon habitable? Has the moon ever been inhabitable?"

"Good!" replied Nicholl. "First let us see whether the moon is habitable."

"To tell the truth, I know nothing about it," answered Michel.

"And I answer in the negative," continued Barbicane. "In her actual state, with her surrounding atmosphere certainly very much reduced, her seas for the most part dried up, her insufficient supply of water restricted, vegetation, sudden alternations of cold and heat, her days and nights of 354 hours—the moon does not seem habitable to me, nor does she seem propitious to animal development, nor sufficient for the wants of existence as we understand it."

"Agreed," replied Nicholl. "But is not the moon habitable for creatures differently organized from ourselves?"

"That question is more difficult to answer, but I will try; and I ask Nicholl if motion appears to him to be a necessary result of life, whatever be its organization?"

"Without a doubt!" answered Nicholl.

"Then, my worthy companion, I would answer that we have observed the lunar continent at a distance of 500 yards at most, and that nothing seemed to us to move on the moon's surface. The presence of any kind of life would have been betrayed by its attendant marks, such as divers buildings, and even by ruins. And what have we seen? Everywhere and always the geological works of nature, never the work of man. If, then, there exist representatives of the animal kingdom on the moon, they must have fled to those unfathomable cavities which the eye cannot reach; which I cannot admit, for they must have left traces of their passage on those plains which the atmosphere must cover, however slightly raised it may be. These traces are nowhere visible. There remains but one hypothesis, that of a living race to which motion, which is life, is foreign."

"One might as well say, living creatures which do not live," replied Michel.

"Just so," said Barbicane, "which for us has no meaning."

"Then we may form our opinion?" said Michel.

"Yes," replied Nicholl.

"Very well," continued Michel Ardan, "the Scientific Commission assembled in the projectile of the Gun Club, after having founded their argument on facts recently observed, decide unanimously upon the question of the habitability of the moon—'No! the moon is not habitable.'"

This decision was consigned by President Barbicane to his notebook, where the process of the sitting of the 6th of December may be seen.

"Now," said Nicholl, "let us attack the second question, an indispensable complement of the first. I ask the honorable commission, if the moon is not habitable, has she ever been inhabited, Citizen Barbicane?"

"My friends," replied Barbicane, "I did not undertake this journey in order to form an opinion on the past habitability of our satellite; but I will add that our personal observations only confirm me in this opinion. I believe, indeed I affirm, that the moon has been inhabited by a human race organized like our own; that she has produced animals anatomically formed like the terrestrial animals: but I add that these races, human and animal, have had their day, and are now forever extinct!"

"Then," asked Michel, "the moon must be older than the earth?"

"No!" said Barbicane decidedly, "but a world which has grown old quicker, and whose formation and deformation have been more rapid. Relatively, the organizing force of matter has been much more violent in the interior of the moon than in the interior of the terrestrial globe. The actual state of this cracked, twisted, and burst disc abundantly proves this. The moon and the earth were nothing but gaseous masses originally. These gases have passed into a liquid state under different influences, and the solid masses have been formed later. But most certainly our sphere was still gaseous or liquid, when the moon was solidified by cooling, and had become habitable."

"I believe it," said Nicholl.

"Then," continued Barbicane, "an atmosphere surrounded it, the waters contained within this gaseous envelope could not evaporate. Under the influence of air, water, light, solar heat, and central heat, vegetation took possession of the continents prepared to receive it, and certainly life showed itself about this period, for nature does not expend herself in vain; and a world so wonderfully formed for habitation must necessarily be inhabited."

"But," said Nicholl, "many phenomena inherent in our satellite might cramp the expansion of the animal and vegetable kingdom. For example, its days and nights of 354 hours?"

"At the terrestrial poles they last six months," said Michel.

"An argument of little value, since the poles are not inhabited."

"Let us observe, my friends," continued Barbicane, "that if in the actual state of the moon its long nights and long days created differences of temperature insupportable to organization, it was not so at the historical period of time. The atmosphere enveloped the disc with a fluid mantle; vapor deposited itself in the shape of clouds; this natural screen tempered the ardor of the solar rays, and retained the nocturnal radiation. Light, like heat, can diffuse itself in the air; hence an equality between the influences which no longer exists, now that atmosphere has almost entirely disappeared. And now I am going to astonish you."

"Astonish us?" said Michel Ardan.

"I firmly believe that at the period when the moon was inhabited, the nights and days did not last 354 hours!"

"And why?" asked Nicholl quickly.

"Because most probably then the rotary motion of the moon upon her axis was not equal to her revolution, an equality which presents each part of her disc during fifteen days to the action of the solar rays."

"Granted," replied Nicholl, "but why should not these two motions have been equal, as they are really so?"

"Because that equality has only been determined by terrestrial attraction. And who can say that this attraction was powerful enough to alter the motion of the moon at that period when the earth was still fluid?"

"Just so," replied Nicholl; "and who can say that the moon has always been a satellite of the earth?"

"And who can say," exclaimed Michel Ardan, "that the moon did not exist before the earth?"

Their imaginations carried them away into an indefinite field of hypothesis. Barbicane sought to restrain them.

"Those speculations are too high," said he; "problems utterly insoluble. Do not let us enter upon them. Let us only admit the insufficiency of the primordial attraction; and then by the inequality of the two motions of rotation and revolution, the days and nights could have succeeded each other on the moon as they succeed each other on the earth. Besides, even without these conditions, life was possible."

"And so," asked Michel Ardan, "humanity has disappeared from the moon?"

"Yes," replied Barbicane, "after having doubtless remained persistently for millions of centuries; by degrees the atmosphere becoming rarefied, the disc became uninhabitable, as the terrestrial globe will one day become by cooling."

"By cooling?"

"Certainly," replied Barbicane; "as the internal fires became extinguished, and the incandescent matter concentrated itself, the lunar crust cooled. By degrees the consequences of these phenomena showed themselves in the disappearance of organized beings, and by the disappearance of vegetation. Soon the atmosphere was rarefied, probably withdrawn by terrestrial attraction; then aerial departure of respirable air, and disappearance of water by means of evaporation. At this period the moon becoming uninhabitable, was no longer inhabited. It was a dead world, such as we see it to-day."

"And you say that the same fate is in store for the earth?"

"Most probably."

"But when?"

"When the cooling of its crust shall have made it uninhabitable."

"And have they calculated the time which our unfortunate sphere will take to cool?"

"Certainly."

"And you know these calculations?"

"Perfectly."

"But speak, then, my clumsy savant," exclaimed Michel Ardan, "for you make me boil with impatience!"

"Very well, my good Michel," replied Barbicane quietly; "we know what diminution of temperature the earth undergoes in the lapse of a century. And according to certain calculations, this mean temperature will after a period of 400,000 years, be brought down to zero!"

"Four hundred thousand years!" exclaimed Michel. "Ah! I breathe again. Really I was frightened to hear you; I imagined that we had not more than 50,000 years to live."

Barbicane and Nicholl could not help laughing at their companion's uneasiness. Then Nicholl, who wished to end the discussion, put the second question, which had just been considered again.

"Has the moon been inhabited?" he asked.

The answer was unanimously in the affirmative. But during this discussion, fruitful in somewhat hazardous theories, the projectile was rapidly leaving the moon: the lineaments faded away from the travelers' eyes, mountains were confused in the distance; and of all the wonderful, strange, and fantastical form of the earth's satellite, there soon remained nothing but the imperishable remembrance.

XIX

A STRUGGLE AGAINST THE IMPOSSIBLE

FOR a long time Barbicane and his companions looked silently and sadly upon that world which they had only seen from a distance, as Moses saw the land of Canaan, and which they were leaving without a possibility of ever returning to it. The projectile's position with regard to the moon had altered, and the base was now turned to the earth.

This change, which Barbicane verified, did not fail to surprise them. If the projectile was to gravitate round the satellite in an elliptical orbit, why was not its heaviest part turned toward it, as the moon turns hers to the earth? That was a difficult point.

In watching the course of the projectile they could see that on leaving the moon it followed a course analogous to that traced in approaching her. It was describing a very long ellipse, which would most likely extend to the point of equal attraction, where the influences of the earth and its satellite are neutralized.

Such was the conclusion which Barbicane very justly drew from facts already observed, a conviction which his two friends shared with him.

"And when arrived at this dead point, what will become of us?" asked Michel Ardan.

"We don't know," replied Barbicane.

"But one can draw some hypotheses, I suppose?"

"Two," answered Barbicane; "either the projectile's speed will be insufficient, and it will remain forever immovable on this line of double attraction—"

"I prefer the other hypothesis, whatever it may be," interrupted Michel.

"Or," continued Barbicane, "its speed will be sufficient, and it will continue its elliptical course, to gravitate forever around the orb of night."

"A revolution not at all consoling," said Michel, "to pass to the state of humble servants to a moon whom we are accustomed to look upon as our own handmaid. So that is the fate in store for us?"

Neither Barbicane nor Nicholl answered.

"You do not answer," continued Michel impatiently.

"There is nothing to answer," said Nicholl.

"Is there nothing to try?"

"No," answered Barbicane. "Do you pretend to fight against the impossible?"

"Why not? Do one Frenchman and two Americans shrink from such a word?"

"But what would you do?"

"Subdue this motion which is bearing us away."

"Subdue it?"

"Yes," continued Michel, getting animated, "or else alter it, and employ it to the accomplishment of our own ends."

"And how?"

"That is your affair. If artillerymen are not masters of their projectile they are not artillerymen. If the projectile is to command the gunner, we had better ram the gunner into the gun. My faith! fine savants! who do not know what is to become of us after inducing me—"

"Inducing you!" cried Barbicane and Nicholl. "Inducing you! What do you mean by that?"

"No recrimination," said Michel. "I do not complain, the trip has pleased me, and the projectile agrees with me; but let us do all that is humanly possible to do the fall somewhere, even if only on the moon."

"We ask no better, my worthy Michel," replied Barbicane, "but means fail us."

"We cannot alter the motion of the projectile?"

"No."

"Nor diminish its speed?"

"No."

"Not even by lightening it, as they lighten an overloaded vessel?"

"What would you throw out?" said Nicholl. "We have no ballast on board; and indeed it seems to me that if lightened it would go much quicker."

"Slower."

"Quicker."

"Neither slower nor quicker," said Barbicane, wishing to make his two friends agree; "for we float is space, and must no longer consider specific weight."

"Very well," cried Michel Ardan in a decided voice; "then their remains but one thing to do."

"What is it?" asked Nicholl.

"Breakfast," answered the cool, audacious Frenchman, who always brought up this solution at the most difficult juncture.

In any case, if this operation had no influence on the projectile's course, it could at least be tried without inconvenience, and even with success from a stomachic point of view. Certainly Michel had none but good ideas.

They breakfasted then at two in the morning; the hour mattered little. Michel served his usual repast, crowned by a glorious bottle drawn from his private cellar. If ideas did not crowd on their brains, we must despair of the Chambertin of 1853. The repast finished, observation began again. Around the projectile, at an invariable distance, were the objects which had been thrown out. Evidently, in its translatory motion round the moon, it had not passed through any atmosphere, for the specific weight of these different objects would have checked their relative speed.

On the side of the terrestrial sphere nothing was to be seen. The earth was but a day old, having been new the night before at twelve; and two days must elapse before its crescent, freed from the solar rays, would serve as a clock to the Selenites, as in its rotary movement each of its points after twenty-four hours repasses the same lunar meridian.

On the moon's side the sight was different; the orb shone in all her splendor amid innumerable constellations, whose purity could not be troubled by her rays. On the disc, the plains were already returning to the dark tint which is seen from the earth. The other part of the nimbus remained brilliant, and in the midst of this general brilliancy Tycho shone prominently like a sun.

Barbicane had no means of estimating the projectile's speed, but reasoning showed that it must uniformly decrease, according to the laws of mechanical reasoning. Having admitted that the projectile was describing an orbit around the moon, this orbit must necessarily be elliptical; science proves that it must be so. No motive body circulating round an

attracting body fails in this law. Every orbit described in space is elliptical. And why should the projectile of the Gun Club escape this natural
arrangement? In elliptical orbits, the attracting body always occupies
one of the foci; so that at one moment the satellite is nearer, and at another farther from the orb around which it gravitates. When the earth
is nearest the sun she is in her perihelion; and in her aphelion at the
farthest point. Speaking of the moon, she is nearest to the earth in her
perigee, and farthest from it in her apogee. To use analogous expressions, with which the astronomers' language is enriched, if the projectile
remains as a satellite of the moon, we must say that it is in its "apose-
lene" at its farthest point, and in its "periselene" at its nearest. In the
latter case, the projectile would attain its maximum of speed; and in the
former its minimum. It was evidently moving toward its aposelenitical
point; and Barbicane had reason to think that its speed would decrease
up to this point, and then increase by degrees as it neared the moon. This
speed would even become nil, if this point joined that of equal attraction. Barbicane studied the consequences of these different situations,
and thinking what inference he could draw from them, when he was
roughly disturbed by a cry from Michel Ardan.

"By Jove!" he exclaimed, "I must admit we are down-right simpletons!"

"I do not say we are not," replied Barbicane; "but why?"

"Because we have a very simple means of checking this speed which is
bearing us from the moon, and we do not use it!"

"And what is the means?"

"To use the recoil contained in our rockets."

"Done!" said Nicholl.

"We have not used this force yet," said Barbicane, "it is true, but we
will do so."

"When?" asked Michel.

"When the time comes. Observe, my friends, that in the position occupied by the projectile, an oblique position with regard to the lunar disc,
our rockets, in slightly altering its direction, might turn it from the moon
instead of drawing it nearer?"

"Just so," replied Michel.

"Let us wait, then. By some inexplicable influence, the projectile is
turning its base toward the earth. It is probable that at the point of equal
attraction, its conical cap will be directed rigidly toward the moon; at that
moment we may hope that its speed will be nil; then will be the moment
to act, and with the influence of our rockets we may perhaps provoke a fall
directly on the surface of the lunar disc."

"Bravo!" said Michel. "What we did not do, what we could not do on our first passage at the dead point, because the projectile was then endowed with too great a speed."

"Very well reasoned," said Nicholl.

"Let us wait patiently," continued Barbicane. "Putting every chance on our side, and after having so much despaired, I may say I think we shall gain our end."

This conclusion was a signal for Michel Ardan's hips and hurrahs. And none of the audacious boobies remembered the question that they themselves had solved in the negative. No! the moon is not inhabited; no! the moon is probably not habitable. And yet they were going to try everything to reach her.

One single question remained to be solved. At what precise moment the projectile would reach the point of equal attraction, on which the travelers must play their last card. In order to calculate this to within a few seconds, Barbicane had only to refer to his notes, and to reckon the different heights taken on the lunar parallels. Thus the time necessary to travel over the distance between the dead point and the south pole would be equal to the distance separating the north pole from the dead point. The hours representing the time traveled over were carefully noted, and the calculation was easy. Barbicane found that this point would be reached at one in the morning on the night of the 7th-8th of December. So that, if nothing interfered with its course, it would reach the given point in twenty-two hours.

The rockets had primarily been placed to check the fall of the projectile upon the moon, and now they were going to employ them for a directly contrary purpose. In any case they were ready, and they had only to wait for the moment to set fire to them.

"Since there is nothing else to be done," said Nicholl, "I make a proposition."

"What is it?" asked Barbicane.

"I propose to go to sleep."

"What a motion!" exclaimed Michel Ardan.

"It is forty hours since we closed our eyes," said Nicholl. "Some hours of sleep will restore our strength."

"Never," interrupted Michel.

"Well," continued Nicholl, "every one to his taste; I shall go to sleep." And stretching himself on the divan, he soon snored like a forty-eight pounder.

"That Nicholl has a good deal of sense," said Barbicane; "presently I shall follow his example." Some moments after his continued bass supported the captain's baritone.

"Certainly," said Michel Ardan, finding himself alone, "these practical people have sometimes most opportune ideas."

And with his long legs stretched out, and his great arms folded under his head, Michel slept in his turn.

But this sleep could be neither peaceful nor lasting, the minds of these three men were too much occupied, and some hours after, about seven in the morning, all three were on foot at the same instant.

The projectile was still leaving the moon, and turning its conical part more and more toward her.

An explicable phenomenon, but one which happily served Barbicane's ends.

Seventeen hours more, and the moment for action would have arrived.

The day seemed long. However bold the travelers might be, they were greatly impressed by the approach of that moment which would decide all—either precipitate their fall on to the moon, or forever chain them in an immutable orbit. They counted the hours as they passed too slow for their wish; Barbicane and Nicholl were obstinately plunged in their calculations, Michel going and coming between the narrow walls, and watching that impassive moon with a longing eye.

At times recollections of the earth crossed their minds. They saw once more their friends of the Gun Club, and the dearest of all, J. T. Maston. At that moment, the honorable secretary must be filling his post on the Rocky Mountains. If he could see the projectile through the glass of his gigantic telescope, what would he think? After seeing it disappear behind the moon's south pole, he would see them reappear by the north pole! They must therefore be a satellite of a satellite! Had J. T. Maston given this unexpected news to the world? Was this the denouement of this great enterprise?

But the day passed without incident. The terrestrial midnight arrived. The 8th of December was beginning. One hour more, and the point of equal attraction would be reached. What speed would then animate the projectile? They could not estimate it. But no error could vitiate Barbicane's calculations. At one in the morning this speed ought to be and would be nil.

Besides, another phenomenon would mark the projectile's stopping-point on the neutral line. At that spot the two attractions, lunar and terrestrial, would be annulled. Objects would "weigh" no more. This singular fact, which had surprised Barbicane and his companions so much in going, would be repeated on their return under the very same conditions. At this precise moment they must act.

Already the projectile's conical top was sensibly turned toward the lunar disc, presented in such a way as to utilize the whole of the recoil produced by the pressure of the rocket apparatus. The chances were in favor of the travelers. If its speed was utterly annulled on this dead point, a decided movement toward the moon would suffice, however slight, to determine its fall.

"Five minutes to one," said Nicholl.

"All is ready," replied Michel Ardan, directing a lighted match to the flame of the gas.

"Wait!" said Barbicane, holding his chronometer in his hand.

At that moment weight had no effect. The travelers felt in themselves the entire disappearance of it. They were very near the neutral point, if they did not touch it.

"One o'clock," said Barbicane.

Michel Ardan applied the lighted match to a train in communication with the rockets. No detonation was heard in the inside, for there was no air. But, through the scuttles, Barbicane saw a prolonged smoke, the flames of which were immediately extinguished.

The projectile sustained a certain shock, which was sensibly felt in the interior.

The three friends looked and listened without speaking, and scarcely breathing. One might have heard the beating of their hearts amid this perfect silence.

"Are we falling?" asked Michel Ardan, at length.

"No," said Nicholl, "since the bottom of the projectile is not turning to the lunar disc!"

At this moment, Barbicane, quitting his scuttle, turned to his two companions. He was frightfully pale, his forehead wrinkled, and his lips contracted.

"We are falling!" said he.

"Ah!" cried Michel Ardan, "on to the moon?"

"On to the earth!"

"The devil!" exclaimed Michel Ardan, adding philosophically, "well, when we came into this projectile we were very doubtful as to the ease with which we should get out of it!"

And now this fearful fall had begun. The speed retained had borne the projectile beyond the dead point. The explosion of the rockets could not divert its course. This speed in going had carried it over the neutral line, and in returning had done the same thing. The laws of physics condemned it to pass through every point which it had already gone through. It was a terrible fall, from a height of 160,000 miles, and no springs to break it. According to the laws of gunnery, the projectile must strike the earth with a speed equal to that with which it left the mouth of the Columbiad, a speed of 16,000 yards in the last second.

But to give some figures of comparison, it has been reckoned that an object thrown from the top of the towers of Notre Dame, the height of which is only 200 feet, will arrive on the pavement at a speed of 240 miles per hour. Here the projectile must strike the earth with a speed of 115,200 miles per hour.

"We are lost!" said Michel coolly.

"Very well! if we die," answered Barbicane, with a sort of religious enthusiasm, "the results of our travels will be magnificently spread. It is His own secret that God will tell us! In the other life the soul will want to know nothing, either of machines or engines! It will be identified with eternal wisdom!"

"In fact," interrupted Michel Ardan, "the whole of the other world may well console us for the loss of that inferior orb called the moon!"

Barbicane crossed his arms on his breast, with a motion of sublime resignation, saying at the same time:

"The will of heaven be done!"

XX

THE SOUNDINGS OF THE SUSQUEHANNA

WELL, lieutenant, and our soundings?"

"I think, sir, that the operation is nearing its completion," replied Lieutenant Bronsfield. "But who would have thought of finding such a depth so near in shore, and only 200 miles from the American coast?"

"Certainly, Bronsfield, there is a great depression," said Captain Blomsberry. "In this spot there is a submarine valley worn by Humboldt's current, which skirts the coast of America as far as the Straits of Magellan."

"These great depths," continued the lieutenant, "are not favorable for laying telegraphic cables. A level bottom, like that supporting the American cable between Valentia and Newfoundland, is much better."

"I agree with you, Bronsfield. With your permission, lieutenant, where are we now?"

"Sir, at this moment we have 3,508 fathoms of line out, and the ball which draws the sounding lead has not yet touched the bottom; for if so, it would have come up of itself."

"Brook's apparatus is very ingenious," said Captain Blomsberry; "it gives us very exact soundings."

"Touch!" cried at this moment one of the men at the forewheel, who was superintending the operation.

The captain and the lieutenant mounted the quarterdeck.

"What depth have we?" asked the captain.

"Three thousand six hundred and twenty-seven fathoms," replied the lieutenant, entering it in his notebook.

"Well, Bronsfield," said the captain, "I will take down the result. Now haul in the sounding line. It will be the work of some hours. In that time the engineer can light the furnaces, and we shall be ready to start as soon as you have finished. It is ten o'clock, and with your permission, lieutenant, I will turn in."

"Do so, sir; do so!" replied the lieutenant obligingly.

The captain of the Susquehanna, as brave a man as need be, and the humble servant of his officers, returned to his cabin, took a brandy-grog, which earned for the steward no end of praise, and turned in, not without having complimented his servant upon his making beds, and slept a peaceful sleep.

It was then ten at night. The eleventh day of the month of December was drawing to a close in a magnificent night.

The Susquehanna, a corvette of 500 horse-power, of the United States navy, was occupied in taking soundings in the Pacific Ocean about 200 miles off the American coast, following that long peninsula which stretches down the coast of Mexico.

The wind had dropped by degrees. There was no disturbance in the air. The pennant hung motionless from the maintop-gallant-mast truck.

Captain Jonathan Blomsberry (cousin-german of Colonel Blomsberry, one of the most ardent supporters of the Gun Club, who had married an aunt of the captain and daughter of an honorable Kentucky merchant)—Captain Blomsberry could not have wished for finer weather in which to bring to a close his delicate operations of sounding. His corvette had not even felt the great tempest, which by sweeping away the groups of clouds on the Rocky Mountains, had allowed them to observe the course of the famous projectile.

Everything went well, and with all the fervor of a Presbyterian, he did not forget to thank heaven for it. The series of soundings taken by the Susquehanna, had for its aim the finding of a favorable spot for the laying of a submarine cable to connect the Hawaiian Islands with the coast of America.

It was a great undertaking, due to the instigation of a powerful company. Its managing director, the intelligent Cyrus Field, purposed even covering all the islands of Oceanica with a vast electrical network, an immense enterprise, and one worthy of American genius.

To the corvette Susquehanna had been confided the first operations of sounding. It was on the night of the 11th-12th of December, she was in exactly 27@ 7' north latitude, and 41@ 37' west longitude, on the meridian of Washington.

The moon, then in her last quarter, was beginning to rise above the horizon.

After the departure of Captain Blomsberry, the lieutenant and some officers were standing together on the poop. On the appearance of the moon, their thoughts turned to that orb which the eyes of a whole hemisphere were contemplating. The best naval glasses could not have discovered the projectile wandering around its hemisphere, and yet all were pointed toward that brilliant disc which millions of eyes were looking at at the same moment.

"They have been gone ten days," said Lieutenant Bronsfield at last. "What has become of them?"

"They have arrived, lieutenant," exclaimed a young midshipman, "and they are doing what all travelers do when they arrive in a new country, taking a walk!"

"Oh! I am sure of that, if you tell me so, my young friend," said Lieutenant Bronsfield, smiling.

"But," continued another officer, "their arrival cannot be doubted. The projectile was to reach the moon when full on the 5th at midnight. We are now at the 11th of December, which makes six days. And in six times twenty-four hours, without darkness, one would have time to settle comfortably. I fancy I see my brave countrymen encamped at the bottom of some valley, on the borders of a Selenite stream, near a projectile half-buried by its fall amid volcanic rubbish, Captain Nicholl beginning his leveling operations, President Barbicane writing out his notes, and Michel Ardan embalming the lunar solitudes with the perfume of his—"

"Yes! it must be so, it is so!" exclaimed the young midshipman, worked up to a pitch of enthusiasm by this ideal description of his superior officer.

"I should like to believe it," replied the lieutenant, who was quite unmoved. "Unfortunately direct news from the lunar world is still wanting."

"Beg pardon, lieutenant," said the midshipman, "but cannot President Barbicane write?"

A burst of laughter greeted this answer.

"No letters!" continued the young man quickly. "The postal administration has something to see to there."

"Might it not be the telegraphic service that is at fault?" asked one of the officers ironically.

"Not necessarily," replied the midshipman, not at all confused. "But it is very easy to set up a graphic communication with the earth."

"And how?"

"By means of the telescope at Long's Peak. You know it brings the moon to within four miles of the Rocky Mountains, and that it shows objects on its surface of only nine feet in diameter. Very well; let our industrious friends construct a giant alphabet; let them write words three fathoms long, and sentences three miles long, and then they can send us news of themselves."

The young midshipman, who had a certain amount of imagination, was loudly applauded; Lieutenant Bronsfield allowing that the idea was possible, but observing that if by these means they could receive news from the lunar world they could not send any from the terrestrial, unless the Selenites had instruments fit for taking distant observations at their disposal.

"Evidently," said one of the officers; "but what has become of the travelers? what they have done, what they have seen, that above all must interest us. Besides, if the experiment has succeeded (which I do not doubt), they will try it again. The Columbiad is still sunk in the soil of Florida. It is now only a question of powder and shot; and every time the moon is at her zenith a cargo of visitors may be sent to her."

"It is clear," replied Lieutenant Bronsfield, "that J. T. Maston will one day join his friends."

"If he will have me," cried the midshipman, "I am ready!"

"Oh! volunteers will not be wanting," answered Bronsfield; "and if it were allowed, half of the earth's inhabitants would emigrate to the moon!"

This conversation between the officers of the Susquehanna was kept up until nearly one in the morning. We cannot say what blundering systems were broached, what inconsistent theories advanced by these bold spirits. Since Barbicane's attempt, nothing seemed impossible to the Americans. They had already designed an expedition, not only of savants, but of a whole colony toward the Selenite borders, and a complete army, consisting of infantry, artillery, and cavalry, to conquer the lunar world.

At one in the morning, the hauling in of the sounding-line was not yet completed; 1,670 fathoms were still out, which would entail some hours' work. According to the commander's orders, the fires had been lighted, and steam was being got up. The Susquehanna could have started that very instant.

At that moment (it was seventeen minutes past one in the morning) Lieutenant Bronsfield was preparing to leave the watch and return to his cabin, when his attention was attracted by a distant hissing noise. His comrades and himself first thought that this hissing was caused by the letting off of steam; but lifting their heads, they found that the noise was produced in the highest regions of the air. They had not time to question each other before the hissing became frightfully intense, and suddenly there appeared to their dazzled eyes an enormous meteor, ignited by the rapidity of its course and its friction through the atmospheric strata.

This fiery mass grew larger to their eyes, and fell, with the noise of thunder, upon the bowsprit, which it smashed close to the stem, and buried itself in the waves with a deafening roar!

A few feet nearer, and the Susquehanna would have foundered with all on board!

At this instant Captain Blomsberry appeared, half-dressed, and rushing on to the forecastle-deck, whither all the officers had hurried, exclaimed, "With your permission, gentlemen, what has happened?"

And the midshipman, making himself as it were the echo of the body, cried, "Commander, it is 'they' come back again!"

XXI

J. T. Maston Recalled

"IT is 'they' come back again!" the young midshipman had said, and every one had understood him. No one doubted but that the meteor was the projectile of the Gun Club. As to the travelers which it enclosed, opinions were divided regarding their fate.

"They are dead!" said one.

"They are alive!" said another; "the crater is deep, and the shock was deadened."

"But they must have wanted air," continued a third speaker; "they must have died of suffocation."

"Burned!" replied a fourth; "the projectile was nothing but an incandescent mass as it crossed the atmosphere."

"What does it matter!" they exclaimed unanimously; "living or dead, we must pull them out!"

But Captain Blomsberry had assembled his officers, and "with their permission," was holding a council. They must decide upon something to be done immediately. The more hasty ones were for fishing up the projectile. A difficult operation, though not an impossible one. But the corvette had no proper machinery, which must be both fixed and powerful; so it was resolved that they should put in at the nearest port, and give information to the Gun Club of the projectile's fall.

This determination was unanimous. The choice of the port had to be discussed. The neighboring coast had no anchorage on 27@ latitude. Higher up, above the peninsula of Monterey, stands the important town from which it takes its name; but, seated on the borders of a perfect desert, it was not connected with the interior by a network of telegraphic wires, and electricity alone could spread these important news fast enough.

Some degrees above opened the bay of San Francisco. Through the capital of the gold country communication would be easy with the heart of the Union. And in less than two days the Susquehanna, by putting on high pressure, could arrive in that port. She must therefore start at once.

The fires were made up; they could set off immediately. Two thousand fathoms of line were still out, which Captain Blomsberry, not wishing to lose precious time in hauling in, resolved to cut.

"we will fasten the end to a buoy," said he, "and that buoy will show us the exact spot where the projectile fell."

"Besides," replied Lieutenant Bronsfield, "we have our situation exact—27@ 7' north latitude and 41@ 37' west longitude."

"Well, Mr. Bronsfield," replied the captain, "now, with your permission, we will have the line cut."

A strong buoy, strengthened by a couple of spars, was thrown into the ocean. The end of the rope was carefully lashed to it; and, left solely to the rise and fall of the billows, the buoy would not sensibly deviate from the spot.

At this moment the engineer sent to inform the captain that steam was up and they could start, for which agreeable communication the captain thanked him. The course was then given north-northeast, and the corvette, wearing, steered at full steam direct for San Francisco. It was three in the morning.

Four hundred and fifty miles to cross; it was nothing for a good vessel like the Susquehanna. In thirty-six hours she had covered that distance; and on the 14th of December, at twenty-seven minutes past one at night, she entered the bay of San Francisco.

At the sight of a ship of the national navy arriving at full speed, with her bowsprit broken, public curiosity was greatly roused. A dense crowd soon assembled on the quay, waiting for them to disembark.

After casting anchor, Captain Blomsberry and Lieutenant Bronsfield entered an eight-pared cutter, which soon brought them to land.

They jumped on to the quay.

"The telegraph?" they asked, without answering one of the thousand questions addressed to them.

The officer of the port conducted them to the telegraph office through a concourse of spectators. Blomsberry and Bronsfield entered, while the crowd crushed each other at the door.

Some minutes later a fourfold telegram was sent out—the first to the Naval Secretary at Washington; the second to the vice-president of the Gun Club, Baltimore; the third to the Hon. J. T. Maston, Long's Peak, Rocky Mountains; and the fourth to the sub-director of the Cambridge Observatory, Massachusetts.

It was worded as follows:

In 20@ 7' north latitude, and 41@ 37' west longitude, on the 12th of December, at seventeen minutes past one in the morning, the projectile of the Columbiad fell into the Pacific. Send instructions.

BLOMSBERRY, *Commander Susquehanna.*

Five minutes afterward the whole town of San Francisco learned the news. Before six in the evening the different States of the Union had heard the great catastrophe; and after midnight, by the cable, the whole of Europe knew the result of the great American experiment. We will not attempt to picture the effect produced on the entire world by that unexpected denouement.

On receipt of the telegram the Naval Secretary telegraphed to the Susquehanna to wait in the bay of San Francisco without extinguishing her fires. Day and night she must be ready to put to sea.

The Cambridge observatory called a special meeting; and, with that composure which distinguishes learned bodies in general, peacefully discussed the scientific bearings of the question. At the Gun Club there was an explosion. All the gunners were assembled. Vice-President the Hon. Wilcome was in the act of reading the premature dispatch, in which J. T. Maston and Belfast announced that the projectile had just been seen in the gigantic reflector of Long's Peak, and also that it was held by lunar attraction, and was playing the part of under satellite to the lunar world.

We know the truth on that point.

But on the arrival of Blomsberry's dispatch, so decidedly contradicting J. T. Maston's telegram, two parties were formed in the bosom of the Gun Club. On one side were those who admitted the fall of the projectile, and consequently the return of the travelers; on the other, those who believed in the observations of Long's Peak, concluded that the commander of the Susquehanna had made a mistake. To the latter the pretended projectile was nothing but a meteor! nothing but a meteor, a shooting globe, which in its fall had smashed the bows of the corvette. It was difficult to answer this argument, for the speed with which it was animated must have made observation very difficult. The commander of the Susquehanna and her officers might have made a mistake in all good faith; one argument however, was in their favor, namely, that if the projectile had fallen on the earth, its place of meeting with the terrestrial globe could only take place on this 27@ north latitude, and (taking into consideration the time that had elapsed, and the rotary motion of the earth) between the 41@ and the 42@ of west longitude. In any case, it was decided in the Gun Club that Blomsberry brothers, Bilsby, and Major Elphinstone should go straight to San Francisco, and consult as to the means of raising the projectile from the depths of the ocean.

These devoted men set off at once; and the railroad, which will soon cross the whole of Central America, took them as far as St. Louis, where the swift mail-coaches awaited them. Almost at the same moment in which the Secretary of Marine, the vice-president of the Gun Club, and the sub-director of the Observatory received the dispatch from San Francisco, the Honorable J. T. Maston was undergoing the greatest excitement he had ever experienced in his life, an excitement which even the bursting of his pet gun, which had more than once nearly cost him his life, had not caused him. We may remember that the secretary of the Gun Club had started soon after the projectile (and almost as quickly) for the station on Long's Peak, in the Rocky Mountains, J. Belfast, director of the Cambridge Observatory, accompanying him. Arrived there, the two friends had installed themselves at once, never quitting the summit of their enormous telescope. We know that this gigantic instrument had been set up according to the reflecting system, called by the English "front view." This arrangement subjected all objects to but one reflection, making the view consequently much clearer; the result was that, when they were taking observation, J. T. Maston and Belfast were placed in the upper part of the instrument and not in the lower, which they reached by a circular staircase, a masterpiece of lightness, while below them opened a metal well terminated by the metallic mirror, which measured two hundred and eighty feet in depth.

It was on a narrow platform placed above the telescope that the two savants passed their existence, execrating the day which hid the moon from their eyes, and the clouds which obstinately veiled her during the night.

What, then, was their delight when, after some days of waiting, on the night of the 5th of December, they saw the vehicle which was bearing their friends into space! To this delight succeeded a great deception, when, trusting to a cursory observation, they launched their first telegram to the world, erroneously affirming that the projectile had become a satellite of the moon, gravitating in an immutable orbit.

From that moment it had never shown itself to their eyes—a disappearance all the more easily explained, as it was then passing behind the moon's invisible disc; but when it was time for it to reappear on the visible disc, one may imagine the impatience of the fuming J. T. Maston and his not less impatient companion. Each minute of the night they thought they saw the projectile once more, and they did not see it. Hence constant discussions and violent disputes between them, Belfast affirming that the projectile could not be seen, J. T. Maston maintaining that "it had put his eyes out."

"It is the projectile!" repeated J. T. Maston.

"No," answered Belfast; "it is an avalanche detached from a lunar mountain."

"Well, we shall see it to-morrow."

"No, we shall not see it any more. It is carried into space."

"Yes!"

"No!"

And at these moments, when contradictions rained like hail, the well-known irritability of the secretary of the Gun Club constituted a permanent danger for the Honorable Belfast. The existence of these two together would soon have become impossible; but an unforseen event cut short their everlasting discussions.

During the night, from the 14th to the 15th of December, the two irreconcilable friends were busy observing the lunar disc, J. T. Maston abusing the learned Belfast as usual, who was by his side; the secretary of the Gun Club maintaining for the thousandth time that he had just seen the projectile, and adding that he could see Michel Ardan's face looking through one of the scuttles, at the same time enforcing his argument by a series of gestures which his formidable hook rendered very unpleasant.

At this moment Belfast's servant appeared on the platform (it was ten at night) and gave him a dispatch. It was the commander of the Susquehanna's telegram.

Belfast tore the envelope and read, and uttered a cry.

"What!" said J. T. Maston.

"The projectile!"

"Well!"

"Has fallen to the earth!"

Another cry, this time a perfect howl, answered him. He turned toward J. T. Maston. The unfortunate man, imprudently leaning over the metal tube, had disappeared in the immense telescope. A fall of two hundred and eighty feet! Belfast, dismayed, rushed to the orifice of the reflector.

He breathed. J. T. Maston, caught by his metal hook, was holding on by one of the rings which bound the telescope together, uttering fearful cries.

Belfast called. Help was brought, tackle was let down, and they hoisted up, not without some trouble, the imprudent secretary of the Gun Club.

He reappeared at the upper orifice without hurt.

"Ah!" said he, "if I had broken the mirror?"

"You would have paid for it," replied Belfast severely.

"And that cursed projectile has fallen?" asked J. T. Maston.

"Into the Pacific!"

"Let us go!"

A quarter of an hour after the two savants were descending the declivity of the Rocky Mountains; and two days after, at the same time as their friends of the Gun Club, they arrived at San Francisco, having killed five horses on the road.

Elphinstone, the brothers Blomsberry, and Bilsby rushed toward them on their arrival.

"What shall we do?" they exclaimed.

"Fish up the projectile," replied J. T. Maston, "and the sooner the better."

XXII

RECOVERED FROM THE SEA

THE spot where the projectile sank under the waves was exactly known; but the machinery to grasp it and bring it to the surface of the ocean was still wanting. It must first be invented, then made. American engineers could not be troubled with such trifles. The grappling-irons once fixed, by their help they were sure to raise it in spite of its weight, which was lessened by the density of the liquid in which it was plunged.

But fishing-up the projectile was not the only thing to be thought of. They must act promptly in the interest of the travelers. No one doubted that they were still living.

"Yes," repeated J. T. Maston incessantly, whose confidence gained over everybody, "our friends are clever people, and they cannot have fallen like simpletons. They are alive, quite alive; but we must make haste if we wish to find them so. Food and water do not trouble me; they have enough for a long while. But air, air, that is what they will soon want; so quick, quick!"

And they did go quick. They fitted up the Susquehanna for her new destination. Her powerful machinery was brought to bear upon the hauling-chains. The aluminum projectile only weighed 19,250 pounds, a weight very inferior to that of the transatlantic cable which had been drawn up under similar conditions. The only difficulty was in fishing up a cylindro-conical projectile, the walls of which were so smooth as to offer no hold for the hooks. On that account Engineer Murchison hastened to San Francisco, and had some enormous grappling-irons fixed on an automatic system, which would never let the projectile go if it once succeeded in seizing it in its powerful claws. Diving-dresses were also prepared, which through this impervious covering allowed the divers to observe the bottom of the sea. He also had put on board an apparatus of compressed air very cleverly designed. There were perfect chambers pierced with scuttles, which, with water let into certain compartments, could draw it down into great depths. These apparatuses were at San Francisco, where they had been used in the construction of a submarine breakwater; and very fortunately it was so, for there was no time to construct any. But in spite of the perfection of the machinery, in spite of the ingenuity of the savants entrusted with the use of them, the success of the operation was far from being certain. How great were the chances against them, the projectile being 20,000 feet under the water! And if even it was brought to the surface, how would the travelers have borne the terrible shock which 20,000 feet of water had perhaps not sufficiently broken? At any rate they must act quickly. J. T. Maston hurried the workmen day and night. He was ready to don the diving-dress himself, or try the air apparatus, in order to reconnoiter the situation of his courageous friends.

But in spite of all the diligence displayed in preparing the different engines, in spite of the considerable sum placed at the disposal of the Gun Club by the Government of the Union, five long days (five centuries!)

elapsed before the preparations were complete. During this time public opinion was excited to the highest pitch. Telegrams were exchanged incessantly throughout the entire world by means of wires and electric cables. The saving of Barbicane, Nicholl, and Michel Ardan was an international affair. Every one who had subscribed to the Gun Club was directly interested in the welfare of the travelers.

At length the hauling-chains, the air-chambers, and the automatic grappling-irons were put on board. J. T. Maston, Engineer Murchison, and the delegates of the Gun Club, were already in their cabins. They had but to start, which they did on the 21st of December, at eight o'clock at night, the corvette meeting with a beautiful sea, a northeasterly wind, and rather sharp cold. The whole population of San Francisco was gathered on the quay, greatly excited but silent, reserving their hurrahs for the return. Steam was fully up, and the screw of the Susquehanna carried them briskly out of the bay.

It is needless to relate the conversations on board between the officers, sailors, and passengers. All these men had but one thought. All these hearts beat under the same emotion. While they were hastening to help them, what were Barbicane and his companions doing? What had become of them? Were they able to attempt any bold maneuver to regain their liberty? None could say. The truth is that every attempt must have failed! Immersed nearly four miles under the ocean, this metal prison defied every effort of its prisoners.

On the 23rd inst., at eight in the morning, after a rapid passage, the Susquehanna was due at the fatal spot. They must wait till twelve to take the reckoning exactly. The buoy to which the sounding line had been lashed had not yet been recognized.

At twelve, Captain Blomsberry, assisted by his officers who superintended the observations, took the reckoning in the presence of the delegates of the Gun Club. Then there was a moment of anxiety. Her position decided, the Susquehanna was found to be some minutes westward of the spot where the projectile had disappeared beneath the waves.

The ship's course was then changed so as to reach this exact point.

At forty-seven minutes past twelve they reached the buoy; it was in perfect condition, and must have shifted but little.

"At last!" exclaimed J. T. Maston.

"Shall we begin?" asked Captain Blomsberry.

"Without losing a second."

Every precaution was taken to keep the corvette almost completely motionless. Before trying to seize the projectile, Engineer Murchison wanted to find its exact position at the bottom of the ocean. The submarine apparatus destined for this expedition was supplied with air. The working of these engines was not without danger, for at 20,000 feet below the surface of the water, and under such great pressure, they were exposed to fracture, the consequences of which would be dreadful.

J. T. Maston, the brothers Blomsberry, and Engineer Murchison, without heeding these dangers, took their places in the air-chamber. The commander, posted on his bridge, superintended the operation, ready to stop or haul in the chains on the slightest signal. The screw had been shipped, and the whole power of the machinery collected on the capstan would have quickly drawn the apparatus on board. The descent began at twenty-five minutes past one at night, and the chamber, drawn under by the reservoirs full of water, disappeared from the surface of the ocean.

The emotion of the officers and sailors on board was now divided between the prisoners in the projectile and the prisoners in the submarine apparatus. As to the latter, they forgot themselves, and, glued to the windows of the scuttles, attentively watched the liquid mass through which they were passing.

The descent was rapid. At seventeen minutes past two, J. T. Maston and his companions had reached the bottom of the Pacific; but they saw nothing but an arid desert, no longer animated by either fauna or flora. By the light of their lamps, furnished with powerful reflectors, they could see the dark beds of the ocean for a considerable extent of view, but the projectile was nowhere to be seen.

The impatience of these bold divers cannot be described, and having an electrical communication with the corvette, they made a signal already agreed upon, and for the space of a mile the Susquehanna moved their chamber along some yards above the bottom.

Thus they explored the whole submarine plain, deceived at every turn by optical illusions which almost broke their hearts. Here a rock, there a projection from the ground, seemed to be the much-sought-for projectile; but their mistake was soon discovered, and then they were in despair.

"But where are they? where are they?" cried J. T. Maston. And the poor man called loudly upon Nicholl, Barbicane, and Michel Ardan, as if his unfortunate friends could either hear or answer him through such an impenetrable medium! The search continued under these conditions until the vitiated air compelled the divers to ascend.

The hauling in began about six in the evening, and was not ended before midnight.

"To-morrow," said J. T. Maston, as he set foot on the bridge of the corvette.

"Yes," answered Captain Blomsberry.

"And on another spot?"

"Yes."

J. T. Maston did not doubt of their final success, but his companions, no longer upheld by the excitement of the first hours, understood all the difficulty of the enterprise. What seemed easy at San Francisco, seemed here in the wide ocean almost impossible. The chances of success diminished in rapid proportion; and it was from chance alone that the meeting with the projectile might be expected.

The next day, the 24th, in spite of the fatigue of the previous day, the operation was renewed. The corvette advanced some minutes to westward, and the apparatus, provided with air, bore the same explorers to the depths of the ocean.

The whole day passed in fruitless research; the bed of the sea was a desert. The 25th brought no other result, nor the 26th.

It was disheartening. They thought of those unfortunates shut up in the projectile for twenty-six days. Perhaps at that moment they were experiencing the first approach of suffocation; that is, if they had escaped the dangers of their fall. The air was spent, and doubtless with the air all their morale.

"The air, possibly," answered J. T. Maston resolutely, "but their morale never!"

On the 28th, after two more days of search, all hope was gone. This projectile was but an atom in the immensity of the ocean. They must give up all idea of finding it.

But J. T. Maston would not hear of going away. He would not abandon the place without at least discovering the tomb of his friends. But Commander Blomsberry could no longer persist, and in spite of the exclamations of the worthy secretary, was obliged to give the order to sail.

On the 29th of December, at nine A.M., the Susquehanna, heading northeast, resumed her course to the bay of San Francisco.

It was ten in the morning; the corvette was under half-steam, as it was regretting to leave the spot where the catastrophe had taken place, when a sailor, perched on the main-top-gallant crosstrees, watching the sea, cried suddenly:

"A buoy on the lee bow!"

The officers looked in the direction indicated, and by the help of their glasses saw that the object signalled had the appearance of one of those buoys which are used to mark the passages of bays or rivers. But, singularly to say, a flag floating on the wind surmounted its cone, which emerged five or six feet out of water. This buoy shone under the rays of the sun as if it had been made of plates of silver. Commander Blomsberry, J. T. Maston, and the delegates of the Gun Club were mounted on the bridge, examining this object straying at random on the waves.

All looked with feverish anxiety, but in silence. None dared give expression to the thoughts which came to the minds of all.

The corvette approached to within two cables' lengths of the object.

A shudder ran through the whole crew. That flag was the American flag!

At this moment a perfect howling was heard; it was the brave J. T. Maston who had just fallen all in a heap. Forgetting on the one hand that his right arm had been replaced by an iron hook, and on the other that a simple gutta-percha cap covered his brain-box, he had given himself a formidable blow.

They hurried toward him, picked him up, restored him to life. And what were his first words?

"Ah! trebly brutes! quadruply idiots! quintuply boobies that we are!"

"What is it?" exclaimed everyone around him.

"What is it?"

"Come, speak!"

"It is, simpletons," howled the terrible secretary, "it is that the projectile only weighs 19,250 pounds!"

"Well?"

"And that it displaces twenty-eight tons, or in other words 56,000 pounds, and that consequently it floats!"

Ah! what stress the worthy man had laid on the verb "float!" And it was true! All, yes! all these savants had forgotten this fundamental law, namely, that on account of its specific lightness, the projectile, after having been drawn by its fall to the greatest depths of the ocean, must naturally return to the surface. And now it was floating quietly at the mercy of the waves.

The boats were put to sea. J. T. Maston and his friends had rushed into them! Excitement was at its height! Every heart beat loudly while they advanced to the projectile. What did it contain? Living or dead?

Living, yes! living, at least unless death had struck Barbicane and his two friends since they had hoisted the flag. Profound silence reigned on the boats. All were breathless. Eyes no longer saw. One of the scuttles of the projectile was open. Some pieces of glass remained in the frame, showing that it had been broken. This scuttle was actually five feet above the water.

A boat came alongside, that of J. T. Maston, and J. T. Maston rushed to the broken window.

At that moment they heard a clear and merry voice, the voice of Michel Ardan, exclaiming in an accent of triumph:

"White all, Barbicane, white all!"

Barbicane, Michel Ardan, and Nicholl were playing at dominoes!

XXIII

THE END

WE may remember the intense sympathy which had accompanied the travelers on their departure. If at the beginning of the enterprise they had excited such emotion both in the old and new world, with what enthusiasm would they be received on their return! The millions of spectators which had beset the peninsula of Florida, would they not rush to meet these sublime adventurers? Those legions of strangers, hurrying from all parts of the globe toward the American shores, would they leave the Union without having seen Barbicane, Nicholl, and Michel Ardan? No! and the ardent passion of the public was bound to respond worthily to the greatness of the enterprise. Human creatures who had left the terrestrial sphere, and returned after this strange voyage into celestial space, could not fail to be received as the prophet Elias would be if he came back to earth. To see them first, and then to hear them, such was the universal longing.

Barbicane, Michel Ardan, Nicholl, and the delegates of the Gun Club, returning without delay to Baltimore, were received with indescribable enthusiasm. The notes of President Barbicane's voyage were ready to be given to the public. The New York Herald bought the manuscript at a price not yet known, but which must have been very high. Indeed, during the publication of "A Journey to the Moon," the sale of this paper amounted to five millions of copies. Three days after the return of the travelers to the earth, the slightest detail of their expedition was known. There remained nothing more but to see the heroes of this superhuman enterprise.

The expedition of Barbicane and his friends round the moon had enabled them to correct the many admitted theories regarding the ter-

restrial satellite. These savants had observed de visu, and under particular circumstances. They knew what systems should be rejected, what
retained with regard to the formation of that orb, its origin, its habitability. Its past, present, and future had even given up their last secrets.
Who could advance objections against conscientious observers, who at
less than twenty-four miles distance had marked that curious mountain
of Tycho, the strangest system of lunar orography? How answer those
savants whose sight had penetrated the abyss of Pluto's circle? How con-
tradict those bold ones whom the chances of their enterprise had borne
over that invisible face of the disc, which no human eye until then had
ever seen? It was now their turn to impose some limit on that selenographic science, which had reconstructed the lunar world as Cuvier did
the skeleton of a fossil, and say, "The moon was this, a habitable world,
inhabited before the earth. The moon is that, a world uninhabitable, and
now uninhabited."

To celebrate the return of its most illustrious member and his two
companions, the Gun Club decided upon giving a banquet, but a banquet worthy of the conquerors, worthy of the American people, and under such conditions that all the inhabitants of the Union could directly
take part in it.

All the head lines of railroads in the States were joined by flying rails;
and on all the platforms, lined with the same flags, and decorated with
the same ornaments, were tables laid and all served alike. At certain hours,
successively calculated, marked by electric clocks which beat the seconds
at the same time, the population were invited to take their places at the
banquet tables. For four days, from the 5th to the 9th of January, the
trains were stopped as they are on Sundays on the railways of the United
States, and every road was open. One engine only at full speed, drawing
a triumphal carriage, had the right of traveling for those four days on the
railroads of the United States.

The engine was manned by a driver and a stoker, and bore, by special
favor, the Hon. J. T. Maston, secretary of the Gun Club. The carriage was
reserved for President Barbicane, Colonel Nicholl, and Michel Ardan. At
the whistle of the driver, amid the hurrahs, and all the admiring vociferations of the American language, the train left the platform of Baltimore.
It traveled at a speed of one hundred and sixty miles in the hour. But what
was this speed compared with that which had carried the three heroes
from the mouth of the Columbiad?

Thus they sped from one town to the other, finding whole popula-
tions at table on their road, saluting them with the same acclamations,
lavishing the same bravos! They traveled in this way through the east of

the Union, Pennsylvania, Connecticut, Massachusetts, Vermont, Maine, and New Hampshire; the north and west by New York, Ohio, Michigan, and Wisconsin; returning to the south by Illinois, Missouri, Arkansas, Texas, and Louisiana; they went to the southeast by Alabama and Florida, going up by Georgia and the Carolinas, visiting the center by Tennessee, Kentucky, Virginia, and Indiana, and, after quitting the Washington station, re-entered Baltimore, where for four days one would have thought that the United States of America were seated at one immense banquet, saluting them simultaneously with the same hurrahs! The apotheosis was worthy of these three heroes whom fable would have placed in the rank of demigods.

And now will this attempt, unprecedented in the annals of travels, lead to any practical result? Will direct communication with the moon ever be established? Will they ever lay the foundation of a traveling service through the solar world? Will they go from one planet to another, from Jupiter to Mercury, and after awhile from one star to another, from the Polar to Sirius? Will this means of locomotion allow us to visit those suns which swarm in the firmament?

To such questions no answer can be given. But knowing the bold ingenuity of the Anglo-Saxon race, no one would be astonished if the Americans seek to make some use of President Barbicane's attempt.

Thus, some time after the return of the travelers, the public received with marked favor the announcement of a company, limited, with a capital of a hundred million of dollars, divided into a hundred thousand shares of a thousand dollars each, under the name of the "National Company of Interstellary Communication." President, Barbicane; vice-president, Captain Nicholl; secretary, J. T. Maston; director of movements, Michel Ardan.

And as it is part of the American temperament to foresee everything in business, even failure, the Honorable Harry Trolloppe, judge commissioner, and Francis Drayton, magistrate, were nominated beforehand!

■ ■ ■ ■ ■ ■ ■ ■ ■ ■

More Titles from Phoenix Pick

9 781604 502503